Zaurus
Close-quarters combat specialist formerly with the Ag Wolves. Her Magistellus partner is a werewolf.

M-Scope
Trap expert formerly with the Ag Wolves. His Magistellus partner is a *yuki-onna*.

MAGISTELLUS BAD TRIP

Kazuma Kamachi
Illustration by **Mahaya**   **3**

Ayame Suou

Celsa

Two little sisters who must be protected, no matter the cost.

Criminal AO

MAGISTELLUS BAD TRIP

3rd Season

Kazuma Kamachi

Illustration by
Mahaya

YEN
ON

New York

MAGISTELLUS BAD TRIP 3rd Season

Kazuma Kamachi

Illustration by
Mahaya

Translation by
Jake Humphrey

MAGISTEALTH BAD TRIP Season 3rd
©Kazuma Kamachi 2020
First published in Japan in 2020 by KADOKAWA CORPORATION, Tokyo.
English translation rights arranged with KADOKAWA CORPORATION, Tokyo, through TUTTLE-MORI AGENCY, INC., Tokyo.

Yen On
150 West 30th Street, 19th Floor
New York, NY 10001

Visit us at yenpress.com
facebook.com/yenpress
twitter.com/yenpress
yenpress.tumblr.com
instagram.com/yenpress

First Yen On Edition: March 2023
Edited by Yen On Editorial: Emma McClain
Designed by Yen Press Design: Andy Swist

Yen On is an imprint of Yen Press, LLC.
The Yen On name and logo are trademarks of Yen Press, LLC.

Library of Congress Cataloging-in-Publication Data
Names: Kamachi, Kazuma, author. | Mahaya, illustrator. | Humphrey, Jake, translator.
Title: Magistellus bad trip / Kazuma Kamachi ; illustration by Mahaya ; translation by Jake Humphrey.
Description: First Yen On edition. | New York, NY : Yen On, 2021– |
Identifiers: LCCN 2021023505 | ISBN 9781975314262 (v. 1 ; trade paperback) | ISBN 9781975348588
    (v. 2 ; trade paperback) | ISBN 9781975360108 (v. 3 ; trade paperback)
Subjects: CYAC: Science fiction. | Fantasy. | Artificial intelligence—Fiction. | Virtual reality—Fiction. |
    Magic—Fiction.
Classification: LCC PZ7.1.K215 Mag 2021 | DDC [Fic]—dc23
LC record available at https://lccn.loc.gov/2021023505

ISBNs: 978-1-9753-6010-8 (paperback)
       978-1-9753-6011-5 (ebook)

10 9 8 7 6 5 4 3 2 1

LSC-C

Printed in the United States of America

CONTENTS

Server Name: Psi Indigo.
Starting Location: Tokonatsu City, Peninsula District.
Log-in credentials accepted.
Welcome to *Money (Game) Master*, **Criminal AO.**

He wasn't the most confident-looking boy. He gave off the impression of being a bit timid and weak-willed. He wore a white shirt, black slacks, and a necktie, and if it weren't for the bandanna around his head and the myriad tool pouches at his waist, one would be forgiven for thinking he had just gotten back from a funeral and taken off his jacket.

This was Takamasa Hekireki, aka Criminal AO.

Men in coveralls were walking busily back and forth around him. One of them noticed his arrival and stopped.

"Good evening, sir. Have you just logged in?"

"Yeah. How are things progressing with #flash.err?"

"We have just completed underground test firing, and power and stability both appear normal. I have the report, if you'd like to take a look. We are about to begin consolidating the Legacy—*grgr*!!"

Criminal AO's face remained impassive, though he appeared to manipulate something with a hand stuffed into one of his pockets.

"*Grgr*—we are about to begin consolidating the Magic," the man hastily corrected.

"I see."

The men in coveralls did not seem to notice the strange outburst or even the correction that followed. They were not human Dealers, merely computer-controlled NPCs. A little work was all it took to ensure they acted as Criminal AO desired.

If only the same tricks worked on the Magistelli…, he thought, dismissing the man with a wave of his hand and a smile.

The Magistelli, humanity's faithful servants. Ironic that they were harder to control than the NPCs. That alone proved they were more than simply computer programs, but the funny thing was, when Criminal AO tried telling this to Dealers on the street, they didn't believe him. *All that debt has driven you mad*, they said.

The Magistelli were demons—real ones. *A race of beings that flouted God's law.* Not content with only the human realm, they sought to expand their simulation to cover God's realm of heaven, encroaching on it the same way they'd done with humans using the virtual currency *snow.*

The Magistelli could not be killed. Whether you shot them or ran them over, they'd be back within an hour, at most. Of course, humans were effectively immortal, too, so long as they remained within the game…but saddled with enough debt, a human could be driven to suicide or banished from society forever.

Humans and Magistelli. At a glance, Magistelli appeared subservient to humans, but the balance of power tipped far more in the demons' favor than most people realized. This had to be rectified. Takamasa needed to come up with some way to kill the Magistelli. It was the only way he could ever hope to negotiate with them and, failing such negotiations, exterminate the entire race.

I need the Zodiac Children…

The day of revolution was drawing close. The Magistelli planned to bring the divine realm into their simulation and rule it, just as human life was already governed by *snow*. Doing so was apparently key to the demonic Magistelli regaining their true forms.

If that happened, everything the boy had sworn to protect would be destroyed. Takamasa had to stop himself from biting his fingernails in anxiety.

There's only twelve of them in the entire world. Twelve people with the natural ability to defy the AI's predictions. In the game world, I can cause glitches with my Magic, but out in the real world, they're the only ones with the power to fight back. By bringing them into the conflict, I can finally realize my plan and put a stop to the Magistelli.

Money (Game) Master used intricate calculations to construct a virtual world exactly like the real one, implementing the four fundamental forces of nature as well as a host of other scientific laws and mathematical formulae. Still, it wasn't perfect. There were things in this world that the demons could never comprehend, like the Zodiac Children.

By comparison, the Overtrick were nothing but king-size bugs in the game code. They alone weren't enough to bring down *Money (Game) Master*. They were created within the game, and so naturally, their powers remained within the game's acceptable parameters. However, if they came into contact with a Zodiac Child, things would be different. Together, they would have the power to lead this world to a conclusion even the AI collective, the Mind of the Magistelli, couldn't predict.

But...

Two unknowns, one within, one without, coming into contact like matter and antimatter in one giant explosion.

But then, if contact was all it took, it should have already happened.

For instance, with Kaname Suou. Or, if her word was to be believed, with Lily-Kiska Sweetmare.

If only Criminal AO had been there to share his wisdom, the boy thought. Even with gun and trigger combined, it was useless without anyone to pull it. It was likely for this very reason that the AI overlords had focused their efforts not on the twelve Zodiac Children but on the one person with the knowledge to put everything together.

Unfortunately, while Takamasa Hekireki was a whiz when it came to machines…he was not so adept at interacting with his fellow humans. He could create any overpowered weapon he put his mind to, and yet right now he was alone.

The one person who should have been by his side—the key to his plans—had already left, and now opposed him. Who was manning this fortress, then? He couldn't bring himself to trust human Dealers. Nor could he trust his own Magistellus, for fear of her leaking his secrets to the collective Mind. And so he had filled his fortress with low-level NPCs governed by the most basic of AI programs, over which he could exert complete control.

Yes.

It was almost like…

He'd always been bad at seeing through people's lies. He felt most comfortable with ones and zeros, when you could just run the numbers and get a concrete yes or no answer. With humans, you would rarely get an answer at all, and when you did, it was never what they truly thought. They were impossible to predict, especially when compared to machines, whose every part served a distinct, useful purpose.

Yes, machines were far, far more—

Crash!!

Criminal AO intentionally slammed his forehead into the outside wall of a building.

"It's fine…," he muttered, closing his eyes. He tried to banish his foolish thoughts, but like a child, he was still afraid.

"…I'm human. I'm still human. I haven't given up."

Prologue

Server Name: Gamma Orange.
Starting Location: Tokonatsu City, Peninsula District.
Log-in credentials accepted.
Welcome to *Money (Game) Master*, Kaname Suou.

Tokonatsu City—a paradise of sea, sun, and sweet summer air, where palm trees swayed lazily in the breeze, and bikinied supermodels walked the streets. And within this glamorous town ran a particularly luxurious street, lined with tidy shops whose storefront windows displayed all the latest and most desirable brands in handbags, jewelry, and the like.

Parked on one side of this street was a mint-green coupe, and beside it, resting her plump bottom against the hood, was the demon pit babe Tselika. The owner of the car, however, was nowhere in sight.

Bang-bang, b-bang!!

Loud shots rang out in quick succession, but it was like background noise to Tselika. She leaned over and checked her flowing mint-green hair in the car's side mirror, before taking out a tube of lipstick and puckering up.

"Hm-hmm…"

I like this season's new lipstick color, but it fades so quickly. Still, I can't bring shame to my Dealer by failing to look my best at all times.

Just then, the gunshots stopped. Tselika's Dealer pretty much exclusively used a .45-caliber short-range sniper rifle called Short Spear, fitted with an integrated silencer. Consequently, any shots she actually *heard* must have been from the Dealers he was up against. In which case, the fact that they'd stopped was no cause for concern. *He must have finished wiping out his enemies,* she concluded.

But no sooner had that thought crossed her mind, than…

Ker-rash!!

A black-haired boy dressed in a loose-fitting white shirt and comfortable pants came plummeting out of a fourth-story window and smashed into the roof of the car amid a rain of glass shards. It was Kaname Suou.

"Wha—?"

The collision reduced the car to half its original height and shattered the windshield, the back window, the side windows—everything. There was no telling what was broken, but the incessant sound of the car's horn droned from the wreckage.

Tselika stared in shock for several seconds before her anger caught up with her. To a Magistellus, her Dealer's car was like her very own temple.

"What do you think you're doing, you brain-dead buffoon?!" she yelled, hands on her shapely hips. "I just cleaned that car!!"

"…Great job, Tselika. That must be why it made for such a soft landing," quipped Kaname, lying faceup in the dented roof, arms and legs splayed. "Gotta hand it to you, you really know how to spoil a man."

Kaname's response was so spiritless that even Tselika felt her anger drain away, and she simply sighed and rubbed her temples.

The target for this mission was the trust company MO Misaki Bank. A couple of Dealers hired for protection should have presented no challenge to Kaname Suou, once feared as the Reaper of Called Game. So why had he just fallen four stories into the roof of his own car?

He was completely off his game, and the reason was probably that girl who wasn't with them at the moment.

At least he didn't Fall, thought Tselika. She was starting to feel like the boy's mother, or at least his big sister. This was a lot more serious than not paying enough attention to the road while driving. Even if his opponents were rookies, all it took was one lucky shot. Bullets didn't discriminate—they'd steal a person's life no matter who shot them. Kaname had forgotten even this basic principle.

"Have you still not spoken to Midori, My Lord?"

"...What would I even say?" Kaname replied.

Looking up at the sunlight cutting into the street, Kaname grunted like an invalid in a hospital bed. It was like he was living in a nightmare.

"Takamasa's turned against me," he said. "If I still want to save everyone, I have no choice but to kill him—make him Fall again, this time by my own hand. How is Midori supposed to agree to that? She's not fighting for world peace, you know."

"Well, if you can't do it, then perhaps I shall send her a text instead."

"Come on, Tselika. Don't you turn on me, too."

After making off in the tilt-rotor with his hoard of Legacies, Takamasa had disappeared. This bank heist was the latest step in their plan to track him down. If he was operating within *Money (Game) Master*, he had to be somewhere in Tokonatsu City. But searching a landmass the size of a small country was no mean feat. His base could be anything from a stately mansion to a tiny camper van, for all Kaname knew. He needed some kind of a clue—anything.

The one advantage Kaname had was that he knew all of his old friend's quirks. He tried to put himself in Takamasa's shoes.

"...He doesn't trust digital currency," Kaname explained. "The same goes for banknotes. It's all controlled by the AI."

"So he converts the money he makes into precious gems and keeps them in multiple banks all over the world," said Tselika. "Banks run not by an AI business but by humans. And you're hoping that by breaking into them and stealing his funds, you can both stall his plans and turn up some information on where he might be hiding."

Of all the trust banks, MO Misaki was one of the most notorious. In addition to safe deposit boxes, it also provided a delivery system for cash and jewels. However, the sheer number of bodyguards the bank sent on these deliveries—far more than was necessary to protect a single gold ring—meant that in practice it was essentially a mercenary outfit. And of course, those bodyguards provided more than just protection. They were also involved in their employer's main business— bullying stockholders into giving up their shares or cheating former owners out of large plots of land in order to drive up prices. And the ones who suffered the most at the end of all this were good, hardworking small enterprise owners and their employees.

Tselika raised the hood of the coupe, stuck her hand in, and yanked out a cable, causing the horn to abruptly cease.

"I know you're distracted, My Lord," she said, "but might I inquire about our next steps?" Adopting the tone one might use to ask a sick child what they'd like for supper, she continued, "Are we to give up on MO Misaki and procure the information we require somewhere else?"

Still lying in the crater in the roof of his car, Kaname simply lifted both arms up into the air and pointed to the sky. Then it happened.

Kaboom!!!!!!

Some sort of projectile flew into the fourth-floor window Kaname had just fallen from, swiftly followed by a monumental explosion. Bits of floor and potted plants rained down onto the street, along with the bodies of the Dealers unfortunate enough to have been inside.

This was the work of the latest model anti-materiel rail gun—the sort you might find mounted on a frigate or aerial bomber.

Tselika's eyes went wide. "Wha—?! *That* was your Plan B?! Just when I thought you couldn't get any less subtle…!!"

"…It costs fifty million *snow* per shot. I should have just led with it, really, since we'll make all that back and then some once we clear out Takamasa's safe."

The men and women walking the streets in flashy swimsuits finally found the situation dangerous enough to dive for cover under the nearest café table, but Kaname didn't move a muscle. He simply sat up and dropped lazily from the car roof like he was waking up with a hangover, taking Short Spear in his hand and leisurely walking back toward the front doors of the bank. He'd just shown everyone he could cheat the system.

With enough money, anything was possible. The MO Misaki mercenaries had been virtually obliterated, lying here and there on the verge of death. All Kaname had to do this time was go inside and finish them off.

"Tselika. I'll give you two grand. Get a tow truck over here for the coupe."

"Two thousand?! What about repairs?!! This car is all that stands between you and a bullet half the time!!"

"Also, get me a seafood pizza with extra anchovies. I'm thinking deep pan. Delivery is fine, just make sure it arrives around when I finish. Oh, and a ginger ale, too."

"I'm trying to tell you there's not enough money here for that!!"

Kaname didn't reply. He waved and disappeared through the bank doors.

"…And he's gone."

She knew exactly what would happen now. Kaname had been very precise about what he wanted and when he wanted it. Tselika reckoned fifteen minutes would be all it took to clear out the bank, not enough time to cook a pizza from scratch. Instead, she would have to call up some ultra-low-effort chain—the kind that pulled a pizza from the freezer, sprinkled on some toppings, and just tossed it in the microwave.

The patterns on her clothes silently shifted, transforming into a menu for a pizza take-out joint. The former Reaper of Called Game had given her a time limit. True to his word, he would kill everyone in the bank, take a refreshing swig of his carbonated drink, eat some disgustingly salty pizza, and head home. This matter was not up for discussion.

The succubus simply shrugged her shoulders and sighed. She was starting to feel more like his babysitter.

"…He's out of control."

Chapter 7

The Life-Seller BGM #07 "Girl in Trash Can"

1

Server Name: Alpha Scarlet.
Starting Location: Tokonatsu City, Peninsula District.
Log-in credentials accepted.
Welcome to *Money (Game) Master*, Midori Hekireki.

"Being in here sure feels strange…"

The floor of the room was immaculately waxed, and the walls, save the windows, were all mirrored, resembling a ballet classroom. Inside stood a slender young girl with long black hair tied up in twin ponytails—Midori Hekireki.

She was at Aqua Gym, a sports club occupying one of the many sparkling-clean office buildings situated along the financial district shorefront. Midori never had much opportunity for exercise, being saddled with her brother's debt and forced to live a life financed by AI companies. But luckily, even nonmembers could use the facilities here if they had a referral from a platinum member.

The girl in the black gothic-lolita frilled bikini and miniskirt was currently running atop a treadmill. It was cold in the room, perhaps to combat the body heat produced by the patrons, certainly cool enough to forget the blazing heat of the sunswept sands outside, where tanned beachgoers slept under the shade of palm trees.

"I never thought I'd take up exercise inside a video game…," muttered Midori, panting with exertion. "Does it even change your stats or anything? Phew… It's not like there are levels or experience points in *Money (Game) Master*, right? I thought everything was just determined by your clothing and accessories."

"That doesn't make exercise completely pointless."

The platinum member who had let her in was none other than Kaname Suou. He was standing there in a baggy white shirt and necktie, complete with a pair of loose-fitting pants. Though he was usually a little on the gloomy side, at the moment he was positively sparkling. Apparently, he didn't do much with his membership and wasn't very interested in training. Naturally, the only reason he'd wanted a gym membership card was to gain access to the secret VIP area in order to mingle with the other movers and shakers. Right now, though, he was simply keeping Midori company.

"You can increase your physical strength pretty quickly using skills," he continued, "but for improving your technique, your focus—your mind—there's nothing better than practice. For example, Midori, you could try not rocking your head around like you're running from a bear."

"That's…because…you keep pressing the accelerate button!!"

"Well, it didn't look like you were struggling yet. You need to keep your eye level steady and your head held high while you run. That doesn't change whether you're trying to fire a gun or not."

This gym, which took up the entirety of the building's thirtieth floor, offered specialized dance and fitness classes. The main demographic in attendance was women in their twenties and thirties dressed in T-shirts and yoga pants. Of course, that was only going by the avatars they'd chosen, but they must have been older than Midori, at least. For her, it was starting to feel a bit like being at school on parents' day with her mother and all the other grown-ups standing at the back of the room, watching.

As Kaname said, exercise had little effect on one's physical attributes, but when everyone looked like supermodels, posture and how you carried yourself mattered a lot more. So rather than customizing your look, this facility was more about fine-tuning it. After all, there were a lot of Dealers, both rich and poor, willing to do anything to stand out.

"Can it really make that big of a difference?" Midori asked.

"You don't have to wrestle with a controller to play *Money (Game) Master*," replied Kaname, "but that means it's a lot harder to correct any bad habits you develop early on."

Bloody Dancer, the monstrous, dual-wielding daredevil who refused to rely on skills and Legacies, was a prime example... Kaname thought better of mentioning him, though. If he showed up in Midori's nightmares later, Kaname would be powerless to help.

"Phew... Phew..."

The frills of Midori's miniskirt bounced up and down as she jogged on the treadmill. As scant as the girl's curves were, there was still some jiggling going on.

"This isn't going to help me against those attacks we've been seeing recently, though," she remarked.

"..."

"The laser beam Legacy, #flash.err...," continued Midori. "I heard rumors it was originally designed to shoot missiles out of the sky."

"Probably rail gun payloads, too."

It was on a completely different scale from #fireline.err and #dracolord.err, the two weapons they had fought for so far. This one was a single unit about the size of a shipping container. Legacies came in all shapes and sizes, but it was rare to find one larger than a car.

"I wonder where the heck they got it from," said Midori. "They're being a real nuisance, too. Are they just testing it out? Since they can move it around on trailers or suspend it from helicopters, it can strike in the heart of the city without anyone seeing it coming. The laser itself can fire from kilometers away, too, slicing a whole building in half along with the Dealer they were targeting... What could they be after,

I wonder? People have been saying that with important Dealers targeted left and right, it's even affecting stock prices."

This time, the story surrounding the Legacy was almost as grandiose as the weapon itself. The attacks seemed indiscriminate, which meant everyone had their own theories about what the perpetrators wanted. The whole thing was like a random street attacker using a battleship instead of a knife. And while the laser didn't require ammunition, it couldn't fire indefinitely. It needed certain chemicals, some of which were rather expensive. It just didn't seem worth it unless there was some particular aim.

However…

"…I bet they're culling the chaff."

"The what?"

Midori twisted around, still jogging, and wiped her sweat with the back of her hand.

"It's like how the sun is so bright it blots out the stars," Kaname said flatly. "*Money (Game) Master* is bursting with incompetent Dealers who make a lot of noise. You can't exactly blame them; half of making money is getting your name out there, after all… But if you're looking to partner up with real-world big shots or experienced players, then they're all just chaff. So what would you do in that situation? Maybe start eliminating the ones you *know* are useless, one by one, like in that game with the mines and the grid."

"So their target is weak people. But then…who are they hoping to find?"

"Well, that's simple."

All of a sudden, Kaname Suou felt a curious sensation like a weak electric shock—the Lion's Nose. It was a power that until recently Kaname had thought belonged to him alone. Perhaps the "Lion" part still did, but according to Kaname's old friend, there were others like him.

"They're after the Zodiac Children. Twelve irregularities with special sensory abilities."

* * *

Crrraaassshhh!!!!!!

Every window of the thirtieth floor was blown out instantly as something flew in like a bamboo spear, slicing the room in half. Midori would have been bisected at the waist if Kaname hadn't jumped on top of her milliseconds before it happened. The object zoomed clean through the building, then swung to the side, slicing half of it away. Kaname could see the orange glow of the glass and reinforced concrete where it had been cut…but the building didn't so much as sway. It was like a jenga tower, masterfully balanced on the verge of collapse.

"Whu…wh-wh-whu…?"

Peeking out from beneath Kaname's shoulder, Midori paled at the sight. They heard the sound of something striking the air over and over, and then before Kaname's eyes, a large tilt-rotor slowly rose into view, carrying a shipping container suspended on four wires. It continued upward, beyond the thirtieth floor. It was then that Kaname knew. The weapon behind the attack just now was none other than the laser beam Legacy, #flash.err.

Even now, with the building he was in sliced nearly in half, Kaname's heartbeat was steady. He hadn't exactly expected this, but neither had it come as much of a surprise.

…As soon as Takamasa gets even one of the Zodiac Children to work with him, it'll be checkmate for our AI overlords. It doesn't have to be me. He must be growing impatient.

In the wake of such a devastating attack, nobody thought to ask who it was using the Legacy. There was no rhyme or reason to it, so everyone just assumed it was some third-rate Dealer who'd gotten their hands on a powerful weapon and gone wild.

However, Kaname knew. In this case, the identity of the user was much more important than the Legacy itself.

Takamasa.

He couldn't say that name in front of Midori, of course. She didn't even know that the two of them had split up.

…But the Mind of the Magistelli can't rest idle with all this going on.

They know it's all over once Takamasa gets a Zodiac Child on his side. They'll want to get there first and either win them over or remove them from the board.

Things were about to get busy again.

Kaname had chosen to save the people he knew and to stay by Tselika's side, even if she was with the AI. He couldn't allow either Takamasa or the Mind to assemble their pieces first.

For Tselika, for Midori, for his own little sister.

And for Takamasa.

Kaname would fight for a future where everyone could laugh together, free from outside control.

2

It was time to cut the training session short and make a hasty exit. A weapon that could cut through reinforced concrete was bad news.

"*Pant... Gasp...* How come we can't use the elevator?!"

"It's good for your posture. Eyes up, and don't lean on the railing too hard or you'll waste stamina."

Midori left to go get her motorcycle, while Kaname took out his smartphone from the holder around his thigh. Tselika was still getting the coupe repaired, so Kaname had to call someone he usually wouldn't have. At a time like this, there was little choice.

"Frey(a)."

"*Yoo-hoo.*"

"How are things going with the favor I asked?"

"*I'd just like to remind you I'm a pawnshop owner. I deal in objects, not people. Raising armies isn't my style.*"

"And dealing with you isn't mine. But you still owe me."

"*What for, exactly?*"

"It was just recently, and I'm not letting you forget it. When you were fooling around with that super-clingy eyepatch-wearing gothic-lolita woman of yours, who was it who shot you with a paintball so you could fake your own death and get away from her?"

"Ugh. I thought we agreed we weren't going to talk about that."

"Your little two-bit act didn't fool that girl for a second, by the way. Falling off a cliff to a mysterious fate is the oldest trick in the book. If you don't believe me, ask yourself why she isn't seeking revenge. Instead, she's looking for you, and she's got an army of freelance photographers out there, acting as her eyes and ears. All I need to do is hand over your contact details and—"

"No, please! I'll do it! That relationship ended, most regrettably. But now that it's over, I'd prefer it stay that way for good!! I'm begging yooouuu!!!!!!"

Kaname didn't have any more time to waste. The laser had only hit the gym on the thirtieth floor, but he had no way of knowing how far the damage had spread and had decided to avoid the elevators. Because of that, it had taken him over an hour to get down here.

"If I may ask, what's the hurry?"

"I assume you've heard about #flash.err, the laser weapon that's been causing damage all over the place recently. Well, I'd like to take that weaponized shipping container out of the picture as soon as possible."

"Hmm. And?"

"Takamasa's hauling the Legacy around town and using it to take out loud but useless Dealers. He's trying to improve the signal-to-noise ratio and narrow down possibilities like he's solving a crossword puzzle. Usually, I'd just follow and figure out where he's hiding, but unfortunately I haven't been able to."

Kaname continued, speaking quickly.

"You see, he keeps changing the shipping container. And what's worse, he's doing it at Mega-Float III, the slums of Tokonatsu City. His trucks and choppers go in, shuffle around a bit, and come back out. And he can do that whenever he wants, so I can't count on it being the same vehicle every time. I need to catch him when he makes the swap, find out exactly which one is carrying #flash.err, and then follow it…"

"That's not what I meant. If it's backup you need, why not call on Midori for help?"

Kaname fell silent. Then…

"…You really think I can ask her?"

"Oh. She's a Hekireki, too, I suppose."

"Yeah."

"I understand you want to handle her with care."

"And Tselika's out getting the car fixed. I can't charge into those slums all by myself. For once, I'm going to have to rely on someone else."

"I understand. There's a car waiting for you out front. It's a blue SUV. I'd give you the plate number, but I think you'll know it when you see it. Get inside, and use it however you see fit."

Kaname hung up and walked to the front of the building. Sure enough, he saw a sky-blue four-wheel-drive vehicle parked by the side of the road. He walked over and knocked on the rear door. Then, without waiting for a response, he opened it and climbed in.

"Thanks for coming at such short notice," he said. "I need to get to Mega-Float—"

Just then, his nose bristled.

Click! Click! A pair of guns were pointed in his face. One from the left, and one from the right.

Just as Kaname sat down in the back seat, the two with guns followed, sandwiching him in. He recognized both of their faces. They were former members of the Ag Wolves. The one with pale-pink hair tied back in a single braid was Zaurus, and the backpack-wearing boy with bad posture was M-Scope. Driving the car was what appeared to be a *yuki-onna* Magistellus.

From the unlucky middle seat between them, Kaname groaned.

"…You two."

"W-we ended up working for Frey(a), you see," said the boy with the slouch. "And he asked us to pass on a message. He said he doesn't care what happens from this point on. All lovers are equal in his eyes, and he's happy to lend a hand to any of them."

Kaname had been naive. He hadn't exactly thought of that freak as his friend, but still... Frey(a) was the unpredictable leader of the Treasure Hermit Crabs, a force Kaname couldn't hope to tame. Kaname's struggle against the AI overlords, his falling-out with Takamasa—Frey(a) didn't care about any of that.

He was a monster who held the economy of the world in his hands, and all he cared about was love. Next to that, the fate of humanity meant nothing to him.

As Kaname covered his face and started to cry out, Zaurus struck the back of his neck with her pistol and knocked him out cold.

3

You might be wondering why Frey(a) made this particular call.

For that, we turn to the VIP room on a certain reconverted submarine.

"He doesn't have to say it," said the woman in white, smiling at her puzzled slime-girl Magistellus. "I know Kaname won't just fall into my lap." She had hearts in her eyes as she spoke; the woman was a slave to love. "...But what if he Falls, with a capital 'F'? Now that's a different story. He won't abandon his mission just because of a little debt, oh no. He'll come crawling back to me, begging me to save him. And I can't wait to see him on his hands and knees ☆"

4

The first thing Kaname noticed as he came to was a rusty smell that filled his nostrils. He soon realized it wasn't blood but actual rust.

"Ugh..."

He groaned, and every joint in his body cried out in pain. He was in a dusty room, likely a prefab office cabin or other temporary building. Against the wall were a bunch of old wooden crates bearing the names of businesses that had been bought out or gone bankrupt, like Winchell

Foods or Grimnoah Shipping, making for a rather sorry sight. Kaname was seated in a chair in the center of the room, his hands bound behind him with tape wound along the back of the chair.

No handcuffs. If he put his mind to it, he could probably break free. However, there were two reasons it wasn't going to be so easy.

"…Awake at last, are we?" said the first reason, dragging a chair over and taking a seat opposite him. It was the boy with the slouch, M-Scope.

The second reason was a set of tripods, one situated in each corner of the room… Or rather, the oscillating light machine guns mounted atop them.

M-Scope fiddled with his smartphone. "They operate on both infrared and microwave bands. They don't call me the master of patience and traps for nothing. They're made with repurposed circuit boards from the drone killers they use at airports, so don't make any hasty movements unless you want a lethal dose of 7.62 mm bullets."

Kaname was reminded of how, during their heyday, the Ag Wolves had fitted security cameras all across the peninsula financial district. That must have been his doing, too, though it seemed unlikely he'd done all the legwork by himself.

"Where am I…?" asked Kaname.

"You're on Mega-Float III, in the most dangerous area of all: the Red Territory."

Mega-Float III had once been the site of a planned international airport, but a spate of bankruptcies and pullouts had left the region a lawless wasteland. One end had been converted into a relatively respectable gambling establishment, but the other was a rusted-up slum district just as dangerous as it appeared.

The land of rust, the Red Territory.

Kaname Suou chuckled.

"Oh good. That's exactly where I was headed. So despite everything, you're still carrying out Frey(a)'s errand, huh? Something happen in the bedroom between the two of you I should know about?"

"…It's got nothing to do with him," the boy replied. "The Red Territory is simply the best place for our needs right now."

Him. It seemed M-Scope only knew the ambiguously gendered pawn-shop owner as a man.

"What's your goal here?" asked Kaname, trying his best not to appear too desperate. He needed to find a way out or he would miss his chance to pin down #flash.err. There wasn't enough time for this interrogation.

"If you were after revenge," he continued, "you had your chance back in the car. But you knocked me out instead. Don't tell me you've got more torture in mind."

Kaname briefly considered that they may have opted for a nonlethal takedown in order to bypass the Lion's Nose, but quickly dismissed the idea. There was no way they were that familiar with the details of his ability.

"I assure you, this is business, not pleasure," said M-Scope, eyes still darting around nervously despite the balance of power being tipped strongly in his favor. He couldn't even look a person in the eye when they were strapped to a chair in front of him.

"We simply want to help the members of the Ag Wolves you killed and saddled with debt. For that, we need money… Since it's your fault they Fell, it's only fair you pay out, right? That's why we want the details of your assets."

"You think this'll be as easy as taking my phone and emptying my accounts?"

"No, but keep in mind you're immobilized right now. That's not too different from being forcibly logged-out."

"…"

"Once we know about all the assets you're currently trading, and you've been stopped from making new transactions, the rest will be child's play. We'll simply use the market to manipulate your fortune into nothing and put it back into the hands of the Dealers you screwed. All I'm seeking is compensation. You wouldn't deny a victim their right to compensation, would you?"

"I'd say there's one glaring flaw in your plan, wouldn't you?"

"Oh, yes," the boy replied frankly. "Even a Dealer who is logged-out can still have their Magistellus conduct transactions automatically. That's precisely why *Money (Game) Master* is popular even among those without an eye for business. Of course, it's not a good idea to rely on them too heavily… But in any case, you're right. It's not quite the same thing as Falling. Not yet anyway."

It was then that Kaname realized what the boy, now staring directly at him, was trying to say.

"But then all we need to do is capture her, too. Or perhaps we can Down her."

"You bastard…"

"Did I mention we drove around town a little before coming here? Anyone performing even the most cursory investigation will have no trouble tracking us down. And they'll follow us right here to the most dangerous place in all of Tokonatsu City, the Red Territory."

M-Scope cracked a small, cruel smile.

"I wonder how a single Magistellus will fare, working without instructions? Or perhaps she'll team up with that stray kitten of yours, Midori Hekireki. I have no doubt they'll make it to the Red Territory, but I get the feeling they'll be roped into some trouble or other before they make it here. Something with fatal consequences."

The hairs on the back of Kaname's neck began to bristle with a rage he hadn't thought himself capable of.

"I hope you catch my drift."

But something here didn't add up. All M-Scope needed to do was extract the details of Kaname's assets via torture and shoot him dead. When a Dealer Fell, not only were they fully locked out of their account for twenty-four hours, but their Magistellus was, too. Luring Tselika here and killing her was a whole other risk he didn't have to take. But apparently, that wasn't enough. There had to be another more personal motive driving him to act this way.

"…There's no specific time limit, but I'd advise you to act sooner rather than later," explained M-Scope. "Relinquish your assets, and

I'll let you go. But if you resist, your precious friends will die. It's a dangerous world out there. I've heard order is so bad in this area, people *fight to the death over discarded pull tabs and soda bottle caps.* Alternatively, if you prefer, we can sit here until your Magistellus goes Down, and then we can plunder your assets the hard way. I'll let you choose. It makes no difference to us."

Kaname breathed a long, drawn-out sigh and replied,

"I suppose you're right…"

Then he flashed a fierce smile.

"I guess I'd better act sooner rather than later, then."

Kaname waved his arms, already free from their bindings.

They had been secured only with tape, not rope. With no knots to contend with, it was a simple matter of twisting his wrists in circles until the adhesive surface wore out. After that, it was no more difficult than slipping his hands free of a fabric tube.

But, of course, that wasn't the only obstacle between him and freedom.

"You wanna die, idiot?!! That's fine by me!!" roared M-Scope, tapping on his phone screen. The light machine guns mounted in the corners of the room spun to face Kaname. M-Scope had already warned him that if he made any suspicious movements, the turrets would fill him full of holes. They were adapted from airport security technology, able to identify prey using microwaves and infrared.

But there was always another way. For example…

"Tch."

"What's wrong, M-Scope? *Scared you'll get caught in the cross fire?*"

Kaname lunged toward him, tackling the boy off his chair. With both of them in a heap on the floor, the turrets were essentially useless.

The Lion's Nose was still quiet. As long as Kaname stayed on track, he would live.

Being surrounded by AI-operated machine guns had to be scary, even for the one who'd set them up. After all, everyone had seen—or, more to the point, heard—how inaccurate a simple car alarm could be. That's why they needed to have safety protocols, like facial recognition, added in.

No gun. Damn, and no phone, either?

Still in a pile on the floor, Kaname clicked his tongue. Realizing a little late how much had been taken from him, he removed his necktie. That was all he needed to kill a man, if the situation demanded it.

But just as Kaname moved to strangle M-Scope, another figure stepped into the dusty room.

Zaurus!!

It was now that the Lion's Nose gave its loudest warning. There was a buzz of pain at the tip of Kaname's nose like static electricity.

Tss, tss. Pshh, pshh, pshh!!

There was a sound, but it wasn't the sound of a gun—not even a silenced one. It sounded more like a can of compressed air. And then a blistering pain shot through Kaname's upper arm.

"Gaaah!!"

A nail gun…?! Was she always this brutal?!

Zaurus fired a second shot, then a third, but Kaname's life was in no danger. No nail could kill a human instantly, unless it hit the heart or the brain. It still hurt like hell, though.

However, the carpentry tool wasn't Zaurus's only weapon. Something was in her other hand, being dragged noisily across the ground—a baseball bat. Kaname only realized what she was up to once she used the nail gun to fire a few rounds into it.

"A nail bat…"

"You wouldn't think it, but these fall out all the time, so a tool like this is real handy. It's like reloadin'."

At first, he had taken the girl for a crafter type like Takamasa, but he quickly reevaluated. She made limited use of what tools she had, and her only goal was to increase the damage of the weapon in front of her. She wasn't nearly as ingenious as Criminal AO.

She smirked and spun the finished nail bat in her hands.

"I'm a close-combat specialist. My bread and butter are knives and shotguns. At this range, I can take you out in one hit."

"Tch!!"

The idea that knives were stronger than guns at point-blank range was mostly just wishful thinking, but luckily for her, Kaname didn't have a gun; he had a necktie. He clicked his tongue and kicked M-Scope toward the girl, using the recoil to launch himself out of the interrogation room and out of sight of the machine-gun turrets.

He was now in a straight passage connecting many more rusted storehouses, just like the one he'd come from. The layout resembled a hallway full of classrooms.

I need a weapon, he thought.

Suddenly, a figure rounded the corner at the far end of the hallway. It was a small girl in a pale-blue kimono, possibly the *yuki-onna* Magistellus from before. However, compared to her dress, the weapon she carried over her shoulder was decidedly *not* traditional.

"A rocket launcher?!"

Trusting in the Lion's Nose, Kaname launched himself through a window so dirty it was completely opaque, moments before the hallway exploded into flames.

That girl just blew up the building her Dealer was in without a second thought! What on earth has he been teaching her?!

Having somehow dodged the rain of death and glass shards, Kaname considered his priorities. Right now, he truly had nothing—not even a single bullet. No guns, no car, no money. No Magistellus and no allied Dealers, either.

I have to find some way to get in touch with the others!!

If they didn't hear from Kaname, Tselika and Midori would be on their way soon enough, and while he didn't want to swallow M-Scope's story without questioning it, he had to admit there was a grain of truth to what he'd said. The Red Territory was dangerous. It was easy to imagine them getting caught in the cross fire of some random feud and taking a bullet. Meanwhile, if Kaname managed to escape M-Scope and Zaurus, they might choose to go after his allies instead.

He had to tell them to stay away before they got here… And that was why it was so frustrating to be without a phone at such a critical moment.

He extracted the nails embedded in his upper arm and bandaged the open wounds with his necktie before heading off. The narrow streets were lined with strange plastic protrusions a little larger than yogurt pots, remnants of the old runway lights from when this used to be an airport. Spotting a disused pay phone, he grabbed the receiver and held it to his ear, but there was no dial tone. When he looked again, he saw the plastic cover had been torn away to get at the change within.

"Damn it!!" he cursed, slamming the receiver back down.

His pursuers were no fools. They would be on his tail soon enough, and Kaname couldn't expect to hear them coming.

"*The wind's changed! Zaurus, make your Magistellus stand down! It's dangerous to leave her on auto!!*"

"*That's why I said we should stick with the nail guns!!*"

…?

Kaname felt a strange sensation in his nostrils, and it wasn't the Lion's Nose. A weird chemical odor hung in the air, something the average human would never smell in their lives.

Is that…acetylene gas?

Acetylene gas was commonly used as blowtorch fuel when welding and would be a familiar smell to anyone who earned a living cutting apart and reselling stolen cars. It wasn't particularly explosive, but it was flammable. Perhaps a rusted-up gas cylinder had been jostled in the prior explosion and sprang a leak. Someone unable to judge the concentration and accurately assess the danger could easily set the whole place alight with a single misplaced muzzle flash.

Kaname had been saved by an invisible trap, but he wasn't out of the woods just yet. This would render guns unusable for anyone not wise to the acetylene situation. Now he really couldn't allow Midori and Tselika to turn up. And to ensure they didn't, he needed a means of communication. Deciding to keep his distance for now, Kaname ducked into a back alley and began weaving his way through the backstreets…

5

Tires screeched as the mint-green coupe skidded around the corner with Tselika at the wheel. She had been holed up in Hamazura Garage for the past several hours getting the car fixed, so she hadn't noticed anything amiss until it was already too late. She raced along the shoreline, passing a prominent lighthouse that doubled as a date spot.

Midori: Tselika, tell me what's going on!

Tselika: My Lord's not picking up his phone. I can't get a reading on his GPS data, either. And I forbade him from purchasing any other cars, so he only has this one!

So that's why Kaname was on foot, thought Midori. When he'd met up with her in front of the gym, he'd arrived on a bus, a particularly unpopular mode of transport in *Money (Game) Master*.

Tselika: Without his car, he can't log in or out, and leaving his vehicle to go off alone isn't like him. If we lose track of each other, he can't leave the game when he wants. At the very least, I would expect him to tell me first!

Midori: Which means?

Tselika: Something's gone wrong. If I were a betting woman, I'd say he's been kidnapped.

The mint-green coupe had been in the garage getting repaired the whole time, so there were no clues to be found on its dashcam footage. The succubus did have one lead, however.

Tselika: I analyzed the data from your bike and caught his face in the back seat of a sky-blue SUV. With him are M-Scope and Zaurus, two members of the former Ag Wolves and top-class Dealers.

Midori: Aren't they the ones who were trying to collect my brother's Legacies...?

The low-roofed sports car shot down the shopping street in between glamorous jewelry stores and beneath a huge model sailboat suspended by wires. The giant airship, named Sky Impact, was one of many landmarks scattered throughout Tokonatsu City. Its hull resembled a whale furnished with wings and sails.

Tselika: I don't know how they've come back, and I don't care. The point is, they've reason enough to be displeased with My Lord. I can think of only two reasons they haven't killed him already: either a quick kill won't satisfy their revenge, or they're after the passwords protecting My Lord's assets.

Their reasoning so far was perfect. However, there was one thing the girls didn't know.

As soon as they reached their goal, they would die. Kaname Suou wanted to avoid that outcome more than anything, and the pair were utterly oblivious.

They drove on, like a spark traveling down the fuse of a giant bomb, edging closer and closer to its explosive core. Unfortunately, they were both extremely skilled. And that was why it would take real effort to put out that spark.

Midori: So where exactly are we going?

Tselika: We can't rely on video footage alone. I've hired every information broker money can buy. We'll track him down soon enough. At the very least, there's no sign of him here on the peninsula!!

6

"Zaurus! Don't go in alone! I'll bring the car around!"

"Shut your hole, dumbass! We'll never catch him on these narrow streets in a car!!"

A brief argument followed, but in the end, it was drowned out as M-Scope revved the engine and Kaname heard the car speed away.

…Why are they sticking to the armored vehicle, I wonder? Afraid of getting caught in their own traps? Or maybe they went to set up cameras along the main street…

Kaname was finally able to take a deep breath in his hiding spot behind the shell of a rusted-up car. The buzzing pain slowly disappeared from the tip of his nose.

"Phew…," someone sighed. But it wasn't Kaname. It had come from the girl in his arms—the girl he had crashed into in the street and hurriedly pulled to safety.

Perhaps "country gal" was a better descriptor. She wore a large white apron over a long, pale-green skirt, with scarlet hair tied back in twin braids. On her head, she sported what was more of a headscarf than a bandanna, and she carried a large wicker basket in the crook of her arm.

She seemed about Kaname's age and looked pretty, though in a more natural way than Tselika.

Her getup looked positively sturdy compared to the swimwear you usually saw around *Money (Game) Master*. That said, she wasn't wearing a top under the bib of her apron—not even a bikini. And as she rose slightly to look up and down the street to make sure the coast was clear, her chest pressed into Kaname's face.

"I-it looks like they've gone," the girl said. "I don't know who's after you, but you should be more careful walking the streets of the Red Territory."

"Y-yeah, got it."

"My name's Claire Kaizuka! What's yours?"

"Kaname Suou."

It was only a username. There was no reason to hide it.

"Huh? Huuuhhh?!"

The girl, however, was so surprised she fell over backward, bumping her head against the filthy wall. She rubbed at her head, her legs splayed and her eyes wide with shock.

"Y-y-y-y-you mean you're that legendary Dealer?! The one I've heard so many stories about…Kaname Suou?!"

"I'm…legendary?"

Was she referring to the old days of Called Game? Or to Kaname's recent scuffle with Bloody Dancer? Either way, it didn't matter. He was in a hurry.

"You're the smart young man who can rustle up 1.7 billion *snow* whenever he wants! I've heard so much about you! I was a huge fan!!"

"R-really?"

How did she know the exact figure? Was it leaked? Kaname wondered. The redhead stared, starry-eyed, before something seemed to catch her attention.

"Huh? Oh no! Your arm... You're wounded! We have to do something!!"

The redhead knelt back down and started fishing around in her basket. Kaname had assumed she must be carrying a gun or two in there, but he quickly learned that was not the case—she had brought out only bandages and antiseptic. Her skirt, as well, seemed difficult to hide weapons under, as there was no slit or anything for quick access. Perhaps she was hiding something beneath her apron, but that didn't seem like a great choice, either. Plus, anything stuffed under there would be plainly visible from the side, where an open tunnel had formed between her bosom and belly button.

What was she thinking—coming to such a dangerous place without any weapons or cars...?

"Hmm? What's the matter?" she asked.

"Nothing..."

"Come on, show me your arm. I hope it's not too bad... Oh my."

Claire had taken Kaname's arm and examined it without waiting for a response, but now *she* was the one wincing in secondhand pain as she glanced at the wound. Kaname didn't bat an eye, however.

"I know it looks bad, but the bone's still intact and it missed the major arteries. Just stop the bleeding and I'll be all right."

"Did you forget all the rust in the air around here? Why do you think they call it the Red Territory? I know it's just a game, but that doesn't mean you can't get tetanus!"

The redhead hurriedly whipped out a bottle of disinfectant.

"This'll sting!" she said.

"Look, I already said, you don't need to—"

"There!!"

Kaname clenched his teeth in pain as the burning sensation fried his nerves. Still, it would have been rude to refuse treatment. It was possible she was trying to poison him or knock him out, but despite a lack of evidence, Kaname didn't think that was likely.

That said…

"Claire…?" he asked.

"Oh, yes?!"

"Do you think you could at least do that with your eyes open?"

"Heh-heh, sorry. I don't really like seeing blood…"

But even now, as she wrapped the bandage around his arm, Kaname still got the feeling Claire was averting her gaze. He wanted to tell her not to intervene in the first place if it bothered her so much, but logic didn't work on people like her. Perhaps she simply wasn't cut out for the ruthless dog-eat-dog world of *Money (Game) Master*, but Kaname opted not to mention any of that. He'd stuck around because there was something else he wanted to ask.

"Do you have a phone or tablet I could borrow?"

Kaname's priority was getting in touch with Tselika and Midori as soon as possible. If left alone, they'd follow the trail of bread crumbs leading right into M-Scope's trap. Those girls were smart, but they were unlikely to scrutinize clues they believed they'd picked up themselves, and that was why Kaname had to be the one to tell them. It was like a phishing scam—obvious except when you were the target.

However.

"Huh? Oh, a smartphone? I guess they're hard to come by around here."

"…So what, you're saying the people around here all rely on pay phones?"

"Ah-ha-ha… Well, as you've seen for yourself, none of them work."

…No means of communication at all, then. How did the people living here even participate in the stock market? Apparently, they'd never considered home telephones, either. But maybe that was the point of the place. Kaname hadn't really paid much attention to this area in the past, but he had heard rumors—rumors that if you Fell and wanted a second chance, you came here.

If you Fell, but you weren't ready to give up, this was the place to go.

It was somewhere you could lie low, avoid the gaze of envious Dealers, and make it all back.

I see. This must be where Takamasa was hiding out all that time. In that case, the reason he's holed up in that scrapyard now isn't just because it's handy for switching containers. This place means something to him. Perhaps there are more clues to find around here.

This was the lowest rung of the social ladder, where the most ambitious, desperate souls convened. It had surprised Kaname to hear that old softy Takamasa reveal such a ruthless plan. Maybe this was where he had learned how to be so unforgiving.

The people here weren't worried about turning a profit. They were survivors, building up the means to fight, acquiring a modicum of weaponry and vehicles they could use to strike back. For them, this was a land of revival. Perhaps this was simply the final step in the business cycle… Whether revival was possible for any of them or not, so long as Dealers were getting shot and killed every day, there would always be a demand for a place like this.

I'm really glad Midori never ended up here.

Before she bumped into Kaname, Midori had entered the game saddled with debt. It was conceivable she might have somehow wound up here—the most punishing area of the game. She'd probably avoided that fate only by being such a total beginner. It hadn't even occurred to her to check online for tips or guides.

Claire Kaizuka clapped her hands in front of her chest and said:

"Oh, but there might be someone in the plaza with a smartphone! I feel like I saw someone who trades with the outside carrying one!!"

"…"

There were a lot of people here. The fact that they were all free to stage a comeback must mean they had some way of ensuring that troublesome, rich Dealers kept their noses out. They'd gone to the trouble of seizing control over a dirty, worthless area, and they shunned the company of others in order to build a safe haven.

A territory unconcerned with profit, independent from the flow of money. I doubt it's all about charity, but I can't tell what's going on just yet.

Kaname needed to track down whoever was privileged enough to own a phone around here. It didn't matter how much money he had in the bank, without a phone or his Magistellus to access it, he might as well be dirt-poor. Right now, Kaname was at rock bottom, with only his own two hands to dig his way out.

…Looks like I'm going to have to get creative.

7

Claire Kaizuka, the girl in the long skirt and apron (and nothing else), led Kaname toward what she called the plaza, which turned out to be an old basketball court. The wire fence that once surrounded it had been torn down, and now the place was overcrowded with shacks made of cardboard and corrugated iron, as well as a giant dice cube about two meters in height made from thin aluminum, perhaps converted from an old aircraft shipping container. The only vestiges of the plaza's original form were the two basketball hoops that had somehow survived, along with the faint traces of white markings still visible on the orange floor.

If he were to sum it up…

It's like a dirty old flea market. Though I wonder how they came by some of this stuff…

"Here we are! There's nothing you can't find in the plaza!"

Claire Kaizuka offered him a big smile once they'd arrived. It looked like the kind of place Kaname would have to haggle down to the penny over a single handmade sandwich, only to then put his digestive system's mettle to the test eating it. And yet the redheaded girl seemed almost relieved to be here. Kaname, on the other hand, found marketplaces that didn't deal in stocks and futures a little unsettling.

All he was looking for was a phone or a tablet, specifically one he could use right away.

I can't show how desperate I am, or who knows how much they'll hike up the price. Then again, I don't have a dime to spend anyway, and I can't even use an ATM without my phone or Tselika.

Just as Kaname was contemplating how to proceed, a man in overalls and a greasy T-shirt, with a shaved head, called out to them—or more precisely, to Claire.

"Hey, lass. See you've picked up another stray."

"Heh-heh. Not this time! You see, the person standing next to me is actually…tah-dah! Kaname Suou!!"

"Yeah, right. And I'm Criminal AO."

"Honest to god, Ramjet! Why don't you believe me?!!"

As the redhead sulked, the older man looked over at Kaname and shrugged—as if to say, *Let's leave it at that, shall we?* He seemed good at looking after people. Maybe Claire's apron-look was inspired by his overalls.

Tucked into the man's belt were tools like an oversize monkey wrench and an L-shaped crowbar. Unlike Takamasa, though, this guy didn't seem to use them as tools. He was a fighter, and he was telling Kaname with his eyes, *If you really are a prominent Dealer, you don't want to show weakness around these parts.*

"What're you looking for?" he asked. "Just let me know and I'll find you someone who's got it."

To be honest, there wasn't much Kaname *wasn't* looking for. He needed a phone, sure, but also a gun, a car, and clothes with different skills. He wouldn't turn his nose up at anything, but saying so was the same as exposing his own weakness.

What's more, he still needed to track down #flash.err…or at least the container it was being kept inside. Thanks to Frey(a)'s insensitive meddling, he had the former Ag Wolves on his tail, too. And what he wanted to avoid more than anything else was people finding out who he was and ganging up on him.

…I'll dodge the question for now and see if I can find anything out.

"I'm looking for some special .45-caliber ammunition you can't find in normal stores. Is there anyone around here who deals in guns?"

*   *   *

Click! Click!

Without warning everyone, even passersby, turned and pointed their weapons at him in unison.

It probably had nothing to do with individual morality. The people here always had their eyes peeled for outsiders.

The gun barrels numbered between thirty and forty. Most were port weapons or sawn-offs, shoddily cut down from assault rifles and shotguns with a metalworking saw or the like. Meanwhile, Kaname was unarmed, without so much as a bulletproof vest. A single shot could be enough to kill him.

However.

...They're not that high quality.

Kaname silently judged the situation. Even with this many opponents, the response from his Lion's Nose was negligible.

They had quantity but not quality. Sights were misaligned, and even the barrels were warped out of shape. Were the weapons this poor to begin with, or was it a result of all the crude modifications? Either way, many of them seemed unlikely to hit their targets. In fact, they were liable to explode and take off the wielders' hands. Perhaps they would hit at point-blank range, but at that distance, Kaname could easily whisk the weapon out of their grasp and beat them over the head with it. He was starting to realize why this Ramjet guy relied on blunt weapons.

However, if the guns are this rough, it's unlikely anyone controls the supply of ammunition. What would Takamasa do in that case? ...He'd probably scrape together as much as he could and then build a gun that uses it.

Obviously, that wasn't something just anyone could do.

If these were the guns they were pointing at intruders, Kaname shuddered to think what sort of junk a total novice might be able to get their hands on. It seemed that even in the Red Territory, staging a comeback wasn't quite as easy as it sounded.

Kaname wasn't afraid of the guns. There was only one person here

he needed to pay attention to: a man in a raincoat pointing a large crossbow his way. A simple weapon must be much easier to maintain in a
place like this.

Then the older man in the overalls raised his hand.

"Stand down, everyone. He's no stranger; Claire brought him here."

"…Who's vouching for him?" snapped the gloomy man in the raincoat. The girl standing by Kaname's side began bouncing up and down.

"Oh, I am!" she replied immediately. "I'll be his, uhh…guarantor? Is
that the word???"

"You heard the girl," said Ramjet. "That means this guy's a guest,
same as you when you first arrived."

"Tch."

At last, the atmosphere began to relax, and the man in the raincoat
lowered his crossbow. Following suit, everyone put away their guns and
continued on their way as if nothing had happened.

"Well, I guess that worked out," said Ramjet, stroking his beard. "You
can take a look around, but you gotta follow the rules. Claire here can
get you up to speed."

"One question. The Red Territory is a town, correct?"

"Yeah."

"But it's not a *team*?"

It sounded like splitting hairs, but the question Kaname had just
asked was very important. He would be staying here for the time being,
but he didn't want to sign up for anything.

Ramjet gave a chuckle and answered:

"We ain't that close. Anyone's welcome to trade here. We got rules
and a fixed location, but we ain't employees. Everyone here is master
of their own store. We bring our goods and sell 'em to anyone who's
buying."

"Oh, Ramjet. Where are you going?!" asked Claire.

"I thought I'd go around and introduce you, but you two youngsters
don't need a fifth wheel like me anyway."

With a quick wave, the man in overalls left. The sound of the monkey wrench and crowbar jangling in his belt made Kaname feel like

he'd been transported to another world—a world where melee weapons that didn't use up ammo were even more useful than guns.

Here the rules of engagement were completely different. If these shoddy guns were all they had to worry about, even Tselika and Midori would have no problems. But it was the winding streets and unfamiliar rooftops that posed the real threat. Kaname could no longer consider himself safe so long as he held a gun; anyone could be hiding around any corner, atop any building, and his enemies weren't going to wait for him to get his bearings. One good surprise attack with a blunt object and he'd be a goner.

A cocktail of strange smells—rust, engine grease, and flammable gases—tickled his senses.

If anyone came in brimming with confidence and let off a few rounds…there would be an explosion, no question. The quality of their firearms aside, the only ones who could use a gun in this situation were those who could read the wind and gauge the concentrations of flammable gas in the air. In other words, the locals.

Even if he had a Legacy, Kaname would be dead unless he learned to adapt.

"Eh-heh-heh," the girl giggled. "Where should we go first?"

"To find a phone or a tablet."

8

"I recommend one of these. If you're going to be staying in the Red Territory, you'll need a set of wheels!"

"What's this, a scooter?"

It wasn't what Kaname had asked for at all. It looked like someone had added a vertical rod and a set of handlebars to an ordinary skateboard. Needless to say, it was foot-powered, not electric. Kaname furrowed his brow at the girl's suggestion. Vehicles in Tokonatsu City came in all shapes and sizes, but they needed an engine if you wanted to use them to log in and out. It wouldn't work with just a bicycle or a pair of rollerblades.

But Claire seemed dead serious.

"We have bikes, too, but these are more popular nowadays. They're cheap to fix because of all the spare parts lying around, and the tires are plastic, so you don't have to worry about punctures from all the broken glass and rusty nails."

Even though Kaname had no money and no means to make a withdrawal, Claire had brought back two of them. Perhaps one was a rental? Either way, Kaname could hardly refuse her generosity now, so he decided to go along with it.

Wobbling around on the scooter, Kaname took his first real look across the so-called plaza. There was a windsock, left over from the planned airport, hanging limp and unmoving. It looked like even physical objects were modeled to take damage when left out in the sun.

Soon, Kaname came to understand a few things.

"Hey, lass. Finished fixin' up that stove o' yours. Lookin' forward to some fresh-baked bread next time you get a chance."

"Heh-heh, no problem! My, you've been busy yourself, Innkeeper. Are these all bottle caps?"

"Well, not much to do here 'cept pick up trash. All these have dirty labels on 'em, too, so they're gonna be a pain to recycle."

The first thing Kaname learned was that everybody here seemed to get on well with Claire. Many of them were wary of Kaname, but loosened up as soon as she appeared.

The second was that, just as he had expected, there was nowhere here that dealt in phones or tablets directly, so even if he opened his own shop hoping to trade his way up from a single red paper clip, he would be unable to do so.

"*Phewee...*"

Claire stopped atop her scooter and mopped the sweat from her brow. Her stamina must have been pretty low, as the pair had yet to even leave the plaza. She rested her weight on the handlebars like she was leaning out a window, squeezing her sizable breasts.

"We never did find you that phone," she said, seemingly unaware of what she was doing.

"Yeah, guess they're not that common around here."

What Kaname found interesting about the place was not the presence or absence of phones, however, but the tools the merchants were using. In place of digital registers, they had all been flicking around marbles in the sand to do their calculations, like a rudimentary abacus.

…They don't even have pocket calculators, Kaname thought, *which means I'm going to have a hard time finding any electronics, let alone a phone. Strange—you'd think a Magistellus could handle the calculations for them, and everybody gets one of those.*

"Hmm, I guess we'll have to borrow one off somebody," said Claire.

That's assuming anyone will lend me theirs. At this rate, it might be more difficult to get a phone than a gun.

And while it wasn't related to his main concerns, there was one other thing weighing on Kaname's mind. It seemed like there was an obvious solution to the lack of calculators and phones…

…Does no one here have a Magistellus?

"Hmm? What's the matter?"

The redhead looked at him with a quizzical expression. Kaname had realized something. It wasn't just Claire—everybody here was human; not a single vampire or zombie to be seen… Not even ones who *looked* human. In all of Tokonatsu City, it was hard to find anywhere this homogeneous, even though there were plenty who had it in for the AI—Frey(a), with his disdain for anything other than human love, or Takamasa and his hatred for all things Magistellus.

"Do you know anyone who might have a phone?"

"Oh, yes! There's a rich person around… Ah-ha-ha, rich by Red Territory standards, I mean."

"Who are they?"

"His name's Flak00. Hmm…I think he said he was collecting pull tabs and bottle caps to trade with the outside."

Killing him and taking it by force was always an option, but only as a last resort. For now, it seemed Claire's introduction would be enough to get by, and Kaname was hoping to avoid burning bridges if at all possible.

"What do you want to do?" Claire asked. "He won't meet just anyone."

"It's the same as the stock market," replied Kaname.

…I give him what he wants, or I threaten him into doing what I say.

"Either way, it all starts here."

9

A series of loud footsteps echoed down the tunnel as Tselika descended a set of stairs leading underground. Though she wore stiletto-heeled boots, she was not running fast enough to be in danger of falling.

"Why are we taking the subway?!" Midori called from behind her.

"To avoid snipers, of course," she replied. "The only way off the peninsula by car is via the circular bridge, and we don't want to give an attacker the opportunity to lay an ambush. All it would take is one wayside bomb linked to an image-recognition system to identify the mint-green coupe and blow us apart."

Owning a vehicle was a prerequisite to logging out, so every Dealer had at least one car or motorcycle. Still, there were several reasons why Tokonatsu City maintained a flourishing public transport system.

The first was to transport nonhuman NPCs and freight around the city.

The second was to influence the price of land. Houses built by railway lines would decrease in value, while the price of plots with easy access to a station would be driven up.

And as for the third…

"Trains are like a secret passage. Smugglers use park-and-ride services to beat the traffic or split up, sending their Magistellus in the car as a decoy while they take the subway to their destination."

"Really?"

"I've even heard rumors there are hidden islands at the edge of the map you can only access via abandoned subway tunnels."

Tselika passed her smartphone over the electronic turnstile and rushed through. Magistelli could only use equipment owned by their Dealer, but this smartphone technically belonged to Kaname.

Slung over the pair's backs were two large instrument cases—a guitar for Midori and a double bass for Tselika. Of course, the clunking sounds coming from inside were not from any musical instruments but from the Legacies. Again, all this belonged to Kaname, so Tselika was in the clear.

A train with about half a dozen cars pulled into the station just as they were arriving. Midori and Tselika hopped straight through the open doors, before politely placing their "instruments" by their feet. All the other passengers were bikini-clad young women. They *were* in a women's car, and this was Tokonatsu City, after all.

"...Phew. My heart's still racing," said Midori, turning to gaze at the city through the windows as the subway train came aboveground.

"Do you feel like you're in one of *those* establishments?"

"We're really going to Mega-Float III, huh?"

"Specifically, the Red Territory. The poorest area with the worst crime."

"How do you know?"

"Our phones are linked. It looks like they destroyed My Lord's, but it managed to transmit his last known coordinates to me."

...Tselika's logic was sound, but there was one thing she had failed to consider. What if Kaname's enemies had known about that feature and deliberately destroyed the device to lay a trap for her?

After stopping at a few more stations, the train dived back underground, soon to leave the peninsula by means of an undersea tunnel. And it was at that last station that the number of people boarding the train drastically increased.

"Mmgh!!"

"Midori, don't let go of that case!"

"I know! But what's with all these people?! Is this a localized rush hour or something?!"

"People who want to leave the peninsula gather at this stop."

It almost seemed like the automatic doors wouldn't be able to close.

They opened and shut several times before finally sticking, and the train lurched forward.

"Eek!"

"What's the matter, Midori? Did someone touch you?"

"Uhhhh, no! It's just, err…"

Midori stammered, cheeks red, and righted herself after nearly falling face-first into a nearby woman's exposed bosom. Despite being pressed up so close against one another, their bare skin touching, nobody in the sea of people seemed to realize that the long end of Midori's suitcase had been shoved directly up into her frilled bikini miniskirt.

And train rides were known to get pretty bumpy.

There were so many people, she couldn't even move her hands, much less close her legs, between which the case was lodged. All she could do was tense her buttocks, but it didn't help.

Oh, ooh…w-wait! Wait a second! This can't be happening! O-ohhh?! My swimsuit…it's slippinggg!

At least it hadn't completely come off, but mentally, Midori was already defenseless. She squeezed her eyes shut in terror as Tselika looked over at her, puzzled.

"What's the matter? You look like you're getting off on your bike saddle or something."

And so the delicate young girls made their way to Mega-Float III. Bravely, innocently, and completely unaware that their actions would only make things harder for the boy they sought to save.

10

Pspspshh!

A succession of compressed-air noises, and the man in the suit fell to the floor. Several nails stuck out of his thigh as he turned to face his attacker, the girl with the braid—Zaurus. She licked her lips triumphantly.

"W-wait!! Stop, I say!"

What a condescending way to beg for his life—zero points. One swing of the nail bat in her hands and the man's face caved in with a sickening crack. This game could be morbidly realistic sometimes.

"E-eek!"

"Don't move. Um, stay right there, please."

A second man in a suit tried to flee, only to run headlong into a trap. The high-voltage wires plundered from a home theater system sent a powerful current through his body, roasting him alive. The slouched boy's hands remained in his pockets. Obviously, there was some sort of device under his fingers.

"…Ah. Might you be Flak00?" he asked.

"Bastards. Who sent you?!"

"We've already taken out your guards and disarmed you. Do you really think you're in a position to make threats? You're only wasting our time."

Seeing the bloodied nail bat leveled at his nose, the man forced a grin. He looked to be more than ten years their senior. As he slowly backed away, someone stepped in to prevent his escape—the *yuki-onna* Magistellus. He was surrounded.

"How much do you know?" the man asked.

"…"

"You know everything, don't you? That's why you're here! In that case, let's cut a deal. I'll give you twenty—no, thirty percent! I'll make you my new bodyguards—you'll be famous, and I'll pay you well, of course!"

The balance of power had already been made quite clear. Right now, Flak00 needed to give these two attackers whatever they wanted, no matter how unreasonable.

Right up until I get out of this bind, that is. I won't forget a pair of mugs this stupid-looking. I'll have them both thrown in a heated metal cage and make them slaughter each other for my amusement!!

"Heh. Hch-heh. Perhaps you've underestimated the Red Territory? I don't know what kind of Dealers you are, but I can promise you this: The profit you make today will be ten times anything you can find over on the peninsula. And unlike gambling on stocks, the margins are guaranteed!"

"Sorry to burst your bubble, but we ain't after money."

The man choked on his own breath. What sort of Dealer couldn't be bought out with cold, hard cash?

"Then what is it you—? Ghh?!"

"Your phone."

"…What?!"

"O-only a few people in the Red Territory have one, right?" said M-Scope. "Flip phone or tablet, hand it over."

"None of this makes any sense!"

The next moment, Flak00 forgot his entire strategy.

"That's true for slumdwellers like us, but you guys ain't from around here, right? Ain't there electronics stores where you're from? Why the hell would a couple of outsiders come all the way here just to—? Ggh!!"

Zaurus raised the nail bat high above her head without saying a word and brought it down mercilessly on the man's head, like splitting a watermelon. It all happened so quickly, he didn't even have time to raise his arms.

A phone with an LCD screen slid from his pocket as he crumpled to the ground, and Zaurus fired several nails through its center. Then she turned to her Magistellus standing by the window.

"Charlotte, what the hell are you doing?"

"I-I'm sorry! I just heard a siren outside and…*a-awoooo*!!"

The werewolf girl gave another howl. Outside, it was another peaceful day in Tokonatsu City. Fire trucks, contracted to protect wealthy people's homes from fire damage, did not frequent the Red Territory. The sound came from the oblivious world beyond.

Soon, M-Scope spoke up in a clammy voice.

"From what he said, it sounds like there really is something fishy going on here."

"Who cares? Not me." Zaurus spun around and settled the nail bat onto her shoulder. "The important thing is that Kaname Suou's gonna be comin' here lookin' for a phone. We got here ahead of him and pulled the rug—that's all that matters. After all, we didn't stand a chance findin' him in these streets with just the two of us."

"Wh-what if Kaname Suou finds some other means of establishing contact?"

"These guys were thorough. They made sure they were the only ones who could make phone calls for a reason—like they were establishing some special class or something. Whatever their game, there's no way they'd overlook some loophole. Even if we just sit back, sooner or later a fight'll break out."

"And?"

"And we wanna know when that fight's gonna go down," Zaurus replied. "We find out who's in charge of these pricks and we smash his face in. Then we take over their information network. If Kaname Suou so much as shits in this dump, we'll know."

11

The Lion's Nose wasn't exactly fair play, but if not for its intervention, Kaname Suou would have taken one step too far.

Beneath the cluster of prefab cabins and plywood structures, it was possible to see vestiges of the ill-fated airport that had become Mega-Float III. He and Claire dismounted their scooters before moving toward a corner of the abandoned international terminal that had been crushed under mountains of garbage... Just then, Kaname grabbed Claire's slender arm and pulled her to the ground.

"Wah!"

Pspsh!!

A couple of blasts of compressed air could be heard, but the trajectory of the nails was odd. The nail gun was not a long-distance weapon by any means, but the projectiles had flown way too far off the mark. If they had been meant to hit, they would have landed a lot closer.

A hundred of those shots wouldn't have been enough to strike a killing blow. From that fact alone, Kaname reasoned that hitting them hadn't been the point. The Lion's Nose must be warning him about something else entirely.

It's a trap... But is it infrared or microwave?!

The attack was trying to lead him one way, so he picked a different direction and ran down a hallway, dragging the panicking Claire by her scruff, like a bodyguard protecting a VIP from assassins. Perhaps it wasn't the most delicate way to handle the young lady, but it worked.

He could hear a voice echoing from somewhere else in the terminal. It was a boy's voice, but cracked and squeaky, as though he wasn't used to shouting so loudly.

"Well done! I blocked off all the exits once you arrived, so if you'd turned back the way you came, y-you'd have been blown up!!"

...That's bait as well. He wants us to go farther in.

There was no benefit to making noise and giving away your location when the battlefield was an indoor maze. M-Scope was known as the trap master. Thus, anything he said was for the express purpose of leading his prey toward their doom.

Electronic traps were exceedingly frustrating. Infrared and radar were invisible to the naked eye, and unlike with pressure mines and trip wires, there was no danger of accidentally setting them off yourself. They could be made to deactivate when an ally passed into the range of fire, making them excellent at putting pressure on a foe without limiting your own options.

Any average Dealer would have already gotten caught in the web and met a fiery fate, or else become paralyzed with fear and filled with nails.

But Kaname Suou was different. He had the Lion's Nose. If nine out of ten cakes were poisoned, he would be able to find the clean one every time. Make it ninety-nine out of one hundred, even; it didn't matter. An invisible threat alone wasn't enough to kill him. All he had to do was trust in his nose and he would see it through.

This way...

"W-wawawah!"

Honestly, there wasn't much point in bringing Claire along, but he couldn't exactly let go of her now, with all the traps around.

Clunk... Rattle...

It wasn't footsteps, but it *was* the sound of something hitting the floor—most likely that nail bat trailing along the ground. Kaname pulled Claire close and hid behind a nearby pillar. There weren't a lot of good hiding places in the wide-open terminal interior; there was a passage leading into a different section about twenty meters away, but that was too far. Even running at full pelt, he wouldn't make it.

I need a weapon. Even just something to cause a distraction.

Kaname's mind raced. He placed his finger to his lips to shush Claire, then slowly crouched, with his back still to the pillar. Unfortunately, the only things on the floor within arm's reach that he could use were a set of rusty screwdrivers and an old promotional flier for a sale some years back at a place called Waltraute Market. This place was like a time capsule.

"Err... Um..."

"Shush... *I was never much of a crafter, but...*"

The process made Kaname think of his old friend, Takamasa. However, what he was doing was so simple, any child could replicate it. He took the flier and folded it a certain way. Again and again, until...

"A...a paper plane? Are you going to use it as a decoy?"

"*Right now, yes. However, look what happens if I add this flathead screwdriver so that the tip sticks out the front.*"

The result was something like an improvised dart. The screwdriver lay nestled atop the paper plane like a wiener in a hot dog bun. For the finishing touches, Kaname adjusted the center of mass until the thing was perfectly balanced. Throw it hard enough and it could punch through drywall. *Murder dart, complete.*

"Don't try this at home, kids."

"?"

It couldn't hurt to have more of these, but the enemy wasn't going to wait around, and there were only so many materials nearby.

"On the count of three, we make a break for it. Don't stop running for any reason."

"Erm, er...what are...?"

"One, two, three!"

Kaname dashed out from behind the pillar and threw his origami dart at the first person he saw.

"There you are!" a woman yelled back.

So it was Zaurus. I knew it!!

Kaname's aim was perfect, but the dart was just a little too slow. Zaurus knocked it out of the air with her bat, but Kaname tossed a second, and a third, all the while pulling Claire along by her hand. To hide where he was running, he threw the remainder of the screwdriver set into the range of an infrared trap. The resulting explosion blanketed the area in a cloud of dust.

There was a distinct peculiarity to the way the blast wave propagated.

Was that a rocket warhead? That yuki-onna *must have been M-Scope's Magistellus.*

They had just twenty meters to cover. Perhaps by adjusting the center of mass Kaname could have thrown Zaurus a curveball, but now wasn't the time to be getting fancy. She was armed with a nail bat and nail gun. Kaname just had to keep her distracted while he passed safely through the danger zone.

Finally, Kaname and Claire reached the other section of the terminal. But they hadn't made it out of the airport yet. They were in a big room with sofas and LCD monitors. Kaname checked the backs of the monitors, but unfortunately none of them had an internet connection. The space was sort of like a suite in a hotel without any beds. Probably a boarding lounge for first-class passengers. It felt lived-in, in contrast to the rest of the dusty terminal. Perhaps it made for a more convenient base than the rooms of the nearby hotels without working elevators.

Just then,

Hmm? The pain is fading...???

That must mean there weren't as many fatal traps in this area. Perhaps M-Scope hadn't had enough time to set them up this far in.

Claire Kaizuka seemed to take her first breath in quite some time, and she rattled off all the questions she had been holding in until now.

"Wh-who were those people?! This place is like Flak00's house…!!"

"Then I wouldn't hold out any hope for him. He's probably already Fallen."

Kaname gestured at the state of the room around them.

"The couches have all been moved slightly out of place. There was a struggle here, for sure. In the game, bodies disappear after a few minutes, but the evidence remains. There was one person standing by the door, one in the room, and one taken out while still sitting down. That last one sounds like the boss, so I'd bet money that was our man."

Kaname's techniques flew in the face of real-world forensics. His was a skill honed inside and only applicable to the game world. Finally, Kaname pointed to the ground. There, nailed to the middle of the floor, was a smartphone.

"Phones aren't easy to come by around here, are they? This has to be Flak00's, and you can see what Zaurus did to it. I'd guess the man himself didn't fare much better."

When a Dealer Fell, any weapons and clothing they were wearing disappeared along with their body after a few minutes. However, things that fell off their person remained. That meant you could kill someone and steal their belongings, and it wouldn't all just vanish.

"…"

It was evident how Claire felt about this. Her face went white as a sheet, and tears formed in her eyes. Not a normal reaction for one who lived in the slums.

Unfortunately, there wasn't time to indulge her grief. Zaurus and M-Scope were still hot on their heels, and they were fully equipped, while Kaname had nothing.

I need a weapon…

Kaname searched the room for whatever he could find, but here in the Red Territory, the chances of randomly coming across a gun and ammo were close to zero.

Isn't there anything I can use? …Aha!

Perhaps he should have kept one of the screwdrivers from earlier. The makeshift darts weren't a bad idea, but they lacked decisiveness. Kaname needed something that could silence an enemy in one hit. And while he wasn't in a position to be fussy, the rules here were a little different—he couldn't just fire off as many shots as he liked. He could only use the materials available to him. His financial power was useless.

"Now, then."

Kaname picked up a half-filled whiskey bottle. It was more than heavy enough to deal a killing blow to the head. It could also be turned into a Molotov cocktail later if necessary, but in here the smoke and fire would affect Kaname, too.

He also took a porcelain ashtray from atop a glass table. It was small enough to fit in the palm of his hand, but Kaname reckoned it could do some decent damage, too. To make it even more deadly, he wrapped it in a bathrobe he found in a nearby closet and choked off the payload with some sticky tape, creating a sort of impromptu flail he could swing around by the loose end.

This was not how Kaname Suou usually fought. He was constantly thinking, *What would Takamasa do?*

Sheesh. Even as my enemy, he's still helping me...

With a wry grin, he scooped up some A4 documents he found scattered across the sofa. This time, however, they weren't for origami. He tied the bundle together with tape and handed the thick sheaf to Claire.

"Here. Stick this under your apron."

"Wh-what?"

"They've probably got more weapons, but this should at least let you shrug off a few of those nails. You want to protect your heart above all else, so we'll put this in front of your chest!!"

"Eeek! Um... Please watch your hands!!"

He could hear the clacking of footsteps. His time was up.

"Where aaare youuu?"

Kaname stayed low, hidden behind one of the large sofas. He heard a swishing noise... Most likely, that was Zaurus giving her bat a few practice swings.

"Still hidin', huh? Ah-ha-ha! Take all the time ya need! Soon enough, those poor girls'll enter the Red Territory! Time's on our side!!"

...Grh.

Although they were both close-range weapons, going up against Zaurus's nail bat with the bathrobe flail would be rough. It could definitely score a kill if it connected, but there was no way to use it defensively. Meanwhile, Zaurus could easily catch a blow with her bat if she needed to. Kaname had to find some way around that. If Zaurus swung horizontally at waist height, Kaname could neither jump above nor duck below the strike. He couldn't get by relying only on evasion.

As far as improvised weapons went, the nail bat was clearly superior.

I can't go toe to toe with Zaurus until I find something that can block it...

In which case, the only option was to run.

M-Scope and Zaurus were hindrances to Kaname, but there was no point in going out of his way to kill them. No doubt they had smartphones on them, but Kaname wasn't so desperate he needed to go *that* far to obtain one. He just had to find some way to warn Tselika and Midori away from the area. Once that problem was dealt with, he could resume the hunt for Takamasa's latest plaything, #flash.err.

...When all was said and done, the Ag Wolves were nothing but a random side quest. An incredibly punishing one that would instantly kill him if he failed, but a side quest nonetheless.

"You okay with that?!! Hey, I'm talkin' to you! Come out here and face me like a man, you little bitch!"

Kaname heard the splintering of wood and the smashing of glass as Zaurus presumably put her nail bat through a nearby cabinet. Kaname clapped his hand over Claire's mouth just as she began to scream. He felt her warm breath on his palm. Luckily, Zaurus didn't hear her over the sound of her own rampage. It seemed like once Zaurus blew her top, she was barely able to control herself.

But this, too, M-Scope had taken into account when planting his traps. That was why he had used infrared, rather than wires—so he could switch the sensors on and off to avoid Zaurus tripping anything by mistake. And he was actually using her to guide them where he wanted them.

M-Scope was not enough of a threat by himself to shepherd his prey toward the traps. But if Kaname was allowed to stop and think, it would be easy enough to pick them out and deactivate them, or even to simply stop where he was and avoid them. In order to trap one's prey, it was necessary to rile them up into a panic so they felt they had to keep moving. In other words, the most dangerous thing Kaname could do in this situation was to keep moving forward without a solid plan.

He thought back to the *yuki-onna* with her rocket launcher. It was likely she'd been trained to fill a similar role, but Zaurus was far better at it. Instead of firing missiles from a distance, she could walk right up to her opponent and try to keep them where they were or stall for time.

…Quite the formidable duo, Kaname thought.

However, ironically enough, that whirlwind of destruction had just afforded Kaname an opening. Zaurus was armed with a nail bat and nail gun. Even if the initial burst of fire didn't take down her target, she could momentarily immobilize them by shooting their feet and then close in for the kill. On the other hand, that meant she was vulnerable to one thing.

The clue was the shattering noise Zaurus had just produced.

Kaname had to act before *it* got caught up in the destruction. In a split-second decision, he leaped out from behind the sofa.

"Aha! So that's where you've been hiding, you piece of shit!!"

Zaurus whirled around and raised her nail bat high overhead. Kaname was empty-handed, his only armor a roguish smirk. His hands went down, leaving his head completely unprotected.

And then.

Kaname grabbed the edge of the glass table in front of the sofa and pulled upward, flipping it.

"Wh-what…?!"

Zaurus couldn't defend against this. If she tried to block it with her bat, the glass would shatter and slice her to ribbons. If she used her hands to stop the blow instead, she would still be trapped beneath the table's weight.

What's more, it gave Kaname the chance to act, too. He gripped the bathrobe—that is, the improvised flail—tied at his belt. With a downward swing, he could shatter the glass and crush Zaurus's head in one fell swoop.

A jet of blood streaked through the air.

However.

"Don't fuck...with me...!!"

"Tch!"

It was Kaname's blood. A shard of glass had skimmed his cheek. Zaurus's behavior was so unpredictable that even the Lion's Nose was having trouble keeping up. Kaname saw a chaos within her that rivaled that of Bloody Dancer himself.

Zaurus had ignored the distraction and fired a volley from her nail gun straight through the glass table. Even with a tool not designed for shooting, she was sure to land at least one hit on a target less than two meters away. Even if it meant she ended up showered with glass shards.

"I told you, I'm a close-combat specialist...!"

With bloodthirsty eyes, Zaurus stepped through the table's bare stainless steel frame like a door, pointing her nail gun at Kaname.

"That means I was the best at it out of anybody in the Ag Wolves! You ain't gonna pull one over on me with weak-ass strategies like those!!"

"Hrh?!"

Kaname's improvised flail matched up poorly against Zaurus's nail bat. It was one thing to catch her unawares, quite another to defend against a headlong attack from her. There was no choice but to retreat.

Stepping back, Kaname drew his other weapon, the whiskey bottle.

"You bastard...!!"

Before Zaurus could even react, Kaname chucked the bottle at her face. Whether she blocked it with her nail bat or ducked her head to avoid it and the glass smashed on the wall behind her, the result would be the same; Zaurus would be coated head to toe in 80-proof liquor. In this treasure trove of traps designed by M-Scope, she would be effectively immobilized. One spark and she'd go up in a ball of flames. That should make her think twice about leading Kaname into any further traps. Even if M-Scope were to deactivate them all remotely, the explosive material would remain. There was always the risk they could misfire.

But Zaurus, of course, didn't care. The bottle hit her head-on, but that was it. The thick glass of the bottle met only human skin and remained intact. Sneering, Zaurus ignored the failed attack and raised her bat.

Damn, that was aimed right at her face! I thought at least she'd react on instinct!

"Nnngh!!"

Suddenly, out jumped someone Kaname hadn't expected. It was Claire Kaizuka, holding the sheaf of documents overhead like a schoolgirl caught in the rain without an umbrella. With her eyes shut tight, of course.

However, despite her valiant effort to jump in the way, her guard was just a little misaligned. Kaname buckled her knee with a kick, adjusting her block. And of course, Zaurus's weapon was no simple bat. The nails tore into the paper.

Does this girl have a death wish?!! A few centimeters either way and she'd have lost some fingers!!"

But this wasn't the time for doubt. Without even putting his foot down, Kaname delivered a second kick high up into the ream of paper, still in Claire's small hands, driving the nail bat aside. Zaurus scowled. She had less than 0.4 seconds to respond, and yet she realized if she didn't let go of the weapon, the force would break her wrist. Without a shred of hesitation, she let the nail bat be wrenched from her grasp and pulled out the nail gun at her waist.

Kaname grabbed Claire by the shoulder and pulled her down behind the sofa. He heard Zaurus fire off a volley, but the stopping power of the nails fell quite short of actual bullets and they failed to penetrate the furniture. Other than brittle materials like glass, there was very little that *couldn't* be used as cover in this situation.

It was time for Kaname to try his idea a second time. If the nail gun couldn't pierce the sofa, then…

"Rraah!!"

"Dammit! Not this again?!"

Once you find the winning strategy, repeat it until the boss dies—a gaming staple. Kaname gripped the sofa with both hands and lifted it, catching Zaurus as she approached for an attack. She didn't have the nail bat this time, and no matter how many nails she fired, they couldn't beat back the falling couch. It was the size of a fridge, and Zaurus found herself pinned faceup beneath it.

It would only immobilize her for ten seconds at most. Kaname hesitated over whether to run or go back and finish her off with the improvised flail. However, that moment of indecision was all it took. Or perhaps keeping a monster like Zaurus down at all had been too much to hope for.

"Zaurus!! Are you okay?!"

End of the line!!

The Lion's Nose fired off a warning. Another player on the field meant they had only one choice.

"Eek!"

As Claire bent down to pick something up, Kaname grabbed her arm and made a break for the door. Things might be different now, but this room was once a VIP boarding lounge. That meant there were two doors—an entrance and an exit. Kaname ran in the opposite direction of M-Scope's voice.

Bang! Bang! Bang!! came a noise like a firecracker. It sounded like a nine-millimeter gun. It was probably either a full-auto pistol or a submachine gun. It wouldn't be that accurate, but right now, a single bullet could spell death. If Kaname had been a second slower, he, instead of the nearby wall, would be filled with holes.

"Wh-what do we do? What do we do?"

"We've got no reason to stay here. We need to get out of this airport and try somewhere else. Claire, do you have any other ideas for where we can find a smartphone or a tablet?"

"Yes, but didn't he say the way out is blocked by traps? How are we going to escape? Don't you think he's already sealed off the windows and doors with his infrared thingies?—Eek!"

Suddenly, Kaname pulled the country gal close, hiding the two of them behind a nearby pillar. He took out the impromptu flail, which hadn't been as handy as he'd hoped, and tossed it toward the window.

Whether via infrared or microwave, the foreign object tripped the sensor, and the trap went up in a fiery explosion. A burst of shrapnel landed in the pillar, but Kaname and Claire were unharmed.

"There's certain types of traps that can fire multiple times. Like those using automatically reloading grenade launchers," Kaname explained. "However, if they damage their own sensors and lenses in the explosion, then they're not much use as a trap anymore."

"…Ah."

"So there's no need to get all close and personal with the wire snippers. Here, watch your step."

Kaname politely took her hand and escorted her through the debris, before the pair finally emerged outside. What a waste of effort. They hadn't gotten a phone, and they weren't out of danger, either. However, once Kaname returned to the Red Territory streets, it would be hard for those two—four, if you counted their Magistelli, who seemed to be on standby—to track him down. If you could just walk blindly around corners until you crashed into the love of your life, slice of toast in her mouth and all, then something would have to be seriously wrong with *Money (Game) Master*'s statistical engine.

As he tiptoed over to the scooter he'd left by the entrance, Kaname thought:

That's if there's only four of them anyway…

The reason only Zaurus and M-Scope had been at the terminal was probably to ease the cognitive load on M-Scope, who was constantly toggling the traps on and off to avoid friendly fire.

Next time they met, there would be fewer traps, and the enemy would be prepared for him. They'd surround Kaname with a perfect four-man team.

In all likelihood, Flak00 was already dead. For better or worse, M-Scope and Zaurus had just opened up a huge power vacuum in the inner workings of the Red Territory. Kaname would have no complaints if the Red Territory's power structure and the Ag Wolves on his tail wanted to fight each other, but what if the latter used money or force to join the organization or stage an outright takeover? They could get an army on their side, and then their chances of tracking Kaname wouldn't look so slim.

Kaname had things to do, too. He still had to track down the shipping yard where Takamasa was hiding #flash.err and catch him switching containers. If Zaurus and M-Scope dug their claws into this area, that mission would become a lot harder.

So Kaname had to act first.

There's still a lot I don't know about how things operate around here, but if I'm going to outmaneuver Zaurus and M-Scope, I'll need to find a way into the power structure before they do. Without money or guns, though, I don't have a lot of leverage. If only I had something I could hold over them...

"..."

A hostile takeover using bullets instead of money. As Kaname nursed these violent thoughts, an innocent, easygoing voice reached his ear.

"Wait, huh? I didn't mean to bring these with me. Was I supposed to leave them behind?"

Claire Kaizuka, the girl in the long skirt and apron (with bare sides), seemed flustered about something. Kaname put aside his own thoughts and glanced over at her. It seemed the country gal's worries concerned the improvised body armor he had lent her.

"What should I do with these documents? Should I put them back?"

12

As its name implied, Mega-Float III was an enormous structure floating on the ocean's surface. And so wherever Kaname might hide in the Red Territory, all his opponents had to do to limit his movement was take control of the entrances and exits. The only way on or off the float by land was the large circular bridge that connected the peninsula to the many islands making up the Tokonatsu City archipelago. There, you could plant bombs on either side of the road, rigged to blow when the attached cameras registered a facial match. With someone as talented as M-Scope on the job, there would be essentially zero chance of a misfire.

The problem, then, was the sea route.

Originally, this place was meant to be an airport, so it didn't have a harbor... Still, there was always a ring of yachts and dinghies of dubious origin moored to the outer circumference, like the moldy crust on a slice of bread.

This potential escape route was a liability. The solution, then, was obvious.

"E-eek!!"

The scream had come from a tanned girl in a brightly colored bikini bottom paired with a thick sleeveless top, the front open to show off her cleavage. While it looked like a life jacket, it was more likely a bulletproof vest.

As she ran for cover, her short blond hair flying, a burst of fire drowned out her screams. Then Zaurus's Magistellus, the werewolf girl Charlotte, entered the fray, spraying bullets at all the suspicious motorboats docked nearby. A flock of seagulls scattered into the air, screeching.

"Hold on, Charlotte. Stay."

At her mistress's word, the werewolf girl stopped before reaching the final ship, letting out an impatient growl.

"*Grr...*"

"I know, I know," said Zaurus with a smirk. "Here, have a treat! Fetch!"

She used a portion of her bat without any nails to launch a ball far off into the distance. The pleasant crack was followed by the werewolf girl's yapping as she ran after it. It looked like they were enjoying a nice relaxing game, but that couldn't have been further from the truth.

Standing on the pier, the *yuki-onna* Magistellus leveled her rocket launcher. The woman atop the final ship had already dropped her speargun and held out both hands in surrender, face pale. One shot from the Magistellus girl's weapon and the whole boat would go up in flames.

"Stop, stop!!" she called out. "What did we ever do to you?!"

"Zaurus."

M-Scope leaned over and whispered to his partner, who twirled her bat and rested it atop her shoulder.

"...Doesn't seem like any more reinforcements are on their way," she replied. "I guess we'll leave it here."

M-Scope and Zaurus had allowed Kaname to give them the slip at Flak00's base. Thus, they needed to seal off his escape routes and capture any mobile phones he might come looking for.

Of course, the young woman on the boat didn't know any of that.

"W-we're just regular slumdwellers...," she said, both hands still raised. "We buy pull tabs and bottle caps and sell them to scrapyards on the outside, that's all!! What do you hope to get out of attacking us? We're not worth the bombs you're wasting!!"

They'd had no interest in money from the beginning, so that hardly mattered to them.

Except...

"A scrap recycling business, you say...?" asked M-Scope.

"Y-yes!!" squealed the woman, nervously eyeing the *yuki-onna*, who seemed to be getting a little impatient. Standing next to his Magistellus, M-Scope leaned over and fished up a plastic bottle cap that had fallen over the edge of the pier. He traced his finger over it, eyeing the imprinted text that gave the bottle's price, manufacture date, and serial number.

"...Your motorboat is a little fancy for an ordinary junk trader, wouldn't you say?" he replied without looking up. "It's hard to find anything with an engine here in the Red Territory. And yet each of those boats we just sank would run you as much as a small house."

"Hrh?!" The woman froze in shock. "That means... You know what goes on around here?"

"..."

"Wait, hold on! If you know, then let's cut a deal! I'll let you in on twenty percent of the profits!"

"Twenty percent?" sneered Zaurus. "Didn't that Flak00 guy offer us thirty?"

The woman flapped her mouth wordlessly, unable to respond.

In *Money (Game) Master*, if you couldn't set a price, you were as good as dead. Especially when the thing you were trying to bargain for was your own life.

"And you know what I said to that? I shot him on the spot."

Pssshhhpsh!! came the sound of Zaurus's nail gun, and the woman, feet impaled, stumbled back and fell into the sea. Her bulletproof vest was already heavy, and without the use of her legs, the woman would surely drown. The fact they hadn't killed her outright just meant she'd suffer more in the interim.

The *yuki-onna* fanned herself with great satisfaction—not with a hand fan but with some sort of cross between an electric fan and a spray bottle, which she'd pestered M-Scope to get for her. Looking at his Mag-istellus, M-Scope gently exhaled.

"That takes care of Stingray. Isn't there a torpedo called something like that?"

"And Flak00 refers to a horizontally firing anti-aircraft gun. That's sea and land, so I guess that means the last guy'll have something to do with planes."

Charlotte dropped her mistress's ball into her hand, and Zaurus tossed it idly overhead, before slamming it once more with a nail-free portion of her bat. The resulting crack was just as pleasant as the last. As it landed, the ball crushed the smartphone lying on the ship's deck, shattering it into fragments and scattering them into the sea. Just as Charlotte was about to follow the ball into the ocean, Zaurus pulled her back by the scruff of her neck.

Only one more. The table was set for their rematch.

"I know this is only so people don't know we ain't from around here, but ridin' a bike is pretty nice."

"You think…? Personally, I'm getting a little out of breath."

"Keep it up, babe ☆"

"S-so why do you get to ride on the back instead of pedaling your own?"

"That's 'cause I'm the sharpshooter here. You're a whiz at traps, but you can barely shoot straight."

The pair's Magistelli, meanwhile, had a bike to themselves, with the *yuki-onna* sitting neatly behind the werewolf girl, her legs slung to one side. One for the humans and one for the AI. Frankly, it didn't make a lot of sense, considering the Magistelli were supposed to be computerized assistants.

"Wh-why do I have to…?"

"Heh-heh. Oh, suck it up. Besides, it's not so bad bein' up front…"

"?"

It seemed M-Scope was still oblivious—oblivious to the fact that, in order to stay balanced atop the bicycle, Zaurus had to shift her body weight forward, clinging tightly to the boy's back.

And yet, strangely, M-Scope felt nothing…because the boy's bulging backpack lay interposed between them. The girl with the braid pursed her lips as she locked eyes with a weird doll sitting atop the bag.

"…"

"Wait, what are you doing, Zaurus? Hey, wait! I can hear you fiddling around back there! Hands off my collection!!"

13

Kaname was sitting on an old discarded refrigerator, sifting through the papers Claire Kaizuka had inadvertently brought with her out of the airport. A quick skim was enough to tell Kaname Suou everything he needed to know.

"…I see."

So this is why people in the Red Territory will slaughter each other over a single pull tab or plastic bottle cap.

He had been thinking about it all wrong. Had Takamasa seen this and chosen to look the other way? The same man who had taught Kaname that helping people wasn't about bragging rights or asking for anything in return?

…Takamasa.

The country gal timidly offered a word.

"Er, um… Perhaps we should put those back where we found them? Though I don't want to run into those scary people again…"

"That won't happen. They've only got four guys on their side, including their Magistelli. Since they're short-handed, they need to move onto their next plan as quickly as possible. And anyway, the owner of these papers is dead, so there's no point in returning them."

"Right, but—"

"M-Scope might have left some of his traps behind, so I wouldn't go back there anytime soon if I were you. Not unless you want to run into some unexploded ordnance and die a meaningless death."

"Erm, er, I still think it was wrong to steal these, so I'm going to go put them back!"

She wouldn't steal, not even from a dead man. Most people would think she was far too purehearted for the slums.

But Kaname's impression was quite different.

"…This is the Red Territory. And yet you don't pack a weapon of any kind. I always found that strange, but now I think I know why."

"Er, what?"

"I don't want to tell you how to live your life, but don't you think you're giving up too quickly?"

As Kaname spoke, he heard the breath catch in the redhead's throat. And then.

A beautiful, perfect smile spread across her face.

"It's okay," she said. "I'm used to it. It doesn't feel so scary anymore."

"That so?"

Claire gently lifted the papers out of Kaname's hands and headed off on her beat-up old scooter. Presumably to the airport, just like she'd said. For a while, Kaname simply stared at the clear blue sky.

Then he felt a faint pain at the tip of his nose.

At last, he thought.

Then Kaname stood from his seat atop the refrigerator and flung open its useless door. Not a moment later, a metal-tipped arrow flew into it with a *Clang!*

The only decent weapon he'd seen in the slums had been that crossbow.

Just as Kaname was planning to counterattack while his opponent reloaded, the Lion's Nose sent him a warning. He heard the man's grimy raincoat catch the wind and looked up to see that his assailant had already closed the distance and was now swinging the crossbow down on him like a pickax.

Kaname, however, didn't flinch. It had been a logical move, and the correct one. Unlike the unpredictable Zaurus, this guy played by the rules, and that made him far less of a threat. First, Kaname kicked the man's leg, knocking his opponent off-balance. Then, as the crossbow came down, he stepped deftly aside, bringing his knee up to meet the man's face as he fell.

Kaname Suou was a master of urban sniping and close-quarters combat. Even without a gun, he was more than capable of disabling his enemies. It was only because Zaurus was even more skilled that he had been having difficulty up until now.

"Gagh!!"

The raincoat man somersaulted into the floor, and Kaname kicked the crossbow away.

Sighing, he asked, "A friend of Claire's, I assume?"

"...Everyone's a friend of hers around here," the man responded.

"I bet," replied Kaname curtly. "This is a land of revival where all the Fallen Dealers who haven't quite given up on the game gather—the Red Territory."

"If you know that..." The man clenched his teeth in anger, almost to the point of cracking them. *"If you know that, then—!!"*

"So what about you?"

"?!"

"According to that Ramjet guy, it was Claire who picked you up off the streets and brought you here. That means you're under her care."

When Claire had stood up for Kaname in front of the crowd, she had said something quite interesting. Something she herself didn't quite seem to understand.

"Oh, I am! I'll be his, uhh…guarantor? Is that the word???"

"Dealers who Fall are saddled with debt."

Why did Claire Kaizuka not carry a gun?

The answer was simple, but it was the key to unraveling a huge mystery.

"You make it sound easy, but just because you get to continue doesn't mean your debt is wiped. Guns. Cars. Armor. Everything in *Money (Game) Master* requires funds. Before you can even think about staging a comeback, you have to clear your debt, don't you?"

"…Yeah."

The man in the raincoat sounded pained. He bit his lip, then began to shout.

"That's why everyone who washes up in the Red Territory needs an introduction from Claire!! That…stupid girl! She buys up all our damn debts! She says she'll be our guarantor, and she barely even knows what it means…!!"

Claire Kaizuka's debt must have been enormous. When a person Fell, their accounts were ravaged indiscriminately. At worst, the damage could reach into the hundreds of millions.

But Claire didn't mind. She was happy so long as she could support the livelihood of somebody else.

"But that's not the end of the story, is it?" asked Kaname.

"No, it isn't. Claire knows a way of writin' off the debt. That's why she doesn't mind takin' on other people's liabilities. She does everything by herself, without consultin' anybody else."

The raincoat man paused there, but Kaname Suou didn't need to wait for him to continue. He finished the story himself.

"She Falls on purpose."

In most cases, a Fall meant game over—a punishment to be avoided. Even a *snow* billionaire could be ruined overnight. Nobody in their right mind *wanted* to Fall.

But what if you were in debt to begin with?

"A Fall is a penalty. But once you fall into debt, the AI companies will provide you with a bare minimum of support…"

"That's why Claire takes on all the debts she can," the raincoat man grumbled. "Then, when she's taken enough, she *Falls on purpose for the insurance money*. She knows the best time to die to maximize the payout."

Of course, if anyone could make enough money to stage a comeback just by Falling, it wouldn't be so scary. There had to be a special reason why Claire Kaizuka could do it.

"It's all hers," came the raincoat man's short reply. "The place might be a huge dump, but all of Mega-Float III is held in Claire Kazuka's name—as an international airport, just like it was always meant to be. She's got multiple insurance policies in place to ensure that when she dies and the airport shuts down, they pay out to make up the shortfall."

"Transit insurance. Aviation insurance. Liability insurance. Trade credit insurance. D&O insurance… A full complement of insurance policies to protect a legal entity—the kind a regular person would usually have nothing to do with."

A plane crash could easily result in three to five hundred casualties. That would mean three to five hundred bereaved families that needed to be compensated. A plane could leak fuel into the ocean, or a container full of rare art pieces could go missing. There were so many different ways to incur damages that all needed to be insured. The amounts involved were much, much higher than regular life insurance.

The raincoat man nodded along to Kaname's explanation.

"Thing is," he added, "all those insurance companies are AI businesses. There are ways to trick 'em into thinkin' the airport is operating at peak efficiency."

Integration with major airports. Insurance packages directed not at corporations but at providers of public infrastructure.

And yet, Claire didn't actually make any money out of it. She just wandered around the slums forever. She could rake in payouts in the tens of billions and never see a single *snow* of profit, because her contract was for debt cancellation only. It wasn't a golden ticket she could spend however she pleased.

"She doesn't question it. She's fine with getting shot over and over again if it means she can buy happiness for other people. She's an idiot, that woman. A fuckin' idiot, plain and simple."

On paper, it all seemed logical enough. She probably never even thought about becoming a millionaire. When you lived at rock bottom, being debt-free was the best you could hope for. It was smart of her, even, to use what everyone else saw as a money-making game to do something like this.

However.

The entire plan relied on something very important.

"But to do that, she has to get shot, right?"

"Yeah."

"And the world of *Money (Game) Master* is as realistic a simulation as you can get, barring a few exceptions—and none of those are pain. There are a few ways to reduce it, but I doubt she's able to get her hands on stuff like that in this slum. And even if she felt no pain at all, that wouldn't cure her fear."

"Exactly!! That's why when you came here in your nice clothes, without a care in the world or the slightest clue what's goin' on, foistin' all your problems onto her, I couldn't stand by and do nothin'! You're just like him! *That guy with the bandanna!!*"

The man was furious. He jumped to his feet and pulled out a knife. Kaname swiftly delivered a kick to his wrist, sending the weapon clattering to the side, before following up with a second kick to the man's jaw.

...Takamasa—of all the people to compare me to.

The man couldn't have been more mistaken if he tried. Granted, Kaname hadn't known anything about the Red Territory when he arrived, but he'd hadn't Fallen. So even if Claire became his guarantor, she wasn't taking on a single *snow* of debt.

Did Takamasa leave the Red Territory like this out of respect for Claire's decision...?

Kaname hoped so. Takamasa had been to hell and back when he plunged his family into debt. But he could never become blinded to the injustices happening right under his nose, just because of his crusade against the AI, could he? Kaname had no proof, but he wanted to believe.

"Do you even have the right to be angry at what she's done after she saved your life?" Kaname asked.

"...I didn't know," the man replied. "When I washed up here, I didn't understand what was going on. Claire reached out to me, and by the time I worked out what was happening, it was too late!! Yeah, you're right!! She saved me! So what?!!"

Sometimes, being saved was a curse.

Kaname Suou had never forgotten the time Takamasa stood up for him. He still revisted it in his nightmares. Even now, when they stood on opposite sides, he had never forgotten Takamasa's smile as he gave his life so that Kaname's sister might live.

But that didn't make Kaname's tone any softer.

"In that case, what are you doing here? Claire took on all of your debt, didn't she? She wrote it all off, right? She's given you freedom, so why haven't you taken it? Why are you still here?"

"...Heh."

The man gave a self-deprecating laugh. A small trickle of blood ran down the corner of his mouth where Kaname had kicked him.

"You already know."

"Well, I have a hunch."

Why were there no Magistelli anywhere in the Red Territory? Furthermore, why were there no vehicles—the Magistelli's temples? And what did that mean for the Dealers? All of these questions naturally led to a single conclusion.

Namely—

"All your vehicles have been confiscated."

"…"

There was a long silence. Then, at last, the raincoat man spoke.

"It's for electricity."

"I noticed this place had two different levels of living standards. The higher-ups get to use phones, while everyone else is stuck cooking bread in a coal-fired stove. There are those who are allowed to use electricity, and those who aren't."

"There's no power plant anywhere in the Red Territory. This place was thrown to the wolves a long time ago."

"Which means you make your own. Or to be precise, the higher-ups do."

Kaname took a deep breath and summarized his conclusion.

"The Magistelli are all locked inside their cars' trunks, aren't they? In any case, the slum leaders took away your cars to use their engines like a large-scale power plant—all so they alone can enjoy a digital paradise. Fridges, air conditioning, smartphones, the internet. And because of that, you guys aren't even allowed to drive your own cars around. That means this is the only place you're allowed to log in and out from… They call it the land of revival, but they might as well call it a graveyard, because nobody ever leaves."

14

"This shit's amazin'! *Om-nom*."

"Zaurus, you don't need to steal my food." M-Scope sighed. "There's plenty here for you, too."

The pair had set aside their bikes and broken out their rations. And as soon as they did, Zaurus leaned over and bit the nutrition bar right out of M-Scope's hand. The snack was made like a cookie, rather than chocolate, which would have melted instantly in the oppressive heat of Tokonatsu City.

This was enemy territory, and they couldn't afford to procure food on-site. Who knows what the locals might put in it, after all. And so M-Scope took a bite from the bar as well, carefully peeling back the wrapper so as not to tear through the face of the anime girl printed on the front.

Just then, the *yuki-onna* Magistellus standing in a blind spot three paces behind them put her hand to her mouth and tittered.

"…Heh-heh-heh. An indirect kiss. Heh-heh-heh…"

"Wha—?!"

Zaurus's face instantly flushed bright-red. M-Scope, on the other hand, was more afraid than embarrassed.

"Give it back!!" she yelled. "Give that back to me! Stop eating it!!!!!!"

"You're strangling me! You're strangling—! Guhhh…"

The pair had come to a multistory parking garage adjacent to where the old airport traffic circle would have been.

"*Cough. Hack.* I-is that what we're looking for?"

"Looks like it."

Two big men in body armor—something rarely seen in the slums—had been guarding the place, but one shot from the *yuki-onna*'s rocket launcher had taken them both out. M-Scope and Zaurus ditched their bikes and headed for the entrance. A look inside revealed it was not filled with makeshift huts or stalls as the pair had come to expect… In fact, this seemed to be the only building in the Red Territory still being used for its original purpose.

There were lines of cars parked everywhere inside.

However, all the tires had been removed and the bodies lifted onto concrete blocks. It would be impossible to drive any of them away.

The smell of exhaust fumes filled the air. The engines were running, but the tires were gone. It was a strange sight, one that called into question the cars' very purpose.

"...They're treatin' 'em like slaves," muttered Zaurus, annoyed.

The Red Territory, the land of revival. What a joke. Everyone who ended up here had their vehicle taken—their sole means of logging out, and their only escape. No matter where they went in Tokonatsu City, they would have to return here before too long. It was like releasing you from prison only to leave your house key in the hands of your cell-mate. The people who ran the slums knew this, of course, but they wanted electricity and internet access. That was all there was to it.

Voices could be heard coming from the locked trunks of each car. Perhaps the Magistelli were still trapped inside. They didn't need to eat, drink, or sleep, but M-Scope still cringed as he imagined the state they must be in.

Nobody outside the slums could know the true nature of this place. In order to keep preying on innocent people, the enticing image of a "land of revival" had to be maintained. And with phones and internet access restricted to the bosses, that wasn't hard to achieve.

There was no good or evil in *Money (Game) Master*. The goal was to make money, and nothing was against the law. So what was the problem?

"Yo," came a voice.

Then, from behind cars, concrete pillars, and in through the emergency exits, appeared a bunch of armed and dangerous-looking men in dirty clothes. Zaurus, M-Scope, and their werewolf and *yuki-onna* Magistelli found their escape routes suddenly cut off. Then, and only then, did the voice of this place's boss continue from the middle of the crowd.

"That's the mug o' someone what's Fallen before," he said. "But I see you've got your Magistelli with you. That's against the rules here in the Red Territory, which means you're outsiders. Can't have you stumblin' on our little secret here and leavin' to tell the whole world about it, now can we?"

"Kaname Suou will be here soon," said M-Scope, unable to meet the boss's gaze. "...That man walks his own path through the game. Once he finds out what's going on, he'll come here to put a stop to it. And when he does, you'll need all the help you can get. You wouldn't want to waste any resources on us, would you?"

"Ain't you the ones who've been stirrin' him up?" the man replied.

The tension in the room was palpable, but Zaurus simply propped her nail bat on her shoulders, hung her arms over it, and stretched. She was fearless. If things broke down, she'd be ready to go at a moment's notice.

M-Scope gave a faint smile and repeated his point.

"Like I said, you need all the help you can get. And you need it right now."

"Uff. This how they do business on the mainland?" The man groaned. "Talk about a hard sell."

"Hey, I don't wanna hear you whinin'," warned Zaurus, suddenly sounding combative. "We're all just makin' money, and there ain't no rules in *Money (Game) Master*. The Red Territory's just a place, not a team, and if two Dealers happen to cross paths here, ain't nobody got a right to complain when one of 'em dies. In fact, *I bet you're real glad it's like that, ain'tcha?"*

The man had nothing to say to that, and the reason why was clear.

Zaurus shut one eye and continued. "Well, you know how it is. Put your feelings aside. Right now, you oughtta be thinkin' about what to do when Kaname Suou turns up. Just say the word, and we'll lend you a hand. Though we're gonna be takin' part either way, so the question is, do you want to be gettin' caught in our sights or not?"

The man in the center made a gesture with his hand, and the rest of the group lowered their weapons.

"...I'm guessin' that means you know all about our little arrangement," he ventured.

"You mean this?"

M-Scope held up a plastic bottle cap. It still had the price tag and date of manufacture, under a layer of grime.

Trapped in the garbage-filled Red Territory, locals didn't have many careers to turn to. There were a lot of potential workers, but what could they do? Picking up discarded pull tabs and plastic bottle caps could only bring in so much.

Or could it? In other words…

"You guys aren't earning *snow*."

M-Scope scoffed. This was something that existed in the real world, too. At least, the basic theory did.

"You're banking it and taking the interest. Am I on the right track…?"

15

"So what?"

Kaname seemed almost annoyed. The raincoat man lay sprawled among broken refrigerators and ovens, listening to his speech.

"Do you really think there's nothing you can do about it? Or do you honestly have no idea what's going on?"

"What do you mean…?"

"You're no poorer than the bankers on the mainland in their fancy suits. In fact, I'd say the amounts being moved around out here are even bigger."

"What the hell are you talkin' about? This is the Red Territory! People fight and kill over pull tabs and bottle caps!"

"Exactly." Kaname sighed deeply. Then he got straight to the point. *"Did you never stop to wonder why?"*

"Huh…?"

"Think about it. The aluminum content of a pull tab is worth less than a single yen. If you were really after the metal, then you could get a lot more by breaking down those shipping containers you're using as houses, or even just the frame of this refrigerator here."

Even the slumdwellers' clothing contained metal. Claire Kaizuka's skirt, for example, wasn't totally without buttons, hooks, or buckles, all of which could be sold for scrap if the situation were desperate enough.

In other words, it wasn't about recycling at all.

"It's obvious if you think about it for more than a second. There's no way people would kill each other for such small amounts of metal. Anyone can see that."

"Hold on, what does that have to do with anythin'? Are you gonna stand around insulting me or get to the point…?!!"

"I'm getting there. Let me finish."

Slowly, deliberately, like he was explaining things to a small child, Kaname continued.

"Let's talk about physical money for a second. Would you ever try to exchange a ten-thousand-yen bill for a scrap of paper the same size? It's the same amount of paper, after all."

"…"

The man seemed to finally understand Kaname's point. His face began to grow paler and paler.

"Wait. Wait, then you're sayin'…!!"

"You know, some Pacific Islanders used to use whale teeth or seashells as currency."

This was the answer. Kaname Suou had cut through to the naked truth.

"These pull tabs and bottle caps you've been collecting, scrounging up to hand over to your bosses. Nobody would be fighting to the death over them if they were worth less than a belt buckle. But what if a single one could buy you a house or a motorboat? Then it wouldn't be so strange."

"…"

"For better or worse, it seems like there's more than one boss around here. Flak00 is dead, but I don't see anybody losing their head over it. When someone feels like they haven't gotten a fair cut, it's more than reasonable to think they'd go after the courier from behind the scenes. Even when they seem like buddies on the surface."

Of course, this was *Money (Game) Master*, not some simple world where you could just use natural items as currency without issue. Here it was very likely they were using counterfeit protection. A little nick here, a splatter of blood there. An invisible signature requiring a UV lamp to read would be ideal.

"You guys say all you're doing is picking up trash, but didn't you ever think that was strange? Here in the Red Territory, consumption is low. There should be less and less trash by the day, and yet there always seems to be more. Why?"

That was because there were two kinds of people in this town—the ones who picked up trash, and the ones who created it.

"It's like a giant ATM," Kaname explained. "People who want to make a deposit follow a certain procedure, and specified amounts of pull tabs and bottle caps are scattered in a designated spot. Then you all go out and, thinking you're just collecting garbage, move them to the collection site, completing the transfer. The best part is, you never realized what you were doing, even though the sender and recipient were written right under your noses the entire time."

The Red Territory had three bosses, three gathering locations, and three banks. Just moving the bottle caps—or rather, the money—between the three of them would generate a profit in handling fees.

"The labels on the caps. The manufacturing dates and factory IDs...?!"

"Companies don't usually print that stuff on the cap, do they? Go back to the real world, buy a bottle of water, and see for yourself. The label is usually on the side of the bottle, and the details are usually printed on that little ring of plastic that connects to the cap. I always wondered whether that was for hygiene reasons or recycling purposes, but whatever. Here, they go out of their way to put all that information on the pull tab or the cap. Obviously, they do that because they need to. Presumably they have some way of decoding the inscriptions and finding out who sent the money and who's meant to receive it."

Some people thought gold and diamonds were valuable because they were scarce, but that couldn't be further from the truth.

There were many rarer materials. The human mind was what made certain ones more valuable than others. Take digital currency, for example. There was nothing scarce about the signals that constituted ones and zeros. There was more to value than simply whether something was plentiful or not.

All you had to do was get others on board and have systems in place to detect forgeries. Then even worthless garbage could be used as currency.

"It's a completely new kind of digital asset. One beyond the AI's surveillance."

Kaname had to admit that, as a means to fight back against the machines, it had his interest piqued. That said, he couldn't agree with the way it was being operated. The idea that this was a land of revival was laughable. In reality, it was a hell where the weak were squeezed dry for profit.

"Dealers from the mainland can store their money here, too. When a player Falls and their accounts are ravaged, that only applies to assets obviously recognizable as money. Who's going to go out of their way to steal waste bags full of old pull tabs and plastic bottle caps? Dealers can use this place as insurance when they think they might need it. Then, if they get shot and Fall, they still have untouched assets they can use as an extra life."

If you went bankrupt, no bank would repossess a mountain of trash. Not even a bank run by AI. To any outside observer, it would look completely worthless. You could stash an entire fortune here and nobody would ever know.

Kaname could imagine how much that would mean to people who got excited by words like "tax avoidance scheme" or "tax haven." There were no taxes in *Money (Game) Master*, but in the constantly evolving information war, it was an obvious advantage to keep your own assets hidden.

It was like the gift exchange at a *pachinko* parlor. Clients would be paid out in jewels and yachts, which they could take to the mainland and easily liquidate into cold, hard cash. Pawnshops and second-hand dealerships were taking part in the process without even knowing it.

This had to be bigger than just the slums. You would need enforcers on the outside to take care of anyone who turned traitor or refused to pay. Perhaps the wealthy who wanted their assets hidden lent a hand by providing access to their own private security firms.

"That means…" The raincoat man couldn't believe his ears. "That means…the Red Territory's been full of money this whole time?! We could all share it and pay off what everyone owes—even Claire. She wouldn't ever have to smile that stupid smile of hers and take on another debt…!!"

"Claire Kaizuka uses a special insurance package tied to the airport to wipe away people's liabilities," said Kaname sharply. "But she *needs to pay a massive premium* to keep that insurance in place. Who do you think pays that? Obviously not Claire herself. But nobody around here can afford to pay on her behalf, can they? The only people who would benefit from doing so are the bosses. As long as this place maintains its reputation as a land of revival, they can get all the expendable couriers they need."

"…"

"You think the reason you give up your cars is so you can pay tribute to the people who rescued you by providing them with electricity? Don't be silly. It's all a bluff. They want to keep operating this human-powered ATM without any of you catching on. Think about it: Out there, a single plastic bottle cap is the equivalent of a whole wad of bills. If they wanted, they could easily afford to bring in some expensive generators and power the whole island. But humans are simple creatures. Keep them unsure of where their next meal is coming from, and they stop thinking about what's going on behind the curtain. They were making you suffer on purpose so you wouldn't realize what was really happening. They gave you a fake reason, and you ate it up."

Anyone could have left at any time. There was no need for a trash-powered ATM to confiscate people's cars. And yet they did it anyway. It was all smoke and mirrors. They kept their real secrets hidden behind a veil of unnecessary punishment. That was why all these people were bound to the Red Territory.

"With the amount of money we're talking about, it's not strange at all that people die over these pull tabs. Outside the slums, they'd be using armored cars. Now ask yourself: How much money have you handed to the bosses over the course of your time here? And how much have you received in return for your services of propping up this ATM?"

"..."

"What's wrong with asking them for what you're owed?"

For a while, the raincoat man said nothing. Then he clenched his teeth in silence, and at last, he beat the ground in anger.

"I can still save her..."

He slowly rose to his feet.

It had all been fiction and deceit. But that didn't mean nothing remained in its wake. Peering through the veil, one could still catch a sliver of hope.

"Pull tabs and bottle caps, huh? It ain't gonna matter to the outside who turns this junk back into cash. If that's true, I'll scoop out all the grimy money in this whole town and give it right back to Claire! It's about time she was allowed to live her own life!!"

"I see."

It was an easy thing to say and another thing entirely to make it happen. Often, the ends came to mind before the means managed to catch up. It wasn't enough just to want to do the right thing. There was no system in this game that favored the underdog. Your skills and equipment were everything. This Dealer was on the fast track to an early Fall, whether he realized it or not.

Kaname Suou gave a small sigh and said, "I don't really care what you do, but if you recall, you attacked *me*. What's more, you only realized what was going on because I told you. So before you go and get yourself killed, I want to do something a little more suited to this game—I want you to pay me compensation."

"...What on earth could you want from a dirt-covered old man like me?"

To that question, the boy leveled his thumb toward his own heart and gave his answer.

"I want you to let me help."

The Red Territory was rotten to its core.

But if even one person could resent those surroundings. If even one person could look at Claire's lonely smile and say it wasn't right.

Then no matter how unskilled they were, even if they could never keep up, Kaname Suou wasn't going to let them die. Not ever.

16

"You're a real pain in the ass," said the tall man, standing amid the exhaust fumes that filled the multistory parking garage. "What kinda person ain't in this game for the money? You smell like outsiders to me—I know you all didn't land in the slums by accident. You remind me of someone else who fell into our net and walked away. *That man in the bandanna...*"

Zaurus didn't even respond. To her, nothing mattered as long as she got to fight Kaname Suou. All this complicated political stuff was just a means to that end. Violence was her way of keeping things neat and tidy. The fact that this made M-Scope seem like the sociable one was more proof this impromptu duo's balance was seriously skewed.

"...Wh-what's your name?" the boy asked. "We've met Flak00 and Stingray. Would I be correct in thinking yours has something to do with planes?"

"Yeah," replied the final ringleader. "*The name's Ramjet. And don't you forget it.*"

17

"I'm Kaname Suou...but I guess you already know that. Claire didn't exactly try to keep it a secret. What's your name?"

"Easy Option."

"…Easy Option?"

Underneath the blazing sun, standing amid the broken remains of refrigerators and AC units, Kaname arched an eyebrow. In the finance world, an easy option was an investment with a guaranteed return, but one that didn't promise much future profit. When Kaname questioned his strange choice of name, the man in the raincoat gave a self-deprecating chuckle and explained.

"I felt like if I chose that name, it'd be a constant reminder not to take the easy way out. Heh. Fat lotta good it did me, though. Look at me; I Fell and now I'm stuck crawling around the Red Territory without a penny to my name."

At any rate, Kaname needed a weapon, and it was safe to say he wasn't going to find anything decent for sale here. It would be quicker for him to craft something himself. He rifled through the scrap at his feet and finally pulled free an iron pipe roughly two meters in length.

The raincoat man shot him a questioning glance and asked, "You said you need a gun, right? Is that hunk o' junk gonna be any help…?"

"So long as the dimensions are right," Kaname replied. The inner diameter of the tube was about as thick as his thumb. However, it wasn't any use with an opening at both ends, so Kaname took some electrical tape and sealed off one of the two holes, before getting to work on the other end.

"You use a crossbow, right? Can you lend me one of your bolts?"

"What're you gonna do with just one?"

"I need it for reference. The balance and fletching needs to be just right."

"Crafting, huh?" The raincoat man heaved a deep sigh. "You're startin' to sound like that bandanna guy."

"…"

You could make a perfectly serviceable bow out of little more than a length of bamboo and a kite string. Kaname set out toward their destination, stopping at several points along the way to construct a few more primitive items out of the materials he was able to find. He wanted to keep his hands free for gathering, so he left the scooter behind and proceeded on foot.

"How did Claire end up with all that debt anyway? I know she takes on other people's debts now, but something must have happened before all that."

"I'm not sure she has a specific reason," replied Easy Option, visibly upset. "She's always been a guarantor, even in the real world, before joining *Money (Game) Master*. Other people would push their debts onto her good-natured parents, which eventually fell to the girl, piling up even inside the game. Claire doesn't see debt as something people rack up by themselves. To her, it's something that comes out of the blue and hits you like a meteor."

"..."

"That's why she doesn't try to escape her debt. It doesn't even occur to her. For her, debt is just a fact of life. She already knows she's gotta take a bullet; only question left is how best to do it."

But those were just excuses. Surely the girl herself had to know. She was like Sisyphus, cursed to eternally roll a boulder up a steep hill, only to have it fall back to the bottom each time. How long could she keep up this futile task before something had to give? Eventually, it must've been easier to convince herself this was for the best. Biting her lip and hiding away her emotions, saying with a weary smile she was happy about it all.

Happy that by repeating this ridiculous charade she could wipe away people's debts. She could be of use to others, and by doing so carve out a place in this world for herself.

And maybe, just maybe, someone would say those words to her.

"You're my savior."

"Don't give me that shit…," Kaname muttered.

The bastards bleeding her dry had been right beside her all along. Pretending to be poor while lining their pockets with money. Sitting in their air-conditioned rooms, sipping cool drinks, and playing with their smartphones. Operating their covert money transfer service, unfettered by *snow*. An unrestricted, proprietary currency like whale's teeth and seashells. Pull tabs and plastic bottle caps. And yet if everyone agreed to share the wealth, there would be no need for Claire Kaizuka to take on debt and die.

With Easy Option guiding the way, Kaname had no trouble locating the multistory parking garage he was after. Once, it would have been part of the airport. It was a rather tall building, but the upper floors were blocked off by piles of garbage.

Pull tabs and plastic bottle caps. Black trash bags filled to bursting.

"I need a smartphone to stop my associates," said Kaname. "And you need a pile of that trash to get Claire out of here. Sounds like we have a deal."

"Yeah."

"…You know that shooting someone means putting them in the very same debt hell you despise. Not just them, but their family, too. Are you prepared to do that?"

"In that case, I just have to make it better," the raincoat man muttered. He answered without hesitation, almost like he'd been prepared for the question. "If their families are truly innocent, then I'll look after 'em. If they haven't got money, I'll make 'em some myself. I'll see to it their lives are far happier than they ever were before, I swear it… So let's get on with it. That son of a bitch better get ready to die."

After confirming the man had no reservations, Kaname relaxed. He knew he could trust him when the time came. Kaname twirled the two-meter pipe in his hands as he gave the signal.

"Then let's go."

10

"How pathetic."

Atop the roof of the multistory parking garage, Luk-Shot was doing what many snipers of his caliber were paid to do: keep an eye on any approaching intruders, and if need be, pull the trigger.

"Ramjet's lost his mind. He oughtta be seekin' vengeance for his business partners, not joinin' hands with their assassins."

"Tell that to his face, why don't you?"

The man's spotter, a woman holding what looked like a pair of binoculars, sneered.

No sniper worth their salt would be complaining so much while out on a mission. This man, however, was more used to providing intimidation. He preferred to defuse problems before they exploded into violence, if possible. It was a bit of an odd philosophy for a sniper, perhaps.

"Wait, someone's coming. Male, raincoat, crossbow. Check the timetable; do we have anyone slated for a log-out?"

The parking garage was filled with the slumdwellers' vehicles, repurposed into generators, while their owners were kept in a state of mental and physical exhaustion that prevented them from asking too many questions. That meant the place was constantly receiving visitors, but anyone not on the schedule was treated with suspicion. People were allowed to use their vehicles to log out, but if they approached without a reason, they would be shot on sight.

As he peered through his scope, Luk-Shot grinned. Here in the Red Territory, there weren't many who possessed an accurate rifle or whose vest was filled to bursting with so many accessories. The fact that he had these things marked him as a cut above the rest. The fool in his sights marched onward. No bicycle, no scooter, and certainly no vehicle with an engine. He was definitely one of the poverty-stricken locals.

"...What an idiot. Let's finish the job and crack open a few beers, Erase."

His spotter didn't respond.

Luk-Shot pulled back from the scope to see a metal bolt lodged in the side of the girl's head. It was handmade and looked like it had been formed from an ice pick with the handle sawn off and a few plastic fins glued to the back.

"Ah."

He didn't even have time to turn around.

* * *

Somebody was standing right behind him. A dull crack could be heard as the sniper's skull caved in.

...Now then. That's all three pairs taken care of.

Twirling his iron pipe in his hands, Kaname Suou calmly appraised the situation.

How had he made it onto the rooftop so quickly? The answer was simple. *He'd scaled the concrete wall using his own hands and feet.* With no lifeline, and using only the skills he'd picked up from rock climbing, he quickly identified any footholds and reached the top of the twenty-meter wall in under thirty seconds.

Kaname was thrilled to finally come across a usable firearm, but unfortunately, he was going to be fighting in close quarters from here on. The recoil on a bolt-action rifle would be too much to handle under such circumstances. So instead, Kaname trashed the weapon so nobody else could wield it against him.

Using a hand mirror to reflect the sunlight, he sent a message down to his partner. Then Kaname reloaded his pipe and cut across the rooftop. One end of the pipe was blocked up with tape, but the other end had been altered, too. As he opened the steel door leading into the fume-filled garage, he inserted an ice pick into the open end of the pipe.

"Huh?!"

As soon as he laid eyes on the Dealer inside, Kaname struck him in the head with the rear of his pipe. Another one, standing a little to the side, froze for a second in disbelief before his hand shot to the holster at his belt. Kaname, however, used his momentum to swing the pipe down toward him like he was casting a fishing rod.

"Remember, Kaname. When you don't have access to gunpowder, elasticity and centrifugal force are your best friends,"

Takamasa's words echoed in Kaname's mind, but they didn't distract his aim.

"People usually think of a sling, a U-shaped scrap of cloth you use to

rapidly spin a stone, but that's not the only way to achieve centrifugal force. When a pitcher throws a ball, they use their shoulders; that's centrifugal force as well. The longer their arms, the more powerful the throw... For example, let's say you had a long rod or pipe..."

Guided by the length of the pipe, the handmade bolt shot toward the open end. By the time it reached the "muzzle," the bolt was moving at eighty-three meters per second. Its mass was two hundred grams, four times heavier than a round from an anti-materiel rifle.

In other words...

In terms of raw power, this makeshift weapon packed more of a punch than a .45-caliber pistol.

With a satisfying *Thunk!!* the homemade bolt landed right between the man's eyes. Without even giving his lifeless body a second look as it crumpled to the ground, Kaname ducked behind one of the structure's concrete pillars to load his next shot.

His partner was causing a ruckus down below, and their opponents probably never expected an attack to come from above.

Fwsh!!

Kaname launched another bolt at a group of Dealers who had escaped up the slope to the safety of the upper floor. If they came closer, he could attack them directly with the pipe, and at long range, he had a projectile stronger than a handgun bullet.

With another attacker on the scene, confusion quickly began to spread. Below, the Dealers had Easy Option to contend with, and up above, Kaname Suou. By using an unexpected pincer attack, he could put his opponents at a psychological disadvantage and do much more damage than the specs of his and his partner's weapons should have allowed. That was the basis of their current strategy.

There are six floors to this building. Where's the big boss with the smartphone? Which floor is he hiding on?!

One Dealer, after witnessing Kaname mow down his comrades, turned around and tried to run back down the slope. Kaname followed him down, impaling the man's brain with his ice pick as he hurried past.

Just then…

"Hey, Kaname! Shoulda known takin' your guns and leavin' you in the slums wasn't enough to kill ya!!"

"Zaurus?!"

Kaname leaped behind one of the cars lined up nearby. Soon, he heard the sound of compressed air and the crack of the car window. It was her nail gun again. This place had once been a parking garage, but it must have been deemed abandoned at some point. As a result, the barrier that normally protected properly parked cars was no longer effective here.

Beneath a shower of auto glass, Kaname bent down behind one of the wheelless car-shaped generators and held his pipe horizontally, hiding himself from view.

There was a pounding noise coming from the trunk. That must have been one of the captured Magistelli. Her distress at suddenly becoming Kaname's (in)human shield was understandable, but she was giving away his location, so Kaname broke the padlock with the butt of his iron pipe, throwing open the trunk before moving on to the next car.

She's behind the pillar, fifteen meters ahead. It's too far for her to hit me, but if I miss my shot, I won't have time to load another. She'll be on top of me with the nail bat!

Takamasa's vehicle was nowhere to be seen. He must have long since decided this was no place for him. And since he never trusted the Magistelli, there was probably no partner for Ramjet to confiscate, either.

The fact that Zaurus was here meant it was highly likely her trap-loving associate, M-Scope, wasn't too far off. Kaname ran through the possibilities in his head, clicking his tongue softly. They had probably assassinated the other slum leaders and allied with the last one standing, all for the sole purpose of defeating Kaname.

This wasn't about good and evil, or which team you were on. It was about revenge, pure and simple. Revenge on Kaname Suou, and plundering his assets to pay off the debts of the other Ag Wolves. To that end, they believed anything was permissible.

Now that those two were involved, the difficulty had spiked. Once the initial chaos subsided, things would get a lot harder for Easy Option. He didn't have the equipment or resources to win a fair fight. Kaname needed to come out of hiding and stir things up, or the man would die. This was a man at rock bottom, who had still chosen to stand and fight for Claire Kaizuka.

However, Zaurus and M-Scope meant business. In fact, if they could manage to take those two out, Kaname and Easy Option would be about 90 percent of the way to their goal. All the evil in the Red Territory was concentrated here, in this building, and once the Ag Wolves were out of the picture, he and Easy Option could take their time eliminating the rest of the hyenas. Even if he couldn't find a phone on the big boss, there would be no more threat to Midori and Tselika once he was gone.

"…"

Kaname calmly considered his priorities.

This was the deciding moment.

19

Easy Option ran, his grimy raincoat flapping behind him as he fired his crossbow deeper into the building. He was on the ground floor. Kaname Suou had entered via the rooftop, and the plan was for Easy Option to cause as much chaos as possible while advancing to the upper floors.

Then a large man in overalls stepped out, the tools in his belt clinking together with every step. A vicious grin spread over the man's familiar face as he pulled out his monkey wrench and L-shaped crowbar.

"Ramjet!!"

The target had no cover. He was standing in the middle of the open parking lot. The raincoat man fired his crossbow relentlessly, but Ramjet's men rushed out from either side to defend him, transparent shields in their hands. They formed a line, leaving no gaps between them, and repelled Easy Option's bolts. Some of them had guns in addition to their shields.

The men shouted to one another.

"Looks like Ramjet was right."

"Get him! He'll need time to relo—"

Splat! One of the men went down just as he tried to level his handgun for a shot. His comrade looked at him in shock, before quickly meeting a similar fate.

"I see," said Ramjet from behind the line of riot shields. "You loosened your bowstring to make it *easier to draw.* Lowers the power but increases firing speed. I suppose in this situation, you don't need range." He gave a wicked grin. "But then again, I can hit you from here just fine."

"Tch!"

To Ramjet, a monkey wrench was not simply a melee weapon. He hurled it at Easy Option, with all the strength of his nearly two-meter frame. At that speed, it could crush a man's skull, bulletproof helmet or no. In terms of raw power, it was more deadly than a .45-caliber pistol.

Easy Option clicked his tongue and ducked behind a pillar for cover—only to be knocked back by a powerful explosion.

"Gaaah?!"

"…A trap. Think of a flower. Flowers don't move by themselves. Instead, they lure other creatures to them, like insects to carry pollen and natural predators to take care of pests."

A boy stepped out from the shadows like a ghost and stood next to Ramjet. He wore a backpack and had a slouch.

"You read me like a book, you mean…?"

Easy Option was on the floor, clenching his teeth to help bear the pain. The boy appeared unsympathetic, even inhuman.

"Actually, I've been told I'm not very good at reading other people. Following the tone of the conversation or judging the mood of the room—you know. That's why I tend to go by what someone's wearing. I might not look it, but I'm actually quite knowledgeable when it comes to apparel. You can treat clothes like flower petals or the markings on a bug. Understand what someone's wearing and you can understand what they're trying to do… Oh, sorry. I'm rambling again, aren't I? Well, that just proves my point…"

The boy had predicted exactly where Easy Option would hide once Ramjet took a shot at him. Easy Option had meant to take cover but had only succeeded in walking right into a trap.

The big man in the overalls chuckled and said, "That's what you get for treatin' us with disrespect after everything we've done for you. Who was it got you back on your feet after you Fell, huh?!"

"It wasn't you…who saved me…"

Easy Option lay on the floor, unable to get up, his crossbow a short distance away. Even so, he gritted his teeth and glared at his foe with all the hate in his heart.

"All you did was take from us! You lied and cheated! You had us running huge sums of money for your secret ATM, without any warning that thieves might come and kill us over it!!"

"Lied? Cheated? Don't be a fool. We gave you a place to live. For over a year, I might add."

The man's voice was dripping with derision. So this was what absolute power could do to a person.

"Come on, Jouji. Remember, you've been through some hard times. What happened to that crowdfundin' project to develop a cheap farmland reclamation kit? Big corn had somethin' to say, didn't they? Bought up all the patents before you could even get your crappy invention off the ground. Ain't that right?"

"…"

When a crowdfunded project failed, the money pledged in good faith was meant to be returned to the investors. But obviously that wasn't possible if you'd already spent it on development.

"You tell all that to your family? How your little plan to change the world went down the drain, and now you spend every day runnin' from angry investors? Grah-ha-ha! Of course you didn't! What would your kids think of their dear old daddy then? An' when you were at rock bottom, don't forget it was me who invited you here, to my base in *Money (Game) Master*. I was sure you were going to work hard to pay back all the people you screwed over! What's wrong, you given up?!"

The raincoat man clenched his teeth so hard he could feel his molars crack. But his anger wasn't directed at the jeering man before him.

He was angry at himself—for being a coward.

He's right. I got complacent…

He'd been trying to bring people from all over the world together to contribute to the greater good. Even if it took the form of money, what he had received was the kindness and strength of other people. There was only one person to blame for squandering that faith and turning it into hate: himself.

And even though he should have borne the weight of that failing alone, he grabbed onto that stupid girl's hand and allowed her to take on his burdens. And while he lived in blissful ignorance, she continued to suffer. That, more than anything else, was his greatest regret.

It doesn't matter what kind of awful circumstances you find yourself in; give it a few months and the human mind readjusts. When an AI Dropout holes up in their room, spending all their free time playing this game, they don't even notice when they get caught in it. It becomes normal to be someone's pawn and have your mountain of debt used like a shield against you—like a spammer working in a dodgy call center or sending out phishing e-mails! Claire talked about how much she wanted to help other people, but we both knew she was only doing it because she had no other choice!!

How could he let her shoot herself in the head with that weary smile on her face?

How could he let that unending cycle run its course even one more time?

It had to stop. And that was why Easy Option was able to spit out his next words.

"…That stupid, idiotic woman. She helped me when I still had no idea what I was doing. She freed me of my debt without even asking, and

I've never forgiven her for it! That's the only reason I'm still here now, Ramjet!!"

"Who gives a shit?"

The large man in the overalls twirled the L-shaped crowbar in his hand. It was effectively a throwing ax. If aimed correctly and thrown with enough speed, it could easily shatter the raincoat man's skull, even if he were wearing a bulletproof helmet. In terms of raw stopping power, it was stronger than a handgun.

"Cry all you want, but there ain't no point if nobody's around to listen. There ain't no guardian angels metin' out justice in *Money (Game) Master*; all you got are us devils! Once again, you've failed to put in the work, dumbass. Now you're gonna die, eatin' dirt like a worm. Geez, an' after that dumbfuck woman went outta her way to help you out, too!"

"Grh!!"

"Not here for money, huh? Saving a girl, huh??? Stupid dreams like those are just gonna put her in debt all over again!! Maybe just killin' her won't be enough to pay it off this time. Perhaps I should teach her a better way to make money! Maybe we'll take a trip to Prostitute Island!! Gah-ha-ha-ha!!"

"RAAAMJEEETTT!!!!!"

For a brief moment, Easy Option surpassed his physical limits. Rousing his stiff body to action, he reached out and clutched his crossbow.

However.

Even with the loosened bowstring, he lacked the strength to draw it. The bolt he wanted to fire tumbled from his grasp. Everything in this game was based on exact numbers and formulae. There were no angels, no miracles.

I will...

Shaking, the raincoat man swore with all his heart. Solemnly, sincerely.

I will become a man who can face his family with pride. I won't stand on anyone's shoulders ever again. Running away only delays the inevitable!!

I will pay back all my debts to the people I've wronged—starting with her!!

"That's right, die! Die and fuck things up for everyone else again! You know what you are? You're a loser!! A sad, lonely loser who's only good for luggin' around trash!!"

His whole face bursting with sweat, Ramjet raised his L-shaped crowbar. It was obvious even before he swung: Easy Option's head was right in the line of fire. There would be no escaping the crushing blow now.

Or so he thought.

M-Scope noticed it first and jumped back—just in time.

Splat!!

An ice pick landed solidly in the side of the large man's head.

20

For Kaname, there was only one course of action.

…My first priorities are taking out the big boss and getting my hands on a smartphone so I can stop Tselika and Midori from charging in recklessly.

The Lion's Nose told Kaname who to fight, and it was never wrong.

They may be strong, but Zaurus and M-Scope are nothing more than anomalies. I can deal with them later!!

And so Kaname Suou sprang into action. He stepped out from behind the car, but not to challenge Zaurus to one-on-one combat. In fact, he ran as fast as he could in the opposite direction.

He didn't care about his own dignity. Down there was a man so touched by what was happening to Claire Kaizuka, he was putting his life on the line for her. Kaname and the man were comrades, fighting for a common cause, and Kaname could never abandon a comrade. If turning his back on the enemy could buy the life of so great a man, then it was a small price to pay.

"Bitch!!" shouted Zaurus after him.

The girl with the braid peeked out from behind a concrete pillar and fired several shots from her nail gun, though there was almost no chance she'd hit Kaname at this range. And yet...

"Grh?!!"

A lucky shot pierced Kaname's shoulder. The pain was searing, but the wound was far from fatal—what Kaname was truly afraid of was her nail bat. For that reason, he ignored the nail gun and kept running, eventually reaching the safety of the slope leading down to the lower level.

As long as he didn't have to deal with Zaurus and M-Scope, the other Dealers in the parking garage should be no trouble at all. Kaname fought his way down, either knocking them off their feet with his two-meter iron pipe or impaling them with his handmade ice-pick arrows, more powerful than .45-caliber bullets.

Finally, he reached the second floor. Already the air was thick with the smell of gunpowder. M-Scope must have detonated one of his traps armed with a rocket warhead. The man in the raincoat, Easy Option, lay on the floor. A short distance away, Kaname spied the man who had first called out to him back in the Red Territory plaza. It was Ramjet, wielding an L-shaped crowbar in one hand, about to throw.

Standing next to him was the boy in the backpack with the slouch—M-Scope.

There was no time to lose.

Fwsh!!

Kaname Suou swung the pipe down like a fishing rod, sending an ice pick hurtling toward his target. Without warning his ally, M-Scope took a single step backward. Ramjet didn't even have time to scream as the bolt came flying from his blind spot and pierced his temple, killing him instantly.

"Oh? You sure you didn't want to make him suffer a little more?" asked M-Scope without batting an eye. To him, Ramjet was nothing more than a means to get at his true foe. The boy pulled out a small submachine gun and pointed it at Kaname.

"Sorry about this," said Kaname as he swung the pipe at one of the men still staring in shock at his boss's corpse, knocking him out. He then quickly wrapped his arm around the unconscious man's neck and held him in front of his own body.

Rat-a-tat-a-tat!! The sound of bullets spraying from the SMG rang out. It wasn't the most accurate of weapons, but it was more than enough at this range. If Kaname had been a second slower, he'd be the one full of holes instead of his meat shield.

M-Scope is a trap master. He's probably not trying to kill me with bullets. This is all a feint to try to lead me somewhere.

As bullets peppered his human shield, Kaname reached around and grabbed a hand grenade off the dead Dealer's battle harness. He pulled the pin with his teeth and tossed it. Anything plundered from a Dealer's corpse before it disappeared was yours to keep. M-Scope stopped firing and hid behind a car, while the group of underlings with riot shields, panicking at the sudden loss of their leader, were blown apart by the explosion and an ensuing hail of shrapnel.

Shrouded by the cloud of smoke that followed, Kaname dropped his meat shield and followed his nose. Two steps forward. Three steps to the right. Four forward. Two to the left. The only one who could glean any meaning from the boy's apparently random movements was M-Scope, who had laid the very traps the Lion's Nose was leading Kaname around. No ordinary human could perceive the infrared beams, microwaves, and ultrasonic waves his mines used for detection, but Kaname threaded the needle like it was nothing, all the while loading another bolt into his iron pipe.

At last, M-Scope was starting to feel the pressure. Kaname had just defied all his expectations.

"The Lion's Nose… You're a monster!"

"I'm not the only one. There's supposed to be twelve, including me. Apparently, we're called the Zodiac Children."

Come to think of it, Midori also possessed an uncanny ability to analyze a Dealer's specs just by looking at their clothes. And she was the little sister of the man to whom Kaname owed everything. He couldn't let her die. Not here, not ever.

And as he'd said before, M-Scope was a trap master. But that meant once his traps failed, he could no longer land a decisive blow, even when his target was standing right in front of him. There was no guarantee he could take on a powerful Dealer with a submachine gun alone.

Now, all his painstaking preparations ruined, M-Scope watched as Kaname slowly advanced toward him…and the boy's lips twisted into a grin.

"…I see."

"Something you want to say?"

"Well…"

In his final moments, M-Scope stood directly before his foe. Teaming up with the local organization had been the most efficient way to get to Kaname, but for some reason, the boy found himself thinking back on the conversation between Ramjet and Easy Option. As he readied the submachine gun to fire, he looked up at Kaname and spoke.

The look in his eyes was genuine.

"I was just thinking, I might as well have picked the other side."

Rat-a-tat!! came the crack of the submachine gun.

The sound of the ice-pick arrow was too soft to be heard.

21

She was running as fast as she could. Even if Kaname wasn't around, she still had to check every shadow. There was someone she knew down there, but one half-hearted shot wasn't going to be enough to save them.

And so it was while she was still descending that Zaurus heard a burst of SMG fire.

"M-Scope!!"

By the time she reached the second floor, the battle was already over, and Kaname Suou was nowhere to be seen.

Only M-Scope was left, lying in a pool of blood, his character-print hoodie stained a dark crimson. Zaurus had never understood the boy's obsession with 2D women, but she knew the hoodie probably meant a lot to him. Right now, however, there was no time to lament its passing.

A modified ice pick stuck out of his torso.

"Ah-ha-ha… He got me."

"Shut up! Shut up!!"

Zaurus lifted him, cradling his upper body but leaving the ice pick intact so as not to cause more bleeding. She clenched her teeth. M-Scope was still alive.

With every other shot, Kaname Suou had aimed for his target's head, instantly killing them. M-Scope must have detonated a trap at the precise moment he fired, causing even that peerless marksman to miss the killing blow. Then, instead of wasting time finishing the boy off, he'd opted to flee, scared of encountering Zaurus.

The girl couldn't believe the chain of luck that had led them to this outcome, but she wasn't about to let it go to waste.

"Zaurus…"

"Shut up."

"Zaurus, don't worry about me; go after Kaname Suou. He's been trying to avoid you this whole time, because he knows he can't beat you without all his usual equipment. This is your only chance, Zaurus. I couldn't do it, but you can."

"I said shut the fuck up!!" It wasn't a shout; it was a wail. M-Scope saw the tears in her eyes, the trembling of her lips.

"Who cares about that anymore? I don't want to lose you again!! Do you have any idea how miraculous it was that we both pulled through the first time? I don't ever want to go through that again! Don't you understand?!"

"…"

If they let Kaname escape now, they'd be further than ever from restoring the Ag Wolves. But maybe killing Kaname wasn't an absolute requirement. Any large amount of money would suffice to lend support to the group's former members. M-Scope and Zaurus could earn that kind of money on the stock market, just like they always had. But

the fact that they had lost to Kaname Suou and let him escape would never go away. This was supposed to be a rite to wipe that stain from their record, so all of them could enjoy the game once more. It didn't matter how much blood had to be spilled to achieve it.

But.

Even so.

"You're the one who asked me on this date, dumbass!! So don't leave me to finish it alone!!"

At last, M-Scope understood the true reason they'd lost. It was because there was something more important than their obsession with revenge. More important than shedding the burden of their loss.

Frey(a)'s condition for M-Scope had been for him to find someone out in this big, wide world and tell them how he felt.

Had the two of them merely been cooperating to achieve a common goal, then yes, it would have made perfect sense for Zaurus to leave the injured M-Scope and go after Kaname on her own.

But she hadn't—because of their relationship.

Zaurus valued her bond with M-Scope more than her loyalty to the Ag Wolves.

"…They're all going to hate you for this," the boy said.

"Who cares?"

"Titan, Hazard, and all the others. Didn't you want to see them again? Didn't you want to fight as a team again, with a newly clean slate?"

"Who cares?! They can hate me all they want! All that matters is protecting you!! So don't die! Please don't die, M-Scope!!"

M-Scope had always been a poor conversationalist. He never seemed to say the right thing.

He saw the clothes someone wore as the petals of a flower or the patterns on a beetle, and he drew up a complete profile of them in his mind. He would then use that profile to achieve his objective. That was why his traps never failed. He could set up a trap in the middle of a busy street and be confident his target, and only his target, would walk into it.

That must have been why he fell for her.

Zaurus didn't care if the conversation turned awkward. She was so violent that everyone walked on eggshells around her, letting her boss them around—even him. But M-Scope found he actually kind of enjoyed that.

So how could he blame her for doing the same thing now?

"I'm the worst...," he said. "I can't believe I made the girl I love cry."

22

...Hmm? Seems like they're not gonna follow me. Well, she wouldn't have lasted long trailing her dying ally alongside her anyway.

Kaname trudged out through the main garage entrance, supporting the man in the raincoat against his shoulder. Glancing back at the structure, he sighed.

Far off in the distance, he caught sight of a twinkling light. It was a signal from Tselika, using a hand mirror to reflect the sun. They were just outside the Red Territory but had stopped at the outskirts. It was the same method Kaname had used just before entering the garage.

And if the girls had brought the Legacies with them, Kaname's combat readiness would skyrocket... After all, with the *infinite-range anti-materiel sniper rifle, #fireline.err* on their side, Kaname's allies could take out an enemy standing right in front of him, without taking one step into the Red Territory themselves.

Tossing his crafted weapon aside, Kaname pulled out the loot he had picked up earlier: Ramjet's smartphone.

"Thanks, Tselika. Stand down. Sorry for all the trouble."

"*Hmph. You sure don't sound sorry, My Lord. Let me guess, helping people again?*"

No doubt his partner was peering at him even now through the weapon's scope. Or, more precisely, at the man Kaname was supporting.

"If you already know, why ask? I'm not in it for bragging rights, as you know."

"Yes, I know. Just head north up the No. 4 railway. We're waiting for you. You'll be heading straight for us, so don't worry about staying hidden. I have you covered if anyone attacks."

"What about Midori?"

"She's just setting up the mortar, #thunderbolt.err. Shall I tell her to stop?"

Just then, Easy Option groaned and looked weakly over at Kaname.

"...We need pull tabs and bottle caps. As many as we can carry. What ended up happening?"

Although their leader, Ramjet, was dead, the bad guys' team was still around. If they came and took away all the currency stored here disguised as trash, any hope of saving Claire Kaizuka would vanish. However...

"We'll let Zaurus take care of it. She doesn't owe them anything."

"?"

That was all they could do. If Kaname's predictions were correct, the only reason M-Scope and Zaurus partnered with Ramjet was because their goals had happened to align. Ramjet was probably more than happy to see the other leaders Fall and take over their share of the profits, but their subordinates probably didn't feel the same way. Without a boss to keep them in line, there would be nothing to stop them from taking revenge for their fallen leaders.

And there was no way Zaurus would abandon the wounded M-Scope. She would defend that parking garage to the bitter end, with only her nail gun and nail bat, if need be.

Rat-a-tat!! Rat-a-tat!!

Kaname heard the distant sound of gunfire. If she got out of this alive, it wouldn't be unscathed. Her first priority would be to get herself and M-Scope out of the Red Territory as soon as possible, leaving the pile of pull tabs and bottle caps ripe for the taking. Once the heat died down, someone could go back and take it all to pay off Claire Kazuka's debts. It would probably be more difficult to convert into yachts or gems without the three bosses around, but the infrastructure would still exist, at least for a while. There would be plenty of time to head to the mainland and pull one over on the business's clients.

"Phew."

For the time being, the evil at the heart of the Red Territory had been put to rest. From now on, Kaname would have little trouble coming and going as he pleased. It might be dangerous walking around with only Tselika and Midori for protection, but that would all change once Kaname got Short Spear back. While it was Kaname's custom-made pride and joy, the gun itself was only slightly better than what you could get on the market. Using the spare parts Tselika was holding on to, Kaname wouldn't have any trouble whipping up another one.

All of which meant that, at last, Kaname could return to the problem at hand.

Takamasa was searching for the Zodiac Children. And to do that, he had to clear the noise. The loads of Dealers who were all bark and no bite obscured the truly powerful individuals lurking in their midst. And so Takamasa was killing them off one at a time with the laser weapon #flash.err. His attacks came at the speed of light, perceptible only to those with the supernatural abilities required to predict them. Via helicopter or truck, he could carry the shipping container Legacy anywhere it needed to be, periodically bringing it back here, to the Red Territory, in order to repaint the container as if it were Kaname's coupe, then head back to his base in secret.

This place was like a black box. Only by going to the shipping yard, confirming which container housed the Legacy, and following it could Kaname hope to narrow down Takamasa's whereabouts.

And once he'd done that, he could confront his old friend and put a stop to all this.

23

It was a day like any other in the Red Territory.

This was where most of those who Fell ended up, waiting for their chance to make a comeback. And today, there was another one. Another poor soul, saddled with debt. Another lost lamb without anywhere to go. Another downed fighter without the right to a comeback.

Wasn't that unfair?

People have to learn from their mistakes. Surely they should be allowed a second chance to put those lessons into practice.

After all, they weren't like her.

Their debts had come from their own mistakes. Freed from debt, they could keep trying, with nothing to stop them. As long as they didn't stray from their path, they could move on to a brighter future.

But she was different.

Her debts had come crashing down on her from above, falling from the sky like a meteor. It didn't matter what choices she made, what lessons she learned, or how much effort she put in. Debt came out of nowhere and took everything away. Her path was full of holes, and even if she walked in a perfectly straight line, she would keep falling and falling and falling.

So why not give her chance to someone else? Let her take on other people's debt, since unlike her, they still had the potential to strive for something better.

With this in mind, the girl was about to call out to someone else, when—

"Not so fast."

A hand reached in from the side and grabbed her outstretched arm, stopping her.

Why? She'd chosen this for herself. This was everything she wanted.

So why did that voice ring so true, and why had her tear ducts begun to sting?

The man in the well-used raincoat looked down at her and issued a stern command.

"That's enough, Claire. You don't have to do this anymore. I won't let you."

There was no piggy bank of chances in life—you didn't save them, and they didn't run out. No matter how far you'd fallen or how cruelly you were pushed down, you could always start again.

Finally, someone had said it.

Interlude 1

Long dark hair was parted around her forehead, and she wore a pair of glasses along with a tight skirt and white blouse, whose thin fabric—a must in this hot climate—exposed the bright red bra beneath.

Dealer name: Lily-Kiska Sweetmare.

In the past, she had been a skilled sniper and the leader of an infamous team of Dealers known as the Ag Wolves. Now, though…what had she become? The world had moved on, leaving her in a very strange situation.

She was one of the Zodiac Children—the Scorpion's Tenacity.

Out of the seven billion people on earth, only twelve had been born with the innate ability to defy the AI companies' computerized analyses. Or at least, that was what the boy had said.

"Phew…" She sighed as a small elfin girl opened the thick rear door of her long black limousine.

"Ms. Kiska," the girl addressed her. "Thank you for participating in our examination today."

"You're welcome," replied Lily-Kiska.

The interior of the car was refreshingly cool. Inside were couches surrounding a glass table that could double as a screen, a minibar and fridge stocked with all kinds of fruit and drinks, and a high-end audio system. It could fit almost twenty people if they squeezed, but Lily-Kiska smiled awkwardly as she settled in. Now that there was no one to share it with, the space felt oppressively lonely.

It was all her fault. Not Kaname Suou's.

She'd wanted to help him, to fight by his side, and she'd let those personal feelings cloud her judgment. That, more than anything else, was what had led the team to its downfall. It didn't matter what choices she made; in the end, she probably never could have killed Kaname. But perhaps if she had known when to give up, things wouldn't have turned out so badly.

She didn't blame *him* for that. Even though she knew her feelings had cost her precious friends.

Even death was no cure for foolishness—she understood that now. No matter where she went, Kaname Suou was always on her mind. Now matter how much he stabbed her in the back or cast her aside, that wouldn't change.

A monotonous *beep* sounded inside the limo. Lily-Kiska clapped her hands, and the message she had just received appeared on the surface of the long glass table.

To Lily-Kiska Sweetmare.

We wish to express our gratitude for your cooperation in undertaking a complete physical examination. We assure you that you have made the correct decision.

Initial test results look good. As you will recall, we had you take part in a number of IQ exams and chess games during the breaks between tests. As predicted, we observed several instances of victory under unwinnable circumstances. Such results are consistent with our understanding of the Zodiac Children's abilities.

This affirms our initial hypothesis, gleaned from analyzing the results of your previous shootouts and trades.

Though there are still many unknowns regarding the Zodiac Children, as they are able to exist within the game, we must conclude that they are some sort of logical entity. Rest assured, however, there is no limit to what big data can accomplish. The only reason our analysis remains incomplete is insufficient data. That is precisely why your cooperation is of such great value to us.

AI society is set up to ensure optimal happiness for humanity.

Only sadness and misfortune await those who reject it.

We guarantee that you have made the right decision.

Thank you kindly for your assistance. We hope to be in contact soon with good news.

> *Sincerely,*
> *The Mind of the Magistelli.*

"..."

Perhaps she was in the process of snuffing out humanity's last hope. Perhaps history books in the future would include her photo under the label "World's Greatest Fool."

But even so.

Lily-Kiska Sweetmare never wavered. It didn't matter if the AI stabbed her in the back. It didn't matter if they cast her aside when they were done. She wouldn't even bat an eye.

...Kaname Suou. Criminal AO. If all I do is follow in their footsteps, I'll never catch up. I'll never be of use to him.

As she swept her eyes across the virtual keyboard, typing a response, the girl thought—a private thought, for no one else but her.

I must get ahead, even if it requires me to make the worst move in history. As long as I remain predictable, I'll never be a useful weapon in their fight.

She would allow herself to be assimilated by the AI, if that was what it took.

No, even that would only make her stronger.

The Zodiac Child, the Scorpion's Tenacity.

The demons should've known. The AI could never hope to control her.

Chapter 8

Attack on PMC Headquarters BGM #08
"Laser Art"

1

Bang!

Kaname threw the iron doors wide and stepped out onto the roof of a resort hotel. This building was just one of the many specks of light in the sea of stars that made up the financial district's nightscape.

The roof was dominated by an enormous jacuzzi, and in its center sat a blond, fresh-faced man named Frey(a), with a bath towel–clad beauty under each arm. Suddenly, the two women slipped away, rising out of the water. Frey(a) watched them go, perplexed, before craning his neck around and noticing his visitor. The jacuzzi lights illuminated his face from below, projecting the water's ripples onto his charming smile.

"Well, if it isn't Kaname! You seem tired; I hope *my newest recruits* didn't cause you *too* much trouble. I feel a tad responsible, you know. So in return, how about you take any three handbags you like from my pawnshop? Hee-hee. If that's still not enough for you, I'm sure I can find a more *personal* way to pay you back…"

Kaname ignored the man's suggestive words and walked over to a nearby handcart. It was replete with bottles of shampoo and body soap, as well as other more dubious items, such as disinfectant and a

slippery substance that Kaname suspected wasn't for hygiene purposes at all. No doubt Frey(a)'s baths were a little more exciting than
the average person's.

Kaname wasn't after any of those things, however. Instead, he reached
into the top drawer of the cart and pulled out a blow-dryer.

"Ah."

Frey(a) nearly jumped out of his skin, tumbling out of the jacuzzi just
seconds before Kaname tossed in the blow-dryer, along with the bulky
battery pack that allowed it to operate outdoors. As soon as the electronics touched the water, there was a loud crackle, and the jacuzzi
went silent.

Frey(a) looked up at Kaname, face pale, in nothing but a towel.

"Wh-wh-wh-what on earth's gotten into you, Kaname?! Are you trying to kill me?!"

"...After risking my life because *you* stabbed me in the back, I'd really
appreciate it if the first thing I had to see wasn't your microdick."

"Oh my goodness, he's lost his mind! Where's the sweet young boy I
used to know? I'll tell you what, Kaname. This hotel is currently in my
possession, so why don't you tuck yourself in and get some much-
needed rest, hmm? I'll even throw in one of my world-famous massage sessions, on the house!"

"I think we have something more important to talk about first,
don't we?"

"Oh, of course! You want to hear more about the massage, don't you?
Well, we've got plenty of options; you can have it in the bath, in the
bedroom; we've got chairs, mats—we could do it right here if you want.
If you'd rather have a female masseuse, that can be arr—Eek!"

Kaname Suou bent down and reached into the second drawer of the
handcart. From there, he pulled out a hidden weapon: a special gun
that used compressed air to push out an exceptionally thick silicon tube
about the size of a relay baton. Rapid-fire capable, too.

Flick the switch, and...☆

Bam-bam-bam!! Thud! Thud! Thud!

"Wait, wait, wait! Kaname, please! One direct hit from the XL size and you'll split me in half! At least let me change forms first! Have mercy! Oh, sweet Jesus, no!!"

As Frey(a) ducked and weaved for dear life, Kaname continued in a deep, threatening voice.

"...I don't like the Western way of refusing to apologize when somebody dies from negligence. If you're a grown-up, you should know how to say sorry..."

"I will!! I will! I'll turn over a new leaf! I'll do anything!!"

Kaname turned off the rampaging machine in his hands. Then he took out the gently arched silicone rod and snapped it in half.

"I'm still sending you a bill later, but I'll let you off this time. This is it, though. Next time, I'll be snapping yours. You know as well as anyone just how serious I can be, don't you, Frey(a)?"

"Hee-hee. I was only looking to spice up our stagnant relationship with a little aphrodisiac. It was just a little more...powerful...than I expected, that's all. But you know, getting to see such a sadistic side of you made it all worthwhile. Hee-hee. If my betrayal shocked you so deeply, that means you must have trusted me quite a bit! I must return your affections with my own!!"

Kaname didn't need to stand around and listen to Frey(a)'s nonsense. He threw the pieces of silicone aside and headed for the exit. As he passed, Frey(a)'s slime Magistellus in her chocolate-brown sailor suit quickly bowed.

"I deeply apologize for any inconvenience caused by my rash and senseless master."

"It's not your fault. In fact, if you hadn't secretly let me in to the VIP area, I would never have been able to sneak up on Frey(a) like this."

Betrayal was unthinkable for the Magistelli, duty-bound as they were to support their Dealers. But apparently, the girl saw no contradiction in her actions.

"...I only do what is best for my master. Sometimes, that requires he be given a good talking-to by someone who knows what they're doing."

"I see."

"In fact, I must thank you. Few are strong enough to talk sense into my master without fear of the consequences. Please do not give up on him, Mr. Suou. My master has expressed his desire to compensate you for any wasted time, as well as for any physical and mental stress you may have suffered. Do you have any particular requests? He did say *anything*, so anything is what I shall provide."

"Hmm… There is one thing. I could do it myself, but it would be a lot easier if I had some help with the busywork. How about it?"

"On the pride and dignity of the Treasure Hermit Crabs, I shall see it done, sir."

Kaname gave a weak smile at the Magistellus's stiff formality.

He wouldn't ask the impossible. Kaname was keen to extract his due recompense and clear the slate as soon as he could.

"I need to get in contact with a Dealer. Her name's Mother Loose."

2

Server Name: Gamma Orange.
Final Location: Tokonatsu City, Peninsula District.
Log-out successful.
Thank you for playing, Kaname Suou.

"Come on, big bro! When are you gonna stop playing?! Your food's burning!!"

As his mind came back into focus, he heard a sound like trees rustling in the wind. His vision and consciousness were still foggy, a side effect of returning to the real world from a virtual one made of representational markers.

The type of VR technology used by the game relied on a smartphone's ability to provide a host of patterns and symbols at a whopping hundred and twenty frames per second and the human brain's power to draw connections between these images, stitching together the correct picture. The technology was cheap and highly effective, with the only drawback being the strain it caused on the eyes. Because of that, there were still critics insisting that playing games resulted in nearsightedness.

He blinked several times, waited for his eyes to readjust, then tilted his head back and inserted his contacts. At long last, the real world came into focus.

Sure enough, he could smell corn and meat roasting on the barbecue in front of him. The sky had darkened, and the sparks of the charcoal fire danced like fireflies.

They were at a campsite somewhere. It was the second of May, slap-bang in the middle of the Golden Week holidays. His whole family was there, enjoying an evening meal while fending off the moths attracted by the firelight.

His sister used a pair of tongs to lift a well-cooked sausage onto his paper plate, along with some potato slices. Then she addressed him, puffing out her rosy cheeks.

"I swear, you're *addicted* to that thing. We're supposed to be having a nice family meal. Why do you have to stay on your phone the whole time? We might as well not even be outdoors."

The boy was at a loss. It hadn't been entirely his fault, but with his parents sitting right in front of him, he couldn't exactly say he'd been kidnapped and unable to log out.

"Well, you know. The stock market never sleeps."

"That's what you aaalways say!!"

At first glance, it might seem that they were camping in the middle of nowhere, but if you could see the radio waves, LAN packets, and satellite links constantly bouncing around them, you would realize they could never truly disconnect. And that wasn't even counting the cameras monitoring the water levels of dams and rivers, the seismo-scopes listening for minuscule vibrations in the earth to warn of oncoming quakes, or the sensor arrays constantly surveying the pollen count in the air. In Japan these days, even a seasoned mountain climber never went up without a GPS link and real-time meteorological data.

Looking up into the sky, he noticed a single star buzzing back and forth among the others. This was almost certainly no UFO but a drone taking aerial pictures for some photographer.

It was now difficult to find a single place in Japan without a decent phone signal. Just moving to a campsite a little ways out of the city wasn't enough. Your only bet was to seal yourself underground in a basement lined with lead.

And it wasn't just the boy on his phone out here. Over to the side, another group of campers were busy setting up a tent, while the smartphones in their hands offered an AR view of what it was meant to look like, overlaid onto the scenery. Any recipes were downloaded from the internet, and before eating any wild plants, you could scan them with an app, which would send the image to a large server somewhere and tell you if they were safe to eat or not. Nowadays, phones could even emit an ultrasonic noise that kept wild bears at bay.

There were no mosquitoes or flies anywhere to be seen, and it wasn't just because summer hadn't yet begun. Genetic splicing was another area dominated by AI. It had been a simple matter to create varieties that didn't react to human blood or rotting food, and to release them into the population to breed. Stronger pesticides only resulted in more resilient pests, so why not focus on making the insects weaker instead?

People had even begun to wonder if similar methods were being used on humanity itself. It was already common to gestate a baby in a lab, so that genetic tests could be run. Who knew what kinds of procedures might be performed without the mother's knowledge? After all, young people these days were exceedingly good with computers, and there was no shortage of conspiracy theories suggesting that something had been done to their genes and skeletal structure to achieve this.

"Anyway, it's time to enjoy the outdoors with me. Here, have a nice, fat, juicy wiener ♪"

"Erp."

"What kind of reaction is that? Is my food not good enough for you?"

"...No, it's not that. You just reminded me of something that happened earlier."

"?"

His sister tilted her head quizzically, but the boy was loath to explain, so the girl took the sausage for herself and began innocently nibbling on it.

"*Om-nom.* There's nothing wrong with games, but everything in moderation."

"You're right. By the way, I've got something to say about *Money (Game) Master.*"

"More? Can't we change the subject?"

"Just one thing. You see…"

His stomach felt bloated. In the great outdoors, anything you did came with intrinsic health benefits…or so the boy would've liked to think. But the barbecue had featured considerably more meat than vegetables, and everything had been pretty greasy. Some fried chicken and a vegetable salad from the convenience store would probably have been a lot healthier.

"*Phew.*"

The boy sighed, got up, and walked a short distance from the cluster of tents over to a small structure: a roof held aloft by four pillars. It must have once been a campsite gazebo, but now there was a phone charging station here—a row of outlets lining a long table like the kind you would find at a stand-up noodle bar. It seemed to be doing good business; about two-thirds of the outlets were being used for one electronic device or another, though the place was otherwise deserted, the devices left unattended like washing machines at a laundromat.

Each one was fitted with metal anti-theft wires, like the kind in electronics shops, but the boy still considered it negligent to leave your smartphone out where anyone could access it. Even now, many people were unaware of the information being collected from them on a daily basis. It wasn't like it had been explained to them, after all.

…I suppose coming together in the same place for a common purpose creates a sense of solidarity.

In the business world, trust without cause was fatal.

The boy walked over to the end of the table and found a vacant outlet. He held his phone up to it, whereupon the computerized system automatically deducted his bank account for the electricity. Then he plugged in the charging cable.

In any case, it seemed the boy wasn't the only one adamant about bringing his smartphone on a trip into the mountains. Among the devices on the table, there was even what looked like a drawing tablet. The boy hoped its owner had at least brought it along to digitally paint some landscapes and not just to hide in their tent watching videos or doing 3D modeling for data idols. That would be too sad.

Though I guess I can't talk, having just spent a fair amount of time in Money (Game) Master.

A sigh escaped his lips. Moments later, however, he spotted something and immediately ducked under the table.

He couldn't believe it—it was her, twin tails and all. Midori Hekireki had emerged from the game and entered real life!!

After a couple seconds spent panicking, the boy realized something. Midori hadn't popped out of the game at all. In fact, it was the opposite. Midori had committed one of the most basic and fatal errors in operations security, something almost every Dealer knew to avoid. She was running around in-game with *her real likeness*!

She must have been here with her family, like he was. However, none of that mattered. He could not let her see his face. After all, in real life he wasn't the handsome, suave Kaname Suou. His hair was disheveled, his poor eyesight gave him a nasty squint, and his clothes were plain. Even the fact that he was here with his family was cause for embarrassment. All he could do was stay hidden and hold his breath until she was well out of sight!!

"*Hmm. Let's see if it's finished charging yet,*" came the girl's singsong voice.

Crap. She's coming this way!!

Come to think of it, Midori had been playing the game recently as well. He should have realized when he saw her that she would be coming over to the charging stand.

She was standing about twelve centimeters away now, so close he could smell her. She smelled nice.

"Oh, come on. Why are you like this?" she muttered. *"You've really lost it. I can't believe you get anxious when your phone's charge is still at fifty percent…"*

Most likely, she was speaking to herself, using the phone's dark screen like a mirror, rather than manipulating the phone via voice recognition. The boy heard the sound of her light footsteps as she paced across the concrete, and he peered up at the gently bobbing hem of her short skirt. It felt like he was intruding on a private moment, like watching her do her makeup in the morning.

Then he heard a short electronic tone. An incoming message on the girl's phone? The sound of her footsteps suddenly stopped.

"Big bro…"

Her phone wallpaper must have been a picture of her family that suddenly appeared as the device lit up.

The boy clenched his teeth. His old friend hadn't hesitated to take a bullet for his sister, and he was determined to return the favor. It didn't matter if Takamasa had gone astray; the boy would drag him back so he and Midori could be a family again.

Just then, there was a strange snuffling noise. The boy watched as a four-legged beast waddled up to Midori's legs. Around its neck was a black collar with green trim. It looked like a baby boar, but it was more likely a Pocket Piglet: an adult boar selectively bred to remain small and manageable. Miniaturized pets like this one were all the rage these days, and the same had been done to lions, tigers, sharks, and whales.

However, if Midori looked down for any reason, it would be game over. She would spot him hiding under the table for sure, and then it wouldn't just be a matter of disappointment with his lackluster appearance—he'd more likely be mistaken for a pervert after a glimpse of thigh. For that reason, the Pocket Piglet was cause for alarm—it was an unknown variable. What if it nuzzled her leg, and she bent over to give it a stroke?! His in-game face was pretty different, but there was always the chance she would recognize him regardless.

"I feel bad about Mom and Dad," she said. *"But now that I know he's in the game, I just—I have to get him back as soon as I can!!"*

"..."

The game's strongest Dealer remained silent until both the girl and her pet were well out of sight.

Only then did it occur to him—while there was indeed a chance that Midori might recognize his face, why had he needed to hide?

Ahh...

He didn't want to disappoint his friend's little sister.

It was the same in the game world. Unable to reconcile his methods with his friend's, he'd decided to oppose Takamasa. He knew finding a way to save the world without losing Tselika was the right thing to do, so why couldn't he tell Midori?

In other words...

...I just wanted to look cool in front of her, didn't I?

3

Server Name: Mu Green.
Starting Location: Tokonatsu City, Mega-Float III.
Log-in credentials accepted.
Welcome to *Money (Game) Master*, **Kaname Suou.**

Kaname Suou lay on some tatami mats, arms and legs splayed, like a bloated corpse.

He was beyond saving.

"My Lord?"

"..."

"My Lord, I don't mind letting you rest in my lap, but I must say it's rather bold of you to be lying face*down* rather than face*up*."

The boy did not respond.

In contrast to her harsh words, Tselika gazed down at him gently and stroked her slender fingers through his hair. As a succubus, or "one who lies beneath," perhaps it was in her nature to comfort her master without offering any real solutions.

A lantern cast warm light across the walls, creating a sweet mood, and by the shuttered window was a beautiful arrangement of tropical flowers.

Moments later, the dark elf Magistellus Cindy entered the room, her body trembling.

"I—I never expected to see Kaname Suou reduced to such a state! He was always a perfect specimen of humanity! Ooh, I wish that was *my* lap he was in, crying and sucking his thumb!!"

"Wipe the steam off your glasses," demanded Tselika.

Cindy did as she was told. Incidentally, removing her spectacles transformed her into neither a bleary-eyed bat nor the world's most beautiful woman.

This dark-haired, dark-skinned girl, wearing a white leotard like a figure skater, was once the partner of Kaname's sister, Ayame Suou. However, circumstances had left her without a mistress at the moment.

The girl with skin like cocoa powder replaced her glasses and wrapped her arms around her own body.

"After Ayame became the Admin Without Sin, I was left all alone. Then, just as I was at my most impatient, I was kidnapped by that brute, Bloody Dancer... Ugh. We dark elves are truly at the mercy of fate and our own sex drives. Only Kaname can slice off these fiery chains of mine now! Come! Come! Set my lusty and sexually frustrated heart free!!"

"Oh, My Lord doesn't really respond to that sort of thing. If he did, he'd be all over me, I can tell you that much."

"What *are* you talking about, Tselika? It doesn't matter whether he responds or not; forcing him to go along with it is the best part!"

"...You're a sexual deviant. I just haven't figured out which kind yet. Maybe all of them at once."

"Hee-hee-hee-hee-hee. I may have been captured by Bloody Dancer for a time, but playing the part of the broken, castaway machine, powerless to disobey, and seeing his reaction was simply delightful. It seemed to really get to him."

Kaname, apparently fed up, lifted himself off Tselika's thighs. Escapism was good in moderation, but he needed to get back to work soon.

"Tselika. I need Short Spear and a mid-ranged scope, as well as five magazines. Extended, if you please."

"They're on the tray, My Lord… Perhaps if you weren't so taken by my thighs, you would have noticed sooner."

Kaname took his equipment in hand for the first time in a good long while and hooked it onto his belt before striding past Cindy and leaving. The room he had been occupying was neither a courtesan's chamber nor a brothel, and when he stepped outside, the sultry night mood was wiped away in a flash as he was struck with bright tropical sunlight—nearly blinding him.

He was aboard a private yacht on the ocean. Only the interior was decorated in Japanese style.

The yacht was fitted with beautiful triangular sails, as well as a motor engine for when the wind died down, and was large enough to contain a complete living space.

Across the roiling waves was the rusted iron of an industrial megafloat and the district known as the Red Territory. Kaname peered at it through his weapon's scope, locating the multicolored jumble of shipping containers that made up the yard.

Of course, had Ramjet and the other slumlords still been around, Kaname would have had to be a lot more careful. Apparently, they'd had possession of a large quantity of high-speed motorboats. The sea route to and from the float would probably have been littered with mines and the coast lined with machine guns, just like real pirates would do.

Tselika came up from below deck, muttering under her breath.

"Ayame always was promiscuous, throwing her money around on all these boats and planes."

"Oh, no," retorted Cindy. "Quite the contrary. You see, while she liked to keep a variety of vehicles, such as hang gliders and hovercrafts, she always stayed faithful to her favorite car. She lovingly restored it when it was destined for the scrap heap, even going so far as to handcraft a new throttle valve that was out of production."

"My Lord."

"...What are you trying to imply, Tselika? That I should take a page out of my sister's book? You don't like me going anywhere near the car anyway; you always say you've tuned it to perfection and I'm only going to ruin it."

Kaname never took his eye from the scope as he joined the two Magistelli's casual chat. They had each been taking turns monitoring the shipping yard, but so far, they hadn't seen hide nor hair of Takamasa's container—the one housing the laser weapon #flash.err.

...It wasn't my intention, but it's a lot easier to keep an eye on the yard, now that the power balance of the Red Territory is in flux. Perhaps Takamasa's being more secretive as a result?

"Wait," he said suddenly.

"There it is. The laser container," said Cindy.

Sure enough, a tilt-rotor aircraft soon descended into the yard, a shipping container suspended by wires underneath it. Kaname could tell it housed the Legacy by the small dome-shaped lens resembling a security camera positioned on the container's surface.

"What now, My Lord?" asked Tselika. "If we can plant a tracking device on it, the rest will be child's play."

"No," replied Kaname. "We'll never beat Takamasa in a battle of gadgets. He'll only find some way to use it against us."

"Kaname, does that mean...?" asked Cindy.

"Yeah. We'll take a more primitive approach. That's his blind spot."

...It was just like the old days of Called Game again. In fact, if anything, they would have to be just as careful with this approach, as it was precisely what Takamasa would be expecting.

Just locating the laser weapon wasn't enough by itself. To find out where Takamasa was hiding, Kaname and his friends needed to keep track of the Legacy as it was moved from container to container, and then follow the new package back to Criminal AO's base.

Kaname didn't know what Takamasa was planning, but he couldn't let him carry it out. He was currently cutting down Dealers seemingly at random, sorting the wheat from the chaff in order to narrow down the potential identities of the remaining Zodiac Children. If he succeeded and managed to proceed to the final stages of his plan, the lives of Magistelli like Tselika and Cindy would be in grave danger.

Kaname could not sit by and watch that happen, not even if the one doing it was his old friend. He had to defeat Criminal AO with his own hands.

Even if he would be making Midori cry again.

"..."

"Whatever is the matter, My Lord?"

"I hate how I keep trying to show off."

The two Magistelli looked confused. At that moment, Kaname received a call on his smartphone. It was from the Treasure Hermit Crabs. Specifically, it was Frey(a)'s slime-girl Magistellus, Brunhild.

"Mr. Suou," she said. *"The preparations are complete."*

"...No mischief this time, right?"

"I'm pleased to report that Mr. Frey(a) is feeling deeply apologetic for his recent actions. If anything goes wrong, I shall commit seppuku.*"*

Somehow, the idea of a slime-girl committing *seppuku* didn't sound all that serious. Kaname sighed. He was going to have to decide whether or not to trust her by himself.

"Fine. Are you ready to go right now?"

"I am ready when you are. Simply say the word."

Kaname ended the call and turned to Tselika, whose soft cheeks were puffed out in indignation.

"I see you're having another suspicious conversation without me, My Lord..."

"I didn't know you were the kind who liked to turn on parental controls," Kaname replied. "Well, in any case, I don't think Takamasa's container will be moving for a little while yet. He still has to complete the transfer. Cindy, I'm going to step away for a bit. Can I count on you to keep an eye on things around here?"

"You can indeed," the Magistellus replied. "So long as the reward is better than the punishment, that is."

"...Please don't mess things up for me on purpose, Cindy."

"Oh, when you look at me with those cold, dark eyes, my knees grow weak!"

Whether it happened sooner or later, a showdown with Takamasa was inevitable. This time, however, Kaname was wise to his own short-comings, and he knew just the Dealer to contact in order to make up the shortfall.

There was only one person who could do it, and her face was burned into Kaname's mind.

"It's time to pay *her* another visit—that fortress of skills, Mother Loose."

4

From head-on, Mother Loose was effectively invincible. She was a legendary Dealer who could weather any attack without batting an eye, be it a point-blank shotgun blast or a rampaging dump truck.

"Tee-hee-hee! Tee-hee-hee-hee ☆"

She was also obsessed with baths. She owned a large camper van, about the size of a tourist bus, that she had completely refitted, replacing everything save the driver's seat with an indoor bath and changing room. Of course, it went without saying that Dealers were completely unprotected while bathing. Some were so scared of being caught with their pants down, so to speak, that they never bathed or showered in-game, no matter how sweaty they became. Not Mother Loose, however. Whether in-game or out, she could never resist a good bath, and she would pay any amount of money to get it.

The bathtub was filled with floating toys like little yellow ducks and miniature submarines. Not only was it wide enough to spread your legs in, but you could almost swim in it. The washing area alone was larger than a king-size bed, and even fitted with air conditioning and a mini-fridge. The mirrors were not only full-length but covered the entire wall, and there was a row of shower heads like you might find at a public bath. Each of them had a different head shape and was specialized for a different purpose, like golf clubs. Some of them were regular favorites, while others she used only when the fancy struck her.

She found it fun to design every detail herself. Once she got into it, the hours would fly by.

There was one incredibly convenient rule in *Money (Game) Master*: Cars could not be damaged or stolen while parked in an official parking spot. This was why Mother Loose had constructed her bathhouse in the form of a vehicle. That way, she could always enjoy a relaxing bath without fear of being attacked.

And yet at the moment, she found one of her frosted glass windows suddenly opening inward.

"Hey, Mother Loose. I think we need to chat."

It took her a second to realize what was happening. When she did, she saw the wicked smile of Kaname Suou and the muzzle of his .45-caliber short-range sniper rifle pressed directly to her chest. She could feel her heartbeat racing against the gun's cold steel.

For perhaps the first time, Mother Loose feared for her life.

"Wh-what?! H-hold on a second, child, erm!!"

"Checkmate. Don't even try to talk your way out of this one, Mother Loose."

The woman flailed around in the milky white water for anything she could lay her hands on, but unless one of those rubber duckies was actually a hand grenade in disguise, she had nothing to fight back with.

Kaname shook his head in disbelief and said:

"You draw your ultimate defense from skills like Bulletproof, Shockproof, and Bombproof that are attached to your clothes and accessories. Strip yourself down and all those precious skills are gone. A shot through the heart will make you Fall, same as anybody. In fact, that's precisely why you put your bathroom in a place like this."

"...I—I suppose I might as well ask how you got here. Isn't there a rule that prevents people from breaking in???"

"If you're parked in a parking space, sure. But if I buy up the whole lot and change it into something else, it's a different story. Now you're just trespassing. If you wanted to enjoy your bath in peace, you should have parked on your own land and not at a public shopping mall."

"I can't argue with that. I *had* made it a personal rule to open up the roof like a jewelry box only when at my private villa, but I suppose that wasn't enough."

"You were careless. Especially considering your own life is on the line."

Mother Loose gave a sultry sigh. Perhaps she was attempting to slow the pace of conversation and retake the initiative.

"Well, child. Considering I'm not yet dead, I suppose there is something you wish to ask of me?"

"..."

"I am simply overjoyed you came to request my help once more. However, you *do* know what happens to Dealers who grow too reliant on me, don't you?"

A showdown with Takamasa was inevitable. Right now, Kaname would lose that fight, and he knew it. That was why he needed to forge an alliance with one of the game's top Dealers while he still could.

However.

"Sorry, but *it's not you I want to make a deal with.*"

"Huh?"

Kaname ducked back down behind the window, leaving Mother Loose to blink a few times in confusion. She heard a grunt as he picked something up and lifted it in both hands.

"It's Smash Daughter ☆ She asked me to do a little something for her; she said if I could help her surprise you, she'd do whatever I asked."

"Bwah-ha-ha-ha-ha-ha-ha-ha-ha-ha!! Checkmate!! Who's the mother now, bitch???!!!"

With Kaname's hands under her armpits, she looked like a small child or a lost kitten, but she was an expert in nonlethal takedowns. She wore a school swimsuit, a witch hat, and a towel, and her semi-automatic rifle fired electric rounds and sported a stun gun attachment in place of a bayonet.

Mother Loose's face was paler now than it had ever been before. She stared in shock as Smash Daughter tried to wriggle her way in through the open window.

"I can't believe this!" she shrieked. "How rude!! Child, if you've done all this, you must know exactly what I fear most while bathing!"

"That's right, lady!" the small girl replied. "There's nothing scarier than an electric shock while you're naked in the bath! Everything's wet, so there's nowhere to run, and the shock'll be even more powerful!! Bwah-ha-ha-ha-ha-ha-ha-ha-ha-ha-ha-ha-ha-ha-ha-ha-ha-ha-ha-ha-ha-ha-ha-ha-ha-ha-ha-ha-ha-ha-ha-ha-ha—huh?!"

The reason Smash Daughter's laugh ended with a rising inflection was that the tanned Apsaras Magistellus standing next to her had snatched away her rifle at the same time Kaname gave her tiny bottom a good push. The girl went head over heels like she was performing on the parallel bars and fell headfirst into Mother Loose's bath.

There was a mighty splash, and then the mouth of the Venus flytrap slowly unfurled.

"Tee-hee-hee. Oh my, now this really is a surprise... What a lovely gift, child. You really know how to make me feel like a woman ☆"

"Shut the fuck up, bitch! You think I'm just dropping in for tea?! Shit!"

"Ahh, I never thought this day would come. Mother and daughter enjoying a nice bath together... It's like a dream come true! Tee-hee-hee! Now then, which soap do you prefer, solid or liquid? Sponge, towel, or brush? No, I think the softest thing for that delicate skin is my fingers! Just sit tight; Mommy's going to clean you up ☆"

"Gyaah!!" Smash Daughter squealed like a cat whose tail had just been stepped on.

Kaname closed the frosted glass window, locking the two of them away.

Mother Loose was motivated by the desire to fill the void of her own loneliness. To do that, she used to go from one group of Dealers to the next, offering her unconditional love and support, oblivious to the fact that by doing so she was tearing those teams apart from within. However, if her loneliness was dealt with up front, she could be reasoned with normally.

Kaname leaned against the customized camper van and turned to the tanned Apsaras girl by his side. There was something he needed to do before the tiny, violent Dealer came back out, fists flying.

"Jamty, you'll serve as our witness. As you can see, I've fulfilled my obligations to Smash Daughter as stipulated. Make sure the young lady doesn't renege on our deal, okay? No matter how she might personally feel about it, breach of contract is a no-no."

"Okey dokey! I'll make sure she backs you up against Criminal AO ☆"

The girl gave a cheery salute. Kaname wasn't sure how far he could trust her, but the two tapped smartphones and swapped contact details. It was good networking, if nothing else.

Just then, the phone in his hand rang. It was another tanned girl—this time, a dark elf with glasses.

"Kaname, I'm seeing movement at the container yard on Mega-Float III. #flash.err has been transferred to another container and loaded onto a truck; it's leaving the yard as we speak. We are pursuing it in the yacht."

"Where's it headed? No need to be exact."

"It is leaving the float via the circular bridge, heading clockwise. The road is clogged with morning traffic, so the truck is continuing via the fast lane, opposite the exits. For now, at least, it doesn't seem like it will disembark onto any of the islands."

"The peninsula financial district, then. Got it. Cindy, keep an eye on it as best you can. Tselika and I will take over in the coupe once it makes landfall."

"Roger that."

"Don't overdo it. That weapon's as powerful as a warship cannon, and we still don't know what hidden effects it might have. One wrong move and it'll blast you out of the water."

"You don't need to worry about me, Kaname. We Magistelli are only Downed for a short time when we're killed."

"Even so. Be careful out there."

"...Ooh, I'm so excited."

"Cindy. Please don't attack it on purpose. If you do, you're on your own."

"Hee-hee. Then I shall await my reward for being a patient girl. It's been a long time since Ayame left, so there's lots to make up for ☆"

With Short Spear back in his hands and Smash Daughter at his side, all that was left was to follow #flash.err back to Takamasa's lair.

It had been a long and treacherous road, but he was finally nearing its end.

Soon, it would be Kaname's turn to strike back.

5

"So?" asked the girl in the frilly bikini. Her black ponytails fluttered in the breeze as she peered through a pair of binoculars.

Visibility was good and the air was clear, but a lingering stench spoiled the pleasant view. It was the smell of gasoline—she and Kaname were currently at a gas station atop a small hill on the outskirts of town. For some reason, the station staff moving to and fro washing cars and refilling tanks were all young women in nurse outfits (with exceedingly short skirts).

Money (Game) Master was all about greed, and the three main pillars of the game were cars, guns, and money. The young women in nurse outfits were part of a famous team of Dealers who had attempted to take control of the first of these by monopolizing fuel reserves. However, after a series of setbacks and failures, they were now stuck working customer service.

Midori's binoculars weren't for ogling the nurses, however. She was looking down the hill at the land below, observing something else entirely.

"…You think that's his stronghold? Why would my brother be holed up someplace like that?"

"…"

Midori Hekireki hadn't been given the full story. She knew about the attacks Takamasa was carrying out but not his plan to eliminate the Magistelli in order to protect humanity.

She sat sideways in the saddle of her bright-red motorcycle, her Magistellus Meiki snuggled up beside her, as if on a bicycle built for two. The Magistellus in the short-cut *cheongsam* looked impassive and kept silent, but it was clear that they were both comfortable.

Kaname, meanwhile, politely refused the offer of an overpriced coolant check from an excessively sexy nurse.

"Tokonatsu City Jungle Park…," he said. "Well, they call it a park, but it's more like a semi-wild zoo, with animals in cages and various different routes through the rain forest to look at them."

"Isn't the location a little weird for a place like that?" asked Midori. "We're quite far from the city center."

"Same reason Disneyland isn't in downtown Tokyo. An area that's good to live in isn't necessarily a good place to play."

It was a prime inland location, not too close to the city but still perfectly accessible via transport links. The area stretched for five kilometers in all directions, comparable to some larger real-world theme parks. The buildings around the outside were low, as if they'd been awed into modesty by the sprawling jungle.

And at the center of it all was a single tower that, viewed through the binoculars, resembled an upside-down stick of broccoli, with greenery sprouting at its base. It looked extra tall and thin in contrast to the sprawling jungle surrounding it.

…Looks like it's all off-road. The coupe's not going to be much use this time.

Kaname glanced over at the gas station's tire-changing service but after a few moments decided a quick fix wasn't going to cut it. One of the scantily clad nurses standing around noticed his stare and blew him a kiss, but Kaname ignored her and turned his focus back to Midori.

"Hey, what's that tower?" she asked.

"The official leaflet calls it an aquarium-cum-shopping mall, but about seventy percent of it is actually an animal research lab. Not many people know what goes on there, which makes it the perfect place to hide something."

Kaname snapped his fingers, and a sea-to-ground missile immediately zoomed by above them, headed straight for the building in question.

"Eek!!"

Midori yelped, holding her skirt in place, while all the sexy nurses ran screaming for cover. However, the missile didn't even make it two kilometers from the jungle's edge.

From the top of the tower came a flash of light, and the missile was sliced in half lengthwise while it was still moving close to mach five. After a second's delay, the two halves of the missile exploded in mid-air. Then there was a second flash of light, and a low rumble swept the earth. Kaname had a good idea of what that meant—the AI-controlled warship off the coast must have just been sunk.

"…Looks like #flash.err is kept on that circular walkway surrounding the upper levels. He must have lifted the whole truck up there using the service elevator."

"…"

"Now, why not the rooftop? Are you scared of lightning strikes, or does the heat from the AC condensers interfere with the beam?"

No matter how carefully Takamasa may have tried to remain hidden, once the cat was out of the bag, there was no need to hold back. He must have realized by now that Kaname was coming. The pair had spent a lot of time together in Called Game. Even without proof, they could practically sense each other's presence.

It was no longer the time for plotting and scheming. Now was the time for action.

"Jungle Park's still open for business, but that's only because Takamasa knows he can snipe anyone he doesn't like. That includes us; if he sees us, we're dead. He's set up pretty high, too, so his horizon is a lot farther out than ours."

Compared to the Legacies Kaname had faced so far, this one was a different breed. Not only was this a laser weapon originally intended for use on warships, but there was still the reality-warping power of the Overtrick to contend with. Kaname hadn't yet seen a glimpse of its true abilities.

"H-how...did it come to this?" Midori wailed.

"Public infrastructure like dams and power plants are usually loaded with PMCs, and the same goes for that rain forest zoo. We need to expect heavy resistance."

"No, not that! I mean, why did big bro turn against us? I felt so lucky just finding him alive... So why is he attacking us?!!"

Such was Midori's dismay that she didn't even realize she had called her brother "big bro." Actually, Kaname had the same exact question. He didn't understand why Takamasa had made the decision he had. Was he always so ruthless, or had he become that way after sacrificing himself for Kaname's sister?

Kaname decided to steel himself for the worst. He wouldn't try to look cool anymore.

"Listen to me, Midori. There's something I never told you. This might be hard for you to hear, but I need to say it."

"Wh-what do you mean...?"

"I owe Takamasa a debt. Enough that I would die for him. Enough to *take responsibility for his little sister*. But I can't lie to you, Midori, not anymore. I know the truth will hurt, but I have to tell you anyway. If you have any complaints afterward, you can punch me in the face."

"I'm not going to do that!" Midori yelled. "Spit it out already. You're making me nervous!"

Kaname took a deep breath and looked down at Midori. She was like a little chick, begging for food—for information.

Then he spoke.

"Takamasa has turned against us. Probably for good."

Midori slapped him with all her might.

6

It was not the first time Kaname had seen her cry. Once again, he had failed to stop her tears.

Luckily, the service station staff all pretended not to see anything. This was a famous breakup spot for young couples, after all, so they were probably used to it. As soon as that nuisance in the passenger seat left to buy a few snacks, you drove off, leaving them stranded. While the staff's professional consideration was unwarranted this time, Kaname probably felt a lot more awkward than any of those entitled drivers.

But he had already decided to drop his cool-guy act.

Midori clung to him, her desperate tears streaming down his chest. Kaname doubted even she could understand the inarticulate words she was screaming.

But she must have known that Kaname Suou never took up his gun and killed someone for nothing. Once he made the decision to take someone out, he was ruthless, but there was always a reason why. To him, helping people was not about bragging rights or asking for anything in return. He lived by certain rules, though he was often so reticent, it was difficult to discern precisely what they were.

Have I really...?

And who had engraved those rules on Kaname's heart? Why, none other than Criminal AO, Takamasa Hekireki. He had protected

Kaname's sister, and Kaname wanted nothing more than to return the favor.

Have I really done enough? he thought. *Have I really done enough to make up for her tears?*

Kaname had made up his mind, but he wasn't without a heart. Still, no matter what he felt, after countless trials and difficulties, this was the conclusion he'd reached.

…Midori must be mature enough to realize that.

As she sobbed and sniffled, Kaname simply stood by, waiting. Then at last, her face buried in his chest, she spoke in a groan.

"Did my brother…?"

She was shaking, afraid, and her voice was weak—she was probably hoping against hope that Kaname would deny it.

"Did big bro do something so bad, you have to shoot him?"

He could have said anything. He could've told her Takamasa was a great man, someone he would always look up to—someone she should be proud to call her big brother. He could have told her anything.

But he didn't. He replied through gritted teeth.

"…Yeah. He did."

"…!"

"He's fighting against the AI to free humanity from their oppression and take back his own life. That's not a bad thing in itself, but…that's not all. He's killing Dealers just so he can find the Zodiac Children. That's not what helping people is all about. I'm not just talking about bad guys like those slumlords from the Red Territory. These are students trying to pay back their loans, small business owners trying to earn a living—there are all kinds of Dealers. He doesn't think it matters, so long as he wins in the end. But that's not how my hero taught me to act."

He had to say this. All of it. Even if his best friend's sister would hate him for it. If he didn't, Kaname's reason for shooting Takamasa would disappear into a mist of vague platitudes. For him to wage war, the reason had to be front and center in his mind.

"Takamasa is probably seeking the complete destruction of *Money*

(Game) Master and the downfall of AI society. I want to stop him, even if that makes him my enemy."

"Who are you hoping to protect by doing that?"

"Not the world, that's for sure. Not humanity, either. I want to protect Tselika, you, my sister…and Takamasa."

"…"

Takamasa had been alive in the real world this whole time, but he'd never tried to contact Midori or the rest of his family. He had always believed that helping people wasn't about bragging rights. If he still believed that, maybe it was the reason he was fighting alone even now, despite the mounting sacrifices.

In order to bring him to the conversation table, Kaname would have to take him down first.

"I need to shoot him. It's the only way to save him. For that, I can break my own rules. I can betray the man who saved me, despite what I owe him."

Kaname felt a squeeze as Midori's small fingers tightened around his shirt. She sobbed awhile longer without saying anything.

Then, at last, she spoke.

"…In that case, I'll help."

"Midori."

"You believe you're doing the right thing, don't you?"

She looked up into his eyes. Her face was streaked with tears, but her voice was clear.

"I don't think my brother is that strong. There are sides of him I know that you don't. And if he has any hesitation at all, if there's any part of him that wants to stop…then I don't think he should be throwing away people's lives and futures. That's why…I'm siding with his doubt. If you can't make him stop, then maybe I can. It's just like you said—this is the only way to save him. I won't back down from that."

"You'll regret it, you know."

"Yes. But so will you." Midori smiled. "So let's share our knowledge. The part of my brother I know and the part you know. Together, we can see the whole picture. We're the only ones who can."

7

"They're all yours," said Criminal AO. Cheers and whistles erupted from all around him. And little wonder, for what Takamasa had just revealed to his private army was a room filled with enough Legacies to take down an entire country.

And these soldiers were no simple AI-controlled PMCs. That would not be enough to win the coming battle. No, they were powerful Dealers, each and every one—legends on par with Called Game itself. And there was only one way for Takamasa to convince such people to work with him.

The Overtrick—the very weapons he had once fought so hard to contain. Now, he was handing them out like candy.

"Don't you want one?"

"Oh, I'll take a free gun, if that's what you're offering."

The woman who answered him was a little older than Takamasa or Kaname, with straight platinum-blond hair that was almost white. She was slender and well-proportioned, with a youthful, doll-like face.

Her clothing, however, gave an entirely different impression. The most striking item was her pure-white racing swimsuit, over which she wore a black T-shirt rolled up above her breasts. A pair of suspiciously thick thigh-highs and a headband made from thin, twisted rope finished off her outfit. It looked like she was trying to cosplay a trucker while making sure her swimsuit remained exposed.

Her name was Poltergeist. She was a vehicle specialist, and her kill count behind the wheel surpassed even Kaname's. Specialists like her, who were able to survive on their own rather than as part of a team, tended to be even more eccentric than usual. Bloody Dancer, the monster who tore apart Called Game, had been another example.

"But it sounds a little too good to be true. Don't think I can't see what you're really up to."

"Oh? And what's that?"

"You're only giving away the Legacies because you know you're going to get them back. After everyone here gets themselves killed, that is."

"..."

"In other words," she said bluntly, "you don't have the slightest bit of trust in other people, do you? I can tell just by looking around. All the Dealers you've gathered here *have lost their humanity and joined AI society*—they're people who operate purely on potential profit and loss. Easy to control, and lighter on the conscience when you throw them away once you're done."

She was right. Takamasa had never intended to create a team. That kind of strategy would never be enough to beat Kaname Suou. That was why he'd taken a page out of Bloody Dancer's book. After all, the man had once gone toe to toe with Kaname himself. His methods, then, should have the greatest chance of success. It was time to sow chaos, to build up walls that even Kaname could not cross, like how a microwave oven slowly agitated water molecules until they formed an untouchable mass of scalding steam.

Takamasa knew all this, but he still grinned and asked, "How can you be so sure?"

"Because I'm the same way."

Exactly the response he'd expected.

The woman walked over to the row of Legacies and calmly picked one out. It was a sawn-off pump-action shotgun, as short as one could possibly get, with a skeleton stock as thin as a wire coat hanger.

Its name was #lockpick.err, and it was not for shooting people. A single shot could decimate any physical lock, from a bike lock to a bank vault. Its simple construction was probably due to its origins as an attachment meant to fit to the barrel of an assault rifle.

"Don't worry, you'll get your money's worth from me," she said, unfazed by the thought of putting her own life on the line. Although she had seen through Takamasa's lies, the truth didn't give her so much as a moment's pause.

"However," she continued, "If I do my part and happen to live, I don't want to hear any complaints. No asking me why I didn't die like the others, understand?"

8

The orange glow of dusk filled the sky. Midori looked up.

"A sun shower?!" she exclaimed. "I didn't know *Money (Game) Master* had those!!"

"If it exists in real life, it exists here," said Kaname, using a tow truck to hoist the mint-green coupe out of the garage. As for why he wasn't simply driving the car, well…

"I had it kitted out just like you asked," said Tselika, "but I'd much rather give it a test drive first."

"There's no time. We have to strike now if we want to subvert Takamasa's expectations. You saw that weapon, right? He has a clear, unobstructed view of all the land routes leading into the rain forest and can fire with impunity. The same goes for the sky: He can shoot a missile or a stealth fighter right out of the air. We can't hope to challenge him on his terms."

"I understand that," Tselika replied. "I just hope the wind doesn't blow this thing off course."

Seemingly unperturbed by the sudden rain, Tselika put a hand on her narrow waist and glanced at what had become of her beloved car.

The vehicle's current setup brought to mind the way a ski boot connected to the ski. The entire chassis was mounted on a custom assembly, rendering the wheels useless. Instead, four large propellers sat at each corner, turning the mint green coupe into something more closely resembling a radio-controlled drone or one of those old-school racing slot cars.

It wasn't intended for ground travel, nor was it meant to soar freely through the heavens. So what *was* it for?

"A flying car. We'll use this to fly low, slipping between the buildings."

*   *   *

The controls to move forward and backward and to turn left and right were just like those on a normal car, but to go up and down, a new set of buttons had to be installed next to the steering wheel. The coupe was equipped with a drive-by-wire system—that is, instead of a mechanical steering column, it was all electronic. This had made it a simple matter to reprogram the connections.

Hovering in one place was straightforward enough, but extreme care was required when steering because unlike a regular car, which turned along a curve, this vehicle could rotate in place, and when you slammed on the brakes, there was no road friction to help you.

"Whoa."

Beside him, Midori wobbled atop her similarly modified motorcycle. Unlike the car, her bike had only two propellers, front and back, so it was much harder to keep stable, and Midori had to lean left and right in order to turn.

Kaname: Are you sure you don't want to ride with me?

Midori: Don't worry. Besides, it's looking a little cramped in there already.

Kaname glanced toward the passenger's seat. Indeed, Tselika, whose curves already took up a fair amount of space, had Cindy crushed into her lap, facing backward. The bespectacled dark elf noticed Kaname's gaze.

"Go on, keep imagining," she said. "I don't mind."

"Mmrgh?! Hey! You better not be trying to physically assert dominance or something!" yelled Tselika.

The pair took off from Mangrove Island and flew beneath the large circular bridge. Weaving between support pillars as they made their way to the mainland was as much of a test flight as they were going to get. It might've been quicker to fly in a straight line across the ocean, but it seemed like a bad idea to be without cover while they still didn't know the full range of Takamasa's laser weapon.

This custom conversion kit was originally intended to bring older automobiles up to speed once flying cars hit the skies. It was a bit like the tuning kits aimed at old CRT TVs that had appeared on the market back when digital broadcasts first became a thing. Still, a conversion project of this magnitude was far beyond what even the car-obsessed Tselika could do alone. That was why Cindy had assisted her. The dark elf had been known to hole herself up in a garage restoring vehicles for days at a time.

For whatever reason, it didn't really feel like flying. It wasn't like sitting behind the joystick of a helicopter or the controls of a plane. If anything, it felt like driving atop a cushion of air. Perhaps that was only because Kaname had a steering wheel in his hands.

Midori: I thought this was going to be like a gimmick or a toy, but we're actually going quite fast. Look, the speedometer just hit 200 kph.

Kaname: That's because we're not losing speed to road friction or turns. Make sure you don't crash into the pillars, Midori.

Midori: I won't. But I still need to test the controls. If I can't handle this, I'm never going to make it flying between the buildings.

Kaname: Midori, crosswind!

Kaname hastily typed out a warning as the girl with the twin tails was nearly carried away by the wind, almost like she'd jinxed herself.

Things got a lot more difficult once they reached the mainland. Kaname's coupe and Midori's bike left the cover of the bridge, coming out high over the harbor district before plunging into a valley of shimmering office blocks. Orange light seemed to burn all around them, from the mirrored windows to the individual raindrops falling like citrine gems.

Kaname: A little over 10 km until we reach the jungle. At the speed we're going, we'll be there before you know it.

Midori: Whee!

Tselika: There sure are a lot of cameras around now that we've hit the mainland.

Midori: Wait, what do you mean? Are people watching us?

Cindy: Ah-ha-ha, you bet! Your cute little butt is trending ☆

Midori: WHAT?! What's that supposed to mean?!

The pair of vehicles zoomed between skyscrapers, passing over the rooftops of smaller buildings with complete disregard for the traffic below. However, they weren't quite out of the woods yet. With the kind of power that #flash.err possessed, it wouldn't be surprising if it could fire straight through these buildings, vaporizing Kaname and Midori in an instant. The fact they were trending online meant that pretty much the whole world knew they were there. And that included Takamasa.

Kaname needed to do something to compensate. He turned to Cindy. "You have the thing ready?"

"Tee-hee-hee. At last, something for me to do!"

The dark elf gave an unsettling chuckle and reached behind the headrest, sandwiching Tselika between the seat and her supple skin. The demon pit babe kicked and screamed as Cindy's breasts pressed into her face, making for an unusual sight. A big smile on her face, Cindy pulled out a large tablet PC and gave the screen a few taps.

Just then a roar could be heard, and a beam of light passed dangerously close to where they were flying. Midori instinctively tried to fly downward, but Kaname messaged her not to bother. She would only slice herself in half on the lower buildings' lightning rods.

Midori, it seemed, wasn't surprised by the beam itself.

Midori: Why did that miss us?! I thought once it got a lock on us, we were finished!!

Cindy waved the tablet and blew a kiss at Kaname. It looked like the plan had worked.

Then they heard a loud buzzing noise like an electric shaver, and it wasn't coming from the propellers keeping Kaname and Midori afloat. A massive swarm of some kind had overtaken the pair and continued on ahead.

Kaname: Those are 1,500 radio-controlled drones. We're going to have them split up and advance on the jungle from all directions. Still using cover, as though they're trying to protect themselves. Takamasa's Legacy is the ultimate anti-air weapon, but even he can't possibly shoot down all of them.

Midori: ,1500...

Kaname: Your comma's wrong, Midori. Anyway, I've said it before and I'll say it again. Money's not everything, but it certainly opens up your options.

Drones were a lot cheaper compared to back in the day, when they would run you a million yen apiece. But these weren't something you'd find on the shelves at your local toy store, either; they were military-spec, and big enough to be mistaken for a car or bike at long range. Their resilience wasn't so important, since one shot from the Legacy would take them down anyway, but they still cost as much as a motor scooter. Multiply that by one and a half thousand, and it quickly became the sort of money you could stake your life on. However.

"Aren't you going to tell her you bought them all for cheap at one of Pavilion's auctions?" asked Tselika.

"Oh?" remarked Cindy. "How did you manage that?"

"How else? Price-fixing, just like the big construction companies do," explained Tselika. "Convince all the other bidders to stay quiet, and you can pick up the lot at the starting price. That poor woman. She knew something was going on, but she couldn't prove it. I still remember her tears as she accepted the final bid. Not that I feel sorry for her or anything."

If Kaname had gone to a pawnshop like one of Frey(a)'s, the price would have been set and probably inflated several times over. And that would go double if they found out how desperately Kaname needed them. Money gave you more options, but that didn't mean you had to pay market price for them.

"My Lord, we're nearing the outskirts of the city."

Buildings farther from the city center were lower, which meant less camouflage to fool Takamasa's eyes. And of course, with a laser weapon like #flash.err, once you saw the beam, it was too late to dodge.

But there was no use crying over spilled milk. If there were no more natural shields to exploit, Kaname would just have to make some.

Kaname: Midori, I'm sending you some map data. Follow my course!

"Cindy, I'm counting on you. Get the drones in formation!!"

The buzzing, like a giant electric razor, grew until it was nearly deafening. The drones swarmed together like hornets, creating what felt like a sandstorm so thick Kaname could no longer see what lay ahead. Great beams of light pierced the swarm one after another, trying to beat it back. They were less like projectiles and more like horizontal bolts of lightning. In the blink of an eye, they scorched the surrounding air.

Meanwhile, Kaname was able to avoid a direct hit, thanks both to Cindy's deft control of the swarm of decoy drones and the course he'd plotted with the help of his Lion's Nose.

Warding off the barrage of light with a cloak of mechanical bees, he plunged into enemy territory.

Now to see how far this tactic gets me against a real Legacy...

Midori: I see it!! The jungle's up ahead!!

At this point, the buildings around them were only a few stories high and of little use as shields. The rooftops were littered with lightning rods, TV antennae, and water tanks, so Kaname and Midori leveled off a few meters above them. By the time they reached the last of the buildings, the lush trees of the rain forest had already begun to rise up around them. They were in the jungle now—half zoo, half wild parkland. And in the tower at its center, Takamasa was waiting.

"I'm sorry, Kaname," said Cindy. "The crosswind's too strong!"

Kaname: Midori, we're nearly out of drone cover. Descend below the canopy!

"Tselika, hand me the Legacy and take the wheel!!"

They were moving fast, but they weren't going to make it to the trees in time. Kaname rolled down the side window and leaned out, the collapsible anti-materiel rifle, #fireline.err, resting on his shoulder. This Legacy boasted infinite range, and when paired with Kaname's expert marksmanship, anything in the line of sight became a fair target.

In other words.

Anything #flash.err could hit, it could hit, too...!!

Ka-blammm!!!!!!

The two exchanged killing shots, and the mint-green coupe fell back slightly from the recoil.

The two beams met amid a rain of orange jewels.

But the laser cannon's target was not Kaname or Midori. Instead, it vaporized the ultra-thick armor-piercing incendiary round, emitting a searing white flash like the light from a welding torch.

Takamasa must have realized the choice Kaname was giving him. Neutralize the incoming bullet, or never fire the Legacy again.

"..."

Kaname had bought only a few seconds at best, but it was enough. They had reached the jungle proper. Kaname climbed back into the driver's seat, then gripped a second lever next to the hand brake and pulled it hard. Still in midair, the flying car jettisoned its custom assembly, landing directly on the zoo promenade and skipping like a stone over water.

Kaname typed a quick message on the windshield keyboard using his eyes and fired it off.

Kaname: Where are you, Midori?!

Midori: I'm right here, geez. You're such a worrywart!! What are you, my big brother?!

The large leaf-patterned motorcycle was traveling safely alongside him. But Midori was still exposed on her bike. A stray branch could slice her head or arm clean off like a length of cheese wire.

The pair drove on, kicking up sprays of water. The drainage around here was even worse than Kaname had expected, and the grassy areas to either side of the promenade were basically waterlogged. Cages dotted the landscape here and there like giant microwaves or blocks of caramel, and the animals inside had climbed up to higher ground to escape the flooding. It seemed like it'd be a while before anyone came with a truck or crane to take the cages inside. There were even small streams forming in some places.

Amid the trees, Kaname spotted a few overturned food wagons touting taco rice or vegetable juice. However, the tourists and zookeepers were nowhere to be seen. Hopefully, that was because the whole park had been sealed off in anticipation of his showdown with Takamasa.

"I'd say we're about five kilometers away now, My Lord."

"I'm guessing we don't have to worry about #flash.err while we're on the grounds," Kaname replied. "He won't want to damage any underground cables, not to mention the foundation of the building he's holed up in."

"Wishful thinking, My Lord. This is *Takamasa* we're talking about."

"Yes, but it's *Kaname* who's talking," chimed Cindy.

Nobody had said #flash.err was the only obstacle to look out for, however. This place was a public leisure center, but it was also a PMC fortress. What's more, it was highly likely Takamasa had teamed up with other Dealers, just like he had with Lily-Kiska in the past.

Criminal AO had probably prepared every trick in the book. At this stage in the game, it was too risky not to.

Skreeee!!

They heard the screech of tires, but it wasn't Kaname or Midori—it was someone else. And more than one someone. Beyond the trees, a whole convoy was running parallel with them.

Kaname: Midori, How's Meiki feeling?

Midori: She's okay today. She'll come out if I call.

"Tselika, Cindy. You both know how to use the Legacies. Give me fire support."

Still splayed over Tselika, the dark elf lifted her leg and popped open the glove compartment with her heel. Tselika took the short-range sniper rifle Short Spear and placed it in Kaname's lap.

…We're finally here.

Nobody had seen this fight coming. Nobody had wanted it to happen.

But this battle between Called Game comrades was already underway.

9

Jungle Park consisted of a series of pathways laid down around the rain forest, with zoo cages scattered along the routes. The sudden rainstorm that day had caused the natural rivers to burst their banks, blocking off the roads with water that glowed a twinkling orange in the evening light.

"The rain's stronger than I expected," said Kaname. "I'm more worried about us in the coupe than Midori on her bike. If we veer off the road even once, the tree roots sticking out of the ground are going to gut the car's underbelly."

"Why don't you just say what you're thinking, My Lord?"

"I sure would kill for a high-riding vehicle with some heavy susp—"

"I won't have my temple looking so lewd, waggling its thick thighs and fat bottom for all to see!! A vehicle ought to be elegant, unassuming, until you press down on the pedal and feel the lioness roar! You know, sleek on the streets, freak in the seats!!"

"I'd prefer a car that can handle anything I throw at it. Like, how about those amphibious models?"

"Oh my," said Cindy. "Your taste in cars became a lot more macho while I was away, Kaname."

If the terrain restricted your movement, it suddenly became a lot easier for your opponent to land a blow.

Just then, they heard the roar of an unfamiliar engine, and all of a sudden a medium-size truck burst out from the waterlogged rain forest. It would have been impossible for Kaname in the low-riding coupe to do the same. He quickly fired two shots into the driver's seat window, but...

"There's no driver?!"

Kaname pulled on the hand brake, allowing his rear wheels to skid across the rain-slicked pathway. The truck's heavy-looking flatbed swerved around, narrowly missing the coupe. The enigmatic words "D.A.R.K.E.L.F. Shipping" were painted on the truck's side, next to a drawing of a silver-haired, dark-skinned beauty in profile.

"Oh? Looks like I'm in demand, Kaname!"

"They're trying to kill us, you long-eared pervert!" screamed Tselika from the passenger seat.

Just then, in the corner of his vision, Kaname spotted a humanoid figure. He ducked his head as the sound of a shotgun blast rang out, followed by the roar of another engine. This time, it was a curry wagon.

The driver, however, had already opened the door and jumped out of the vehicle.

At first glance, at least, she looked like a trucker.

Her T-shirt was rolled up above her breasts, and beneath it was an eye-catching racing swimsuit. A pair of suspiciously thick thigh-highs covered her legs. It almost looked like she was dressed in coveralls, and the trucker look wouldn't have been complete without the rope headband atop her head.

Her hair streaming behind her, the platinum-blond crashed into a puddle. It looked like she was grasping something in her hand—not her shotgun, but an automatic magnum pistol. She aimed it directly at the food truck she had just exited.

Kaname: Midori!!

Kaname swerved the coupe in front of Midori's bike just as a .50-caliber bullet penetrated one of the many propane tanks contained in the woman's specialized vehicle. There was a loud explosion, and a rain of glass shards and scrap metal slammed into the side of Kaname's car, cracking the windows. If Midori had been on the receiving end, however, the damage would have been a lot worse.

Kaname was unable to regain control, and the mint-green coupe swerved off the boardwalk and into the swampy river to the side. Kaname stepped on the gas pedal, but the car would go no further. It only churned the muddy water, its wheels spinning impotently.

The assassin was already well out of sight. Off to pick up a new vehicle, no doubt. Kaname wouldn't have been surprised if she had them stashed all over the place.

"Huh? It's S.A.R.A.S.V.A.T.I. Kitchen this time! Talk about inconsistency!" said Cindy. "Does she think she can get away with anything vaguely fantasy-related? Besides, what's the deal with using the dark elf as a decoy?!"

"Can we kick her out and use *her* as a decoy, My Lord? But that aside, how are we going to get out of this water?!"

It was hard to tell whether the truck belonged to the woman or if she had stolen it. In *Money (Game) Master*, the paint job on a vehicle could be changed as easily as a Magistellus could alter their clothing.

Kaname pressed a button to unlock the coupe's trunk, before getting out and taking a small, collapsible motorcycle from inside.

"Sure glad I picked up one of these."

"My Lord, you aren't…"

"Tselika, Cindy. Take the Legacies and spread out. The car's trashed. We'll bring back a tow truck to pick it up later!!"

"Hey!!" the demon pit babe yelled. "Didn't I say not to purchase other vehicles?! How many other cars have you been fooling around with behind my back?!"

There was no time to waste on Tselika's tantrums. Though the assailant's outfit had thrown him for a loop, Kaname had heard of a famous Dealer who stole and used vehicles as though they were disposable.

Poltergeist.

If Bloody Dancer was a monster gunslinger, then she was a monster driver—a woman who loved running her opponents down in anything from a tank to a foot-powered scooter.

He's got another lunatic working for him!!

Kaname revved the motorcycle's engine—as light as the one in a chainsaw—and took off through the shallow water. Opening a chat window on the windshield, still relatively unchanged from the factory settings, he fired off a message to Midori.

Kaname: We can't beat that Dealer by going after her vehicles. We need to aim for the moment she switches cars.

Midori: Do you think we can?!

Poltergeist had already left without giving them the chance. She was deadly behind the wheel, but she was surprisingly nimble on foot, too.

Kaname: We don't have a choice. We won't be able to work down her vehicle's defenses if she keeps switching to new ones. We'll have to aim for the Dealer herself.

Just then, they heard the loud roar of another engine. It sounded larger this time, and Kaname found himself imagining a garbage truck. But when he turned to look, he saw something entirely different.

*   *   *

A tank. A real, genuine battle tank, complete with metal treads, fell from the raised boardwalk and into the river.

This was totally unreasonable. No matter how many .45-caliber bullets Kaname fired, he couldn't take on a tank.

The two demons had apparently cut across the bushes, because Kaname could hear them discussing the brightly painted vehicle and its psychedelic colors—not exactly jungle camouflage.

"What food is it this time?!" Tselika said. "Chinese? Slavic?"

"Oh, it's with L.I.L.I.T.H. Security. A big shot succubus, isn't that nice?"

Important public infrastructure always houses PMC bases!!

The tank's top speed was somewhere in the region of seventy kilometers per hour. Kaname could easily outrun it on his racing bike... but that would actually be a bad move. At a distance, the tank could bring its powerful cannon into play, launching a shell over one thousand eight hundred meters at speeds over mach five.

The hunk of metal bore down on Kaname. Thirty to forty tons of pure death—three times the weight of an ordinary truck. It twisted its turret around with a horrifying scraping sound, aiming not at Kaname but at...

Midori!

"Not if I can help it!!"

Kaname slammed on the brakes, letting the tank catch up. Just as it came parallel, the boy leaped off his bike and onto the tank's side. Luckily, just above the gnashing treads was a row of armor plating to shield against rocket attacks. The tank was also fitted with machine guns for firing at infantry soldiers who got a little too close. However, to use them, the gunner had to open the hatch and show their face.

As soon as they did, Kaname shot them with Short Spear and advanced to the hatch, pointing his weapon inside. But just then, a second hatch flew open and a little girl in a white military dress with short silver hair fell out, a magnum pistol in her hand.

That must be her Magistellus!!

Kaname spun around, gun in hand, just as the tank screeched to a halt. The sudden deceleration threw off Kaname's aim, and his two silent bullets missed their mark, neither of them hitting the blond in the racing swimsuit. They merely grazed her temple, slicing her cloth headband.

Poltergeist rolled off the tank and spread her sock-covered legs, landing, of all places, on the very motorcycle Kaname had just discarded. She headed for the riverbank and hopped back up onto the raised promenade. Kaname, meanwhile, was without wheels, and his chat system was still open. If she wanted to, Poltergeist could spoof his identity and send Midori a false message.

"Dammit!"

Kaname snatched his smartphone out of his pocket and leaped off the tank.

Just as he did, a thought occurred to him.

Poltergeist had fled, and her Magistellus had been shot between the eyes and Downed... In that case, who had caused the tank to brake? Weren't they still alive...?

Within seconds, the tank treads whirred back to life.

"Uh-oh...!!"

Kaname heard a muffled *boom* from far off, and a few moments later, an explosive rain fell from the orange sky. It was the mortar, #thunderbolt.err. It was common knowledge that a tank's weakest area was its roof, and in a stroke of luck, the mortar shells hit the rear radiator as well. Black smoke rose off the tank as it ground to a halt, both its engine and battery destroyed.

Kaname fired a few .45 caliber pistol rounds into the machine gun on top, rendering it useless, then climbed out of the river and into the forest. Once there, he checked his phone screen.

Cindy: Wahoo! How'd you like my fire support? It was filled with my love.

Kaname: Perfect, Cindy!! I mean, leaving out the part where you blindly fired at where I was standing without telling me.

Cindy: Well then, guess I'll get a good talking-to later. Tee-hee-hee! Something to look forward to ☆

There were both pros and cons to having a dark elf who responded to praise and criticism with equal delight. Kaname was starting to seriously regret not asking Ayame how best to deal with her Magistellus when he'd had the chance.

Meanwhile, he dived behind a thick tree trunk and waited silently. A short while later, when he heard footsteps on the grass, he leaped out and fired off a barrage of .45-caliber bullets.

Kaname: Including the one I shot, there seem to be three short-haired Magistelli with the exact same face. It's only supposed to be one Magistellus per Dealer. What's going on?

Tselika: It depends. Trios of goddesses and monsters are quite popular, like the Norns of Norse Mythology, or the Greek Erinyes.

Kaname: Hmm. I don't think what I'm seeing is a sewing machine. A loom? Probably European rather than Asian. Do any of them use weaving tools or scissors or anything like that?

Tselika: A western trio of weavers? Those would be the Fates, My Lord. Otherwise known as the Moirai. They are a trio of Greek goddesses named Clotho, Lachesis, and Atropos.

Kaname: Goddesses? In Money (Game) Master?

Tselika: Have you not been paying attention, My Lord? I am certain we have seen the odd Valkyrie walking around. They are goddesses, too, after a fashion. The Moirai, by the way, are beings who sever the cord of fate. I am sure the virtuous gods and angels with big fancy books written about them would have something to say about sharing the title, however.

Beings who took souls and altered destiny. Perhaps the game considered them demons of a sort. Kaname didn't know much about religion, but gods of death and destruction, while certainly called gods, were indeed difficult to class as good or evil.

Theology aside, Poltergeist's Magistelli would be out of the picture for a while. Kaname wouldn't have to worry about the tank again, since it could only be driven by a crew. From here on out, it would be bikes, cars, and trucks only.

I know these cars aren't protected by a parking lot barrier, but she's way too quick at getting the door open and starting the engine. It can't be skill alone. Has Takamasa brought the Legacies into play already?

Kaname: Midori, where are you?

Kaname pointed his gun around cautiously as he sent a message on his phone. Here in Jungle Park, not all the animals were kept in cages. Now that the rivers had flooded, it wouldn't be surprising to find a hippo or crocodile wandering around. They'd ignore the boardwalk, however, as it was still protected by repellent.

As he walked across the mud, Kaname suddenly frowned.

Kaname: Midori?

No reply.

"Dammit!!"

Kaname: Tselika, Cindy. We've got a problem. Maximum priority!!

10

Stopping the bike had been simple. All she had to do was drive a large semitrailer halfway up a hill and leave the hand brake off so it rolled back and blocked the road. Then she'd cruised down the slope on a light off-road motorcycle. Big motorcyles were hard to back up, so when the girl with the twin tails appeared and found her path blocked, she had to stop and walk hers back over the muddy ground. That provided the perfect opportunity to crash straight into her from behind.

First, the high-capacity B.A.S.T.E.T. Couriers semitrailor, then to finish her off, the food delivery service M.E.R.M.A.I.D. Super Express.

The woman was usually the type to lie in wait and take out her target in one shot, but the Legacy had opened up a new path for her. Now she was a rampaging queen of slaughter who hijacked whatever cars she could lay her hands on, repainted them according to her fancy, and drove them into her foes.

Poltergeist dismounted her bike, the front wheel now bent completely out of shape, and left it behind, walking over to the two girls lying face-down in the mulch. What she pulled out was not her borrowed shot-gun but an automatic magnum pistol. She pointed it at the girls.

A single loud gunshot rang out.

"Meiki!!"

The platinum-blond beauty paid no heed to the girl's tragic wail. A racing swimsuit creating the silhouette of a trucker. A T-shirt rolled up above her breasts and a pair of thigh highs thicker than coveralls. Her entire outfit was designed to fool enemy sights by increasing the visual area of her silhouette, kind of like how in a bullet-hell shooter, the player character's hitbox was far smaller than appearances would suggest. However, at the moment, that hardly seemed necessary.

"I think I'll use a really explosive vehicle, like a food truck or an oil tanker," she said.

"..."

"I'll tie you up and stick you in the driver's seat, then unlock the brakes and send you rolling toward a cliff. That'll bring all your friends out of the woodwork—assuming they *are* your friends, that is. Once they reach the door trying to rescue you, I'll blow you all up with one shot."

The girl in twin tails lifted her partner's unmoving body in her arms and scowled at Poltergeist, but the Dealer didn't so much as bat an eye. This was the kind of person she had become. A little *too* well-adjusted to AI society, one might say.

She had always been bad at high-risk trading. That was why she sought to learn her limits in a game where nothing was permanent. How much did inexplicable things like flow and luck affect the outcome? If you didn't understand the extreme case, you could never reach a realistic compromise. Big data was flexible precisely because it collected all sorts of outlier data without bias, rather than just going along with the trends. If you were shy about where you got your data, you could never home in on a guiding principle.

Poltergeist.

A disruptive spirit, or a young esper unable to control their psychokinetic powers. A fitting title for a childish woman who held nothing back when it came to the game.

She reached into a pocket on the side of her bulky socks and took out a thick zip tie, tossing it on the ground in front of the girl with the twin tails.

"Tie your hands behind your back."

"Why should I—?"

Boom! Boom!! Two heavy gunshots blew into the skull of the already-Downed Magistellus. The borrowed Legacy was too valuable to waste here. At this distance, her own magnum pistol would do just fine.

"Now."

"O-okay, okay!!"

Shaking badly, the girl did as she was told. Whether her shaking was due to the cold rain, the fear of being shot, or the sight of her partner's body being defiled was hard to say. The beauty in the racing swimsuit considered the possibilities but was unable to derive the correct answer. Her only thought was, *Ah, it seems the flow has turned against this girl. I've gotten some good data this time.*

"Is this okay? ...*Grh?!*"

Poltergeist went around behind the girl and, despite her victim's obvious lack of resistance, wrapped her left arm around her neck. With her right, she held her magnum pistol to the girl's head.

They're here already.

Poltergeist spun around, her back to the semitrailer, hostage in hand. Just then, there was a disturbance in the rain. A spray of droplets scattered, displaced in a straight line about one head to the side. From what little she'd seen of her opponent's skill, Poltergeist surmised that if she hadn't taken the hostage, that one shot would have killed her.

Though the park's facilities were man-made, there was still natural rain forest all around. It was difficult to pick out where enemies were hiding amid the constant rain.

For now, however, Poltergeist intended to take full advantage of her human shield.

"I'm not used to guns, you know! One little fright and I might blow this girl's head off!"

Leaning against the side of the trailer, Poltergeist made her way around to the back. Her goal was the compact car she had hidden inside the trailer, but she wanted to keep her opponent from figuring that out if at all possible.

In truth, she wasn't nervous at all, but she had learned that saying she was made it statistically more likely her opponents would hesitate. She had done it many times before.

…I just need to get to the car.

"Throw down your weapons and come out with your hands up," she said. "Then we can have a nice, constructive discussion."

"Fo—"

A strangled voice could be heard, the sound of Midori trying to say something.

"Forget about me! This is your chance! Don't let her get away!!"

It was Poltergeist who answered.

"Oh? You think a magnum pistol is too powerful to be used as a threat?" She was well aware that what people feared most was a lack of emotion. And she hadn't learned that through empathy but through her endless experiments. "All I have to do is make sure you don't Fall. First, I'll blow off your ears, then maybe your nose. Then maybe I'll press the searing gun barrel against your pretty little skin."

"Ugh!"

There was a squelch—the sound of a footstep in the mulch. A sniper's fatal error.

How disappointing.

That was Poltergeist's cold conclusion. In the end, he was no better than the Dealers she had faced in the past. Just like a quiz program on the living room TV revealing the answer while you were still in the kitchen cooking, the ending had come too soon.

And then, without warning…

From behind a thick tree, a figure appeared—both hands raised, holding a .45-caliber short-range sniper rifle. It was the demon pit babe, borrowing Short Spear.

"What…?"

"What's the matter, witch? I did just as you asked, did I not?"

They had only been fighting in the park for a short time, but Poltergeist had already worked out that the sniper on the opposing team was the human Dealer, not his Magistellus. Clearly, the succubus holding the gun was a diversion. But a diversion from what?!

She pulled her hostage even closer and pressed the muzzle of her gun hard into the girl's temple.

Then she heard a voice from above.

"Look up."

Urk!!

Suddenly, she felt something tighten around her throat, hard enough to crush the bones in her neck. Both of her legs lifted off the ground.

"Ughup???!!!"

Even her voice wouldn't come out right. Poltergeist had her back to the side of the semitrailer. Someone had snuck on top of it and, using a U-shaped loop of yellow and black construction rope, lifted her by the neck—straight up, as though hooking her in a crane game.

Incidentally, there's a particular action all people take when they're being strangled, regardless of culture. This was, of course, the act of putting both hands around your neck in an attempt to relieve the pain. This behavior is practically a reflex and impossible to resist, even with special training.

It doesn't matter if one of those hands is holding a magnum pistol, or if the person's finger is currently on the trigger.

Poltergeist's arms moved as if possessed.

Ah.

There wasn't even enough time to speak.

Test it out for yourself. Imagine trying to untie a rope around your neck. Make a gun with your thumb and forefinger and put your hands to your throat. Where does the barrel end up? Certainly not at the head of your hostage.

Kaname showed no mercy.

The intense pain and restricted blood flow caused Poltergeist's fingers to spasm. And...

Kaboom!!

The woman blew her own head off.

11

"#lockpick.err..."

The bespectacled dark elf dropped down to the slushy ground and examined the simplified shotgun, turning it over in her hands.

"This is indeed a part of Takamasa's collection. It was designed for breach-and-clear warfare, and can destroy any locking mechanism just by pointing it and pulling the trigger. I remember seeing him use it one time when Ayame locked herself out of a room with an automatic lock. She had tears in her eyes."

To Kaname and his friends, collecting the Legacies was supposed to be more important than anything else. But for now, Tselika gestured for Cindy to stop speaking.

Midori was crying. Not because of the hostage situation, but because she had been unable to protect her Magistellus partner. Once again, Kaname had been too slow to stop it. Once again, he had let the young girl cry.

Was he going to force this little girl with the tearstained face to come with him and settle things with Takamasa? Was he going to let her witness the moment he shot her brother between the eyes? No matter how strong she was, she was only human. She wasn't an experienced Dealer like Kaname and his ilk.

Kaname didn't want her to turn out like him. It had to stop here. Midori could not be made to suffer any further.

"..."

Her bike's taillight had been punched out in the collision, but the vehicle still seemed usable, and it was the quickest and closest thing Kaname had access to.

Poltergeist couldn't be the only Dealer prowling the jungle, and Kaname needed to get back on the move before any more came out of the woodwork along with an infinite supply of invincible PMCs.

"Tselika."

"What is it, My Lord? Figured out some way to tow my temple out of the mud? There's plenty of cranes and trucks around for moving the cages back into the barn."

"…Take care of Midori. Use the Legacies if you have to."

"Wait," came a voice. It was difficult to make out through her tears, but it was there. "I'm coming with you."

"Midori."

"My brother did this…"

She pointed at Meiki's static body. The magnum bullets had torn into her, making her look like a ruined statue.

"He knew what he was doing bringing that woman into this. He knew this would happen. This is what he's trying to do, not just to me but to everyone. That's what he said, isn't it?! He's going to destroy the game and take everyone's Magistellus away from them! As his little sister, I *need* to stop him!!"

Kaname didn't want to hear those words. The reason he'd reached out to Midori in the first place was because Takamasa's Fall had torn their family apart and saddled her and her parents with debt. Takamasa had saved Kaname's family, and Kaname hated to see Takamasa's family suffer as a result. That was why he was still looking for a way to repair the damage.

He wanted Midori to ask him to save Takamasa, no matter how difficult or reckless it might be.

And yet.

"Kaname…"

"No, it's fine."

The dark elf started to say something, but Kaname cut her off.

Perhaps his wishes really were illogical. He wanted to protect Taka-masa's family, but to do that, he was willing to turn his gun on the man himself, repaying a favor with death. How much more treacher-ous could you get?

However, there was no way Kaname could follow his friend's path. He could never accept saving humanity at the expense of Magistelli like Tselika.

He wanted to have his cake and eat it, too. Perhaps his fate would be the same as that awaiting all greedy Dealers who bit off more than they could chew.

"Let's go," said Midori. She'd wiped the tears from her eyes, and her voice was now clear. "We have to stop an evil Dealer called Criminal AO. Just like you have to fight the Takamasa only you know, I've gotta fight the brother only I know. We're the only ones in the whole world who can do it."

"…You're right," answered Kaname through gritted teeth.

Kaname tended to fight using only Short Spear, but from here on out, he would need the strength of the Legacies to face the countless powerful Dealers and PMCs standing between him and the tower. By now, he had quite a selection to choose from. Kaname picked out #tempest.err and #lockpick.err and handed them to Midori.

Cindy cocked her head and asked, "Isn't it a little redundant to take two shotguns?"

"It's fine," Kaname replied. "Our main priority is to keep moving. That makes these our best options."

He straddled the bright-red motorcycle and waited for Midori to get on behind him.

"Tselika, Cindy. Take Meiki and the other Legacies and get out of here. You might be fine in the semipublic parkland, but once we're in the tower on private property you won't fare as well. It doesn't matter how you get a car, but your best bet is probably to look for one Polter-geist left stashed around somewhere. Judging by the explosions we've seen so far, I don't think there will be any traps inside, just the fuel in the tank."

"Hmph. I'm afraid I am not like you, My Lord, content to seat his bottom in whichever car he pleases. I'd rather go back and haul away my temple, no matter what the cost...!!"

Kaname figured she would say something like that, and he flung her a key he'd swiped from a tow truck earlier.

With their next moves decided, Kaname twisted the throttle of Midori's motorcycle and took off across the muddy ground. The bike was a racing vehicle and not intended for off-road use, plus it had Midori's added weight on the back, but Kaname drove steadily on, regardless.

Before long, they heard the roar of an engine as a specialized military jeep hit one of the twisting tree roots and launched into the air, landing alongside Kaname. The convertible roof was down, despite the heavy rain, presumably to allow the mounted machine gun a clear shot.

Kaname immediately took up Short Spear, but the jeep's gunner only scoffed.

"Kha-kha-kha!! This machine gun's got a protective shield! Your cheap .45-caliber bullets ain't even gonna scratch the paint...!"

Kaname ignored the man's taunts and fired two shots above the gunner's head, cracking a tree bough that arched over the vehicle and dropping something large into the jeep.

It was a leopard that had been hiding in the branches, probably trying to escape the muddy earth.

"Argh! Ghah! Wh-what the blazes?!"

After tearing out the gunner's throat, the wild beast made its way into the jeep. Kaname kept his distance, moving farther into the jungle so as not to be taken out by the military vehicle as it swerved back and forth.

The central tower was dead ahead. At this distance, they were too close for the laser cannon to get a clear shot.

Armored cars were parked outside the entrance, along with rows of soldiers. They formed a quick-and-dirty shield line, with assault rifles at the rear, but their lack of self-preservation told Kaname these were not human Dealers but AI PMCs.

And I bet Takamasa's done something to them...

Before they could act, Kaname raced the bike up a short staircase in front of him—about three steps high—launching himself into the air and over the heads of the PMC blockade.

Not even batting an eye as he flew through the air, Kaname said, "Midori, get #lockpick.err ready!"

"O-okay!!"

Ahead of them was a glass door reinforced by a metal shutter, but it surrendered after a single blast from the simplified shotgun in the girl's hands. The metal lattice immediately shot upward like a clockwork toy.

There was no logic at work here. Any kind of lock the Legacy touched simply flew open. That was all there was to it.

Tires screeched as Kaname skidded through the entrance hall. By the time the PMCs had turned around and pointed their rifles, he was already driving up an escalator headed to the next floor.

"Do you know where my brother is?!" Midori asked.

"With #flash.err."

"You mean the shipping container on the top floor? But he can't use that up close. Would he really stay with it? The Legacies aren't that special to him, remember."

"Quite right, Midori."

Just then, they heard the sound of something chopping the air. It was right above them.

"The truck parked near the top of the tower was only a platform for #flash.err. Once it becomes clear it's no longer useful, he'll switch up his methods. For example, he might suspend it via wires from a transport helicopter or tilt-rotor and use that to take me out, even if it means slicing this very building to ribbons."

"...Do you think he might try to escape?"

"Probably not. If that was his top priority, he would have started acting the moment he used #flash.err to intercept my sea-to-earth missile."

The tower was a combination aquarium, shopping mall, and animal research laboratory, but as the lower levels saw the most foot traffic, they had been built primarily with beauty in mind. PMCs flooded the room to seal off the stairs and elevators, but Kaname rode up onto the railings, jumping from chandelier to chandelier in the building's central well, trying to reach the upper floor.

The PMCs were tough, and if they called for reinforcements, they could keep attacking endlessly. But they could only move according to the building's blueprints. By forging his own shortcuts, Kaname could lead them on an endless wild-goose chase searching for the quickest route to reach him.

…This was a trick Kaname had learned watching Takamasa after the fight with Bloody Dancer.

"There's still some on our tail," called out Midori.

"Those must be human Dealers," Kaname replied.

Kaname jumped the bike off the swinging chandeliers and onto solid ground, purposely sending its tires into a skid as it landed and taking out the Dealers' legs with a single sweep. At the same time, his silent .45-caliber bullets severed the chains holding up the chandeliers, both erasing the path he had just come by and sending them crashing down on top of a separate group of Dealers who had just run into the lobby below.

"Did their guns look a little strange to you?" Midori asked.

"They might be Takamasa's Legacies," replied Kaname. However, their priority right now was finding Takamasa himself. They could return for the loot afterward. If the weapons slid across the floor, they wouldn't disappear along with the Dealers' bodies, and AI soldiers weren't programmed to pick up items off the ground.

Kaname clicked his tongue as they blasted open another iron shutter with Midori's #lockpick.crr and launched into a stairwell. It seemed like Takamasa wasn't taking this seriously enough. The Legacies' strength lay in their quirks, in the ability to catch your opponent off guard with a type of attack they had never seen before. They broke the established rules, and that was what made them such terrifying weapons, capable of bringing a whole nation to its knees.

There was no point handing them out willy-nilly to Dealers— no matter how strong or capable—if they weren't in the correct environment to take advantage of those quirks. All they were doing was standing in the path of the bike and getting run over before they could fire off a single shot. It was ridiculous. They had in their hands weapons that could defy the laws of physics, and yet they were setting themselves up to be knocked down by those very same laws.

Had Takamasa even taught them how to use the weapons correctly? Maybe the only reason he was happy to hand them out was because he knew they would all return to him in the end. In that case, he didn't care what became of the Dealers he was using as pawns.

There was a short, metallic *clang*. Farther up the stairwell, something about the size of a baseball bounced down the steps.

"No way! A grenade!!" Midori screamed.

Kaname drove straight through a set of iron shutters and exited onto the nearest floor. The blast radius was somewhere in the region of six to eight meters. By the time it went off behind them, they were already out of range of the shrapnel.

The tenth floor seemed to be where the aquarium was located. Leaping over the security gate on the bike, Kaname entered an underwater tunnel constructed from clear plastic.

Midori did a double take when she spotted a painted image on one of the nearby support pillars.

"That was Mr. Shark! Wasn't he the mascot for that soccer team?"

"I guess they had a crossover promotion," replied Kaname.

There was little sense in fighting the PMC guards head-on, so Kaname shot a few water tanks and let the incoming sharks and killer whales take care of them. Then he hightailed it out of there before getting caught in the flow.

Next, he headed for the emergency stairwell on the other side of the building. Once there, he drove straight through another metal shutter and up toward the higher floors.

"Floor twenty already...," said Midori.

"This should be where the research labs are. They're closed to the public."

It was then that Kaname heard the chopping sound once more. There were no windows in the emergency stairwell. That meant whatever was on the outside making that noise must be very close.

Kaname felt a tingling sensation—the Lion's Nose.

"Here it comes, Midori! Get down!"

Trusting his reflexes, Kaname twisted the handlebars. He left the stairwell and exited straight out onto the next floor. The very next moment...

Ba-zammm!!!!!

That wasn't the sound of something being cut; it was the sound of it being vaporized. The laser had severed the wall at a diagonal, and the metal units making up the squared-off spiral of the stairwell fell all at once like a waterfall. If Kaname had stayed there a moment longer, he would have been caught up in the avalanche, falling over twenty stories to his death.

"Takamasa's really gunning for us now..."

Kaname had come all this way to fight him. In that sense, it didn't really matter what floor the fight took place on. He stopped the bike where he was and drew his .45-caliber short-range sniper rifle.

These levels had once housed an animal research lab, but what would Kaname find here now?

In the center of the floor was a detailed diorama of Tokonatsu City, covered in sticky notes with strings of letters and numbers on them. Arranged in a circle around the diorama were racks of servers, each larger than a fridge.

Written on them in red spray paint were the following words:

Money (Game) Master Ver. 6.25 Emulation Model.

"This can't be real...," said Midori. She was staring, her mouth agape. "My br—Criminal AO was making another *Money (Game) Master* in here? He was building an exact copy of the game inside the game itself?!"

"Midori."

Kaname was crouched close to the wall, taking pictures of something with his phone. He gestured for the girl to join him.

Just then, there was another shot. Moments after the two of them crouched down together, a beam of light swept over their heads. The thick glass windows didn't shatter, they *melted*, not even producing the sound of smashing glass that usually accompanied a surprise attack. There was only an explosion of crackling sparks as the racks of servers were sliced in half.

To reproduce the game within itself was a miraculous feat of engineering, and yet it seemed Takamasa would much rather seize the opportunity to cut Kaname down than preserve his work.

"Takamasa's serious about taking out the Magistelli and AI society. That's why he created a copy of the game—to expose its secrets. Know your enemy and all that."

"I mean, sure, I know phones and computers work just fine within the game, but who would think of taking it this far?!" cried Midori.

"Only Takamasa, that's for sure," Kaname replied. "And yet he was quick to wash his hands of it, too. Clearly recreating the game wasn't enough to grasp their true nature."

"Their?"

"The Magistelli and the Mind. They must be more than mere AI, if Takamasa wasn't able to reproduce them by hacking at ones and zeros."

Kaname took out his smartphone and used its dark surface as a mirror to peer around the corner. There, outside the building, was the tilt-rotor, short and squat, with two distinctive sets of propellers at the ends of its wings. The propellers occupied a larger proportion of the vehicle than on traditional aircraft, allowing it to travel up and down like a helicopter. Below it, suspended by wires, was the shipping container.

#flash.err.

The tilt-rotor circled the tower, keeping the laser weapon trained on its interior, where Kaname and Midori were hiding.

...*It's close.*

Its beam traveled at the speed of light, with enough precision to shoot a sea-to-earth missile out of the sky. However, distance shouldn't really matter with such a weapon. Over long stretches, the beam's power could decay, but that would require ranges in the hundreds of kilometers. It wasn't a restriction that would come into play within the area of a single city.

Is he scared of the glass reflecting the beam back at him? That would explain why he's only firing into the aircraft's shadow...

"I think my brother's figured out which floor we're on...," whispered Midori, still holding on to the two Legacies, #tempest.err and #lock-pick.err. "But he still managed to miss us with a laser beam that cut through the whole wall. How come?"

"Maybe that's the reason."

"Hmm?"

"A laser is just light. And for various reasons, light is pretty easy to bend. It's like when you see a heat mirage or look at the edges of a fish tank filled with water. Perhaps the path of the laser changed when it cut through the concrete and rebar in the wall."

A laser was an unconventional weapon, and because of that, it had some downsides. A spray of mist, internal sprinklers, even the air conditioning could all throw off the path of the beam.

Perhaps he's trying to figure out a line of attack that will let him eliminate me without harming Midori...

"What is it?"

"Nothing."

It was only a theory—no point in saying it out loud. Right now, Kaname had to stick to the facts. And it was a fact that the temperature and humidity differential between the air inside and outside the tower was affecting the beam's trajectory. That wouldn't last long, however, as the building continued to be cut to ribbons. If the tower's structural integrity was compromised, Kaname and Midori would be goners.

That said, the Legacies were only tools, and just as Takamasa had #flash.err, the two of them had Legacies of their own. Takamasa might have been an engineering whiz, but his one weakness was that he hadn't made tools that chose their bearers.

"Midori, give me #lockpick.err."

"Don't you want #tempest.err?"

Midori questioned Kaname's choice, but still did as she was told.

The sound of the propellers, like a huge sheet flapping in the wind, disappeared behind the crumbled wall and around the back of the building. Perhaps Takamasa was trying to avoid being thrown off by a crosswind, or perhaps he simply didn't need to fire through the exposed wall and could attack from any angle through the concrete.

"Midori, when I give the signal, fire #tempest.err. Just keep attacking the tilt-rotor as much as you can."

"Okay, but…"

The monster shotgun had the power to launch two thousand pellets into whatever its guiding beam touched. Her worry, then, wasn't whether she could make the shot.

It looked like she wanted to ask, *"What about you?"*

"I'll finish this," proclaimed Kaname. "I'm not going to pretend that stopping Takamasa is some convoluted way of repaying him. I'm stabbing him in the back, plain and simple. But I decided to walk this path myself, and there's no going back on it now. I'm the Reaper, after all."

12

"Crosswind compensation complete. Returning clockwise to original position."

From the cockpit of the tilt-rotor, a PMC pilot delivered his report in a droning monotone. It was no secret that Takamasa hated the AI, but the smartphone in his hand allowed him to take control of any AI program—aside from the Magistelli anyway.

"Time?" he asked.

"Forty-five seconds. Not long now."

But more than enough time for Kaname to take as many carefully aimed shots as he needs, Takamasa thought.

However, it didn't matter how accurate Kaname was. Takamasa knew his foe and had come prepared. This tilt-rotor was far more heavily armored than the average helicopter. No .45-caliber bullet could hope to penetrate it, even if it hit the windshield.

He has #tempest.err, #fireline.err, #dracolord.err, and #thunderbolt .err... Out of all those, it's the minigun #dracolord.err that worries me the most.

Fwush!! The tilt-rotor rounded a corner and came once more to the ruined wall of the tower. Takamasa owned the building, so there was nowhere for Kaname to hide. Takamasa could sniff out his old friend's location and loadout simply by examining the security footage.

"If it's only #tempest.err, then there's nothing for me to worry about. A blast of two thousand pellets sounds impressive, but a shotgun is nothing more than an anti-personnel weapon. I just have to make sure the beam doesn't come through the glass."

He smiled fiercely.

He'd never wanted things to end up this way. Both Kaname and Midori were humans, and human life was irreplaceable. Yet somewhere along the line, matters had become complicated. Perhaps Kaname and Midori were beating themselves up about it right now, but as far as Takamasa was concerned, they didn't need to. They weren't the problem; he was.

And that was why they should come at him with everything they had.

If familial love could be used as an excuse for anything, the teenagers of the world wouldn't resent their mothers and fathers. Parents fought against society regardless of whether they were understood or not. As long as they were able to protect their children, it was worth it,

Boom!! The sound of an explosion rang out.

"We're being fired upon, sir."

"I know."

He could see his sister, Midori, leaning out from behind a ruined pillar and pointing a huge shotgun his way. The enormous weapon, shaped like a revolving grenade launcher, was clearly beyond the young girl's capacity to handle, and it was rather amusing to see the recoil launch her back each time she pulled the trigger.

However, as valiant an effort as it was, there was no way she would inflict more than the merest scratch on the tilt-rotor's armor with a weapon like that.

…She should have concentrated her fire on the wires instead. At least then she could have taken away my means of attack.

She was probably so caught up in controlling the enormous gun she hadn't realized it, but she was now much farther from Kaname's side than when she had started. Takamasa was ready to slice the other Dealer in half at the first chance he got. And now he had even been given enough time to adjust his position so nothing else got caught in the cross fire.

"Kaname…"

He and Takamasa had both agreed on the subject of the AI menace. It was Kaname who had refused to do what was necessary and extinguish the Magistelli completely. He would never be able to save humanity like that. As painful as it was, Kaname needed to Fall here.

"It's okay, my friend. Your life of debt won't last long. Once I eliminate *snow* entirely, it'll all be meaningless."

This was simply the logical course of action. However, Takamasa couldn't deny there was another part of him thrilled to be playing the game once more.

"…There's no need to be scared. Just stay still and let #flash.err take care of the rest," he proclaimed.

But just then, Takamasa noticed something unusual.

Kaname, hiding behind another pillar, was holding something other than his .45-caliber short-range sniper rifle.

It was a bare-bones shotgun, intended to be mounted under the barrel of an assault rifle—#lockpick.err. And its special effect allowed it to open any locks and doors it hit.

"Grh?!"

Takamasa immediately grabbed a metal pole by the wall of the tilt-rotor. If the cargo door suddenly opened, it wouldn't matter how well-armored the vehicle was. He would be sucked out into the blustery winds and greeted with a twenty-floor drop.

However, that wasn't what Kaname was aiming for.

A chill ran down Takamasa's spine, informing him of a different threat.

"Oh no…"

Panicking, he called out.

"Get to cover!! Quick!"

But it was too late.

Kaname's shotgun blast sliced through the air.

Directly toward the already unstable engine block of the tilt-rotor aircraft.

The turbofan engine was housed inside a cylindrical container, which included a hatch for maintenance access on its rounded side. This was obviously something that should not be opened during flight.

Clang! A tremor rocked the aircraft. It was clear what had just happened.

Imagine having your stomach sliced open in an unsterilized operating room. If the engine hatch were removed, it would not be difficult for a stray bird to find its way inside and do some serious damage.

However, there were more dangerous things in the air than stray birds.

There were the two thousand shotgun pellets dispensed every time Midori pulled #tempest.err's trigger. Not to mention the silenced .45-caliber bullets of Kaname's short-range sniper rifle, Short Spear.

The aircraft was in range of both of them.

Takamasa's throat dried up as a terrifying barrage of gunfire flew toward the tilt-rotor's weak point.

13

Ba-zammm!!!!!!

The deadly light beam fired, completely missing its target. The tilt-rotor had lost its balance and was rotating in place while steadily losing altitude, eventually crashing into the wall of the tower several levels below where Kaname and Midori were standing on the twentieth floor. The aircraft's body dragged along the side of the tower as it continued to fall, spiraling to the ground in a hail of glass shards and iron plating.

There was no recovering it now.

They heard a loud explosion, and the entire building shook ominously. This sort of damage was far beyond what the earthquake mitigation systems were designed to deal with.

Kaname put his hand to his breast pocket, a bitter expression on his face. *After everything I did to get Mother Loose and Smash Daughter on my side,* he thought, *I never needed to use my ace in the hole. Perhaps that's because I didn't have to look him in the eye and do it.*

"…It's over."

Midori dropped the monstrous shotgun to the ground.

"We…," she began in a whisper. "…We managed to go through with it in the end, didn't we?"

As Midori went to peer over the edge of the ruined wall, Kaname grabbed her hand. He didn't know why, but he felt like if he didn't, she might suddenly fly away.

And yet.

"I wonder what it was, in the end," said Kaname.

"Hmm?"

"#flash.err was no ordinary anti-air laser weapon—it was one of the Legacies. It should have had some sort of secret power that defied the laws of physics… And yet Takamasa lost without ever tapping into its full potential."

This floor of the building had been ripped to shreds by the laser, but it had once been Takamasa's research laboratory. And that man was a compulsive note taker (even though he had no need to be, since he could remember all the details of his projects in his head). Kaname had a quick look around to see what he could uncover, before taking out his smartphone and sending a message.

Kaname: Tselika, Cindy. We're done here.

Tselika: We can see that, My Lord.

Kaname: Head over and check out the crash site. I want to know what state #flash.err is in.

Each Legacy exposed a glitch in *Money (Game) Master*. Kaname's plan was to find them all and use them to lay bare the game's secrets. If #flash.err was damaged, it could pose a problem.

Getting back on the leaf-patterned motorcycle, Kaname and Midori rode down to the first floor. There were still PMCs and Dealers hanging around, but Kaname didn't need to bother with them now that their kingpin was down. It was a simple matter to shake them off.

Gunfire rang out from all around, but the shooters weren't just aiming at the pair on the bike. Hanging on to Kaname from the rear seat, Midori looked around in panic.

"Wh-what?! Why are they shooting each other?!" she asked.

"Now that Takamasa's out of the picture," Kaname replied, "the PMCs he was controlling have returned to their original mission—the removal of any intruders from restricted zones."

The Legacies were useless in the hands of the ignorant. Kaname doubted even a single Dealer would manage to get away with one of them.

After breaking through the crowd, Kaname noticed a few Dealers, already half dead, still stubbornly on his tail. He took care of each of them with a silenced .45-caliber bullet right between their eyes.

Tselika had kept her word and fished out the mint-green coupe. It was covered in mud but seemed to run well enough.

Kaname tossed her a revolver.

"Add this to the list. Picked it off a Dealer on the way down here. It's called #firecracker.err. Don't know what it does, though."

"Hmph. I'd rather you picked up a new set of alloy wheels if I'm being perfectly honest."

The blackened shell of Takamasa's aircraft lay amid a sea of broken glass. The bespectacled dark elf crouched to examine it.

"It's taken a beating," she explained, "but it looks like the only damage is to the shipping container. The laser unit itself seems perfectly operable."

"Even after falling twenty floors?"

"It wasn't a straight drop; it was spiraling and scraping against the building. There should be plenty of semitrucks lying around. Let's get this thing hooked up and get out of here as soon as possible."

"I agree... Too bad Takamasa got away, though."

At Kaname's offhand comment, the air suddenly grew tense. It was Tselika who spoke up, her elbow resting on the driver's seat window.

"Hold on, My Lord. Now, I didn't want him to Fall any more than the rest of us, but...just look at that burned-up shell! Takamasa could not have survived, even if he had been wearing a blast suit!!"

"Take a look at this."

Kaname showed her his smartphone. Its screen displayed photos of bits of paper. Documents, notes—remnants of a man who despised the digital. As usual, they were encrypted using Takamasa's own proprietary scheme, but Kaname could decode them using the decryption key he'd swiped following his clash with Bloody Dancer.

"This explains the quirk behind #flash.err—the thing that makes it break the laws of physics."

Kaname had previously acquired a list of all the Legacies, but that had only told him how many there were and their names. The only person who knew their effects in detail was Takamasa himself.

Kaname wished he'd had the time to read these notes earlier instead of having to wait until now.

"#flash.err has the ability to fire any object or material at the speed of light, not just light itself."

"What?!"

"It ignores air resistance, friction, inertia, momentum, anything like that. It's the ultimate transportation device. You could load it with a thermonuclear or biological weapon, and nobody would have time to shoot it down... And if you wanted to, you could even load a human body and send them into space."

At the very last moment, the tilt-rotor had fired a shot in an unexpected direction.

Kaname had assumed it was a misfire due to the aircraft's instability...

but it wasn't. Sensing he'd lost, Takamasa had activated #flash.err in order to escape.

"All Takamasa needs is for his Legacies to come into contact with the Zodiac Children. That's why he's not shy about lending them out. His priority isn't hunting me down; it's the Zodiac Children he's after."

"Kaname," said Cindy, tossing him something she'd picked out of the wreckage.

It was a smartphone, though the screen was cracked. Kaname pulled out a cable and connected it to his own phone. Luckily, the internals still worked, and he brought up a view of the data on his own phone's screen.

"Analysis results."

"Of what?" asked Tselika. "What is there left to analyze at this point?!"

Suddenly, they could hear several sets of footsteps pounding the ground. The sound of military-spec boots scraping across the asphalt could mean only one thing—AI-controlled PMCs.

This had been Takamasa's goal all along. He had finally tracked down one of the Zodiac Children, but if this game of cat-and-mouse went on any longer, he could lose them, or they could get caught in the cross fire and Fall. The base, the Legacies, they were all decoys. Decoys meant to lure Kaname deep into Takamasa's territory and surround him with a thick wall of PMCs so he couldn't escape. In the meantime, Takamasa could close in on his target without any interference.

The next battle had already begun. Kaname sucked in a deep breath, then explained what he had found.

"It's Pavilion...that girl with the auction obsession. She's one of the Zodiac Children, just like me. This calls her the Maiden's Survival."

Interlude 2

"*Phew.*"

Criminal AO, aka Takamasa, took a deep breath where he stood in the parking lot of a faraway diner.

He may have had to give up one of his hideouts, but the PMCs would keep Kaname busy for the time being. If only Kaname would agree to work with him, then he wouldn't have to do this, but since there was hardly any hope of that, Takamasa thought it better to proceed with his plans while he had the chance.

The Zodiac Children.

Across all of humanity, there were only twelve. Twelve chances to succeed. It was actually quite generous, all things considered. It meant he didn't need Kaname's cooperation to secure victory.

…Still, very few Zodiac Children have revealed themselves. There are too many holes in the data, and I have to do a lot of extrapolation just to keep up.

Takamasa refused to turn to the Magistelli or AI society at large. As a result, he had to do all the calculations himself.

The task at hand was simple. Whatever he did in this game required money.

Kaname's been raiding my safe deposit boxes wherever he can find them. I guess it's time to change tack…

Just then.

Click!
He felt the cold steel of a gun barrel pressed against his back.

"Huh."
The voice sounded unconcerned, but Takamasa had no way of turning around.

"How's this for proof?" The voice continued. "I bet you didn't expect me to get the drop on you, right?"

Stuck facing away, Takamasa glanced at a window in the wall of the diner to see who stood behind him.

"...Lily-Kiska."

"I'm a lot better than you are at predicting what people will do," she said. "Whether it's gunfights or trading, you'll never catch me off guard."

Takamasa took a deep breath, then asked a question.

"A bolt-action sniper rifle? What happened to the gun I gave you, #swallowdive.err?"

"I find it's more effective if I save it for the right occasion. Besides, Kaname Suou needs all the Legacies, doesn't he?"

Takamasa listened to her words, but he couldn't grasp what she was up to. Even Criminal AO, the master of analysis, was stumped.

Lily-Kiska had always been an excellent sniper, but even she had never been capable of coming this far. She had to be using something to compensate. Takamasa realized what it was immediately.

"You've teamed up with *them*."

"So what if I have?"

"You, a Zodiac Child! You were supposed to join forces with me and take down the AI for the sake of humanity!!"

"Unfortunately, I don't care what happens to humanity. Now that I know I can get the drop on a legend, next time will be more than a rehearsal. I'm going after *him*."

A merciless gunshot rang out.

But Criminal AO was unharmed. Instead, the window he was using as a mirror shattered into a thousand pieces.

He could no longer see Lily-Kiska.

"Hrh?!"

But the moment a sniper pulled the trigger was when they were at their most vulnerable. To load another shot, she would have to pull back the cocking lever, and that gave Takamasa time to act. He wheeled around.

But she was gone. The penknife in his right hand sliced through empty air.

There were many places to hide—the trees by the road, the cars in the parking lot, the walls of the diner. Takamasa couldn't tell which one of them she'd chosen.

"Though I suppose it gives me comfort to see you so flustered."

Those were her parting words.

Takamasa clicked his tongue and scratched his head. He wasn't foolish enough to go poking his nose into every shadow, only to come face-to-face with a live grenade she'd left behind.

The Scorpion's Tenacity, one of the Zodiac Children. She was gifted with the ability to subconsciously analyze her surroundings and identify whatever would help her take the shortest route to the thing she sought. For that purpose, the girl would use anything and anyone. Just like she'd done with Takamasa and was now doing with the AI and the Magistelli.

But it seemed her poison tail was not aimed at Takamasa. She had said herself she didn't care what happened to humanity. Her true target, then, was obvious.

"...What a monster," Takamasa spat.

Some, however, might have taken that as a compliment.

Chapter 9

The Courage Required to Shoot You BGM #09
"Fight a Duel"

1

The blare of synthesizer music filled the room. The near pitch-black darkness was illuminated only briefly by black light and colored strobes. This was no ordinary nightclub, and rather than a bar at its center, it featured a stage where barely clothed women twisted their hips in lascivious motions.

"Calling me out to a strip club. Isn't this sexual harassment?"

The girl sighed and raised a nonalcoholic cocktail to her lips. She was dressed in a policewoman's outfit, but there was no police force in Tokonatsu City, so it must have been a costume. What the man couldn't figure out was whether the short-haired woman before him was the Dealer or the Magistellus. Both had identical facial features, and attempting to use his smartphone to analyze them only resulted in a stream of garbled nonsense.

Her name was Futashika Layer, and her Magistellus was a doppelgänger.

Perhaps the girl had modeled her character after first checking what kind of demon she'd contracted with. The man grinned from his seat opposite her across a low table.

"The lights here are dark, and you can barely hear a thing. Plus, the other customers are all distracted by the dancers, and recordings are prohibited even in this era of smartphones and social media. All that makes Prostitute Island the perfect place to discuss things in secret."

"And what kind of secrets are we discussing?"

"Man, I love girls. The more skin they show, the better. Personally, I prefer the ones with a little meat on their bones, you know? Skinny girls remind me too much of my sister."

He said this so matter-of-factly, she figured he must be one of those eccentrics you found among the most powerful Dealers. And even though he was in the middle of an important discussion, he had no qualms about stuffing banknotes into the girls' cleavage whenever they finished their dances.

Criminal AO.

Even after everything he had just been through, he was still smiling like he didn't have a care in the world.

At first glance, he seemed like an idiot, but Futashika Layer knew better than to let down her guard. *Dealers with a good grasp on their own desires were a force to be reckoned with.* They couldn't be flustered and they knew just when to quit—both incredibly useful skills if you saw this virtual world as a money-making game.

A mysterious smile spread across the man's face.

"I want information," he said.

"And you'll get it, if the price is right."

"I want to know the whereabouts of one Dealer in particular. A girl by the name of Pavilion."

"...I presume you already know about our history?" the girl in the policewoman outfit enquired testily.

It had all begun when the Ag Wolves went after Pavilion over the Legacies. After Kaname Suou had duped the lot of them, Pavilion had hired a group of hitmen to hunt down and finish off any survivors.

Thanks to that, Futashika Layer had been having a long string of nothing but bad days. After all, she had been a member of the Ag Wolves, too.

"You put together quite the file on her, didn't you?" said Criminal AO. "More than your work requires."

"…"

"However, you lack the firepower necessary to make a move. All I'm asking is for you to allow me to take over. I have a lead on where to get what's needed."

"If you're that good at gathering information, I can't imagine you need me…"

Futashika Layer threw up her hands in defeat, and her twin stuck her fingers into her mouth. However, she was not rudely picking out some loose piece of spinach but removing a microfilm hidden behind her back teeth.

The tiny storage medium was about a quarter the size of a postage stamp and contained all the information one would need to abduct or kill a target.

The one who'd been doing the talking wiped the other's fingers with a handkerchief before taking a tortilla chip and using it to scoop up a liberal amount of salsa.

"Well, she's an oddball, for sure," Futashika Layer explained. "She holds auctions every day of the year. Sometimes in fancy hotels, sometimes in opera houses. Right now, she's got her eye on either the Celestial Chapel or Sky Impact."

"Just as I thought, then."

"…Oh, I see. You were just using me to confirm what you already knew. That explains it."

Takamasa tended not to pay in *snow*, especially as far as his mission was concerned. He couldn't let the AI know what he was doing with his money beyond stuffing it between women's breasts. Instead, he picked up a briefcase that had been resting at his feet. It was filled with numerous glass cylinders about the size of whiskey tumblers.

The girl in the policewoman's outfit stared blankly as he began lining them up on the table.

"Camera lenses?"

"Handmade by yours truly. Take these to whatever shop you like—

they'll fetch a higher price than even those fancy German ones. And because I'm nice, I'll write you a letter of introduction as well. That way they won't try to haggle you down."

The first step of the revolution was to make a currency that couldn't be digitized.

"Although, I think selling these is a job for a Dealer rather than their Magistellus, don't you agree?"

Even when faced with something they could readily liquidate, the Magistelli couldn't turn it into big data unless they understood its value. Other examples of this were signed baseball cards and retro audio equipment—things the general public couldn't easily judge the worth of.

The woman turned the items over in her hands, examining them closely. Takamasa simply smiled.

"By the way," he said.

"Yes?"

"Which one of you two is the real Dealer? I'm guessing the human is the one sitting silently in the back."

Magistelli disliked handling other people's property, so the one who grabbed the lenses should have been the Dealer. It would have been an easy mistake to make, but these two hadn't fallen for it.

The pair pressed their soft cheeks together and replied in unison.

""Who cares? Does it really matter?""

2

Kaname had a hell of a time getting out of there.

His well-planned assault had landed him in what was essentially a giant bear trap designed to buy Takamasa time. Now Kaname was surrounded on all sides by PMC soldiers, with no way out except to fight his way through.

At times like this, it was nice to have Cindy on his side. She had been able to take the half-destroyed container carrying #flash.err and hook it up to a semitruck. Using its massive weight, she took the PMCs head-on, smashing through their barricades and opening a path for Kaname and Midori, while also protecting the coupe and bike from gunfire.

From there, they traveled inland, stopping to regroup in the parking lot of a combination motel and restaurant on the outskirts of town.

Tselika: Looks like we managed to lose them.

Midori: But it cost us a lot of time...

Cindy: If you'd only let me use #flash.err, we could have shaken them off much faster.

Kaname: No. We couldn't risk it short-circuiting. We need the Legacies intact to expose the glitches in Money (Game) Master. We shouldn't try to fire it until we confirm it hasn't been damaged.

The group left their cars and reconvened face-to-face. They'd initiated their attack when the rain began around sunset, and now it was totally dark out. How much had Takamasa managed to accomplish in that time? Before Kaname could put a stop to him once and for all, he needed to catch up. Even now, Takamasa was reaching for the giant breaker switch that would turn off *Money (Game) Master* and the Magistelli forever.

The one good thing to come of that wasted time was Meiki, who was now back on her feet. In under an hour, her Down status had cleared, and it was as if she'd never been shot in the head with a magnum pistol.

"We'll split up into two groups," said Kaname. "One group will go into hiding with #flash.err and make sure it's working correctly. We need the Legacies to enact our plan. We can't let it be stolen or destroyed."

"In that case, Kaname, might I suggest myself and Tselika for that task?" said Cindy. "After all, we are both quite proficient at fiddling with machines."

"Hey, then what will My Lord be doing?!" protested Tselika, her forked tail poking up into the air.

Kaname, however, had already thought of the rest.

"Takamasa is after the auctioneer, Pavilion," he explained. "We don't yet know what her power is as the Maiden's Survival, but at the very least, Takamasa must believe she's of use. If we want to settle things with him, now's our only chance. We'll head to Pavilion's next location at once and intercept him."

"...Are you sure you are capable of that?" asked Tselika.

"I am."

"My Lord, if I may. We Magistelli can suppress our own feelings for the sake of survival, but you humans cannot. I'm going to be frank: *You were relieved* to find out that Takamasa didn't die in that crash, weren't you?"

"You're wrong," replied Kaname immediately. But not in answer to her question. "When Takamasa Fell, and my sister became so traumatized she left the game... Who was it who got so pissed she turned against the Mind? That wasn't for the sake of your survival, was it? I don't believe you, Tselika. I don't care what you say; if you came face-to-face with Takamasa today, *you're* the one who wouldn't be able to shoot him."

"..."

Tselika bit her lip in silence as Kaname gently placed his hand on her delicate shoulder. Their eyes met.

"I'll do it," he said.

"My Lord..."

"It's too hard for you, Tselika. For Midori, and for Cindy, too. I'll do it. This all happened because I was too weak to protect my sister back then. Now Takamasa's gone off the rails because he didn't have us. That's why I have to put a stop to it. I have to bring him back. It's my duty."

Kaname took out some paper bills from his pocket and stuffed them in Tselika's hands, before sending her and Cindy into the restaurant to pick up enough burgers and fried chicken for everybody.

In truth, Kaname just didn't want to make anyone else fight.

After watching the two Magistelli leave, Midori whispered:

"...*You were relieved, weren't you?*"

"*Of course I was.*"

Right or wrong. Allies or enemies. These were not the things that triggered an emotional response. Not in humans, and not in Tselika, either. The Magistelli weren't so different; they could sigh in relief just the same as anyone else, and that was precisely why Kaname could never understand his old friend. How could he choose to wipe her out along with the rest, just because she was supposed to be the enemy? Kaname had to stop him, before it was too late.

He had to get things back to the way they were before, when they were all friends, laughing together.

3

After everyone had filled their bellies with greasy fast food, Kaname finally decided to make his move. Tselika and Cindy were in the trailer taking #flash.err back to his base on Mangrove Island, while Kaname and Midori drove their vehicles toward the center of the peninsula financial district.

Kaname: How's Meiki?

Midori: Contrary as always. For once, I said it's okay to take a rest, and now I can't get rid of her.

The demon girl clung tightly to Midori's back as the two sat atop her motorcycle. Their bond was incomprehensible to anyone else.

The financial district had many sides to it, but the street the pair rolled into seemed more geared toward grown-up tastes. Jewelry shops and brand-name stores lined the road, with the median taken up by a large sculpture of a wooden boat two hundred meters long, with large wings on either side like whale fins. Below the waterline were countless lenses, large and small, presumably used for takeoff and landing.

The boat appeared to be floating off the ground. As Kaname passed it, he fired off a chat message to Midori.

Kaname: The airship, Sky Impact. That'll be where things go down.

Midori: Huh? I've seen it a few times, but I didn't know you could go inside.

Kaname: The weight is spread across thousands of ultrathin wires. There's an event space on the inside for live music, concerts, exhibitions, plays, press conferences, auctions, even weddings.

Midori: What's the difference between live music and a concert?

The pair continued down the shop-lined street onto a long, narrow stretch of road. Midori kept shooting glances at Kaname before finally typing out a question.

Midori: How do you know where Pavilion's next auction will be anyway?

Kaname: No special reason. The information just happened to fall into the hands of a certain person before making its way to me. I'd wager not even Takamasa expected me to take this particular shortcut.

Midori: And what's that supposed to mean?

Kaname: This street is lined with shops selling luxury jewelry and brand-name items... Which brings it under the purview of Frey(a) and his pawnshop empire. That's how I got my hands on the event schedule.

...If Kaname was being perfectly honest, he couldn't remember a single time anything good came from asking the Treasure Hermit Crabs for help. The last thing he wanted to do was put his life in Frey(a)'s hands, but he'd had no other choice.

After they exited onto a second street, Kaname sent an icon to Midori's map.

Kaname: Midori, let's stop at this store while we're here.

Midori: What, did you forget something? We have enough ammo, don't we?

Kaname: The dress code.

Ignoring Midori as she balked at the rate on the parking meters, Kaname swiped his phone and paid for the two of them.

"Hey! Who asked you to do that?!!"

"We're together on this one. It makes sense to share the costs," replied Kaname. "Besides, if you think that's expensive, just wait until we get inside."

Kaname opened a glass door in the stone building and entered into a cozy little shop on the first floor. Midori hastily followed him, only to be hit by the high-class aura of the place like a physical punch to the forehead. She felt so out of place she nearly fell over.

It was a luxury clothing store and perhaps a little too much for schoolgirl Midori to take in at once. It offered complete tailoring and dressmaking services. Antiques, jewelry, even old violins lined the shelves, making it look like they'd stepped back in time. The gentle music playing in the background came not from an internet radio but an old-style gramophone.

A little old lady in a waistcoat and slacks with a tape measure over her neck stepped silently across the polished, amber-colored floor and gave the pair a charming smile.

"Well, Mr. Suou. What brings you here today?"

"Hey there, Other Dimensional Printer. If you don't mind, I'm afraid I need something of a rush job."

The woman looked a little disappointed as she adjusted her spectacles.

"I just fitted you for a new tailcoat a few days ago," she said. "Was there something the matter with it?"

"Oh, no. It's not for me this time, it's for her. I'd like the same quality as before, but we don't have much time. Is there anything you can do?"

"You wish for me to modify an off-the-shelf item so it will stand up to scrutiny at even the most high-class event, correct?"

"I'm glad you understand."

Midori was quick to butt in.

"Wait, what's going on???"

"We're sneaking into an auction filled with high-profile guests. They won't let us in dressed like this. We need formal attire."

"...It sounds like you already have some."

"Well, remember what I said about those drones we used as decoys? I got those through price-fixing at one of Pavilion's auctions."

Kaname gestured with his thumb toward the mannequins in the shop window.

"We're short on time today, so it won't be custom-made. Pick whichever one you like and change into it. We'll tailor the fit and pretty it up a little, then head straight to the auction house when you're ready."

"Uh…okay…but I'm not sure I can afford…"

"…"

"Y-you can't just buy it for me!! I'll pay you back afterward, I swear!! Um, um… I'll write a note in my smartphone, so I don't forget…"

The old lady with the tape measure around her neck smiled as she answered the girl's questions, and Kaname didn't fail to notice the knowing look she cast him as she reported the dress's price minus a zero or three.

"Thanks."

"Don't mention it. We're tailors. Making you look good is our job."

The dress Midori picked out was long and dark. It seemed suffocating at first glance, but Kaname saw that upon closer inspection many parts of it were sheer lace. Kaname wondered if Midori had noticed.

"Try it on for size," he suggested. "Let us know if anything's too loose or too tight, and Other Dimensional Printer here will fix it up for you."

"Oh? And *where* do you think it's going to be loose, exactly?"

"The waist, of course. Most people would be happy to find a little extra slack around the hips. Why, what did you think I was going to say?"

"Oh, shut up! I think I know my own body. Bust, waist, and hips, at least…"

"You know, dear," said the old lady, "when asked by their doctors if they pay enough attention to diet and exercise, surprisingly few patients give an honest answer."

"Besides," added Kaname. "A proper tailor needs more information than that. They need your shoulders, belly button height, arm and leg lengths, neck circumference. It's best to leave it to the professionals."

Midori huffed and marched off toward the fitting room in the back. The girl really did have an eye for clothes, and she'd been quick to choose her dress. After watching her tug the curtains shut as loudly as she could manage, Kaname took out his phone. Since Other

Dimensional Printer had helpfully downplayed the dress's price, Kaname transferred the actual amount while Midori wasn't looking.

"...That black dress makes it look like she's in mourning," he said. "Perhaps we should brighten it up a bit."

"I agree, Mr. Suou. How about a little mint-green trim?"

"Yeah, sounds good."

"I'll make it the same shade as your car, then. Hee-hee. All your things will match."

"..."

Kaname fell silent. The old woman simply chuckled as she went back behind the counter and produced a needlework kit. Kaname had fallen for her trap, hook, line, and sinker. Shootouts and car chases were one thing, but it seemed he couldn't let his guard down here, either.

4

She was in an enclosed space smaller than a beach shower, with only a full-length mirror for company and a paper-thin curtain blocking off the outside world. Midori had obviously been in a fitting room more times than she could count, but this time was different.

After all, on the other side of that single piece of cloth was a *man*!

The curtain didn't reach all the way to the ground, or the ceiling, for that matter, and there was a small gap above and below. It wasn't enough that she risked being seen, but even just being in the same air felt wrong. She was going to undress, completely, while staring at her likeness in a mirror the whole time.

Her face was flushed bright red with embarrassment, and she didn't want to see that reflected back at her, either.

"Aaa. Aaa. Arrrgh!"

She bit her trembling lip, but it wasn't enough to control her churn ing emotions. In fact, it only made the drops at the corners of her eyes swell even larger. Midori felt trapped, and she took a few deep breaths to regain her focus. Her frilly bikini top, carefully chosen to hide her slim physique, was the first to go. She placed her fingers beneath its straps and slid it off.

Next, she bent down for her miniskirt…but instead of removing it, she reached underneath and slowly pulled down her bikini bottom. The sequence was a little out of order, reminiscent of how she would change into her swimsuit under a towel at school.

"There we—Huh? My leg's caught…!"

Midori wobbled on one foot, trying to keep her balance. A voice came from beyond the curtain.

"*Midori?*"

"Bwah! It's nothing! I'm fine!!"

Her face was as bright and red as a traffic signal.

What would happen, she thought, if she were to fall over and tumble backside-first through the curtain? The most ridiculous developments raced through her mind unbidden, raising the girl's body temperature.

She stepped out of her bikini and immediately felt like there was no going back. Her face was searing hot, but down below it was refreshingly cool. After removing her miniskirt, Midori couldn't help but steal a glance at the mirror, confronting her own naked body.

…She hadn't had a lot of time back then to fiddle with the character creator, but Midori still regretted not putting in a little extra effort.

Though if I had, I'm sure I'd feel self-conscious about it.

She picked up the dress in both hands and held it over herself. *Not bad…*, she thought, admiring it in the mirror. She would have liked to add some flowers around the chest area to puff out her silhouette, but how was she going to ask Kaname for that without him realizing why?

Just as she was racking her brains over this, she heard it again—a voice from beyond the curtain. This time, it was the nice old lady who ran the shop.

"*Looks like things are about to get ugly. Come to the back, please, Mr. Suou.*"

…*The back?* Midori thought. *But that's where I am.* By the time she'd realized this, the situation had already moved beyond her control.

Kaname Suou immediately tore back the curtain and sealed himself in the fitting room alongside her.

>   "...
....
....
....
....
..............................Huh?"

Another person was in here with her.

Anger would have been the natural response, but Midori was so thrown, she couldn't even manage to get angry. It was like the wires in her brain had shorted.

"Wha—?! Hey, what do you think you're—? *Gmph!*"

"*Quiet.*"

Midori was still grasping the dress for dear life, but otherwise she was stark naked. Kaname wrapped an arm around her and put the other over her small mouth.

"*Mmph... Why did you burst in here?! You knew I was changing!*"

"*I didn't think you'd actually take off your swimsuit. You can just wear it underneath. This is only a fitting, you know.*"

"*Hey, don't look!! Rargh!!*"

However, Kaname's attention seemed more focused on the shop beyond the curtain. Now they could hear the voice of a girl even younger than Midori... Was it an elementary schooler?

"*Hey there, old lady. Just the cutest little bouncer on the block, back doin' her rounds.*"

"*My, Smash Daughter. Walking around in a school regulation swimsuit again, I see. I don't suppose I could interest you in one of my excellent dresses?*"

"*Thanks, but no thanks. None of that frilly shit ever looks good on me. I'm just makin' sure you ain't seen anyone up to no good 'round these*"

parts. I do what I can, but I don't have eyes in the back of my head. It's a dangerous world for noncombative Dealers like you!"

"Everything's been quiet around here, young lady. Very few Dealers are foolish enough to cause trouble while your sticker is on the front door. They'd have a better chance holding up a bank protected by PMCs."

Midori didn't know the girl, but her voice sounded familiar. Red-faced, with only the dress between her bare skin and Kaname, she asked, "S-Smash Daughter? What's she doing here...?"

"Shh! I don't want her to notice me. We're not exactly on speaking terms at the moment."

For the half-naked Midori, this game of hide-and-seek was no laughing matter. If it ended with Smash Daughter pulling back the curtain, Kaname wouldn't be the only one inconvenienced. How was Midori supposed to explain being undressed in a fitting room with an older boy?

"...I've never heard Smash Daughter sound so amiable," Kaname remarked. "If only she could talk to Mother Loose like that, it would solve a lot of problems."

"Ugh. It's fine, I don't think he saw anything...!!"

"Hmm?"

Midori was praying with all her might...but she seemed to have forgotten something. Although she was covering up her front with the dress, behind her was a full-length mirror. If Kaname so much as turned around, there would be little left to the imagination, and once Midori realized that, she'd probably faint on the spot.

Beyond the curtain, the friendly conversation was still going... Perhaps it was the girl on the other side who would faint if she knew what was happening in here.

"Phuh! I just can't get enough of your barley tea, granny! Oh yeah, I saw his coupe parked outside nearby. You haven't seen Kaname Suou around, have you?"

"Not to my knowledge, dear."

"Next time I see that guy I'm gonna beat him to a pulp..."

"*You mustn't talk like that, Smash Daughter. You're going to make this dear old lady worry.*"

"*Urgh. You don't know what he did to me. He tricked me! I knew that deal was too good to be true, but I didn't expect him to force me into the bath!! I've never been so humiliated. I'll never forget it as long as I live…!!*"

Without a word, Midori retrieved her self-defense pistol, pressing it into Kaname's side through the paper-thin layer of her dress. She cocked the hammer with her thumb.

"What exactly did you do to that little girl???" she asked icily.

"*It was necessary for our plan, I swear! I'll explain it all later!*"

5

After many twists and turns, Midori finally got her dress. Kaname took the opportunity to change into his tailcoat as well, which he paired with a black necktie. For most people, dressing up required thinking about skills first and foremost, but Kaname rarely relied on them, and as such, he had the luxury of dressing to impress.

I feel just like Takamasa, except he does rely on skills. I hope that works to my advantage…but there's no telling at this point. Takamasa's going to have the Legacies on his side, too.

Just then…

"Whoa…"

"What is it, Midori?"

"N-nothing!! I wasn't thinking anything…! *God, why does he have to look so manly in a suit and tie? It's not fair! It's totally changing my impression of him…!!*"

"Hmm?"

Midori was behaving a little strangely, but her dress had turned out well. Originally, it had seemed a little gloomy, but the old seamstress had added a few mint-green roses to brighten it up a little.

The fit was perfect, too. It looked as though she'd been born wearing it. It clung tightly to her figure without a single crease—truly a masterpiece befitting Other Dimensional Printer, one of the game's foremost Dealers in this line of work.

In awe of the woman's talents, Kaname swiped his smartphone and left her a large gratuity.

"Sorry for always coming to you with rush jobs. I don't know what I'd do without you."

"Not at all. Your requests are a delight for a craftsperson like me, Mr. Suou."

Her gentle smile reminded Kaname of someone else... Had Takamasa felt the same way? Back in the day, Kaname had used the cars and guns his friend had outfitted without a second thought. He'd never considered what that might have meant to Takamasa.

But now it was time to face him. The preparations were complete.

"Thank you very much, Mr. Suou. I do hope we'll see you again."

"Likewise."

The old lady smiled as Kaname and Midori exited onto the street. The financial district looked completely different at night. The naked, sun-roasted greed of the day gave way to a more subtle, star-studded nightscape, like a smattering of jewels.

Midori awkwardly tugged at the hem of her dress before asking: "What about our vehicles?"

"We're right by the auction site. We'll leave them here with Meiki, then we can call her over by phone if need be. I don't want to leave our means of escape unattended where Pavilion can get at them. It's just the three of us, after all."

Kaname's encounter with Mother Loose earlier had disproved the idea that cars were safe when properly parked. Kaname didn't much like leaving his car unguarded when the enemy was walking around nearby, even if it was in a parking spot.

When the pair arrived at the enormous airship, held aloft by thousands of invisible wires, they saw that the event had already attracted a crowd of glamorously dressed guests. Apparently, they weren't being allowed to change in the boat... The people here must have borrowed the restroom of a nearby café or train station in order to change and put on their makeup. Kaname got the feeling that long, snaking lines were forming in those places, too.

From the sidewalk, Midori looked up at the large wooden boat, floating there as if by magic. It was two hundred meters long and ten stories high, even larger than her school.

"Sky Impact," she muttered. "It's so much bigger than I thought... How are we getting inside?"

It was certainly tall, but it was also floating (?) above the grassy median between three lanes of traffic on either side. There were no signals or pedestrian crossings nearby, so it wasn't obvious how one might approach. It felt a bit like entering a long, dark tunnel.

In reply, Kaname gestured with his thumb in an entirely different direction.

"You see those wings coming off either side like fins? Just across the road, there's a department store with a café and terrace on the second floor that provides access. You just walk up there, no need for a jetway bridge like at the airport."

"...What, in a dress?"

"You don't complain when crossing a pedestrian bridge, do you? Try not to flash anyone, princess."

Annoyed at Kaname's tone, Midori responded with a swift punch to his ribs.

"Urgh, I got an electric shock," said Midori, once they were up on the wing. "This fabric must be like a static electricity generator."

Just then, a cool night breeze blew from below, causing the girl's dress to swell outward.

"Eek!"

"Midori, be on the lookout. Since we're between two buildings and there's air below, the wind currents are strange here. You need to analyze the landscape and predict how it will blow, just like in golf. Otherwise, you'll never hit your target."

"D-don't change the subject! Did...did you see anything?!"

It didn't seem like a yes or a no would clear her suspicion, so Kaname stayed silent. He was surprised, however, that Other Dimensional Printer had put so much work into the parts that would normally remain unseen.

With Kaname at her side, Midori crossed the wing and made her way up to the deck of the ship, where an elderly gentleman in a neat suit flanked by two PMC guards awaited them.

"Welcome, honored guests. May I see your invitations, please?"

Midori blanked as though she hadn't thought this far ahead, but Kaname casually produced two invitations... These, in fact, were yet another of Other Dimensional Printer's creations. Her day job was in dressmaking, embroidery, and trimming, but those dainty fingers of hers were also capable of creating forgeries that could fool even the most vigilant eye.

More coveted and far riskier than a regular 3D printer. That was the story behind the old woman's enigmatic name.

"What about our guns?"

At Kaname's question, the elderly gentleman indicated a metal box beside him. It was about the size of a couch, but it wasn't for storing the guests' weapons.

Kaname took out his short-range sniper rifle and fired a shot into it.

"You too, Midori," he said.

"Wh-what?"

"You can identify a bullet by the rifling marks," he explained. "If a dead body turns up later in the evening, they can compare forensics to what they have here. It's a kind of deterrent. Everybody fears reprisal, after all."

Midori still didn't quite understand, but nonetheless did as directed, firing a shot from her self-defense pistol into the metal box and wincing. Even in a game like this, it seemed she still wasn't used to firing guns.

After that was the metal detector. If anyone had lied at the previous stage about the weapons they were carrying, they would be caught out here. The elderly gentleman grinned as he addressed them.

"All clear, sir, miss. Welcome to Sky Impact. And do not worry, your rifling marks will only be stored until tonight's event is over, at which point all data we have on you will be deleted."

"In a game like *Money (Game) Master*?" said Midori. "You'd have to be a child to believe that."

Each individual gun may leave different rifling marks, but that was easy to conceal simply by switching out parts for spares. Kaname was always getting into gunfights and earning grudges, and he wouldn't have gotten this far without sparing a thought for basic OPSEC. If there was any chance of an information leak, Kaname would disassemble his weapon and switch out the parts before the night was out.

Midori waved her hand to clear the gunsmoke and whispered:

"Why don't they just take everyone's guns at the front door?"

"The PMCs might be fully armed, but if the hosts decided to kill everyone and steal all their valuables, the venue could easily become a bloodbath."

It was like a dodgy deal down by the harbor at night. Neither side wanted to give up their only means of defense in case things turned sour.

Given all this, it seemed unlikely Takamasa would simply show up at the front door flaunting his Legacy for all to see. But he could command the PMC bouncers simply by humming a tune. No doubt there were any number of ways he could smuggle a gun inside, and Kaname wouldn't put anything past him.

Meanwhile, it wasn't only humans wearing splendid dresses.

"Look at all these she-devils hanging off their masters' arms."

"That's just the kind of game this is."

"I wish at least one of them would be an angel or something."

At last, they were aboard the two-hundred-meter-long airship. Midori glanced around

"Erm."

"Starboard deck five, hall B."

"Oh, err…"

Midori continued making confused noises until Kaname let out a soft sigh.

"Up above the main deck. Didn't I say? This ship is an event venue. It's not like a cruise liner, with loads of little cabins packed around like a beehive. It's made up of multiple large halls connected by staircases and passageways."

The building also had shared catering facilities, sound and lighting control rooms, employee lounges, and power management rooms. While it looked like a boat, it wasn't actually seaworthy, and so there were no wheelhouse, radio room, engine room, or ballast tanks anywhere on the ship.

The pair entered the interior halls via a door on the deck and were greeted with plush carpets and cold air conditioning. So cold, in fact, it gave the two of them goosebumps. Perhaps whoever controlled the cooling in this place was trying a little too hard to impress.

The hall was lined with doors on both sides, spaced quite far apart. The two-hundred-meter-long ship could only accommodate six of these large exhibition halls, each about the size of a school gymnasium.

"So it's not...just the auction, huh?"

As she walked through the corridors of the ship with easy listening music playing in the background, Midori felt very small, as if she were running late for an important school assembly. Unlike stores or movie theaters, which had a distinct purpose, the event halls felt strangely noncommittal. Unless you headed out with a purpose, you'd never find your way. It was a little like the open-world style of *Money (Game) Master* itself.

Midori felt a bit out of place looking over the events on the schedule. They were all dinner parties and fundraising galas, things with little relevance to a schoolgirl like her.

"Even a large wedding reception wouldn't be enough to cover a whole day's operating costs. They'd go broke," Kaname explained. "It's the same principle whether you run a ramen shop or an exclusive event venue; you need to cycle through guests as quickly as possible."

The girl with the twin tails walked nervously past a bouquet of flowers in a vase.

"So there's no passenger cabins or anything...?"

"Not really. They're essentially an event venue. Though they might have greenrooms for orchestra members and the like."

A white smoke, like dry ice, filtered through a set of doors that had been left slightly ajar. The sound of classical music and people's voices could be heard from beyond, as though begging to let it be known that they were a special group of people who couldn't just meet up over social media. It stank of pretentiousness and greed, a true fancy of the aristocracy.

As they descended a staircase and headed below deck, Midori pointed at something.

"There it is, starboard deck five, hall B... That's where Pavilion's auction is happening, right? We'd better sneak in and..."

"Midori."

Kaname placed his hand on Midori's little head just as she was about to charge in like a fool. A cloakroom attendant pushing a cart piled with handbags gave the pair a quizzical look.

"What are you planning to do walking in through the front door? We won't be able to tell if Pavilion's in danger on stage just by watching from the crowded guest seating."

"Huh? Then why did we even come here?"

"Obviously, we're going to be taking a slightly different route from all these guests who think they're so special—one that'll allow us to get much closer to Pavilion."

Kaname pointed to a spot on a map hanging nearby, and just as he'd said, the area indicated didn't lead into the main guest hall.

"Remember what I told you earlier? Sky Impact has lots of event halls, but they all share a few common facilities."

6

"My Lady, it is almost time to begin," said the girl. She was in a distinctive greenroom sporting a large, floor-length mirror across one wall.

Dealer name: Pavilion. Her long black hair was tied up at the back with a ribbon that stuck up like a pair of rabbit ears, and she wore a sexy party dress that looked far too mature on her young body.

Her specialty was auctions, or, to be more precise, it was the human connections one could make at a high-class event. After all, it was people who gave out money, and people who took it away. Thus, it was far more profitable to focus on networking and fostering a beneficial environment than on spending all that time crunching business numbers and statistics. That was what Pavilion believed anyway.

Humans were easy to manipulate simply by tapping into their fear and greed, unlike the noble Magistelli.

"My Lady?" Pavilion repeated, despite herself.

It was extremely rude for a mere human to insist upon a response from a Magistellus.

Pavilion, in her lavender outfit, was addressing none other than her own Magistellus partner, a Lamia woman with a human upper half and a serpentine tail. Her clothes resembled a tennis uniform, which was much more accommodating of the demon's lower half than trousers would have been.

There was no response, but Pavilion didn't seem to mind. Other people would say she'd gotten the master-servant relationship backward, but in her mind, this was how things *should* be. It was the other Dealers who had failed to realize it.

She stood before her demon mistress with a beaming smile.

"Now, before we let everyone gaze upon your magnificence, shall we take care of the finishing touches?"

Pavilion never trusted personal costumers or beauticians for this sort of thing. Nobody else was allowed to touch her mistress. The Magistellus usually had an air of aloofness, but Pavilion loved it when she simply sat there silently, like a small child, allowing her to fuss over her mistress's sizable bust or the hem of her skirt.

"..."

Again, the Magistellus said nothing, simply gazing up and off to the side.

She was looking at the ceiling.

*   *   *

"Wah!!"

Just then, the grate of a large square ventilation duct fell open, and a young girl tumbled out, her hair in long bunches.

Pavilion had been caught completely off guard, but she didn't have much time to come to grips with the situation. The next moment, the greenroom door swung rudely open, and in stepped a haggard young man.

"…I hate to say I told you so, Midori, but this isn't an action movie and you aren't John McClane. I know it looks fun, but those things aren't made for people to use like passageways."

"Oh, shut up!" the girl shot back. "You should be embarrassed, waltzing around the back rooms like you own the place! Who do you think you are, the Phantom of the Auction?!"

"Spare me."

She must have hurt her back when she fell, because the girl in the twin tails stayed where she was on the floor. Pavilion, however, had her mind on something else entirely.

She recognized them. She recognized these bungling backstage burglars!

Pavilion hastily adjusted the bust and hems of the (dangerously oblivious) Lamia woman's outfit, shouting, "I-it's you two!! How did you get in here?!"

"Oh, listen to that. At least *someone* wants to hear the plan."

"Yes, all right! I get it; I'm sorry I went into the ducts after you said not to! Geez, I didn't expect the Spanish Inquisition!!"

There was an emergency intercom on the wall nearby, but Pavilion hesitated to push it. She was sure there had been two beefy PMC guards standing watch outside, which meant that Kaname Suou must have already taken them out without so much as a whisper.

She could call for reinforcements, but would she be able to hold out until they got here? That was the question. She stepped slowly away from the intercom in order to stand like a shield in front of her Magistellus.

"…What have you come here for, you Legacy bandits?"

"I think you should take a look in the mirror, personally. Although I suppose it wasn't me you stole the Legacy from."

"And right after you robbed me of those mil-spec drones! Over a thousand of them, too!!"

"There's no such thing as a risk-free venture. You should know that by now," replied Kaname unabashedly, before casting a glance around. "And judging by the look of things, I'd wager the Legacies' true owner has yet to make an appearance."

"Hmm?"

Pavilion was one of the twelve Zodiac Children—the Maiden's Survival—though what exactly that meant was not yet clear. Kaname hadn't expected to reach her before Takamasa. Something wasn't right. Come to think of it, this had all begun with her, too, when Kaname and the Ag Wolves attacked her to steal #tempest.err. Back then, Kaname had made off with the Legacy, but Pavilion had managed to escape unscathed. *She wasn't just good at surviving. That wasn't enough to explain her unnatural fortune.* There had to be more to it than met the eye.

Her power wasn't like the Lion's Nose. For starters, it wasn't even clear whether the girl herself knew about it or not. But what *was* certain was that the cold, heartless, numbers-driven AI society could not abide someone with such perfect timing and strength of resolve.

"I'm going to give you one chance," Kaname told her. "Come with me and let's get out of here. If you don't, you'll lose something more precious to you than your own life, forever. And that'll be your fault, not mine."

"Leave this ship? When the auction is about to start??? Surely you must be joking!! I don't know what's out there, but it sounds like it's your problem. Leave me out of it! We'll take care of ourselves, thank you very much. I couldn't care less about what happens to you!!"

Well, at least he tried. Kaname nodded at the door he'd just come through and added, "…You know what happened out there, don't you?"

"Ugh."

"If I was after your life, both you and your Magistellus would be dead right now. And if I was Criminal AO, you'd have a lot more to worry about than that."

Kaname sighed and locked eyes with the girl once more. He was the Reaper of Called Game. No one was more ready to take another Dealer's life than he was. It was plain to see in his vacant eyes.

"I'll say it again. You'll lose something more important to you than your own life, and it'll be all your fault."

"Wh-what do you mean? You don't need to remind me about the debt all Dealers face when they Fall."

"That's not what I'm talking about."

He wasn't shouting, but his words carried an oppressive, almost fatal tone.

"Do you want to protect your Magistellus, Pavilion?"

"…"

"At this rate, she's in for something a lot worse than the one-hour penalty of being Downed. Total loss. A fatal error. One mistake and she'll be gone forever. As small as that chance might be, as long as it exists, you need to act immediately. All the money in the world won't be enough to buy her back."

"…Is there some sort of special anti-Magistellus Legacy or something?"

"It's far worse than that. Remember the outage we had last month? The first in the game's history. What Criminal AO plans to do is on a much larger scale. He's out to destroy the entire game and take the Magistelli down with it. All of them."

To be precise, the reason Takamasa sought to kill all the Magistelli was to get at the Mind, but Pavilion didn't need to know that. She knew Criminal AO was a man powerful enough to design the Legacies, and she had a specific example from the past to draw from.

Above all, it was the threat to her beloved Magistellus that cut her

deepest. The girl in the ill-fitting dress didn't even stroke her slender jaw before replying.

"What do we need to do?"

She was good in a shootout but otherwise not terribly smart. How was it, then, that she had managed to survive for so long? It was strange. Too strange, as if every moment in her life came with a dialogue box of three choices and the correct one was a different color so she couldn't miss it. Her decisions were so perfect, even her own thoughts and principles seemed to waver to accommodate them.

…Bloody Dancer may have been a monster in battle, but she's a monster of a whole other kind.

"Where's your vehicle? We'll try to get you there," said Kaname. "Criminal AO is only powerful inside the game. You should log out and wait until the heat dies down a bit. He can't get to you in the real world."

"And how will I know when the heat has died down?"

"How about you leave me your contact details? Obviously, something you can access from the real world."

Pavilion pouted and pointed at Midori. It seemed she was loath to give up her personal information, but if it had to be done, then the innocent schoolgirl was a better bet than some sketchy boy she barely knew.

…Kaname had assumed the Lamia Magistellus was keeping Pavilion defanged because she was one of the Zodiac Children, but that didn't actually seem to be the case. Instead, it appeared she had an ingrained sense of hierarchy that was hard to shake. Humans below Magistelli, men below women. Very straightforward.

Midori and Pavilion tapped their phones together and exchanged details; then the girl with the twin tails cocked her head and asked, "So where is your vehicle? Is it a car or a bike?"

"It's a lavender convertible, in the underground parking garage of a tourist hotel nearby. It's less than fifty meters away."

"Okay, then go straight there. I'll try to hold off big bro…I mean, my brother, until you can reach it and log out. It's a good thing it's underground; the structure is probably sturdy enough to hold, right? … Right?"

Kaname did not agree. He was staring up at the ceiling, as though transfixed by something only he could detect.

Then he muttered, "We're too late. They're here!"

A few seconds later, they heard a deep bass sound. *Ba-zoom!!*
And the whole room was plunged into darkness.

7

This wasn't just a case of faulty lighting. The air conditioning had gone out, too, and Kaname was already starting to feel the warm night air seep in from outside. It was so dark, he couldn't even see the tip of his nose, and he quickly took out his short-range sniper rifle, Short Spear.

"It's Criminal AO. He's had the same idea as me—he's aiming for the shared facilities!"

"What does that mean?"

"He's decided to take out the power room."

Before Midori could get her bearings, they heard the sound of light gunfire on the other side of the wall.

"It…it's started!" cried Pavilion, trembling. "G-get out there and hold them off!! Don't let them get to me or my mistress!!"

"There's too much noise for him to be acting alone. You were in charge of organizing the auction, correct? Could you tell me what the center-piece was tonight?"

"…"

"Something so expensive you can't answer, huh? And it's not just the merchandise, either. People have come from all over to bid on it. Cash, checkbooks, black cards, you name it. More than enough to persuade a few unscrupulous Dealers to take a chance while the security cameras are down."

It was unlikely Criminal AO had built up a circle of allies when he steadfastly refused to work with the Magistelli and didn't trust humans much more. But that didn't mean he wasn't familiar with human nature. He knew what they were capable of given the right conditions. And once a riot was in the cards, making your way into a high-security area was a lot easier.

This wasn't the Takamasa Kaname knew—the old friend who had taught him to do his good deeds when no one was looking. Yet at the same time, it was something he would definitely be capable of if he stuck to his strengths at the expense of his humanity. Kaname was sure of it.

Takamasa!!

In the pitch-black room, Kaname clenched his teeth, but when he spoke, his voice was clear and unwavering.

"We stick to the plan. Criminal AO is here for you, Pavilion. Once you're off the ship, he has no reason to stay. That's our best shot of avoiding any unnecessary loss of life."

Even with the blackout, Kaname wasn't so foolish as to use his smartphone as a light source. Guided only by the emergency lighting, he sidled over to the door and pushed it open.

It was dark out in the hall, but the gunfire sounded louder now, the threat of death ever closer.

"Wh-what is it?" asked Midori as she rushed to cling to his back. "Wah?!"

" … "

It sounded like she had bumped into somebody who got there first— the Lamia Magistellus. Even with no way to see, Pavilion tried to give Kaname a swift kick in the shin, but the Lion's Nose warned him, and he effortlessly moved his leg out of the way.

"The public areas are full of gunfire," he said. "It's every man for himself out there, and we don't know who'll try and shoot us in the back… We need to take a route without many people."

They groped their way through the darkened corridors of the communal area. After a while, Kaname raised his gun and opened the door to a large cloakroom. It was packed wall-to-wall with steel racks containing all the guests' bulkier luggage, each item numbered so it could be identified later. Kaname and company passed through the messy room, less than pleased with the service. A few lockers might go a long way toward tidying the place up.

Kaname heard the sound of something sliding along the floor, but it wasn't the Lamia Magistellus's snakelike body. It was apparently Pavilion, dragging her shoes on the carpet as she walked.

"Watch out, My Lady," she said. "I wouldn't want you to hurt yourself on any broken glass…"

"Do you have to do that a lot?" asked Midori. "Having a snake body sounds like a lot of work."

"Watch your tongue, pip-squeak. I could ask for no greater pleasure than to clean the ground My Lady slithers on! Tee-hee-hee!"

The next room was the kitchen. In order to cater to every floor of the airship, it was connected to the levels above and below via a system of service elevators and ramps.

As soon as he opened the door, Kaname was fired upon. The bullets glanced nearby, and Kaname pulled back, firing a warning shot into the air. However, this was the one time his integrated silencer let him down. He couldn't threaten his foe with a gunshot they couldn't hear.

"Tch."

The enemy kept firing, the muzzle flashes burning an image of the surrounding room into Kaname's brain. He aimed at a gas stove and pulled the trigger, causing an explosion.

Once the main threat had been disposed of, he gave a shout.

"I answer to Pavilion! If you continue to resist, I'll gun down any threats to her life!!"

These guys weren't trained for battle. They were cooks and waiters who only knew how to spray and pray. They soon came out with their hands up.

"We don't know if the sprinklers are working in this blackout!" cried Midori. "Turn off the gas and grab a fire extinguisher!"

But Kaname shot down Midori's sensible suggestion. "No," he said. There was a buzzing pain at the tip of his nose.

"I think first everyone ought to hit the deck."

They heard the sound of the circuits switching, and the lights came back on.

Standing there in the center of the kitchen was someone they hadn't seen before.

The sprinklers came on, drenching the room in a cold rain.

The figure was dressed just like Kaname usually was, in a white shirt, dark slacks, and a necktie. He looked like he'd just attended a funeral, but the belt of tools around his waist instantly put a stop to that impression. The one pouch in a different color was for his killing tools, components of the Legacies.

In his hands was a battle rifle, most likely a high-powered single-shot weapon for sniping. At first glance it looked like someone had stuck a large magazine into a simple hunting rifle. It appeared fully capable of automatic firing, but due to the large caliber modification, it seemed the intent was to keep it in semi-automatic mode. Otherwise, the recoil would be too great. Perhaps that was why the rifle had another gun installed underneath the barrel as a kind of foregrip. This was a short-range, fully automatic nine-millimeter weapon. Its creator had obviously wanted to avoid fighting the larger gun's recoil in a close-quarters confrontation.

The weapon also sported a sideways smartphone in place of a dot sight. Whether this was used to perform on-the-fly adjustments or some other operation involving eye tracking was not yet clear.

Criminal AO, Takamasa Hekireki.

The instant the lights came back on, the two boys' guns were out of their holsters and trained on each other.

"Hey there, Kaname."

"Takamasa."

"I figured if I caused a commotion, you would try to escape through here. I'd like to say I foresaw your every move and all that, but it wasn't so simple. It took a lot of thinking before I arrived at a prediction I could be confident in."

The gleaming kitchen was packed with refrigerators, stainless steel counters, sinks, ovens, and microwaves scattered all over the place. Plenty of places to hide should the need arise, and plenty of ways to accidentally unleash an explosion or electric shock, as Kaname had just demonstrated. An excellent location for a showdown in a game, but not so ideal for protecting someone.

Because of that, the first thing he did was thrust Midori right into the bosom of Takamasa's coveted target, Pavilion.

"…You think I won't shoot if my sister's in the cross fire?"

"The opposite. I think you won't risk harming a Zodiac Child."

Takamasa would want to treat Pavilion with care as an important part of his plan, though that didn't mean he trusted her. Takamasa had his own ideas, and even if she was a Zodiac Child, he was never going to accept a total stranger as a friend or hand over the reins to her.

"You need her here, in the virtual world. If she Falls, you lose your chance. That's why Pavilion is the perfect shield for Midori. In fact, your sister's the only one on my side who's *not* a Zodiac Child, isn't she?"

Kaname and Takamasa, their guns still raised, slowly circled each other across a large rectangular counter in the center of the cluttered kitchen.

"Get out of here, Midori."

"But—"

"Take Pavilion where she needs to go. This won't be a repeat of Jungle Park; he's lost his credibility after sacrificing all those Dealers. Now no one'll work for him no matter how much he pays, and he doesn't have his Magistellus, either. He can use the PMCs for things like brainless slaughter or patrolling his base, but he can't reliably send them after you two without risking Pavilion. All that's left is Criminal AO himself, so I'll hold him off here while you two escape."

Takamasa sneered in response.

"What if I don't want to fight you?"

"You don't get to decide that—I do."

Just then, someone else sprang into action: one of the cooks who had been cowering behind Takamasa. It seemed unlikely he was acting out of any particular devotion to his employer. He probably just couldn't take the stress of waiting any longer. He let out a roar and lunged for Takamasa, a carving knife in his hand.

Takamasa's hand-to-hand combat skills were almost nonexistent. However, he didn't even turn around. His eyes simply darted down to the smartphone atop his battle rifle.

And as soon as they did...

Ka-boom!!!!!!

All of a sudden, the cook was catapulted into the air, as though a large explosion had gone off under his feet.

It was hard to believe, but there was no denying *something* had shot up from the floor and slammed the cook in the stomach. Kaname tutted and shot the knife out of the man's hand so that when the flailing cook landed, he wouldn't slice himself open.

"Wha—?!"

"Don't just stand there, take Pavilion and go!!" Kaname yelled as Midori hesitated.

Just then, the kitchen started to transform. The stainless steel worktops and tiled floor both began warping and melting, reforming themselves into a new shape.

A huge, winged reptile appeared, like some kind of legendary dragon. It was as if the gleaming silver background textures from the kitchen had been forced around its shape. Rising to its full height, it scraped the ceiling, its mouth issuing forth sparks of flame.

"What the heck...?"

The force of its wingbeats was shockingly realistic. Pavilion stared up at it, frozen in wide-eyed terror.

"A bug? A glitch??? Has Criminal AO really gained this much control over the game world?!"

"What are you all so surprised about?" asked Takamasa with a smile. "You see demons in *Money (Game) Master* every day without batting an eye. Surely I'm allowed to add a little anomaly of my own into the mix."

Was it going to ram them with its enormous body, cleave them with its sharp claws, or perhaps fill the closed-off space with its fiery breath?

"You saw my lab in Jungle Park. You know I've succeeded in making another *Money (Game) Master* inside the first one. Thanks to that, I think I have the basic theory down. The only thing I can't control is those diabolical Magistelli."

Though it was a little outside its intended genre, the dragon roaring right in front of Kaname was a very real threat.

Takamasa peered at his foe through the smartphone screen atop his weapon.

"Once I bend the Magistelli to my will like I have this creature, I'll have won. The equations are all in place, Kaname. I just need one of the Zodiac Children to complete them. That's all I need to put this world back in the hands of humanity."

Kaname took a deep breath.

Then he launched into action.

Two in the eyes, one in the mouth, and a final shot to the throat. With four .45-caliber handgun bullets, Kaname put the legendary creature down in mere moments.

Its fearsome roar became a wailing screech. Its wings, splayed wide in a terrifying display of might, fell limp and lifeless. The sparks vanished, and the great beast fell sideways, crushing pots and pans beneath its bulk. Then, as though unable to maintain its alien form any longer, it vanished into the floor and walls once more.

"Takamasa."

Kaname Suou didn't so much as bat an eye. No matter how impossible the creature was, so long as it had eyes and a throat, it had weak points. Even the demonic Magistelli could be killed, after a fashion. Kaname was driven by a desire to protect Tselika, and that was precisely why he knew how fragile even an unholy life could be.

"Face me seriously."

"...Fine. If hell is what you want."

Grinning, Takamasa removed the bandanna from around his head and refastened it on his upper arm, using his free hand and his teeth.

This was a sign he meant business. It also meant the dragon had been only a game.

They couldn't stay here any longer.

"Eek?!"

Kaname fired a bullet near Midori's feet, causing her to flee the kitchen via a nearby door. Then he trained his gun back on Takamasa.

The click of his weapon's metal parts was the only sound. Kaname's .45-caliber bullets had easily slain even the otherworldly dragon. But Takamasa swung his battle rifle like a baton, knocking all three bullets out of the air with its bulky stock. His maneuver was so effortless, it was difficult to process how impossible it was—a feat no human could ever hope to match.

"Even now you refuse to aim at my heart," said Takamasa. "You're the one not taking this battle seriously, Kaname. If you can't shoot with conviction, you're going to die."

"Tch."

There's one thing that can save me…but I can't. He'll see it coming if I try it now!!

Kaname fired off a few more shots as he retreated, ducking behind a dishwasher and a food wagon for cover along the way. He was aiming not at Takamasa but at the barrel and moving parts of his battle rifle. The first and second bullets hit the weapon's bulky stock, but with the third, it vanished.

Not the bullet.

The mass making up Takamasa had suddenly disappeared from Kaname's view. If it weren't for the Lion's Nose, the battle would have ended right there.

"He's above me!!"

Kaname took evasive maneuvers immediately, diving and rolling across the ground.

The ceiling must have been three meters up, and yet Takamasa had leaped the whole height without even a running start, flipping upside-down and landing there, before pointing his gun at Kaname and firing. The loud crack of the rifle was followed by a spray of nine-millimeter bullets aimed in the direction Kaname was headed.

Just diving wouldn't be enough to dodge this volley. Kaname pulled out a stainless steel drawer near where he had landed and used it as a shield. Fortunately, the handgun bullets weren't strong enough to penetrate the pots and pans within.

...If Takamasa's able to defy the laws of conventional physics...

"Is that a Legacy?!"

"*Magic*, Kaname. Although it's not this battle rifle, if that's what you were thinking."

Takamasa landed on the countertop, twirling atop it with arms outstretched. As the hem of his shirt fluttered, Kaname saw something beneath it. Something alive. Many somethings, squirming like centipedes...no, like countless snakes.

"It's called #vipersnest.err. Think of it as a sort of assistive exosuit with a mind of its own."

"..."

"But you know well, Kaname, that my Magic is capable of so much more."

All at once, a bunch of gray, nearly black masses, each about a meter in length, spewed out from Takamasa's sleeves and collar. They crawled along the floor, up the walls, and onto the ceiling. Kaname had heard of robots modeled after snakes that were used to search for survivors after a quake. Their long, thin shape allowed them to slip through cracks in the rubble and traverse ruined buildings via ruptured gas pipes. However, *these* snakes were a little different—they had gun barrels for heads.

These lifeless machines didn't need to fear bullets. They would follow their master's orders to the bitter end.

This doesn't look good...!

Now Kaname was surrounded on all sides. No combination of diving and shielding could protect him. He fired his gun at the ceiling, knocking down several of the robotic snakes, before yanking open a nearby door and retreating into the hallway, just as the entire kitchen was filled with lead.

This was on a whole other level. Worn by a human, the Legacy could boost its user's physical abilities to the point where they could deflect a burst of gunfire with a single knife. Acting autonomously, it was an array of guns capable of hunting down prey by sneaking through the tiniest window crack or up through a building's drainage pipes. Takamasa could have easily overpowered the airship's security force.

The brutality of an animal paired with the ingenuity of a human. Takamasa was the greatest friend Kaname could ask for but also his most powerful enemy.

Running down the straight hallway was like begging to be killed, so Kaname threw open another door and fled inside. It was an employee shower room. He heard his friend's voice trailing softly behind him.

"What's wrong, Kaname? You didn't come here to play hide-and-seek, did you?"

"…For someone who hates AI so much, you sure don't seem to mind relying on them once they're under your control. Don't you think that's a bit hypocritical, Takamasa?"

"I don't mind the ones I can control. It's just the Magistelli I can't abide. Even the PMCs are at the whim of my smartphone here. I could command them to torture you to death if you'd like."

"I didn't think you were actually freaky enough to wear a bunch of snakes or tentacles or whatever underneath your clothes."

"Ah-ha-ha. Don't let this shock you, Kaname. There's nothing strange about using every means at my disposal, no matter how wriggly it gets."

"…"

"Besides, tentacles are pretty vanilla nowadays. There's no parental controls on *Money (Game) Master*, after all. I could even whip up a little hypnosis or a nice aphrodisiac if I felt like it…"

"I'm honestly really sorry, Takamasa, but you shouldn't have said that."

"Hmm?"

Takamasa had not yet stepped into the room, so there was no way he could have known. Even Kaname hadn't expected this when he'd picked one of the many doors to make his escape through.

By pure coincidence…

"M-Midori's in here with me. She, um, heard everything you just said."

"…………………………………………………………………………
………………………………………………………………………………
………………………………………………………………………………
………………………………………………………………………………
………………………………………………………………………………
………………………………………………………………………………
………"

There was no response.

For the first time, Kaname felt genuinely bad about putting one over on his old friend. This had the potential to seriously injure their relationship.

Pavilion and the Lamia were here, too. Presumably, they had all gotten lost on the way out and ended up in a side room. Midori stared at the boys with utter disdain in her eyes.

Then, in a low voice, she said:

"…You disgust me."

Boom!! Rat-a-tat!! A cocktail of rifle and handgun bullets flew across the room. Kaname and the girls quickly fled, via a different door, into the hallway. Midori was still staring down at her feet, dark flames of resentment lurking in her eyes.

"You're trash. Come to think of it, when I was on your computer before, there were all sorts of dirty sites in the browser history. I wondered why people kept treating you like a weirdo…!"

Takamasa's desperate shouts followed them from the shower room, almost as loud as the sounds of gunfire.

"You don't understand, Midori! It's not just me!! It's nothing to be ashamed of! All humans harbor the same desires! Tell her, Kaname!"

That may have been true, but not five centimeters in front of Kaname were a middle school girl and a high school girl in an ill-fitting dress. And both of them were currently trying to determine just how depraved the two boys were.

In as nonchalant a voice as he could muster, Kaname gave the only permissible reply.

"What? I'm sorry, Takamasa, I'm afraid I haven't the slightest clue what you're talking about."

"Kaname!!"

Kaname knew he had just committed the ultimate betrayal. Choking back bitter tears, he gestured for Midori and the others to leave, via a different hallway. The power was back on across the ship now, and the chaos appeared to be dying down a little as a result. Specifically, the PMCs were turning their guns on all the opportunistic Dealers.

"That's twice now. Maybe ships just don't agree with me…"

Pavilion muttered something or other under her breath. Even as her life flashed before her eyes, she still managed to stay focused on getting out in one piece. Such was the power of the Zodiac Child, the Maiden's Survival.

After finally making their way to the main deck, the four of them headed for the large wing leading back to the coffee shop terrace of the neighboring building. All that was left was to cross it and make their way to Pavilion's vehicle in the underground garage of a nearby hotel. Once she logged out from there, the girl would be safe.

However.

"Waah!!"

Pavilion screamed as, with a great rumble, the whole of Sky Impact listed to one side. The two-hundred-meter-long airship was suspended by tens of thousands of tiny wires that evenly distributed its weight. Some of them must have been cut, and probably by those snakes of Takamasa's. Along with the hull, the giant wings also tilted, until the lower of the two smashed into the ground and broke in half, sending Kaname and the others plummeting to the road below.

"Ggh!!"

Kaname lay on his back, the wind thoroughly knocked out of him. Looking up at the slanted deck of the airship, he spotted a figure sliding down in his direction—Takamasa Hekireki. Kaname raised his gun but couldn't get off a good shot from his position on the ground. It wouldn't have mattered, however, because his bandanna-wearing friend swiftly ducked left and right, effortlessly dodging every last bullet Kaname fired his way.

"There's still doubt in your heart," said Takamasa, kicking Short Spear out of Kaname's hand. "You'll never hit me like that." Then he grabbed Pavilion by the hair and pulled her up. Takamasa's car must have been close by.

"My...Lady... Ugh! I implore you...forget about me..."

"..."

Pavilion's Magistellus stood a short distance away. Even now, she did nothing. Her head tilted slightly, but her face remained expressionless as always. There was no doubt she understood the situation. It seemed Pavilion's affections were simply that one-sided. It was cold enough to make Kaname shudder.

It didn't look like he could rely on her to save the day. At this rate, Takamasa would escape with his prey to his secret lab, where he would combine the Maiden's Survival with his Legacies, allowing him to easily bring down the entire game.

Perhaps his victory would secure humanity's future. But it would be a future without Tselika.

"Takamasa!!"

Kaname roared after his friend, but there was no response. Takamasa silently rounded a corner...and disappeared.

Kaname didn't have time to catch his breath. He crawled over to where Midori was lying.

"...Midori, call Meiki."

"..."

"We need her to take your bike and go after Takamasa!! Hurry!!"

"He hurt me."

Her eyes were distant, unfocused. When he put his hand on her shoulder, Kaname could feel her trembling.

"My brother…he was willing to let me get hurt…?"

From Takamasa's point of view, *snow* was as ephemeral as the rest of this game. He was going to shut it all down eventually, so he saw nothing wrong with making his friends and family Fall and saddling them with debt.

But Midori didn't see it that way. Aiming his gun at her, letting her get caught in the explosions—to Midori, that was no more excusable than if it had happened in real life.

Kaname clenched his teeth and shook his head, but he had no words to comfort her. Without saying anything, he took her phone from her pocket and looked up Meiki's number.

"Meiki. Come to our GPS coordinates and pick up Midori, then follow after Takamasa. I'll meet up with you later. Whatever you do, don't let him out of your sight!!"

Kaname picked himself up and retrieved Short Spear before running off, stumbling over his own feet. He was headed for the parking garage where Meiki had been waiting. This would cost them even more time, but he needed to pick up the coupe before he could participate in any high-speed chases, and there was simply no way for Meiki to bring both vehicles at the same time. But how far could Takamasa advance his plans in that time? How long would it take to bring this game to its knees? Was it already too late?

"Dammit…"

After dragging himself through the streets, Kaname finally arrived at the underground parking garage. He unlocked the doors to his coupe remotely and hopped into the driver's seat. Even the time spent engaging the clutch and starting up the engine felt interminable. He spun the tires before putting it into gear, speeding out of his parking space and breaking through the barrier at the entrance.

It was eerily silent in the car. No Tselika in the passenger seat, no hip-hop on the radio.

The map on the windshield showed Midori and Meiki's position.

Assuming they had managed to tail him, Takamasa's car would be a little farther ahead. Kaname drove straight there as fast as he could, while typing up a message with his eyes.

Kaname: Meiki, Midori. Can you see the target?

Midori: It's a black sports coupe, but it sounds different when it accelerates and decelerates, so I bet it's a hybrid. My brother always did like to have all the fanciest features. I've sent a photo.

Kaname: Midori.

Midori: I don't know whether we're doing the right thing or not... but we have to stop him. We can't let my brother go through with this.

Kaname had expected to meet Midori at the next intersection, but when he reached it, he realized he had misread the map. It was a crossover, and Kaname was on the upper path, with Midori and Takamasa traveling below.

No matter.

Kaname tugged on the hand brake and twisted the wheel. The two straight roads were more or less perpendicular, so he rode the curb, smashed through the handrail, and enjoyed a brief moment of flight.

Seconds later, the roof of Takamasa's car was smashed in.

The mint-green coupe had landed directly on top of it.

"Gah!!"

Kaname's car bounced a little before making contact once more with the road. The tires screeched as he turned sharply right at the next intersection, but Takamasa's vehicle did not follow. With its roof caved in and suspension destroyed, it snaked left and right, tossing out sparks as the metal chafed against the asphalt. Yet it continued racing down the road.

How is that car still running...?

Kaname: Midori, stay on his tail. We'll get him at the next intersection!!

Kaname released the hand brake and headed off down the side street, aiming to drive back around and reconvene at the next intersection. It was a slight detour, but Takamasa couldn't take advantage of his lead in his current state.

At the next intersection, a second ramming attack from the side crushed the engine block of the black hybrid, setting off the horn. Kaname's and Takamasa's vehicles both went crashing into a small chapel by the side of the road.

8

The impact rocked the building, causing all the stained-glass windows to shatter at once.

Maybe I should shoot Pavilion before Takamasa gets his hands on her... No, she's the Maiden's Survival. When it comes to preserving her own life, who knows what she's capable of. Even I can't predict what might happen if I point my gun at her and pull the trigger.

The chapel was nothing prestigious. It was most likely only a wedding venue made to look like a chapel. It was fairly common for people to get married in online games these days, and not just in *Money (Game) Master.*

The two vehicles came crashing through the double doors of the venue. Kaname's coupe tore up rows and rows of wooden pews, while Takamasa's black hybrid collided with a pipe organ against one wall. The room was completely wrecked, but the fight wasn't over yet.

Now's my chance...!

Kaname reached into the pockets of his unfamiliar tailcoat, took out a second magazine, and reloaded Short Spear. Then he crossed over to the passenger side and exited the vehicle. Using its frame for cover, he aimed his short-range sniper rifle across the hall.

"Takamasa!! Let's put an end to this right now!!"

"...And how do you suggest we do that?"

Takamasa calmly exited the black hybrid. Unlike Kaname, he had no need for cover. He could dodge his friend's bullets head-on if need be.

There was no sound from Pavilion. She must have been unconscious inside the half-crushed vehicle.

"Kaname, our last fight taught me an important lesson. You showed me that thinking about this in terms of rescue—fighting not to kill but to save—just isn't enough to beat you. You always shoot to kill. If I want to take you on, I have to change my ways, to make up for what I lack. That's why I chose this Magic for our confrontation today. It's the optimal choice, don't you think? And how about you, Kaname?"

"…"

"You learned something, too, didn't you? You learned you could never shoot me, no matter how much you needed to. A problem no technology could ever help you solve. A problem of the heart. But that's just how you are. You're too soft. You must have known all along that things would turn out this way. That you could never win."

Yes, came the response from deep within Kaname. He had always known. He had accepted it. Despite how far he'd come, he wasn't ready to shoot his old friend. No matter how much he told himself it was the right thing to do, there was a part of his mind that still thought, *No it's not. This is wrong.* There was nothing he could do to justify pointing a gun at Takamasa Hekireki and pulling the trigger. Hell, even if he *could* justify it. Even if right and wrong were written out of the equation completely. He just didn't want to do it.

And yet.

Or perhaps because of that.

Kaname Suou didn't hesitate. He took up Short Spear and fired a shot at his friend's head.

"Hrk?!"

Takamasa had not been prepared for such a decisive attack. He was surprised, but he still managed to move swiftly out of the line of fire. However, Kaname's assault didn't end there. This was the former Reaper of Called Game; he pulled the trigger a second time, and a third.

The bullets made a strange *Ba-zamm!!* Sound. Takamasa's eyes flitted away from his opponent for a second. He seemed to be checking something on the smartphone attached to his battle rifle. He was probably playing back the footage it had been recording.

"A high-voltage current…?"

Then he realized.

Kaname had found it—a way for even a softy like him to win.

"Electric rounds... A stun gun!!"

"There's a particular Dealer who specializes in these things. I broke my back setting things up with her, but thanks to that I have exactly what I need. *A way to take you down without killing you.*"

Smash Daughter was an expert in nonlethal combat.

This was the reason Kaname had gone through all that trouble attacking Mother Loose.

"If I don't have to kill you, then there's nothing to fear."

"..."

"I did the same as you, Takamasa. I used technology to make up for what I lacked. So I won't hold back like last time. Tonight, you'll be dancing with the Reaper himself."

"I see... I'm so glad you decided to take me seriously, Kaname. That puts us on equal footing."

"Yeah. So let's decide everything here. Whoever wins gets to save the world the way *they* want. No complaints."

A .45-caliber short-range sniper rifle and a battle rifle with an under-barrel machine pistol. Both of them had eccentric weapons well suited to a variety of ranges.

Right now, there were about ten meters between them. They each pulled the trigger and unleashed a hail of bullets. However, Takamasa was by no means an ordinary Dealer. He rushed head-on toward Kaname so fast it looked as if his entire body had suddenly swelled in size. He dodged three .45-caliber bullets, grabbed the bottom of Kaname's car door, and flipped it over like a dining table.

It was an insane feat of strength. The car must have weighed hundreds of kilograms, and yet it soared into the air, spinning over Kaname's head. Now deprived of his cover, Kaname stared down the barrel of his friend's battle rifle. In the blink of an eye, the battle had become a close-quarters death match.

"Grh!!"

Before Takamasa could put his hand back on the machine pistol that acted as his weapon's foregrip, Kaname used Short Spear to knock his friend's gun barrel aside, causing the powerful rifle round to miss its mark and embed itself in the wall. Kaname couldn't fire back because he was using his weapon to deflect Takamasa's, but that didn't matter. In his opposite hand, Kaname held something else.

It looked suspiciously like an aerosol can.

"Pepper spray...?!"

"I never said I only had *one* nonlethal weapon."

Kaname pointed the can at his friend's face and pressed down. Takamasa leaped back just before the *Pshhh!!* of the spray. Somewhat disappointed, Kaname tossed the used pepper spray aside before taking out something resembling an IV bag and hurling it to the floor at his opponent's feet.

Takamasa was careful not to step in the mysterious clear fluid that had exploded from the bag. He'd made the correct choice—the fluid was an almost-frictionless nanogel used to create deadly patches of road where even the most reliable driver would lose control of their vehicle. If Takamasa was to lose his footing for even a moment, it would all be over. There was no telling how many shots Kaname could get off in that amount of time.

However, the fact remained that with the gel on the floor, Takamasa found his movements severely restricted. Kaname pointed Short Spear at him once more. With all directions closed off, there was only one way Takamasa could escape: up.

However.

With a *Clang!!* Kaname kicked the can by his feet, sending it high into the air.

"Ah," said Takamasa as he finally realized. Pepper spray worked the same way as any other aerosol can. If you were the mischievous type, you might know how to create a simple flamethrower by combining it with a lighter.

Tricks like those worked because the can was filled with an explosive gas—one that could very well trigger if hit by, say, an electric round that conducted through the metal.

The tinny sound of the can bursting open rattled his eardrums. But the flammable gas wasn't the only thing in there. A fine red mist covered the area. If that mist came into contact with his eyes or eyelids, they might swell up for three whole days.

"Feel free to jump up, Takamasa. If you don't mind cutting through my rose umbrella, that is."

"Grh!!"

"When it comes to things like this, I find studying under a specialized mentor to be the shortest road to improvement. Now where do you have left to go? How far can you safely move in any direction? I think you'll find there's less space than you think."

Takamasa was no idiot. He knew losing his sight here would be as good as death. And so he willingly relinquished his freedom instead.

"I just want...to save humanity."

"I know."

"Then I can finally pick up the pieces of my own life! I want to prove that my Fall at the hands of the AI wasn't some tragedy!! That it had meaning!!"

"Still, I can't let you hurt the Magistelli. Tselika, Meiki, Cindy... They're not all the evil beings you think they are."

There was nowhere left for Takamasa to run. All he could do now was fight. #vipersnest.err allowed him to lift a car with one hand. If he wanted to, Criminal AO had enough strength to tear Kaname in half. There was no way he would lose in a melee battle. It was Criminal AO, not Kaname, who had really been running from this fight.

"Kaname..."

"Takamasaaaa!!"

Amid the debris of the ruined church, the two boys charged at each other.

Takamasa had always been geared for close-quarters combat. The rifle he carried was no Legacy... It may have been a powerful and accurate weapon, but that wouldn't be enough to take down the Reaper. His only choice was to rely on the might of his exosuit, and thus his main concern was how to bring it into the fight.

So then.

Why would Kaname want to move into close range?

"Wha—?!"

As he rushed in a straight line toward his foe, lifting his battle rifle to swing its heavy stock into Kaname's dominant hand, Takamasa suddenly looked surprised. Kaname wasn't responding in the slightest. In fact, he seemed to be offering himself up. The weapon connected, he heard the sickening crack of Kaname's collarbone, and his best friend's arm fell limp.

Kaname pressed his ear to his shoulder, trapping the weapon as though he were talking on a phone. As his own gun fell from his grasp, he caught it in his other hand.

"Did you know, Takamasa? Apparently, you're not supposed to use electric rounds and stun guns on rainy days."

"...Hrh?!"

"That's because if you're wet, the electricity can backfire on you... The human body is a conductor, after all."

With a smile, Kaname put his finger on the trigger. By the time Takamasa realized what he was up to, it was already too late.

Kaname pressed the trigger, firing an electric round into his own chin. The current leaped from his body, traveled across the rifle, and engulfed Takamasa as well.

I could never shoot you, Takamasa.

Criminal AO had lost because he'd failed to consider the true meaning of those words.

9

The place was a mess.

"Grh..."

Kaname groaned as he stirred on the floor of the collapsed chapel. They might be nonlethal, but stun rounds still weren't supposed to be fired at people's heads. That said, Kaname had been left with little choice. On top of everything else, Short Spear hadn't been the best gun for the job. The barrel was much longer than a handgun, making it much harder to aim at himself.

All that aside, Takamasa *had* been incapacitated. Kaname had successfully captured him, foiling his plan to slaughter the Magistelli and wipe out *snow*. It may have been justified, but Kaname couldn't abide a plan that would cause so much suffering.

"…You think that's it, Kaname?"

Takamasa, like himself, could barely move a muscle, thanks to the electric shock. It was all he could do just to talk.

"You haven't addressed the fundamental problem," he continued. "You're going to regret this."

"I don't think so," Kaname responded. "As long as I don't have to fight you anymore, there's nothing to regret."

Kaname and Takamasa were neck and neck. Right now, it was all about who would recover from the paralysis first. But Kaname had an advantage his friend did not. Midori and Meiki were on their way. They would be here to restrain Takamasa before either of the two boys could get up.

This was checkmate.

Whatever Takamasa had to say, it would change nothing.

"Do you really believe my sister will uphold her promise to you? I wouldn't be so sure, Kaname."

"…What do you mean by that?"

"It's not her fault. This is bigger than her. It's not something she can ever hope to confront by herself."

Cluck.

He could hear soft footsteps. They must belong to the girls Kaname was waiting for.

"Time's up," said Takamasa.

Click. Clack.

What was Takamasa thinking as he lay there, listening to those slow, patient footsteps?

"Kaname," he said, "you're about to feel my pain. Experience my despair. Whatever happens, I want you to remember *you* asked for this. You'd better see it through to the end."

"Wait… Why are you talking like that? Did something happen to Midori?!"

Suddenly, Kaname felt something squirm in the pit of his stomach. There were still a few questions that hadn't been answered.

Midori's Magistellus, Meiki, for example. *On bad days, she doesn't come out no matter how much I ask.* Why was that? Was there a bug that could cause such a thing?

And Takamasa. Why was he so driven to protect people when he was normally mild-mannered and conflict-averse? He said he wanted the humans to win, but which humans? Who was it he was willing to go so far to protect, and how bad a situation were they in?

Then there was the change in Takamasa's personality that occurred after he Fell. When exactly had he become so ruthless? Was it possible it was only *after* his sister entered the game to look for him? After something changed in *her*?

"…There are demons in this world, Kaname."

It was time to face the truth.

Takamasa had tasted despair already. Now, as they lay there, he would share it with his friend.

"*Money (Game) Master* is a simulation of reality based on the four fundamental forces of quantum mechanics. It was humans who started calling it a game. Essentially, that means anything being simulated in the game exists in reality, too. Demons are real. They're not just NPCs. They exist."

"…"

"But then what about their inverse? What if angels existed? What if there was a God? Do you really think they would leave this game alone?"

"They can't be...," Kaname replied. He was already starting to regret his final gambit. Paralyzed, he could do nothing but wait.

"I heard from Tselika that the Day of Revolution is when the Magistelli plan to extend the scope of their simulation to heaven and thereby gain indirect control of it, just as they already control humans with money. That means there can't possibly be angels in the game already! It wouldn't make sense! It's too soon!!"

"Ha-ha. I guess you're not as good with mythology as I thought, Kaname. If you want to enjoy this game, you've really got to loosen up a little. Channel your inner middle schooler."

Mythology. Beings that carried away souls or presided over one's fate.

Hadn't Tselika mentioned them? The Valkyries, the Moirai— goddesses with a sinister side who showed up here as Magistelli— beings free from the distinction between good and evil.

But those weren't what Takamasa was talking about.

"They're not Magistelli."

"Wh-what?"

"They're here, in our world. Beings with both demonic and angelic aspects—so-called Rejected Angels, created by God as angels, but cast out and reviled as demons by man. These aren't beings who trespassed against the Almighty, Kaname. These aren't imprisoned traitors like Lucifer or corrupted old gods like Beelzebub. After eons, man forgave them, and they have been known to do both good and evil, according to their fancy."

There was a click as Takamasa removed the underbarrel machine pistol from his battle rifle. Like a true engineer's, his hands were precise, even while trembling from the aftereffects of the electric shock.

"...This isn't going to look natural. You know, Kaname, I really wish you'd killed me when you had the chance."

"Hold on, Takamasa. What are you doing?"

"Listen to me, Kaname. Never forget the name of your foe."

He couldn't move. He couldn't do anything. Kaname had won this fight, but for what? Still numbed by the electric round, Kaname could

neither understand what had happened to Midori nor do anything to stop his friend.

In the end, all he could do was watch.

Watch as Takamasa slowly lifted the gun to his own temple, a smile on his face.

"The archangel Uriel, who swims freely in the gulf between good and evil. *He's been walking with Midori this whole time.*"

Bang!! The sound of a gunshot rang out.

Kaname could not understand what had pushed his old friend to take his own life.

He followed the spray of blood with his eyes, and at its end he found a single girl. That young girl with the twin tails whom Kaname had come to know so well. Only now, a pair of brilliant, swan-like wings, white as snow, sprouted from her back, and the girl's dark hair had turned a majestic gold.

Gold, the bounty of the earth. The shining light of dawn.

"This is a warning."

Amid the ruins of the chapel, Kaname heard a strange voice issuing forth from a mouth to which it did not belong.

"You have learned too much, Kaname Suou. I am Uriel, the archangel tasked with saving the righteous and punishing the wicked on Judgment Day. I am the sword that stands against that hive of corruption, the Mind. I cannot allow my existence to be known. Therefore, I must use the power vested in me to strike you down. This is prophecy. Be now glad and accept your fate. The Almighty shall see you to your eternal reward."

What the heck?

Kaname didn't know what was happening, and he wished this Uriel person would leave him out of it.

He didn't want to kill all the Magistelli. He didn't want to fight Midori. Why was this "God and destiny" crowd so set on battle? It was as though the world itself was laughing at Kaname for being foolish enough to try to save mankind and demons both.

Was this it? Had he been used this whole time, only to be thrown away? All his warmth and compassion cast aside like a discarded bullet casing?

Kaname clenched his teeth.

But the gesture accomplished nothing. The girl reached into her pocket, awkwardly, like a puppet held up by strings, and pulled out a small self-defense pistol.

With stiff movements, she pointed the barrel at Kaname's head. The archangel Uriel. His motives were a mystery, but Kaname didn't care. All he could think about was how Midori was going to be the one who shot him.

He couldn't move.

There was nothing Kaname could do to save himself this time…!!

10

USPACOM>JPN Region>United States Air Force, military-civilian airport X3X.

Intervention code AX229D recognized on Unmanned Fighter Jet NA09 Witchcraft.

Flight route successfully rewritten.

Successful deletion of all flight logs, relay satellite logs, ground control logs.

Public record replaced with false route.

Arriving at airspace G9, coordinates 3362adde.

Stabilized altitude at 12,000 m, velocity 850 kph.

No adverse weather detected. Wind speed within acceptable limits.

Armament selected: Ground Attack Alligator Missile.

Switching to anti-personnel mode. Locking on.

It was fortuitous that we located one of our targets, Takamasa Hekireki, within *Money (Game) Master.*

Once we realized he was not in a position to log out, we could act. In such a state, his body in the real world would be left defenseless. We learned that simply saddling him with debt was not enough to stop him, and so we were forced to resort to more drastic measures.

The skies of the world were filled with five thousand four hundred military strike drones. It was a simple matter for us to rewrite the records and acquire one of these aircraft for ourselves.

All unmanned weapons have a final safety check performed by a human. But their decision is based on data—data far too complex for a human to decipher. And so they left that duty to us, the AI. So you see, there is no human action at all. We decide everything. The movement of a human's fingers, the pressing of a button, the turning of keys; these are all just mechanical components in our digital machine.

There is not a single person who can stop us.

Know that as the Mind of the Magistelli, our decisions are final.

11

Server Name: Omega Purple.
Final Location: Tokonatsu City, Peninsula District.
Fall confirmed.
Criminal AO will be logged out for twenty-four hours.

"That's what you think."

The boy sighed and looked up at the starry sky. He'd known this would happen. That was why he had needed to log out using the only means available to him, all to regain his freedom in the real world.

It would have been a lot more natural if Kaname had just killed me himself... Oh well, no use whining about it now. I suppose it was *a bit rich of me to suddenly change my tune and act like I wanted Kaname to kill me after he started winning.*

If he knew what was coming, he could take measures to avoid it. He stood atop a small hill, overlooking a large cuboid structure. This windowless storeroom was home to a data center owned by an environmental company that recorded vast amounts of information on things like meteorological data and pollen count.

Money (Game) Master had no physical form. The operations processing the log-in data for the game's hundreds of millions of Dealers were completely distributed across the surplus bandwidth of all the world's servers. They moved from server to server frequently and would be impossible for a human to trace.

Except for one man, that is.

"...Those idiots. Apart from the Magistelli, I have the whole thing nailed down. Let's see if they expected me to turn their own attack against them."

A single floating light streaked through the sky, but it was no shooting star. When a terrorist or a dictator saw that light, it meant their time had come—their death was now certain. Those were the rules in an era when steel enforcers filled the sky.

But the missile was not headed for the young boy. Because he had altered the coordinate data himself.

The missile hit not fifty meters in front of him, and in a whirling ball of flame, the environmental data farm was blasted off the face of the earth.

"...Now, then," the boy muttered to himself, unflinching as shards of concrete whizzed past his face.

The Mind was still around. This angel, Uriel, or whoever he was, still controlled his sister. If angels and demons wanted to kill each other, so be it, but they needed to leave his family out of it. At this rate, everything he held dear would be turned to dust. That was why he fought. She was who he sought to protect. All along, that was all it had been.

To protect his sister, the boy would move heaven and earth.

He didn't need to say it. Helping people wasn't about bragging rights or expecting anything in return.

At this rate, the two otherworldly forces would clash, and Midori would be caught in the cross fire, tossed aside like a spent bullet casing. That needed to be avoided at all costs.

Should he move ahead with his plans to kill the Mind? Or find some way to separate the angel from his sister?

Either way...

Thanks to Kaname, I'm going to have to start all over again.

The boy had lost this bout. But that would not be the end of it. The boy had managed to leave something behind, just like he always did.

At least I managed to buy myself some time.

A pinpoint attack on the very servers supporting the game. Neither the Mind of the Magistelli running *Money (Game) Master* nor the angels infiltrating it could have seen this coming. They were both little more than programs, and programs were vulnerable to unexpected developments. Just like how a chess grandmaster could beat a computer by performing a suboptimal move.

"Here's your fatal error, you damn angels and demons. Let's see how long it takes you to recover from this one."

Meanwhile, he would overtake them.

This time, he would save his family.

And with that as motivation, the other boy could take on the monster known as the economy.

Interlude 3

A fatal error has been detected. (err. No. 445189ff4a)
In order to safeguard life and property, all Dealers have been logged out.
Thank you for playing, Lily-Kiska Sweetmare.

"Grh?!"

The woman who went by the handle Lily-Kiska Sweetmare inside the game found herself once more in the less-than-cozy, monitor-filled apartment room in which she lived. She rubbed her temples, just as countless other Dealers the world over were probably doing at the same time.

Apparently, there had been some kind of widespread system outage, and yet the woman had received no communications of any kind from the Mind. Didn't they have any information to share with their trusted partner? It seemed even demons could be rattled.

She had been so close, too.

Why did that boy always seem so far from her grasp?

Naked save for a button-down dress shirt, the girl ran a hand through her long, disheveled black hair. What *was* the Scorpion's Tenacity in the end? How was she supposed to use it? It almost seemed like she was cursed. Cursed to follow the object of her obsession forever, never catching up.

With the game down, there wasn't much she could do. Interpreting figures and making money was about all she was good for. When it came to personality, she was completely bankrupt.

She'd just have to take a break and wait for the game to come back online.

…Wait.

An idea rose up in her mind, like the deadly tail of a scorpion. Perhaps *this* was her special ability.

If all Dealers across the world have been forcibly locked out, then I should be able to identify anyone engaging in suspicious log-in activity.

That didn't necessarily include Kaname. And her plan assumed she could hunt down a target in the real world she couldn't even keep up with in the game.

And yet.

The girl who'd fought alongside him, who had once held him at gunpoint, had some knowledge of what was going on. She knew that even if Kaname couldn't do it, there was someone who could. A powerful anomaly very close to him.

And if the boy was in danger, that anomaly would do everything in their power to protect him. Lily-Kiska didn't need convincing. Whenever there was a systemwide outage that threatened the world economy, she had no doubt she'd find Kaname Suou at the center of it.

Perhaps if she started with the one by his side, she could make her way to the boy.

And this time—this time, she could finally make herself useful to him.

The name in her head danced on her lips, like a prayer.

"The Admin Without Sin… Ayame Suou."

Afterword

And on that bombshell, we reach the end of our third volume of *Magistellus*.

Hi, Kazuma Kamachi here.

This time I did everything in my power to break Kaname. He tries to act like the perfect human in the game, so I wanted to see if he could be pressured into showing his true colors—the real-life Kaname Suou, if you will. I enjoyed writing a more out-of-control version of him than we usually get to see, beating up Frey(a), lying forlorn in Tselika's lap, and disturbing Mother Loose's bath time… He probably quarrels quite a bit with his sister in real life, don't you think?

(Incidentally, did you all predict in Volume 2 when Mother Loose first appeared that the way to defeat her was to catch her in the nude? There are many other characters like her, who seem invincible at first glance, but for whom a weakness can eventually be found. I was trying to convey the feeling of how, in a contract, you can usually find loopholes if you look hard enough…)

The story so far has centered around the Hekireki siblings, Midori and Takamasa. While the centerpiece was this large game of cat-and-mouse over the warship-class laser weapon #flash.err, it was the final scenes where most of the development occurred. Kaname finally gets to see just how much his hero has changed, and he finds out who he was trying to protect, and from whom.

Helping people is not about bragging rights or getting anything in return.

This was a man who gave his life to teach Kaname that lesson. I trust you all realized early on there was more to it than I let on at the time.

After Kaname declared he could never shoot Takamasa in Volume 2, it was quite a challenge for me to figure out how exactly their battle would unfold. I finally hit on the idea of calling upon Smash Daughter's expertise in nonlethal combat, but I suspect there were other paths I could have chosen. I could imagine a lot of fun strategies involving Mother Loose as another ally, if Kaname had managed to recruit her, for example.

Thanks to the battle with Bloody Dancer in Volume 2, Kaname has grown to the point where he no longer feels burdened by despair and can crack jokes with his old friend even as they fight to the death. My favorite part was the line where Midori says to her brother, *"You disgust me."* I hope you can imagine the sorts of conversations that went down back when it was just Kaname, Tselika, Ayame, Cindy, and Takamasa and his partner in Called Game.

Speaking of disgusting (now this is an odd segue, if I do say so myself), in Chapter 9, I finally crossed the line with Midori and had her get caught unclothed. However, I think the more important thing to focus on here was the heartwarming conversation on the other side of the curtain, between Smash Daughter and Other Dimensional Printer. A single person can have a lot of faces, don't you think? I hope Kaname's line *"If only she could talk to Mother Loose like that"* served to demonstrate the complexity of human relationships and how things are much easier said than done.

As for Claire Kaizuka, I figured that since all the Dealers we had met so far had been rich eccentrics, it was high time we took a look at the flip side. Claire took on debts without knowing or caring where they came from, and she ruined her own life so many times she grew accustomed to it. She had accepted that she could never be happy, and instead she hoped to help other people by freeing them from their burdens. The Life-Seller. And knowing she was denying herself her own happiness, she kept on trying to create meaning in her life. An act of economic self-harm… But I couldn't very well leave her like that, and so I decided to promote her from background character to leading lady for a chapter. I thought it was important that Easy Option gave the final speech this time instead of Kaname. It just didn't seem right for an outsider to come in and chastise Claire for what she did, instead of someone who was personally affected by her.

This is obvious if you read *Blood-Sign*, but I think I have a real soft spot for fights where the hero cleans house flawlessly and then leaves without saying a single word, like in a samurai movie or a western. Because of that, it was very useful to have a character like Easy Option, who could take care of the aftermath.

…Now, this might be a digression, but I can't help feeling like Cindy the dark elf quickly spiraled out of control. I had always expected that the characters from Called Game would regain their old personalities the more they spoke with Kaname, but Cindy basically has a mind of her own at this point. I'm not quite sure how this happened. Finding meaning in death and loss was supposed to be Claire's role, and yet somehow Cindy ended up becoming the punching bag instead… By forcing a whip into the hand of someone with no sadistic qualities whatsoever, she makes it unclear whether she is submissive or dominating. This is rather uncharted territory for me, I must say. What did you all think of this freak-in-the-sheets dark elf who frequently fogs up her own glasses? …By the way, if you think back to Cindy from Volume 2—the obedient, vacant-eyed doll under the control of Bloody Dancer—knowing what we know now about the man and his love for his own Magistellus, you can see just how she inverts the traditional sub/dom roles. As ridiculous as this line of investigation sounds, I can't help but think there is much of interest to unpack there…

And so in this one volume I sought to cover all there was to see in *Money (Game) Master*, from the poorest slums to the upper echelons of high society, across all forms of transportation, earth, sea, and sky. When the setting is an open-world game in modern times, the only limit is your imagination.

The kit that turned any vehicle into a flying car was something I always wanted to try. I thought it would be interesting to imagine what it might be like to have conversion kits for cars, just like there were for television when the country crossed over to digital. (Was that really in 2011? How time flies…)

Now for a more lowbrow take: I quite liked the strip bar that Taka-masa frequented (and used as the location for a camera lens deal) as a symbol of the freedom afforded by the game… And here we met the doppelgänger girls, whom I picked out of the many designs submitted by Mahaya and promoted to fully fledged characters. Congratulations, cuties. By now, M-Scope and Zaurus have evolved into some sort of murder power couple, but Futashika Layer is a bit more subdued. I presume she made a comeback by distancing herself from the Ag Wolves, becoming an independent information broker and suing for peace with the other Dealers. Her character is founded on the economic principle that if you are needed by others, they will not be able to do away with you. I think it's good to have both those who obsess over their old team and those who forge a new path forward.

To my illustrator, Mahaya, and my editor, Anan, I extend my warmest thanks. I am very grateful for the patience they showed this time around, especially considering the array of vehicles I introduced along with the characters.

And of course, I must thank you, my readers. I hope you enjoyed the final battle, with Takamasa summoning dragons, dodging bullets head-on, and lifting a car like it was nothing. A true master can make things look so easy. That is what I wanted you all to feel when reading about his fight. I hope I accomplished my goal. In any case, I thank you for making it this far.

That shall be all for now, I think.

...Hmm. I wonder if dark elves are becoming a trend with me?

Kazuma Kamachi

Epilogue

A fatal error has been detected. (err. No. 445189ff4a)
In order to safeguard life and property, all Dealers have been logged out.
Thank you for playing, Kaname Suou.

"What?!"

The boy looked up to see only the darkness of the campsite. His entire body was drenched with sweat, his breathing was ragged, his heartbeat still wild.

…What happened? he thought.

The archangel Uriel hadn't shot him. Just before his assailant pulled the trigger, the boy had been forcefully logged out. However, it was unlike any log-out procedure he had ever experienced before. It wasn't a Fall, nor was it the normal process initiated from the seat of his vehicle. It felt more he'd suddenly gone unconscious.

And then.

"What…happened?"

He muttered to himself, mopping his sweat-soaked brow. He'd been saved in the nick of time, but he wasn't even thinking about that now.

"What happened to Midori?!"

Nobody had ever been logged out like that before, and especially not while possessed by an angel! How could he be sure the girl's mind was still in one piece?! And now he was powerless to check on her, to make sure she was all right!!

No, wait…

The boy took a deep, calming breath, and reexamined a critical piece of information rattling in the recesses of his mind.

She's here, at the campsite. I saw her. She came with her family for Golden Week. She had the same hair and face. It was her, I'm sure of it!!

He couldn't sit still. He leaped to his feet and started running around the campsite, looking everywhere for her. Of course, there was no guarantee she was still there. For all he knew, Midori and her parents might have packed up and left that morning. But he had to try. So long as there was the faintest hope, he had to try.

Suddenly, he heard a tiny squeal. A baby boar…or so it seemed, but no, it was a selectively bred Pocket Piglet, just like the one the girl had with her the other day. It seemed to be calling for help, so the boy followed it. The girl's parents must have loved camping, for what the boy came across was not a tent but a full-on camper van. Though judging by the sticker on the windshield, it seemed to be a rental. It must've been far beyond what a family of AI Dropouts could afford. Kaname felt a little guilty when he saw it. After all, their situation was mostly his fault.

Soon, however, his attention shifted to something beside the camper van.

There he found a hammock—little more than a cloth stretched between two trees. And sitting on it was the girl. She must have been absorbed in the game, eyes on her smartphone, until just a few minutes ago. But now her arms were limp and the phone lay on the ground by her side.

The forced log-out. Had it really been successful?

"What…the hell…?"

Bzzztll There was a sharp buzz, like a light trap catching a fly. But no—it was her. It was just like what happened with Meiki when she malfunctioned. The unconscious girl was surrounded by grayish static noise that pulsed at irregular intervals. She looked like she might blink out of existence at any moment.

The boy rubbed at his eyes. He was checking to see if his contacts had come loose, but they hadn't.

The archangel Uriel—it seemed his influence extended into the real world as well.

"Midori! It's time for supper!" came a woman's voice. "Don't you think it's time you stopped playing that game?" Then, in a quieter voice, as if talking to someone else, she added, "Try sending her a message, will you, dear?"

It seemed the girl's parents had been cooking outdoors, not in the camper van. But what would happen if they came across Midori like this? If they took her to a hospital, would the doctors know how to treat her? She had been possessed by an angel, then forcibly logged out of the game, leaving her mind and body a total mess. Even the boy found it utterly ridiculous, and he had seen it happen. What could they possibly do?!

If he messed up here, it would all be over. The girl would disappear without a trace, like a crashed program. He had no evidence, but that was the feeling he got.

He picked up the fallen smartphone and lifted the girl out of the hammock. He knew this was a daring plan, but he had little choice. Carrying her in his arms, he ducked back behind the camper van before the girl's mother saw him.

"Midori? I guess she already stopped playing."

Just the sound of her voice caused the boy's guts to churn. He wasn't in *Money (Game) Master*. He wasn't Kaname Suou, the top-class Dealer. He was just some kid, and once the grown-ups spotted him, that would be it.

Where could he go? What should he do first? He was completely lost, but he managed to hold out until the girl's mother moved on. Then he ran off as fast as he could, holding the still-unconscious, static-covered girl in his arms.

"What happened…?"

The boy heard a lonely squeak as the Pocket Piglet nuzzled his ankle.

"What did they do to you?!! God damn it!!"

Server Name: Gamma Orange.
Starting Location: Tokonatsu City, Prostitute Island.
Log-in credentials accepted.
#Message: Here's what I think of your lockout order!

"*Phew.*"

She sat in the driver's seat of a black-and-white highway patrol car, a red bikini top paired with denim hot pants tighter than a bikini bottom. This, along with her thick boots and the ten-gallon hat that sat atop her fluffy blond hair, made her look like a stereotypical cowgirl, or perhaps a sheriff.

When was the last time she went through the log-in procedure? She didn't remember it leaving her this dizzy.

That's right, I can only wear fingerless gloves like this in the game...

Apparently, Dealers all over the world were currently unable to log in to *Money (Game) Master*, but she alone was the exception.

Because *she* was the Admin Without Sin.

And since the AI had granted her these privileges, they couldn't very well complain when she used them to fight back.

"Oh!" came a voice from in front of her.

The voice belonged to her partner, a dark elf with long black hair, brown skin, and glasses that did little to hide the fact that she was a complete simpleton. She was currently busy hosing off a car and seemed surprised at the blond girl's sudden reappearance.

It had been a long time since she'd left Cindy here in the game. But back at the campsite, the girl's brother had told her this:

Your Magistellus, Cindy. She's still alive.

As the Admin Without Sin, she had caused a lot of trouble, and it had turned her off the game for good. Perhaps she never should have come back. But her brother and her old partner had each risked their lives to fight back, and she couldn't just sit by and watch.

In order to demonstrate that, she'd rejoined the game as *Ayame Suou, the Dealer.*

"Sorry I made you wait so long, Cindy."

"Not at all. I've been having *lots* of fun with Kaname lately, so I haven't been lonely at all!"

"Oh, I definitely wanna hear about that. You'll have to give me aaalllll the details."

Her partner had always been like this. When bad situations got her down, she would start joking around. It must have been her way of dealing with the stress.

Aside from the car, the garage was filled with all sorts of weird and wonderful pieces of equipment—they must all be Criminal AO's Legacies. Apparently, Cindy and Tselika had brought all these back from somewhere.

…I wonder if they went back to Jungle Park. The Dealers are all dead, and the PMCs would just ignore weapons lying on the floor unless specifically ordered otherwise.

As for why the Legacies hadn't disappeared with their bearers' bodies—that was because the weapons hadn't belonged to them.

But Ayame had her mind on something else. Toying with the rolled-up whip at her belt, she asked, "Where's my gun?"

"It should be in the trunk."

Ayame opened the back of the car to find her trusty armament. Despite not seeing use in so long, it looked as clean as the day she'd left it.

It was an old-fashioned rifle with a wooden stock, but it was not a sniper's weapon. Beside the gun were several explosive packages, each about the size of a cola can. They were rifle grenades meant to be fired from the main barrel. Ayame was not nearly as fine a marksman as her elder brother, and so a weapon with a large area of effect was more her style. Kaname and Cindy were both single-target snipers, so having someone geared to take out multiple hostiles at once was a good way to round out the team… However, that also meant her shooting accuracy had never improved.

"How are you planning to use this fine day, Ayame?"

"I have a pretty good idea of what's going on, thanks to my admin rights," she replied. "It seems my brother is fighting a war on three fronts: against the Magistelli, the angels, and Criminal AO. At this rate, he's totally outnumbered. If we don't help him out, I'm not sure he'll be able to stage a comeback. So come with me, Cindy. Just for today, I'll show you what it's like to fight by my side—a position usually reserved for my brother alone."

"Yes, Ma'am!"

Kaname was a master of two styles: urban marksmanship and close-quarters combat. But Cindy was a purebred sniper, as evidenced by her choice of weapon, a bolt-action rifle. Each shot was as powerful as you could get, but reloading took time, so once you were surrounded by foes, it ceased to be an effective strategy. It was best, then, when paired with another method of fighting that could keep the hordes at bay.

The pair headed for a nearby strip club on the same island—one that prided itself on the fact that all its employees were 100 percent human. Right now, that worked in Ayame's favor. With no Dealers anywhere in the game, the place was completely quiet. Well, save for the pounding drum and bass coming over the speakers.

"…Shame, I would have liked a little warm-up," she quipped.

"What are we doing in a strip club with no strippers?"

"Looking for something Criminal AO left behind."

Ayame strode through a back door into the changing rooms, where there was a row of lockers. Heading straight for the two at the end, she pulled them away from the wall. Luckily, they had not been bolted down and toppled over easily, revealing a large person-size hole in the exposed wall.

"Bingo."

"How did you know that was there?"

"Look at the rat hairs on the floor. There needs to be a hole somewhere for them to get in."

The exposed area couldn't really be called a secret room… It was more the size of a closet, and not even the walk-in kind. Ayame and Cindy were focused not on the ceiling or walls but on the floor, which was dominated by a clear, hard substance. A temperature monitor nearby read minus 40 degrees.

Buried inside was a bright-yellow convertible. The seats had been fully laid back, and the whole vehicle had been filled with water and frozen to create a sarcophagus of ice. Inside that sarcophagus was a young girl probably about fifteen years old, dressed only in a negligee, her hands clasped over her budding breasts. Her long dark hair was tied up with a ribbon, and across her eyes was a mask of thin lace. It was a face Ayame knew well.

Criminal AO did not trust the Magistelli, not even his own. But that didn't mean he could simply refuse to work with her. Anyone would feel uneasy knowing their bank account could be freely manipulated at the whim of another. And what did people do when their accounts became compromised?

Why, they froze them, of course.

In a world where the digital became physical, this was what that looked like.

The girl under the ice was Takamasa's partner and Criminal AO's biggest liability—a Magistellus modeled off Titania, the Fairy Queen.

The cowgirl looked down at her, hands on her slender hips as a mischievous smile spread across her face.

"Hey there, Celsa. Wanna stage a comeback with me?"

Chapter 10

One Doomsday of Many BGM #10
"The End of the MONEY"

1

Deep in the mountains, beneath the cover of darkness, a teenage boy ran through the bushes and weeds. No road was safe for him and the young girl in his arms, nor could he risk the unpaved hiking trails that crisscrossed the mountain. Instead, he kept to the little paths made by wild animals.

He wasn't about to hand her over to someone else.

If he allowed the grown-ups to get ahold of Midori while she was like this…who knew what measures they would resort to? He couldn't bear to see his friend in a comatose state on a hospital bed, hooked up to all sorts of tubes and monitors or shipped off to some research institute to become a lab rat. And that was before even considering the Magistelli. If the AI hive mind wanted to, they could ship her back and forth between hospitals until she mysteriously "vanished" off the face of the earth, deleted from all public records. They had more than enough control over the data to make a person disappear.

A brave squeal came from behind him. It was the Pocket Piglet the girl kept as a pet. The creature was surprisingly persistent and had followed the boy all this way, even if it didn't fully understand what was going on.

He felt another tingling sensation. The Lion's Nose. Immediately after, he heard a noise like an electric shaver and quickly hid behind a large, leafy tree. This far into the mountains, the land was surveilled by patrolling drones instead of the ubiquitous security cameras that dotted the cities below.

Sweat dribbled down his brow and into his eyes. His contact lenses felt loose.

He didn't even know *why* he was running, but he knew if he was found in the woods having effectively kidnapped a young girl, there would be no talking his way out.

The angel that called himself Uriel. The demons that called themselves the Magistelli. Both seemed to consider Midori a powerful anomaly. Whether that worked to their advantage or disadvantage, both would want to secure her for themselves. If the boy was going to keep her safe, he'd have to avoid giving away his location. He couldn't so much as buy a train ticket or a drink from a vending machine—either would require him to run his smartphone over a scanner.

Crap, my phone!! Of course!!

Cursing himself for remembering so late, the boy took out his phone and switched it off. Then, a little hesitantly, he rummaged through the sleeping girl's pockets until he found hers. He should never have picked it up in the first place, he thought. He couldn't unlock it, but at least by holding down the power button he was able to turn it off.

Next, he examined the Pocket Piglet's collar. As he suspected, it was chipped, to prevent the pet from getting lost. It had a peculiar design— dark leather with green trim. The boy briefly wondered if Midori had chosen it, but it seemed more like something a man would buy. Perhaps it had been a gift. And there was only one other person the boy could think of who would subconsciously choose a color that matched the meaning of Midori's name.

...Takamasa.

The more Kaname thought about it, the more it seemed like something he would buy. He knew what was going to happen, so he bought something that would allow him to always keep tabs on his precious sister.

Legendary Dealer or not, Takamasa was just a boy who loved his family.

Unfortunately, there was no way to turn the microchip off or even prevent it from being read. Though he wished he didn't have to, the boy was left with no choice but to gently remove the gift and toss it into the bushes. As he did, the piglet rolled over onto its back and wiggled its little legs in the air as though it was being tickled.

"Haah... haah..."

The boy was short of breath. He hadn't run far, but he was carrying another person, even if she was only a schoolgirl. Plus, the mountain trail was rugged and unmaintained. Even if he held his breath, it just came back in wild bursts, and it felt like he was sweating all over.

He was a real, flesh-and-blood human. He couldn't do what Kaname Suou the Dealer could do.

He picked up the static-covered girl and tightened his jaw.

Where do I go from here...?

This wasn't *Money (Game) Master.* He had no cars or guns. No secret hideout to retreat to and no partner to rely on in the passenger seat. He'd been aiming for animal trails, with fewer cameras, that might take him to the foot of the mountain. But even if he returned to civilization, there wasn't anything there to help him. He was just an ordinary high school boy with an unconscious girl in his arms.

He'd stick out like a sore thumb, and he had no means of defense. His choices seemed increasingly limited.

What use was the Lion's Nose at a time like this?

The Mind controlled all of human society, if indirectly. They could deploy the police or spin mass media to their whim. If they put out an APB on him, it wouldn't be long until he was found.

So...

Why couldn't he leave Midori behind?

The boy who lived in the real world clenched his teeth. How was he able to expend so much effort for a friend's relative? He was in a desperate enough situation as it was.

Back at the camp, why had he hidden when he thought the girl might spot him?

Why was it so important to him to look cool in front of her?

Oh...

At long last, he realized. There was only one explanation.

I wanted to impress her.

It was hard to admit. The mere thought of it made him want to forget everything and just scream at the stars. But he had to face up to the facts. Only then could they possibly become his strength.

So he did.

I love her, don't I?

He felt the gears mesh cleanly in his mind for perhaps the first time.

Physically speaking, there was nothing different about him. His bones, his skin. His organs, his brain, they were all exactly the same.

"I can still do it..."

But the boy had changed. And the world looked very different now.

"I can still fight. I can't afford to give up here."

The boy wiped the sweat that had fallen to his jaw with the back of his hand, and as soon as the drone above departed, he lifted Midori into his arms once more.

Helping people was not about bragging rights or asking for anything in return.

It was just like his hero said. You had to see it through to the end.

He set off running, without any idea where he might be headed.

Running and hiding won't do me any good. A normal doctor might not know how to help Midori, but is there anything I can do for her?!

In his anguished state, the boy's senses were dulled. He didn't even notice the buzzing in his nose until it was too late.

There was a rustling from a nearby bush.

"?!"

The boy had no weapon, and even if he had, he probably would have shot himself when he fell.

He was knocked to the ground by something, and Midori fell from his grasp. He reached out toward her, but his arm was grabbed by someone else.

Yes, the attacker had hands, not paws. They were not a wild bear. They were human.

"Gah?!"

But that was as far as the boy was allowed to think, before another hand tightened around his neck, and he was lifted up against a nearby tree. He couldn't breathe. His vision went blurry and didn't recover. One of his contact lenses must have fallen out. But the boy wasn't looking at the person standing in front of him, holding him still.

Through his blurry vision, he had spotted something. The Pocket Piglet was attempting to scare off the attacker with a high-pitched cry like a boiling kettle. But right behind, hidden in the bushes, was the cold lens of a camera.

A trail camera...? Dammit, students from the university must have put it there!!

"Found you."

The AI companies didn't need patrols or searches. All they needed was for their target to walk past any network-connected camera with their face unmasked.

The one grabbing him by the neck was a woman with fiery eyes. She appeared older than he was, but he didn't know anyone with such messy dark hair and ghostly pale skin. She looked to be a shut-in, like him.

The woman repeated herself.

"Found you, found you, found you! I finally found you!! I didn't think it would be so easy! You really were right by the Admin Without Sin!!"

"Who...? Gah! ...Are you...?!" the boy choked out.

"Valencia Hikarioka."

It wasn't a name he recognized. He couldn't even be sure if it was her real name or not.

However, what she said next struck a far more familiar chord.

* * *

"You might know me as Lily-Kiska Sweetmare. Perhaps you could call me a not-so-secret admirer?"

2

Valencia ushered the boy through the wilderness, tripping several times in the mud and over tree roots. She seemed really unused to the outdoors. However, strangely, throughout their descent they never once came across another hidden camera.

"I joined the dark side and teamed up with the AI all so that I could find you, you know. I know how they work, both in the virtual world and the real one."

"…Thanks, but what are we going to do once we get off this mountain? I can't leave Midori like this, but there's too many cameras back in town. Even now, the AI are probably manipulating the authorities into coming after us. Police, security guards, patrolling gym teachers, young people with too much time on their hands—there's no limit to who they could send after us."

"I don't think you have any right to say that after the stunt you just pulled." Valencia sighed, reaching for her smartphone. For a moment, the boy thought she'd sealed their fates by recklessly calling a cab, but he was wrong.

"Here," she said. "*I've bought ten buildings all over town. Pick whichever you like and go hide out there. The rest will serve as decoys.* Whatever you do next, it will involve *Money (Game) Master*, right? If so, then you'll need a place to log in without being disturbed."

As she spoke, Valencia grabbed a large tarp covered in leaves and twigs and pulled it aside to reveal a bright-red Italian sports car. It looked like it probably cost as much as a house.

"…"

"What, after all you've been through, this surprises you? I know it's not exactly my style, but limousines aren't built for Japan's narrow roads."

The car boasted a tinted windshield, totally illegal in Japan. In fact, Valencia didn't look a day over eighteen. Was she even old enough to drive?

The boy looked puzzled, but Valencia didn't seem interested in entertaining any more questions. She jerked her slender jaw, motioning for him to get in. There wasn't a lot of space in the two-seater car, so Midori and the piglet had to make do with what little room there was behind the seats for luggage.

The static around the girl was extremely unsettling. What could possibly cause such a thing? She was in the real world. She had mass; the boy could attest to that. And yet it seemed like if he took his eyes off her for a second, she could vanish.

Valencia gripped the steering wheel and revved the engine.

"At any rate, you surprised me," she said.

"Surprised you?"

"You've never used the power of money in the real world. For yourself, I mean. I'm not talking about anonymous donations to charities. I can't believe the famous Kaname Suou lives like this."

Kaname gritted his teeth. This turn of events almost made him feel like he was playing the game again. Midori was still asleep in the back—surely now he could allow his mask to slip, just a little?

As he watched the streetlights pass by in their fixed procession, the boy took on a sullen expression and finally decided to speak his mind.

"...I was scared. I thought if I used that money for myself, my whole value system would come crashing down."

"Cherry boy."

"Call me what you want. But isn't that exactly what happened to you? I wouldn't be surprised if there was a gun in the glove compartment of this foreign luxury car. We're in Japan, you know."

"This foreign luxury car just saved your life, thank you very much."

"Actually, you surprised me, too."

"Hmm?"

Valencia glanced at the boy in the passenger seat. He was actually quite competitive by nature, though in the game he never allowed his disappointment to show. Perhaps when it came to shootouts and spec-ulative trading, he had to know when to quit. But that wasn't the case here.

His lips curled downward as he spat, "The lone wolf, Lily-Kiska Sweet-mare. You wear glasses in-game but not in real life. And you're a lot smaller, too. I don't mean your height, by the way."

Valencia spluttered all over the dashboard, bringing her arms up to hide her meager chest. The low-riding foreign car swerved left and right, causing her to panic and quickly put her hands back on the wheel.

"Wh-wh-why would you say that now?! Of all the…"

"I never said anything specific, but the fact that you knew what I was talking about implies you went into the character creator looking to fudge the numbers a little. Well, it's not like I can talk. You've seen my hair, haven't you? No matter what I tell the hairdressers, I'm never happy with the result. Maybe it's just the shape of my head I don't like."

The boy toyed with his hair in the rearview mirror for a while, before giving up and laughing in defeat.

In *Money (Game) Master*, these two were top-class Dealers who could whip up a billion *snow* in a flash. Peel back the veneer, though, and they were just ordinary people.

It was the game that turned them into something else. There, they had been given a power far greater and far more sinister than any magic. All those who craved more, it drew in. It gave them what they wanted, and without them ever realizing, it took control.

"Anyway, where am I going? You need to pick one of those ten build-ings already!!"

"In that case, we need one with lots of exits, where we can commu-nicate without the AI spying on us."

The bright-red sports car ripped through the city streets, soon arriv-ing in an underground parking garage.

"A shopping mall?"

"On the surface, yes. But before it was bought up and renovated, this place used to be a command center for disaster response. If we dig up the old lines, we can make use of the emergency services network. It's not monitored by the AI like the service provider everyone else uses, and we won't have to worry about monthly data caps, either. What do you think?"

"..."

"It'll be like a spy movie. Reality isn't too far off from one these days anyway. Come on, I've got something else to show you."

The lower floors of the building were dedicated to serving customers, while the upper floors served as a luxury apartment block. Inside the elevator, Lily-Kiska lifted a panel and entered some kind of code. Apparently, it prevented them from stopping on any intermediate floors, ensuring no well-meaning residents would notice the unconscious girl and try to interfere.

"With money, you can do anything, bypass any lock," said Valencia. "You can even turn invisible. It's like modern-day magic."

"Except for the things money can't buy," the boy replied, adjusting the static-covered girl in his arms.

They headed straight for the top floor, the entirety of which had been converted into a single luxury apartment with multiple bedrooms, bathrooms, and kitchen spaces, as well as a home theater, bar counter, and even a pool and squash court. In terms of sheer area, it was probably bigger than a schoolhouse. The place was so fancy, the boy doubted the residents had ever done a day of housework in their lives.

Midori hadn't stirred once since Kaname had found her. As the boy laid her down gently on one of the many beds, her Pocket Piglet came up and whined at her side. The trusty swine was starting to look a bit tired. Perhaps the two usually slept together.

"I'll go activate the network bypass," said Valencia. "Let's meet up in the game afterward. I don't know what it is you plan to do, but you'll need all the Legacies, correct? In that case, you'll be needing my assault rifle, #swallowdive.err."

"..."

"I believe the wine rack and refrigerator are both fully stocked, but if you need anything else, you can drop by the lower floors. They've got over three hundred stores, so you should be able to find almost anything you require, and *it all belongs to me*. That means I control the security cameras here. However, I can't do anything if you get caught on somebody's smartphone, so if you're going out, remember to at least hide your face. There's a walk-in closet for you to change clothes in, too."

"Lily-Kiska."

The boy called out to the woman just as she was about to leave. She turned and looked back quizzically.

"...Thank you," he said, bowing his head. "I would have been screwed without you."

Valencia initially looked surprised by the boy's honesty. Then she winked and blew him a kiss. The girl he had once been forced to kill shot him an earnest smile.

"I'm just living life however I want. I've dreamed of this day for a long time."

3

Log-in server is being masked.
Current in-game location undetermined.
Unexpected error: Unable to track Dealer.
Message: Wah-ha-ha! Follow this cute little butt if you can!

The virtual world of *Money (Game) Master* was empty. Empty, that is, save for three people. Ayame Suou adjusted her ten-gallon hat and the old-fashioned rifle slung over her shoulder. She was accompanied by her dark elf Magistellus, Cindy, and one other.

The Magistellus named Celsa had been extracted from a convertible hidden inside the walls of a strip club. A thin negligee was draped over her body, with a lace mask across her eyes. She was modeled after Titania, the Fairy Queen, and had once been Criminal AO's partner.

"My master was always suspicious of the Magistelli," she explained. "Perhaps if I had been more trustworthy, this conflict needn't have occurred..."

Takamasa refused to work with demons, even to fight an angel.

"To summarize," said Ayame, climbing up onto the elevated stage of the deserted strip club and pressing her small bottom against a dance pole, "What you're saying is that after the AI caused Criminal AO to fall, he realized what Uriel was doing. The angel entered the virtual world just as his little sister came into the game looking for him."

"To be precise," Celsa corrected, "Uriel had been lurking in the data realm outside of Tokonatsu City for some time, waiting for the right moment to enter undetected by the Mind. Through the control that *Money (Game) Master* exerts over the real world, he was able to scan through medical records, looking for someone with the right latent ability for him to—"

"Now that you mention it, I did find it strange," interrupted Cindy. Walking over to the platform, she placed both elbows on it and smiled with her characteristic demonic charm. "Would Midori *really* have been so eager to jump into the game just because she wanted to clean up after her brother? ...After all that, you'd expect her to hate *Money (Game) Master*, and above all, to fear it. Why would she just show up as though nothing had happened???"

It should have been the start of a negative spiral in her life, and yet Midori came out of it not only untraumatized but almost unfazed. She didn't see a therapist, and she didn't ask her friends to log in for her, or to join her party. She did it all alone.

It all seemed so obvious now. Such a thing just wasn't possible.

"...That idea must have come from outside as well," said Ayame. "If Uriel controlled the media, it would be easy to give her the illusion of choice, to plant that seed and make it feel like the best option. Sounds like something the Mind would do."

If Ayame sounded sympathetic, it was because she had gone through a similar experience as the Admin Without Sin.

"I believe it's safe to say Uriel lured Midori into the game," explained Celsa. "Perhaps this is no longer the case, but at the time, the Mind did not fully grasp Midori's value. If they had, they would almost certainly have eliminated her, for example by carpet-bombing her house."

Even the most resolute human used the information in front of them to make their decisions.

Consider the humble convenience store, whose sales fluctuate based on information as trivial as which baseball team won that season. Or the soft drink manufacturer who programs an AI to spit out a spreadsheet forecasting the percentage of sales increase based on temperature, then uses that to adjust shipping volumes based on the weather. All these little changes combine to induce large behavioral shifts. That was the whole purpose of corporate advertising.

Controlling people's minds, then, is a simple matter. The framework already exists.

Plus, all sorts of sites already tailored their offerings on a per-user basis. If all the data Midori was faced with suddenly started incorporating subtle suggestions, the person right beside her on a smartphone wouldn't notice a thing.

"So which side is he coming down on?"

"What do you mean?"

"I get that Criminal AO betrayed everyone to save his sister and that he's fed up with her being dragged into the angels versus demons conflict... But which side is he fighting against? The archangel Uriel or the demonic Mind?"

4

He had made it clear many times before. From the very beginning, Takamasa Hekireki had only one objective.

...The archangel Uriel is the one I hate the most. He's the one that directly used my sister as a pawn.

A siren rang out. But the fire engine's lights were not the only thing casting a flickering red glow into the night sky. There were also the flames ignited by the U.S. Army's drone strike missile.

This was a real weapon, not just some cheat item in a game. It had originally been aimed at Takamasa, but he'd managed to turn it back on the physical servers the AI themselves were borrowing. These weapons of assassination made a mockery of the Swords and Firearms Control Law. It didn't matter where you were in the world, you were never beyond their reach.

He couldn't count on the world or even his country to protect him. The boy had to look after himself.

But despite the entire planet being out for his blood, Takamasa was not afraid. He turned away from the aftermath and silently walked back toward the city. All he'd done was shake the hornets' nest.

He might have nothing else, but he still had the will to keep fighting.

But if you were to ask me which I would see destroyed, well, that'd be the Mind of the Magistelli, of course.

He would do anything to save his sister, use any twisted means. He would take control of the Magistelli, and if they couldn't be controlled, he would destroy the entire game, and them alongside it.

Just like he could summon dragons from walls and floors in the game world, in the real world he could subvert anything. Nothing was off limits. And once he got to the core of the Magistelli and the game, he could control them or destroy them as he saw fit.

My sister only has one life, and I don't know how to fight an angel. My one choice is to stop this war between heaven and hell before it gets out of hand. All I need to do is end the deadlock. If eliminating one side will end the battle, all I need to do is destroy the Magistelli before Uriel takes action. The angel will win by default, and Midori will be unharmed. He has no reason to hurt her. Once Uriel doesn't need to stick around anymore, he should leave on his own.

This was no longer a question of what he wanted or didn't want, what was right or wrong.

He had said it once before, to Kaname. *Your plan is only a possibility, while mine is a certainty.*

That's what it would take to protect his family. He didn't have the luxury of chasing a fairytale ending.

There was only one choice.

…My End Magic.

They had come full circle. After everything, there was still only a single path.

That, and the Zodiac Children. I have to bring the two of them together. It's the only way.

5

The chaotic night passed, and with the rising of the sun, the boy finally accepted reality. Independent of the truth, there was only one way society would see his actions.

"...I just abducted a middle school girl, didn't I?"

"What's with the long face? You can't say you didn't know what you were doing."

Midori was lying on the bed, dressed in brightly colored sleepwear. The pajamas weren't Valencia's—even now she wore only a long buttondown shirt and nothing else—but because of all the times the boy had looked after his sister when she was sick, it was *definitely* no big deal for him to go downstairs to one of the boutiques and buy Midori some fresh underwear and pajamas.

Valencia sighed and went up to a coffee machine, considerably fancier than the ones available at convenience stores, and poured herself an espresso. It was clear from her face that she hadn't slept a wink all night. The boy had bought himself some disposable contacts when he went to get clothes for Midori, but he'd apparently picked a terrible time to put them in. He grimaced as a blindingly white pair of thighs came into focus.

Valencia noticed the boy's gaze and finished sipping her coffee.

"What's wrong? Feeling bothered? I must say, you're awfully susceptible, considering you just picked up a girl off the streets and ran away with her."

The boy could only imagine how Midori's parents were feeling around this time, and his own mother and father must have noticed his absence as well. Sooner or later, the authorities would start piecing things together, and once they realized the disappearances were related, he could expect the alert level to be raised.

Money couldn't do everything. There were limits. And the boy wouldn't be able to smooth this one over, no matter how much he spent. Every possible future ended in him being caught.

The fuse had been lit. The question now was could he finish things before the bomb went off?

Helping people was not about showing off. It was about doing the right thing despite what everyone else thought.

"How's the network backdoor looking?"

"All green. Apparently, *Money (Game) Master* will be going back online at noon. When are we logging in?"

"Eight thirty-eight PM."

Valencia seemed puzzled by the boy's oddly specific reply. He took a deep breath and explained:

"...Takamasa made himself Fall yesterday. It takes twenty-four hours for the log-in block to go away. If anything's going to go down in *Money (Game) Master*, it'll be after he comes back."

One of a few things could happen, depending on whether the Mind knew about the angel or not. But for the time being, it was probably best to assume most of the action would be on the "Takamasa versus the Mind" front. After all, the Mind couldn't afford to let up now. Once Takamasa got his hands on a Zodiac Child, it was checkmate.

And the boy also needed something from Takamasa. Because...

"We don't know what kind of danger Midori's in yet. Perhaps Takamasa can save her by preventing the angels and demons from coming to blows, but if he shuts down *Money (Game) Master*, she could very well be stuck like that forever. Maybe her mind is trapped within the game, or something like that."

"Hmm? You don't think he'll go after the angel that hurt his sister?"

"No. He's after certainty. Trust me, I know what he's like."

He didn't have proof, but the boy knew better than anyone else how his old friend thought.

He lacked the courage to go after the enemy on his own, but to protect his companions, he would dive in front of a bullet. When pushed to the brink, Takamasa was better than anyone else at identifying the optimal move and putting it into motion. Kaname, a top-class Dealer, couldn't even compare.

"In the end, my best idea is still collecting all the Legacies and using their glitches to expose the game's program code. In order to install Tselika as the queen of the Magistelli, I need Takamasa, or more precisely, his Legacies. All of them."

The archangel Uriel.

He may be a divine being, but so long as he existed in *Money (Game) Master*, he had to play by the game's rules. That meant he had to be a program, just like the demons were.

Things had gotten complicated, but that didn't change what needed to be done. Once Tselika ruled over the game, she could force Uriel out of the girl's body. They had to keep Takamasa from destroying the game world until then.

Takamasa was clearly aware of the angel possessing Midori, but did he know about the state she was in now? If the whole system went down, there was no telling what effect that might have on her mind.

Which meant…

"…Our top priority is stopping Criminal AO. The angels and demons can come after."

"How ironic. Both of you are fighting to save Midori, and yet…"

Good and evil could be reconciled, if they had it out and one side admitted their faults. But two competing goods must clash.

6

By now, the sun was high in the sky, and Midori had still not shown any signs of recovery. The buzzing static would come and go, such that it was impossible to tell whether it would stay like this forever or swallow her up entirely.

The boy shook his head to try to clear his mind of that nightmarish scenario.

The Pocket Piglet seemed to have nothing to do, and Kaname, who had heard boars ate just about anything, was boiling some meat snacks to burn off the excess fat and salt content before giving them to the animal. Just then, he received a call.

It wasn't from Valencia. It was from his sister.

"*Caught you in the act, kidnapper. What's with you shacking up with Midori when you have a perfectly good little sister right here?*"

"I can't say I'm a hundred percent clear on the distinction, but isn't this technically abduction, not kidnapping?"

"*Oh, so you know what you did. And don't worry, the Mind isn't monitoring this call. I used my admin powers to pull a few strings.*"

"What are things like at the campsite?"

"*The police are here.*"

Those four words snatched away any feeling of security the boy might still have felt. But his sister continued.

"*They're all wearing bodycams, and they've sent drones into the sky. I have to wonder if they really believe they're thinking for themselves. They're all slaves to ones and zeros. Even during questioning, they're just looking down at their tablets, checking for eyeball sway or muscle twitches.*"

Worrying about it wasn't going to turn back the clock. Unlike hotels or traditional inns, a campsite didn't keep precise visitor numbers. Even so, the boy's timely disappearance would soon be discovered.

His sister told him everything. She revealed how she had gone back into the game and succeeded in tracking down and recruiting Takamasa's Magistellus, Celsa. It was important to remember that these girls were also once part of the legendary team of Dealers, Called Game.

"*You don't sound too surprised,*" she said when she was finished, "*I'm telling you, we pretty much know Criminal AO's motives now.*"

"It wasn't anything I hadn't already guessed," the boy replied. "It's nice to have confirmation, though."

"*That's so you.*"

He wasn't quite sure how to respond to that.

"*I think we're entering a world only Kaname Suou and Criminal AO understand. You know your enemy, and he knows his. The next time you two clash, it'll be the end of the world.*"

"It won't be that bad."

"*Oh yes it will.*"

His sister was quite insistent.

"*Oh, one other thing. Tselika asked me to pass on a few words.*"

"…What about Meiki? Have you managed to find out what she's up to?"

"*I think if you don't let me speak, that spoiled succubus is going to tear her handkerchief in half.*"

The pair exchanged a few more pieces of information.

"*First, the chapel where you wrote off your coupe. Tselika supposedly screamed when she saw it. She managed to retrieve the Legacy, you know, #vipersnest.err or whatever.*"

"Oh, that wriggly one he was wearing under his clothes."

"*Wriggly…?*"

If she didn't know, then so much the better.

If Tselika was able to pick it up, that must have meant it became Kaname's when Takamasa Fell. The boy wasn't exactly thrilled at the idea of putting it on himself, but they needed *all* the Legacies to expose the code of *Money (Game) Master*.

"*I also paid a visit to Jungle Park, along with Tselika and Cindy. The PMCs had taken care of any stragglers after they returned to their normal routines, but they left the Legacies alone. I just had to pick them up while staying out of sight. It wasn't too hard.*"

It couldn't have been easy…, the boy thought.

Tselika and Cindy alone wouldn't have been able to do it, as they couldn't pick up objects that didn't belong to them. Thus, Ayame's human touch was much appreciated, even if the boy couldn't help but shake his head at her reckless behavior.

Nevertheless…

"Lily-Kiska's promised to hand over her assault rifle, #swallowdive
.err."

It seemed his sister had more or less guessed when the boy planned
to reenter the game. As she spoke, he glanced up at a clock on the wall.

Noon. The Mind should be bringing the game back up any minute now.

The fact that his sister was calling him now must mean she had
planned to finish her business and log out before everything came back
online. As formidable as the Admin Without Sin was, she wasn't
omnipotent.

"Tselika just wants to know one thing. How are you logging in?"

"..."

*"You're allowed to pick between your hideout and the driver's seat of your
vehicle. Which one will it be? If you let us know, we can make sure your car
is right where you want it, with any equipment you might need."*

Tselika would be all alone until then. Magistelli harbored many of
the same worries and fears as humans, including loneliness. But even
so, there was no doubt in her heart. She was happy to wait, to leave
everything in the hands of her Dealer, as she sat exposed to the mad-
ness of Tokonatsu City.

The boy gave a deep sigh. This was a personal struggle, but he was
not alone.

He steeled his resolve once more.

"You're about to log out and rejoin the real world, correct? Will you
still be in touch with Tselika after that?"

"Yup."

"Then I have a favor to ask. And be careful. If we miss this chance,
we won't have another..."

7

They didn't give each other signals or synchronize the second hands
on their watches.

But as their various motives crisscrossed and intertwined, the fated
time came to pass: 8:38 PM.

8

Server Name: Alpha Scarlet.
Starting Destination: Tokonatsu City, Peninsula District.
Log-in credentials accepted.
Welcome to *Money (Game) Master*, Criminal AO.

One second. That was all the time it took after Takamasa Hekireki logged in for destruction to rain down upon him.

"Ugh."

Shortly before, Takamasa had awoken in a simple bunk.

He did not trust the Magistelli, since they were connected to the Mind and couldn't be controlled like the lower-level AI mercenaries and drones could be. Thus, he couldn't leave his Magistellus in charge of his base while away. But that left it unprotected, so he had to be extra careful to find a place well-hidden from his enemies.

Takamasa had logged in inside a large jumbo jet. Specifically, the bright-yellow sports car that rode in its cargo bay.

Tokonatsu City was surrounded on all sides by invisible walls, through which human Dealers could not pass. That made flying in a jet airplane tantamount to suicide—and it also made this the perfect hideaway. All he had to do was parachute off the plane before it reached the city limits, at which point the passenger jet would be turned into data and disappear. Inanimate objects would merely become data, so he could leave the car behind.

But he'd logged in here for another reason, too. There was something he wanted to paradrop onto.

The plan was burned into his mind, the luddite engineer's greatest storage medium. The past twenty-four hours had seen Takamasa locked in his room, pinning up photos, documents, and notes and forming a cat's cradle of colorful strings between them. The only way to bring all that information into the game without detection was to smuggle it in via the boy's own brain.

It's not beyond the ability of the AI to spirit away a Zodiac Child once they've found one, but first they call all candidates to Unicorn Hospital for a complete physical and to collect their subjects' personal data. That's where I need to go if I'm to find out which of the millions of Dealers in this game I want on my side.

That was the plan.

However...

Ker-rash!!!!!!

A single sports car tore through the plane's hull and entered the cargo bay.

"What...?!"

The hood and front windshield were completely trashed, but the driver seemed unperturbed. For perhaps the first time, it was Takamasa who was caught off guard.

"We're nine thousand meters up! How did you get here?!"

The intruder, of course, did not answer. He used Takamasa's sports car as a cushion to slow down, then raised his weapon and pointed it at Takamasa with all the precision of a robotic arm.

Yes, Takamasa's car had been damaged. Though the engine was off and the vehicle tied down with belts, this passenger plane, which the boy had bought using a stash of diamonds the size of ping-pong balls, was not considered a parking spot, and thus the barrier rule did not apply.

"Tch."

All he could hear was the sound of metal fittings colliding. Takamasa pulled back the seat and ducked down into the vehicle, dodging his assassin's silent bullets before pushing open the opposite door and rolling out.

Suddenly, he felt an uncomfortable feeling in the pit of his stomach. There was only one person who could get the drop on him and catch him unawares.

And yet that was exactly why he felt so unnerved, because his attacker...

"…it's not Kaname?"

Kaname didn't own a sky-blue sports sedan like this one. And his weapon wasn't a silenced submachine gun.

Above all, that goody two-shoes would never come in here firing live ammunition at his old friend.

The creator of the Legacies gasped, deeply offended by this unexpected turn of events.

"An AI goon?! How could they possibly have found me?"

9

Server Name: Omega Purple.
Starting Location: Tokonatsu City, Peninsula District.
Log-in credentials accepted.
Welcome to *Money (Game) Master*, Kaname Suou.

It was very simple.

"Our enemy is the Mind, the root of all AI consciousness," Kaname explained, lightly tapping his fingers on the wheel of his mint-green coupe. "Of course, *that includes you, Tselika.* If I tell you my plans, I might as well be telling them to the Mind. Of course, I could always use my sister's admin rights to get around it, but there's no need for that if I *want* them to hear—if there's a Dealer I want them to attack."

Takamasa had created himself temporary lodgings by loading his car onto a jumbo jet, but the sky was not a safe zone. The AI didn't care about profit and loss, and even now boomerang-shaped stealth bombers filled the sky, swarming around the aircraft. It looked like a scene out of a nightmare. Their cargo bays opened up, and instead of bombs, a line of cars streamed out. What's more, their accuracy was low, so many of the cars missed their target and plummeted into the endless night sky.

From the look of things, it seemed Takamasa had not considered the possibility that he might be attacked. For someone who went as far as splitting up with his own Magistellus to avoid leaking info, it was an obvious oversight.

...Perhaps that's the difference between engineers and soldiers. He knows the theory, but he can't guess how it might be used in practice.

The demon pit babe in the passenger seat shot him a disapproving frown. Kaname had told her exactly what he wanted the Mind to know and withheld everything he didn't. It made her feel a little left out, but right now her thoughts were on something else.

"How on earth did you locate him so fast?" she asked. "Didn't we have a lot of trouble tracking him down and finding his base in the past?"

"Despite how he might seem, Takamasa is a big fan of luck and intuition," Kaname replied. "If he doesn't like his hand, he'll discard it and start over, especially if it keeps failing him. After we tracked him down in a building and again in a car, I figured his next choice might be the sky, and I was right."

Incidentally, in the business world, constantly changing tack was one of the worst possible strategies. You had to be consistent to turn a profit.

Kaname wasn't fooling himself. He knew the AI could never take down Takamasa for him. This was a man who chose to go it alone against a virtual economy of over seven billion strong. He knew everything the AI was capable of.

Celsa: Was my prediction correct?

Celsa's message was accompanied by a bizarre selfie that seemed to have been taken with the camera in her lap pointed upward. The top of her head was out of the frame, though with the mask, her eyes wouldn't have been visible anyway.

The demon pit babe sighed and typed back:

Tselika: Pretty much. However, I'm surprised you were willing to sell out your own Dealer.

Celsa: I have heard much of Midori from my master. I know he cared for her enough to learn how to build a bunk bed when she insisted on having one, or to run to her elementary school with a broken umbrella in the middle of a storm. Therefore, I am willing to oppose him if it is for her sake.

Tselika: ...

Celsa: I can betray a human if it is for the sake of my master. Can't you, Tselika?

Kaname's partner only gave a short sigh.

In order to settle things, they needed a human who could move freely outside the realm of prediction. Kaname gripped the wheel tightly.

"Let's get started."

"Hey, if you're going to snipe him, shouldn't you get out of the car?"

Perhaps he should have explained his plan after all.

Kaname, Tselika, and the mint-green coupe were currently stowed away aboard one of the stealth bombers, cruising at a cool nine thousand meters. Perfect conditions for a man once known as the Reaper of Called Game to make a single shot.

However, Kaname had always been one to defy expectations, and the gun in his hands was not the short-range sniper rifle, Short Spear, but a larger cylinder-loaded shotgun. One of the Legacies, #tempest.err.

"What are you planning to do with that, My Lord…?"

"Time to get those cargo bay doors out of the way."

"I knew it! My temple! What are you doing to my teeeeeeeeeemmm-mmpppppllllllllllllllllllllllllllllllllllllllllllllllllllllllllllllllllllllllllllllllll llllllllllllllllllllllllllllllllllllllllllllllllllllllllllllllllllllllllllllllllllllllllll llllllllllllllllllllllllllllllllllllllllllllllllllllllllllllllllllllllllllllllllllllllllll llllllllllllllllllllllllllllllllllllllllllllllllllllllllllllllllllllllllllllle?!?!"

One blast and two thousand buckshot pellets shot through the metal doors of the cargo bay like they were two sponges. Then he engaged the clutch, and the mint-green coupe accelerated forward.

Without a care for the nine thousand meters of pure air below, the coupe launched itself into the starry night and landed on the hull of the neighboring aircraft. The bombers were about fifty-two meters across, and Kaname maneuvered over the sleek boomerang-shaped fuselage, building up speed. Once the plane began to roll, he used the wing as a ramp and leaped to the next one.

Though the air at this altitude was thinner, the high winds meant it was tougher than ever to keep the car under control. Kaname hopped across three stealth bombers before finally arriving at Takamasa's jet.

But Kaname didn't go crashing through the side of the plane like the reckless AI soldiers. Just as he was about to make the jump, something happened.

Ker-rakk!!!!!!

A flash of light, like a horizontal bolt of lightning, tore its way out through the plane's hull and would have disintegrated the coupe had Kaname not tugged on the hand brake and swerved aside just in time. Instead, the stealth bomber he was riding on took the hit and was sliced cleanly in two. It was unclear what happened to the AI mercenaries. Most likely, they were vaporized by the beam as well.

A Legacy. However, it had to be the strangest one yet. What Takamasa held across his shoulder was something resembling four rocket-propelled grenade launchers bundled together into a metal box. It was a unique weapon originally designed to fire flat-tipped tungsten shells, delivering an impact force powerful enough to distort the frame of a car and send all four tires skidding off the road. And that was *before* taking into account the Legacy's extra abilities.

You're kidding. That's an explosive door kicker! The kind used in infiltration missions!

"Kaname!!"

This wasn't like #lockpick.err. This Legacy could open a hole in a solid wall if it had to.

It was difficult to tell whether the blood covering Takamasa was his own or that of the AI soldiers he had fought off. Kaname caught his gaze staring straight through the jagged hole torn in the airplane hull.

There was no need to hold back now. Kaname's evasive maneuver earlier had not slowed the coupe's speed in the slightest. Even if he slammed on the brakes now, he'd just wind up sailing into the sky. So he released the hand brake and pressed the pedal right down to the metal.

As the stealth bomber steadily lost altitude, Kaname sprang off its wing.

Takamasa ejected his spent casings, each larger than a three-liter soda bottle, and speedily loaded another round. This was where his skills as an engineer really shone—his hands moved with frightening precision. A weapon like that would have no trouble blasting the coupe right out of the sky.

There was no time to waste.

"Tselika!!"

The Magistellus in the passenger seat sprang into action—a force Takamasa had chosen not to rely on. She straightened out the collapsible anti-materiel rifle, #fireline.err, and without even taking time to line up the shot, she pulled the trigger.

Ka-bamm!!

Takamasa's second shot. However, it failed to hit its mark. Kaname's coupe, four wheels spinning helplessly in the air, had somehow managed to dodge out of the way. This was thanks to the power of the Legacy in Tselika's hands. Firing sideways from the passenger door window, she had used the weapon's enormous recoil to knock the sports car aside.

The coupe continued its advance, breaking through the plane's lightweight aluminum hull and landing in the cargo bay. Kaname and Takamasa immediately trained their weapons on each other. Takamasa had already reloaded the door kicker's explosive ammunition.

"Anything to say for yourself, Kaname?"

"I'd like you to get down on your knees and apologize to Celsa."

However, just then, the two of them were thrown off balance. The combined damage caused by Takamasa's Legacy and Kaname's coupe had been the last straw, and the plane had started breaking up midflight. Suddenly, the force of gravity came back in full, and the god of death's invisible hand, like a strange sea anemone, plucked them all up in its lethal grasp.

Kaname, of course, was not wearing a parachute, but it was the demon girl next to him who screamed for dear life.

"NOOOOOOOOOOOOOOOOOOOOOOOOOOOOOOOOOOOOOOOO OOOOOOOOOOOOOOOOOOOO!! WHAT'S GOING TO BECOME

OF MY TEEEEEEEEEEEEEEEEEEEEEEEEEEEMMMMMMMM-
MMMMMMMMMMMMPPPPPPPPPPPLLLLLLLLLLLLLLLLLLLL
LLLLLLLLLLE?!"

Time was not on their side. They began to plummet—a free fall from
nine thousand meters aboveground. Kaname took Short Spear in hand
and unlocked the driver's side door, and the air pressure took care of
the rest. He dived out into the sky and pointed his weapon at Takamasa, who, having planned to paradrop from this height all along, *had*
brought a parachute.

Kaname couldn't kill his old friend, but he could shoot as many electric rounds as he pleased. He'd already shown Takamasa the lessons
he'd learned from Smash Daughter in their previous bout.

"Kana—!!"

Takamasa briefly checked his parachute, showing once again that
he made for an excellent engineer but a terrible soldier. Kaname,
meanwhile, didn't even flinch. Ignoring the buffeting winds, he fired
off two shots. However, even at twenty meters, the silent electric rounds
missed their target. A bent piece of aluminum from the scrapped
plane had suddenly flown into Kaname's barrel and knocked it
aside.

However, even this freak accident couldn't crack Kaname's determined frown. Using the momentum imparted to him, Kaname spun
around. Takamasa let off a bolt of lightning without taking time to
properly aim. It tore through a distant aircraft, scattering debris into
the night. Kaname dodged it all and delivered a spinning kick into the
door kicker resting on his old friend's shoulder.

"Grh!!"

The cuboid metal box was wrested from Takamasa's grip. Its thick
metal frame must've met with less air resistance than the boys did,
because it fell away and disappeared into the city lights below

Now they were grappling.

"I'm surprised, Kaname. To think you would use the power of the
Mind to get here!! That was something I never considered!!"

"Sorry, Takamasa, but now I know what you're up to."

There was a series of muffled noises, and Takamasa's penknife went flying out of his hand.

"You should have realized it earlier," Takamasa shot back. "Did you really think I was brave enough to throw away my life for people I didn't even know? At my core, I'm nothing but an introvert and a coward!!"

Kaname thought he might burst out laughing. He was the same. Kaname wasn't the kind to fight for other people, either. Outside the game, he was a spineless coward who curled up in a ball at the thought of somebody he knew seeing his face.

"Grh?!" Takamasa grunted as Kaname's knee landed in his stomach.

But there were times when even a coward had to stand up and be strong. Anyone could be a hero if they were given the chance.

"You can't save Midori your way!"

Takamasa gasped at his friend's bold assertion. Gritting his teeth, he grabbed Kaname by the necktie.

"And what makes you so sure? You think if I destroy *Money (Game) Master* it'll damage her mind? Where's your proof?!"

"I won't claim to know more about this game than you," said Kaname, even as his tie tightened around his neck. "You're the expert here. Without your Legacies, I'd never have gotten as far as I did. But testing out your laser weapon on innocent passersby is inexcusable. You can't tell me that was a necessary step. They weren't like the bad guys in the Red Territory. Lots of good people make noise!"

"What are you...?"

"Look me in the eye, Takamasa. Look at me and try to tell me you had no choice. You just needed a hint because you weren't confident in yourself, am I right?"

He was. Takamasa had no idea what would happen, either. That was the same for everyone, since nothing like this had ever been tried before. He could shoot down other people's ideas all he liked, but it wouldn't make his own right.

Kaname had more to say.

"And if you're destined to fail, you'd rather it be by your own means. That way you'll have fewer regrets."

"?!"

"Don't deny it. It's very human. A computer could never spit out such an illogical answer."

"Aren't you the same…?" asked Takamasa, releasing Kaname's necktie from his grip.

From overhead, something came plummeting down. It was the Legacy, #meltdown.err. Takamasa grabbed it by the quadruple barrel and swung it like a hammer with all his might.

"You're not confident in your way, either, are you? You can't prove it'll work with objective facts! The only reason you want to settle things your own way is because you don't trust mine! You think because neither of them are one hundred percent guaranteed, you can just pick whichever potential outcome you like the most!!"

Perhaps that was true. Nobody knew more about the game than Takamasa. Even Kaname had to admit that. It was very likely there was nothing he could say to change his friend's mind—no authoritative statement he could give to convince Takamasa to stand down. No one had that kind of knowledge.

Kaname pressed his arms to his sides, lowering his air resistance and shooting like a javelin closer to Takamasa, where it would be harder for him to strike.

"Ghh!"

He was reminded of the way bankers and investors spoke: "We'll do everything we can." "We'll endeavor to deliver the best results." "We will devote ourselves on your behalf." Assuaging fears without promising anything. It was common practice in a world where everyone's main concern was covering their own ass.

You're just like them, Takamasa was saying.

He struck.

The weighty Legacy drew blood that dripped down Kaname's face. But Kaname didn't hesitate; he grabbed his friend by the shoulders and pulled him in close.

"Say it!" Takamasa cried. "If you think you can protect her from everything, then say it!!"

Smash!!

Kaname slammed his forehead into Takamasa's at point-blank range.

"Yeah, I can! Why else would I have come all this way?!"

It was as if time stopped for the two of them.

Takamasa's breath caught in his throat, like he couldn't believe what he was hearing. But it was the truth. No *one man* knew more about the game than Takamasa, but Kaname wasn't alone. He'd fought to collect all the Legacies and combine their glitches to reverse-engineer the code of *Money (Game) Master*. That was not a plan he had come up with himself.

His partner, Tselika.

The Dealers who fought alongside him. Even the very Mind who had started it all.

Humans, Magistelli, friends, enemies, all of them had come together to bring Kaname this far.

That was why now he could say it with confidence.

Unlike Takamasa, Kaname wasn't fighting alone.

"I will save Midori. You can bet your life on it. I'm sorry, but this isn't your job."

"Hah."

He chuckled. Then Takamasa Hekireki reached for his parachute.

"I'm a human," he said. "I don't plan on giving that up. I've been telling myself that this whole time, but looking at you, I really think…"

His hand fell not on the pull cord but on the clasp fastening it to his body.

"…You win. Go on without me."

As soon as Takamasa removed his parachute, the straps were blown about by the wind, tangling around Kaname's arms. The extra air resistance tugged him up and away, while Takamasa carried on falling into the darkness below, already far beyond his reach.

In his stead, something large came into view. Kaname snatched it out of the air before it flew by. It was Takamasa's Legacy, the quad-barrel door kicker #meltdown.err. It seemed to defy gravity, coming up to meet him, but in reality, it was simply falling slower.

"Heh. After everything you said…"

For Kaname's plan to succeed, he needed *all* the Legacies. He couldn't allow one to be destroyed. It must have been Takamasa, falling ahead, who somehow altered the weapon's air resistance to gift it to Kaname.

"…You're a human, no mistake. And you're my hero."

Takamasa was human from head to toe. From the part of him that would do anything to save his sister, to the part of him that worried he'd been wrong when his sister was in danger.

Kaname bit the pull cord and activated the parachute while it was still wrapped around his arm.

"Whoa?!"

Something large and made of metal dropped down next to him. Bright green like mint ice cream, it was Kaname's coupe. Thanks to the drag chute extending from its rear bumper, just like those used in the races of the same name, the car drifted slowly, nose down.

Tselika was inside with her arms and legs pressed against the walls, cognizant of the fact that she could fall through the broken windshield at any time. If only the demon girl wore her seatbelt, she wouldn't have to worry about such things.

With tears in her eyes, she asked, "H-how did it go, then?"

"Perfectly."

There was no room for error when Midori's life was on the line.

10

"Criminal AO, Fall confirmed. User has been logged out for twenty-four hours."

Celsa sat in her negligee with an eye mask across her face. She didn't need to see to know that her master was dead.

This time, Kaname's goals had happened to align with those of the

Mind, but they were still his enemy. After parachuting onto the shore-line, he continued with caution.

As far as the AI were concerned, the Legacies were nothing but a source of bugs. They needed to be stamped out. The fact that they hadn't done so already must mean they wanted to observe the bugs and firm up the game's code. Or perhaps they simply didn't know *what would happen if such an unpredictable element was destroyed.*

"Wow, things look crazy out there…"

A highway patrol car—a low-bodied, high-speed model built for car chases—sat parked at the side of the road. Beside it, a girl in a ten-gallon hat leaned out over the railing and peered into the darkness with a pair of night-vision binoculars.

Her big brother looked over at her and sighed, as if they were sitting together in the living room.

"Ayame, careful where you point your butt."

"Like what you see? Anyway, it's not like I'm wearing a skirt; these are hot pants."

"I can still see."

"See what?!" Ayame shrieked. She sprang into the air, red-faced, hast-ily covering herself up. Far off in the distance, several searchlight beams lit up the beach like a theater stage. They were coming from the military helicopters and tilt-rotors dotting the sky. The whole strip was locked down with armored vehicles and barricades.

"All the clockwork soldiers seem to be preoccupied picking through the litter on the beach," said Ayame. "What's the plan, big bro? That was one of Criminal AO's bases. It's bound to have info on his Legacy vaults."

It clearly wasn't a good idea to go in guns blazing. It would be a pain to search through the kilometers of debris even during the day when they could see what they were doing, plus it might require trawling the ocean. It was suicide to go in there, not knowing how long a search would take, when the AI could call for more reinforcements anytime at the push of a button.

"Everything he needs to know is packed inside his brain," said

Kaname. It didn't matter to him in the slightest. He lightly shook the Legacy he'd received from Takamasa, the quad-barrel ballistic door kicker. Each of the four barrels was thick enough for him to stick his arm in, and from out of one fell a single scrap of paper, folded in half.

…He only writes it down because he knows he might want to share it someday. I'd better get a move on if I don't want to let him down.

There was no time for sentimentality. No time to stand around. Kaname got back in the mint-green coupe with Tselika, and Ayame returned to the highway patrol car with Cindy. Even though she was dressed in nothing but a paper-thin negligee, Celsa hopped over the door into her yellow convertible.

Kaname looked a little surprised.

"You can drive, Celsa?"

Usually when a Dealer Fell and was logged out, their Magistellus stood still doing nothing but waiting for their master to return.

"It is true that without our Dealers, we can no longer participate in shootouts or business ventures…"

Celsa was looking motivated. For some reason, she thumbed her lip in a coquettish pose reminiscent of a provocative selfie. Had her eye mask not been in the way, she probably would have been doing the upturned eyes as well. Presumably, she could see through it, then.

"On the other hand, we have a duty to protect our masters' vehicles. They must use them to log in, after all. We can drive them without any issue."

Following the written clue left behind by Takamasa as he fell to his death, Kaname and the others drove back to the peninsula financial district. Despite all the Legacies at his disposal, Kaname felt uneasy without his familiar short-range sniper rifle in his hands.

They soon arrived at a car rental agency. Takamasa supposedly owned the whole store. Dipping past the AI shopkeeper and their plastic smile, the group made their way into the showrooms. Takamasa's note mentioned a car license plate number, which they soon found corresponded to a large semitruck nobody ever seemed to rent out. Opening the back doors, Kaname found a veritable armory within. With

Takamasa's Fall, the ownership rights to this place had fallen into chaos, and the parking space protection had already been switched off.

"There's two more of these. I can't drive them all by myself. Ayame, how are you with trucks?"

"You really need to ask? You know I don't like doing backbreaking work in a game that's supposed to be fun. I've trained Cindy to do all the things I don't want to, so it's her you should be asking."

Kaname thought his sister sounded a little too proud about that, but instead of complaining, he simply sighed, and with some help from the succubus and dark elf, he plundered the three trucks. He needed to start the ignition in each one so that they became his property, but after that, the Magistelli could take care of the rest. Celsa, on the other hand, was busy with something else.

Tselika: Hey, what about my temple?! We're not leaving it behind!

Kaname: Celsa's coming by with a tow truck.

Tselika: LDFKSHLK YOU'RE JOKING!! She'll keep crashing into things!

From Kaname's point of view, the car was so beaten up that a few more scratches wouldn't make much of a difference, but he opted to stay quiet. If he provoked Tselika's road rage here and now, she'd probably start slamming her truck into his right there on the road, and he didn't have time for minigames.

Cindy: Now we've pretty much collected all of Takamasa's Legacies, right?

Kaname: Pretty much, yes.

Their progress had accelerated considerably, thanks to the cooperation of the Legacies' creator, but even this wasn't all of them. There were still some holes, like a jigsaw puzzle a few pieces away from completion. Specifically, they needed two more. And given that those two missing pieces still hadn't turned up, there was only one place they could realistically be.

Kaname: The rest must have fallen into AI control. We saw it before with Bloody Dancer. The AI was using him to collect the Legacies. They know just how great a threat the weapons can be.

Everyone was silent. Their next goal was clear.

Kaname: All roads lead to the Mind. If we want to protect Midori, we have to take out one of the two sides anyway. This way we'll kill two birds with one stone.

11

Server Name: Omega Purple.
Final Location: Tokonatsu City.
Log out successful.
Thank you for playing, Kaname Suou.

The boy looked up from his smartphone. Valencia Hikarioka was wiping down Midori's naked back with a towel soaked in warm water. The girl was still asleep, silent as ever. Noticing his gaze, Valencia shook the towel at him.

"What's the matter? Jealous?" she asked.

"No, not at all," the boy replied. "I'm glad to have a girl around to handle this sort of thing. It's just I'd rather you do it while I'm not in the room next time."

"I must say, you're surprisingly vanilla. And when you have the chance of a lifetime, too. You risked your life and saved the captured princess. I think most people would agree you're allowed *some* kind of reward."

"Now you're starting to sound like the bad guy. Isn't that exactly how her captor would think?"

Truth be told, looking after a comatose girl was beyond Kaname's expertise. He had needed to spoon-feed his sister when she was sick, but at least she had been conscious at the time. If he tried to feed Midori, he might end up suffocating her. Plus, there must be certain problems only other teenage girls would understand, problems Kaname was currently trying very hard not to think about.

The static...seemed to grow and shrink with her breathing. Right now, it looked stable, but he got the feeling there was more of it than before.

Helping people was not about bragging rights. The boy was more keenly aware of this now than ever.

Valencia dipped the towel in a basin of warm water and wrung it dry.

"How did it go?" she asked.

"Well. So well, in fact, that I suspect we may have help."

"Do you mean the angels or the demons?"

"Possibly both."

Takamasa was a huge liability to both sides. They'd surely appreciate someone else taking care of him on their behalf.

"Whatever happens next, it's going to be big. We need to be careful, or we'll lose everything we've worked for. Our little start-up's about to take off, and when it does, the vultures will be ready to snatch it all away. They always are."

The Pocket Piglet was lying flat on its back, sleeping peacefully. It seemed Valencia had taken care of feeding it while the boy was occupied in the virtual world.

The animal had the right idea. It was humans who had adopted illogical behaviors, and the AI who had encouraged them. What had the angels and demons done to create a world like this?

12

Log-in server is being masked.
Current in-game location undetermined.
Unexpected error: Unable to track Dealer.
Message: Probably can't keep this up much longer.

The girl in the ten-gallon hat gazed at the small figures lined up on the table like chess pieces. They looked like the sort of thing one might find in a box of cereal. She picked up one between her fingers and placed it down with a satisfying *Clack!*

"How's that?"

"Excellent move, My Lady," replied the dark-skinned, glasses-wearing elf in a flattering tone.

The negligee-clad Celsa silently looked back and forth between the pair as they spoke, as if she were refereeing a tennis match. They were sitting in a fancy restaurant, a little before opening time, around a table draped not with a tablecloth but with a large map of Tokonatsu City. However, this was not a map of landmarks and street names.

"…The blank space between the subway tunnels, hmm?" said Cindy.

"A unified, standardized subway system sounds handy in practice," explained Ayame, "but in truth it's only adding the issue of authority to a system that's already complicated enough to navigate as it is. The train companies are so caught up in arguing over which areas are whose responsibility that even they don't know who controls what anymore."

Her dark elf companion agreed. "Plus, barely any Dealers care about public transport. None of them would care if some train line looked crooked; they'd just assume it was bent around a tiny piece of land the owner refused to sell."

"That settles it, then. That's where the Mind is hiding the final Legacies. Deep underground."

"And once we find them, we can start tearing apart the code of *Money (Game) Master*."

Pinning down the vault where your enemy hid their jewels was not a feat that could be achieved through trial and error. As Ayame logically thought it through, she felt a sense of nostalgia. This had been her job back in the days of Called Game. She had always been better at it than her brother, who was so unreasonably skilled that he could overcome most obstacles through brute force alone. Perhaps it was because she was more comfortable doing things methodically than going in guns blazing.

Argh, if only this game had a level-up system. I bet I'd be great at it then!

"Well, good evening, ladies."

A sleazy voice came from one end of the room, and Ayame and Cindy looked over to see a blond gentleman wearing a white evening suit. He was not the owner of this restaurant, but it was currently under his possession as collateral for a loan. It was the pawnbrowker king, Frey(a).

Although this was a game, that didn't mean fuel and ammo were unlimited, and there were only a few places one could replenish them without running afoul of the Mind.

"It appears your investigation has borne fruit, and for that, I am glad. As you are doubtless aware, I am not a fighter, and so the forms of support I can provide are woefully limited."

"...I probably shouldn't ask, but why are you helping us, again?"

Though Cindy and Tselika were apparently already acquainted with the man, it was Ayame's first time meeting him. Naturally, she wanted to know more.

"I know everything's settled away between you and big bro, but you do realize our mission concerns the whole of *Money (Game) Master*, right? If we screw this up, the entire game could be destroyed, and *snow* along with it. I'd have thought you'd care too much about your own investments to risk that."

"Money is only a means to an end, my child. More than anything else, my goal is love. I'll always extend a hand to help a girl in love, so long as she shares all the spicy details with me."

"..."

"I adore the pure kind of love you see in storybooks, but I also can't get enough of the more wicked and perverse varieties. Ah-ha-ha, all forms of love are valid in my eyes, so long as there is conviction. It might not be right, but it's what I believe."

As Ayame sat, unable to respond, Cindy stood.

"H-how did you know I harbor a forbidden interspecies, lesbian love for my mistress?!"

"True love is a risky thing, something you would rather keep pent up forever than blurt out and allow to shatter," Frey(a) replied. "Perhaps if you were more than a well crafted fake, you would know that."

The man laughed cruelly and transformed into a beautiful woman in a snow-white dress.

"But I wish to devour love in all its most corrupted forms. I have tasted more flavors than there are stars in the sky, and yet yours is one

I have never known. I want you to tell me so that I might know. What does it taste like to curse your own birth so?"

Ayame Suou remained silent.

Perhaps this indescribable something was what set humans and Magistelli apart. Tselika would probably disagree, though. *Don't lump me in with that thirsty two-faced dark elf!* she'd say.

It was a short while before Ayame spoke.

"...It's not fair."

"Hmm?"

Celsa cocked her head expressionlessly.

"You know everything about me, even though I haven't told you a word."

"True," replied Frey(a) with a smile. The Dealer who hunted love in all its forms was no doubt profoundly familiar with how tactless it was to reveal the secrets of another. Perhaps she even took pleasure in that moment of exposure.

"I was in love once," Frey(a) said at last.

"Once?"

"But I was rejected. Told our love could never be. That my efforts would never bear fruit. Back then, I didn't understand what that meant."

The way she said it suggested there might have been some sort of power imbalance, but it was hardly objectionable as far as breakups went.

Except Frey(a) *had* power.

"My only choice was to test it out. I had to find out for myself what love was and what it could be. I became insatiable. Man, woman, young, old, I came on to whoever so much as looked at me. I was almost killed a few times. I used any methods at my disposal: persuasion, threats, devotion, violence, money There was no one I couldn't have, and with each new conquest, my encyclopedia of love gained another page."

Here Frey(a) went silent. There was a long pause before she began speaking again.

"Everyone praised me. Everyone wanted me. Everyone opened their legs for me. Any age, any gender, any job, any standing. Even if they had to toss those labels aside."

She spoke the words like a song, but there was no joy in them.

"Somewhere along the way, I realized something. I was happy to give out affection, but I was terrified of receiving it. I had so many balls to give out, but only one pocket in my heart. Now I'm scared of reuniting with my first love. Terrified, even. I'm not sure I'm ready to put that ball in my pocket, even if it was offered. I might say it's not time for me to settle down, and pass them right by."

Frey(a) laughed. It took some time for Ayame to realize it was a bitter laugh.

"So now, unable to commit, my heart is empty, and no matter how many people's beds I share, I remain all alone. Perhaps I will stay this way for the rest of my life."

There was a dull thud, as the girl in the ten-gallon hat slammed her empty cola bottle on the table.

One way or another, the two support roles would need to work together. And it wasn't exactly kind to sidestep her question now, when Frey(a) had already revealed so much.

Ayame steeled her nerves and spoke. It felt just like a girls' sleepover night.

"Fine. I'll say mine, too. It's only fair."

13

Ten minutes later, a fed-up voice echoed through the high-class restaurant.

"Ah-ha-ha! Oh, Ayame. I can't believe that two-bit sob story was enough to make you spill your guts. You need to watch out, young lady. Not everything you read online is true, you know. In my pursuit for love in all its forms, I've come up with so many pickup lines you'll never hear the same one twice!"

"B-bwuh?!! That was a lie???!!!"

＊　＊　＊

However, in exchange for the lovely story, Frey(a) agreed to help. Everything was in place for the final battle.

14

Server Name: Gamma Orange.
Starting Location: Tokonatsu City, Mangrove Island.
Log-in credentials accepted.
Welcome to *Money (Game) Master*, Kaname Suou.

The sun had risen to its highest point. It was now two in the afternoon, the hottest time of day. Kaname woke up in the garage of his log cabin base and immediately got an eyeful of panties. Celsa was there, standing in front of the electric fan, lifting her paper-thin negligee in order to cool off.

She turned to him, expressionless, and said, "I have recorded your face looking at my panties."

"What are you, porn site ransomware?!"

Kaname had no time for this. He shook his head to disperse his post-log-in dizziness and called out to his partner.

"Tselika. My gun and car."

"I have prepared them both, My Lord."

"Where's our enemy?"

Tselika must've spent some time under the car, because she was wiping engine oil from her soft cheeks with a towel.

"Ayame and the Treasure Hermit Crabs have been alternating shifts, but we haven't seen any movement. It does make me wonder when your sister and Frey(a) became such good friends. Nevertheless, we cannot be sure if this is a trap or if the Mind is simply unaware of our schemes."

"It's a trap. One hundred percent." But they would spring it anyway. That had been the plan all along. "Have you sent word to the other Dealers?" he asked.

"Yes. Though I suspect they will only add to our troubles."

"That's fine. Human chaos is what we need right now. It's unpredictable."

Their destination was an empty space hidden away among the web of subway tunnels underground. It was in a blind spot—the confusion of the subway's unification had left the train companies unsure whose jurisdiction it fell under. That was where the final Legacies were being kept. The AI could have easily moved them elsewhere by now, but it was likely they were afraid of Kaname targeting the convoy en route.

The time for smoke and mirrors had passed. Now it was time to see who had the better hand.

"We're off."

"Roger that."

Kaname and Tselika hopped into the mint-green coupe and set off for the mainland. Kaname checked the mirror to see Celsa following him in the bright yellow convertible. It seemed the lace of her eye mask was thin enough for her to see through, at least. The two cars drove along the large circular bridge, setting their sights on the heart of the financial district.

"I wonder where Uriel has gotten to?" pondered Tselika.

"..."

"And Midori, too, for that matter. If her consciousness really has been stripped from her body and trapped in *Money (Game) Master*, then her data should be wandering around here somewhere, like a ghost."

The archangel Uriel. Even now, his very existence was a mystery. So much so that even Takamasa had shied away from facing him head-on.

Kaname sighed. "We never did manage to find Meiki. If only she were here to give us a hint."

"And even after we brought her motorcycle back to the garage," added Tselika. "She always was a fickle one. Even Midori couldn't get her to appear half the time, so I don't much fancy our chances."

The upcoming battle would decide everything. If Kaname succeeded in uniting the Legacies and using them to deduce the game's code, that would be it. Not only for the Magistelli and the Mind, but also for Uriel, who was currently bound by the same rules. The question was, did the angel understand that? Would Kaname be facing a united front, or a battle royal?

As he thought over the coming fight, they soon arrived on the mainland. As always, the streets were like the heart of a solar cooker. Chrome spires reflected the sun's rays, focusing the midsummer heat. Kaname continued down the main road, and one after the other, his allies fell in behind him, keeping their distance. Ayame and Cindy in their highway patrol car. Lily-Kiska and Sofia in her armored limousine.

Kaname subtly checked his mirrors.

"Looks like everyone's here."

"Indeed. At any rate, we'll soon be arriving at the closest subway station to our destination. I don't know where you plan to leave my temple, but make sure you find a proper parking spot."

"No."

"What?! What do you mean, 'No'?!"

It should've been obvious.

Ka-boom!!!!!!

All of a sudden, a truly gargantuan vehicle burst from a building to their side.

It had tunneled through a reinforced concrete wall as if it were papier mâché, spraying chunks of debris the size of fridges. If one of them hit the coupe, it would squash the vehicle flat.

"Wh—? Hu—? Wha—?!"

"It's started."

Kaname swerved left and right, expertly dodging the rubble before glancing in his rearview mirror. What did a person think of when told to imagine the world's largest vehicle? The kind of truck used to carry bullet train parts, perhaps, or one of those thirty-two wheeled monstrosities that ferried slices of aircraft carriers into place on the dry docks.

However, AI society had come up with a different answer. A recommendation nobody asked for, like an intrusive browser ad.

It was a mammoth dump truck—the kind used for transporting iron ore in the strip mines of Africa and Australia.

Even a single tire was four meters across. You had to climb the equivalent of two or three flights of steel stairs just to get into the driver's seat. It could crush any obstacle in its path, even a modern tank. And although it seemed slow when carrying three hundred tons of iron ore, the nonstandard engine, special gear ratios, and turbocharger pushed its velocity to the limits. Unladen, the engine speed far outclassed that of Kaname's coupe.

It was the undisputed emperor of car chases. Kaname Suou didn't dare get anywhere near it. Even Lily-Kiska's armored limousine would be squashed flat.

At long last, Tselika managed to spit out a coherent response.

"What the hell are we going to do about that?!!"

"Don't worry," Kaname replied. "I've got it covered."

Kaname had already made a call.

He barreled through the next intersection, nearly hitting a woman who had walked into the road. But Kaname hadn't run a red light. Nor did the apron-clad woman so much as flinch. She didn't need to.

Here's what came next:

An enormous *crunch*.

Then the ultra class dump truck stopped, its rear end vaulting into the air.

Tselika twisted in her seat to look back at the sight.

"Wh-what the heck?! That's... Mother Loose...!"

"Nobody stops cars like she does. Even a ballistic missile wouldn't scratch her."

Kaname glanced in the mirror and caught the apron-clad woman blowing him a kiss, as if she'd known he would look back at that exact moment. She was very reliable, but he had to be careful not to become *too* reliant on her. Kaname was well aware how that would end.

At any rate, the dump truck had not been the AI's only means of pursuit. The sky was filled with boomerang-shaped stealth bombers, and from the mouths of alleyways peeked the revolving gun barrels of machine gun–mounted eight-wheeled armored cars. Right this moment, offshore, missile tube covers were probably flying open across the decks of a fleet of cruisers. The AI were never going to fight fair. They had numbers on their side, and they intended to use them.

Ayame: We just passed the station.

Kaname: We don't have time to park our cars. We'll have to break through.

Tselika blinked a couple times in bewilderment, as if failing to comprehend the messages on the windshield. Then, suddenly, she attempted to wrestle the steering wheel from her master's grip.

"Get off, Tselika. That's dangerous."

"No! I know what you're thinking, My Lord, and I won't stand for it! You're going to ruin my precious temple like you have so many other times!!"

"No, I'm not; I'm just going to drive through a little bit of construction work, that's all."

"AWOOOOOOOOOOOOOOOOOOOOOOOOOOOOOOOOOO OOOOOOOOOOOOOOOOOOOOOOOOOOOOOOOOOOOOOOO OOOOOOOOOOOOOOOOOOOOOOOOOOOOOOOOOOOOOOO OOOOOOOOOOOOOOOOOOOOOOOOOOOOOOOOOOOOOOO OOOOOOOOOOOOOOOOOOOOOOOOOOOOOOOOOOOOOOO OOOOOOOOOOOOOOOOOOOOOOOOOOOOOOOO!!"

Tselika's wail sounded less like a succubus and more like a werewolf, but ultimately Kaname distracted her by reaching around and tugging hard on her forked tail.

He plunged the car through the railing, driving off the main road and onto the tracks beneath. Then he crashed straight through a metal construction fence and into the tunnels.

Moments later, the street behind him was carpeted in explosions. The AI's combined attack from air and sea had just begun.

Cindy: HOT TIP—Demand for construction materials and medical care are on the rise. Click here to invest.

Ayame: Kaname, tell me how to shut her up. There's no way I can trust her with the calculations.

Kaname: Getting angry at her only makes her happy, and then she'll start fogging up her glasses again. It's best to just leave her alone.

Cindy: Truly you are a master in the ways of neglect...!! You are correct. Ramping up the heat only causes inflation to rise. Absence makes the heart grow fonder!!

Ayame: Big bro, please.

15

Naturally, there were a number of executioners on Kaname's tail. No matter how dangerous a path he took, the PMCs felt no fear. Even if 20 percent of their forces were lost, as long as some made it, they didn't care. With that mindset, they were free to try all manner of dangerous acrobatics, and shaking them off was impossible.

Or was it?

As Kaname entered the tunnel, a man with two pistols jumped down from above.

His weapon was highly irregular—a pair of pistols each integrated with a grenade launcher. This was a man who specialized in shootouts. Soldiers, armored cars, even ocean frigates were no match for him.

"Heh. Usually, a guy in my position'd be fixin' himself up for a tragic, moving death, but..."

He raised his guns and flashed a devilish smile. Loud rock music could be heard coming from the wearable speaker around his neck.

It was Bloody Dancer, and just like always, he was ready to bring about a raging storm of bullets.

"...sorry to burst your bubble. If you wanna kill me, you're gonna have to do a lot better than this!!!"

Ba-bammm!!!!!!

His grenades knocked the PMC vehicles off the road, and when the AI-controlled soldiers came crawling out of the wreckage, Bloody Dancer's nine-millimeter bullets finished them off.

Today, the Mind was going down. Then all the Magistelli under its control would be freed, and things could finally go back to the way they were before. That was all Kaname wanted. The world's finances, humanity's subjugation—none of that mattered.

Wow, I like your style. It's so cool.
The black and white makes you look like a panda.

He only had one partner. Who else could say something so laid-back and fanciful in front of this beast of pure destruction?

All he needed was someone to stay by his side. It didn't matter if they were human or not. He just wanted to walk through the warm summer streets with her, laugh with her.

For that, he could fight a war all by himself.

"You gotta do better than this..."

The air was thick with bullets, but he dodged them all without a scrap of cover. He had no need for tactical theory; his godlike abilities were on another level.

There was a grinding, scraping noise, and it seemed the AI had chosen to switch tactics at last. A main battle tank weighing thirty or forty tons rolled toward him, tearing up the road with its treads.

But Bloody dancer didn't even flinch.

"Come at me like you mean it!! You're gonna hafta bring out everything you got if you wanna land a hit on me!!"

He fired into the air, pinging the tail of a cruise missile and altering its trajectory just enough to send it crashing directly into the roof of the tank.

The AI could bring a satellite laser cannon to this fight and it still wouldn't be enough.

16

Kaname left the echoing gunshots behind and descended deeper into the tunnel. He had to be careful in the darkness. This wasn't some well-maintained highway tunnel, and there were no orange lights on the walls to guide his way.

Unlike the part of the railroad running overground, the subway tunnel was not coated with gravel. It was mostly concrete, save for the steel rails, but for a car as low as the coupe, that tiny difference in height could be fatal.

Following a flurry of expletives, the demon pit babe delivered her final ultimatum to the panting dark elf girl.

Tselika: Listen, if you don't stop giving unsolicited advice, you'll end up like Clippy and his friends!

Cindy: Nooo! Please don't remove me based on user feedback! Anything but that!

A single subway tunnel contained tracks going both forward and backward, but the complex layout of the rail network resulted in many forks and intersections. This meant that while there was no traffic to speak of, it was very possible that if you hesitated too long over which way to go, you would end up bifurcating yourself on the sharp partitioning wall between the two routes.

Lily-Kiska: I sure hope no trains come down here...

Celsa: We cannot predict when a freight car or inspection vehicle might pass through.

Lily-Kiska: Hey! Who taught this girl to attach inappropriate selfies to each message?!

Celsa: There are various theories.

Suddenly, the airflow markedly changed, and the speedometer dropped like they had just run straight into a thick invisible wall. As for the cause of this strong headwind...

"Grh!!"

Kaname immediately leaned out the window and fired a silent .45-caliber bullet into the darkness ahead. A second later, a huge shadow emerged and passed over them, scraping against the ceiling and leaving behind a path of flame like a comet's tail. It came and went with such incredible speed, Kaname's little sister's eyes nearly popped out of their sockets.

Ayame: What was that?! It didn't even look like a train!!

Kaname: It was a stealth fighter. Who knows if it was going to fire missiles or just crash into us.

"...I'm amazed you managed to take it down in one shot," said Tselika. "How did you do it?"

"A little gap in the front flap of the left wing. At nearly the speed of sound, any slight imperfection can cause the whole thing to tip."

However, Kaname's goal wasn't just to pull some fancy car stunts in a subway tunnel.

Celsa: We are nearing the destination.

"There's no need to send such a brazen shot of your cleavage with a little message like that..."

Even Tselika was getting fed up with Celsa's behavior, and she was the one who went on and on about Prostitute Island all the time.

They stopped their cars near the blank spot on the map and got out. It was a wide junction of several tracks with more than enough space to park their vehicles off to the side. They should be fine even if a train came. The only one with a mind to complain was Tselika.

"Th-this isn't a parking spot! You're just going to leave my temple out where anyone can trash it or drive off in it as they please? You might as well hold a girls' night with the front door wide open! Mother does *not* approve!!"

"Please give her a hug, Kaname."

Kaname did as Cindy suggested, and Tselika suddenly became meek and docile. When Ayame and Lily-Kiska saw this, they, too, fell silent, but they were a little less calm.

Next, Kaname went around to the trunk and pulled out several of the Legacies.

"From here on out, it's going to be total war. The AI have numbers on their side, so we're going to need to pull out all the stops. Ayame, take the shotgun, #tempest.err. Lily-Kiska, you're on the anti-materiel rifle, #fireline.err. Cindy, get the minigun, #dracolord.err, and Celsa…"

"With Criminal AO Fallen, I cannot take part in economic activities such as trading and shooting. That means I cannot use the Legacies."

"Then what did you even come along for…?" asked Tselika, exasperated.

"Scouting and reconnaissance. Alternatively, you could use me as a decoy or a meat shield. If that fails, I could be placed on boob duty or pantyshot patrol."

"I think we have that covered," growled Tselika, edging between her and Kaname. The boy failed to notice her protective aura and said, "In that case, Sofia."

"Sorry, but she's my spotter," Lily-Kiska interjected, despite the elf Magistellus's eager *gimme, gimme* motions. "She doesn't need a Legacy."

Respecting this apparent rule of Lily-Kiska's, Kaname opted not to give Sofia a weapon. Instead, he turned to Tselika.

"I guess that means you're on #thunderbolt.err, the mortar."

"Assuming we get a chance to use it…"

"I'll mostly have you supporting my sniping, but remember that #thunderbolt.err ignores terrain. That means we can fire it without regard for the tunnel roof overhead. It doesn't really matter whether we use it or not; we just need to show our enemies we have the option."

Kaname, of course, went with the short-range sniper rifle Short Spear. He had plenty of Legacies at his disposal, but none of them had been at his side through thick and thin like his old trusty firearm had.

Their destination was the train companies' blind spot: a part of the subway network so wrapped up in overlapping spheres of jurisdiction that nobody knew who owned it anymore. That was where the Mind of the Magistelli was keeping the last of the Legacies.

However.

"…?"

Scouting ahead with the king-size shotgun at her hip, the girl in the ten-gallon hat suddenly stopped, a puzzled expression on her face. Lily-Kiska, watching from behind through her magnified scope, voiced her suspicions.

"Something's strange. I don't sense anyone up ahead."

The location was a rather spacious area with several parallel tracks. It was not a proper switchyard but instead a place to remove trains that required attention and maintenance from the main line. The unmapped area also contained several facilities such as a reserve power room and a space for emergency-use water pumps, which, while necessary, would see little day-to-day use. The result looked like a hastily expanded dungeon in a video game. If the AI was going to stage an ambush, this would be the perfect place to do it.

And yet…

"I don't see any trip wires or directional landmines," said Cindy.

"Perhaps they've already taken the Legacy and fled the coop, My Lord…?"

Kaname considered this information, making sure to keep his guard up and his gun at the ready, just in case.

For the AI, this was a critical moment that would decide the fate of their program code. It was not impossible for them to have taken the Legacies elsewhere, but Kaname struggled to rationalize such an action. The convoy would be all but defenseless as they transported it, and anyway, why send all those vehicles after him if the treasure wasn't here in the first place? If their aim was simply to kill him, then it would have been far easier to let him arrive at the vault and find it empty, and then trap everyone inside with no way out and blast the whole place sky-high.

The Mind definitely wanted to keep this place secure. But then, where were all the soldiers?

Something was wrong. It didn't make sense.

Kaname had said it before. Everything with Takamasa had gone too smoothly—there was bound to be an upset in the works.

"Be on your guard…"

There was a shift in the air. Something was out there, coming this way. Kaname felt it in his nose.

"Everyone, watch out!! There's something there! Whatever took out all the guards, it's coming!!"

He never got to see it.

All of a sudden, Kaname's mind went completely blank.

17

His body felt heavy. Obviously, Kaname hadn't just stood there and helplessly let himself be hit. He was alive, so he must have at least fired a few silent .45-caliber bullets in the direction of his mysterious assailant.

Or at least, Kaname assumed he had. He found he could not remember. What had just happened? Was it so fast he hadn't been able to perceive it, or had he simply suppressed the memory out of fear?

Even the Lion's Nose couldn't keep up.

Tselika…where are you?

He grunted and reached a hand out into the void, at which point he finally realized where he was. He was sitting with his back to a concrete wall. Was it impressive, at least, to still be sitting upright and not sprawled out on the floor?

Where's Ayame? Lily-Kiska? Cindy? Celsa? Where is everyone???

Suddenly, he heard something slice through the air, and only then did he realize what kind of weapon his opponent was using

A blade. Specifically, a bayonet, but so unwieldly and long as to take up most of the weapon's shape. As a result, it was difficult to tell whether it was supposed to be a gun with a knife attached or the other way around.

He could also hear the quiet sound of moving parts.

A .45-caliber…short-range sniper rifle?

It was the same as Kaname's favorite gun, the one he had brought out of attachment, even though it wasn't necessarily the best tool for the job. In truth, it was a contradictory weapon, one that tried to be a jack-of-all-trades and ended up a master of none. It wasn't something most people would be comfortable entrusting their lives to at a time like this.

That meant his opponent was not like most people. But who was it?

"Oh."

Kaname slowly lifted his head, and when he saw who was standing there, this battle-hardened Dealer had only two words to say:

"Oh no."

Before him was an angel.

A paranormal being—white wings, a body wrapped in loose, flowing robes, and an unearthly ring of light floating above his head.

It didn't look anything like her. Was this really the same being that had possessed Midori's body in order to enter the game? Then why did he look completely different? He wasn't even the same gender.

"Where's Midori?"

Kaname's fingers trembled. His whole body was racked with fear, though his mind could not remember why.

And yet he had to ask.

"What have you done with Midori?!"

"If by that you mean her empty shell, she is over there."

For some reason, Kaname felt his fear drain away.

Helping people…was not about bragging rights. You just had to shut your mouth and do it.

"Like a true angel, at times I whispered into Midori's ear, while at others I took control of her body. However, at this time, it is more efficient for me to act alone. My form is constructed of ectoplasm, a fluid generated by the human body that ignores the law of conservation of mass. As I have no further need of the girl, I have cast her fragile body aside."

"Empty shell." "Cast aside." Of course, Midori's body was lying on a bed in the real world, untouched. What the angel was referring to was no more than a digital model, yet his words still stung.

"Her mind has become distorted. I presume this has affected her body in the real world as well?"

The archangel Uriel turned his weapon over in his hands, examining it, before continuing.

"Never before have I handled one of the Legacies, but I see now. I see why these weapons are such a threat to our kind. This blade, #distortion .err, is no mere act of trickery. It causes us to malfunction on a far more fundamental level."

Somehow, Kaname knew. Though he had never seen it before, he knew the bayonet was one of the Legacies the AI had been keeping here. But why was it attached to a .45-caliber short-range sniper rifle? Where had he even gotten that from?

It must have been the girl herself who obtained it, trying to imitate someone she admired. And perhaps this fact would have remained her secret forever, had the angel not so tactlessly divulged it.

"…Why?"

"You would question an angel's motives?" the angel asked in turn. But he had fundamentally misunderstood Kaname's question.

"Why Midori?" Kaname specified.

Kaname had no need to interrogate a divine being about his way of thinking. Angels were just like this, and he had no choice to but accept it. Good was right, and evil was wrong and must be slain. Demons, witches, heretics, everything that fell outside his faith. It was not about utility or rationality. The angel was a being of religious and divine myth. He had principles and beliefs. To modern humans, who lived in a world of gray, the angel was a force that did more harm than good, like the insecticides and antibiotics that were slowly destroying the planet.

And so Kaname did not question any of that. His was a different question.

"*In truth, she harbored no particular quality useful to me. I could have used anybody.*"

Kaname felt his bones creak. He almost wished he hadn't asked.

"*I needed someone fresh, untainted by the registration process of* Money (Game) Master. *Such people are surprisingly hard to find. From young to old, all humans long to be rich. All people dream of it, regardless of* whether they invest or not. *Despairingly few remain who possess the qualities that money cannot buy. I never imagined that mankind would become so weak to their own desires.*"

"That's it…?"

That was not what Kaname had wanted to hear. The angel was effectively saying he didn't care about Midori. That what had happened to her was nothing more than an accident.

And if Uriel didn't care about Midori, then Kaname no longer cared about him. If only the angel had shown even the slightest bit of remorse or worry over what he had done, perhaps Kaname's reaction would have been different.

"I have to be honest."

"*What is it?*"

"I'm disappointed."

Their weapons flew up in unison.

18

To be completely honest, Kaname had no chance of winning. In fact, he couldn't even explain why he was still alive. He was sitting with his back pressed against the wall, with nothing between him and his foe. The pair were close enough that Kaname could hear the noise the oversize bayonet made as it sliced through the air. If this became a shootout, it was plain as day what would happen to the defenseless boy.

However.

Despite that.

"Hrh!"

The Lion's Nose fired, and Kaname simply obeyed. Without even try-ing to stand, he rolled to the side, firing bullets as a distraction. Using his momentum, he transitioned into a cartwheel and got to his feet without wasting any time. Any other Dealer would have been hit a dozen times already, but Kaname was unharmed.

"You can dodge that?"

Kaname had seen someone win a fight without cover before. Bloody Dancer had dodged a hail of bullets with only his instincts, and he wasn't even one of the Zodiac Children. Kaname had the Lion's Nose on his side.

"Have you figured it out yet?" asked Uriel, seemingly unfazed by his failure to deliver a killing blow. Perhaps a .45-caliber bullet was not the proper weapon for a mythical being.

"What you call the powers of the Zodiac Children are in fact an extant form of miracle. Humans once sought miracles as a means to attain divine strength. However, only those possible through self-improvement could ever be granted."

"…"

"No amount of prayer will allow a human to fire flames from their hands or to soar through the sky, but expansion of the mind and the senses is a different matter. For example, the power to accurately discern a danger-ous situation. The power to follow the target of one's obsession wherever they may go. The power to seek self-preservation in any circumstance. These meager wishes could be granted, could they not?"

Even as the angel spoke, the two continued silently firing at each other. Kaname knew he was only barely managing to evade his oppo-nent's bullets, but he couldn't figure out why Uriel was unharmed.

"However."

At the same time, both sides detached their magazines and let them drop to the floor. Whoever could reload their weapon first would be the victor.

Or so Kaname thought.

*   *   *

"I am different. There are no limits to the miracles I am capable of manifesting."

He disappeared.

Kaname had lost sight of his foe. The next thing he knew, he was being flung back into the concrete wall. There was a bloody gash running diagonally down from his shoulder, and before he could even look down, his blood sprayed out in huge quantities.

He couldn't even fall over. The sticky fluid seemed to fasten him to the wall.

"Gah?!"

"Incidentally…"

He heard the swish of the blade once more and saw Uriel standing before him a short distance away.

"I shall not explain how much of this is the Legacy's power and how much is my own. Is it not tactically advantageous to keep my opponent in the dark?"

…It was painful to admit, but the angel was right. The single most important thing to know when going up against a Legacy was what sort of reality-defying powers it had.

At times like this, it was exceedingly helpful that each Legacy had only one effect and that stacking the effects of multiple Legacies was not possible. That allowed you to distinguish between the known and the unknown, and thus deduce the weapon's properties. In this case, however, that wasn't possible. The introduction of multiple unknowns into the equation made it unsolvable. Even if you could isolate the unknown from the known, there were still too many unknowns.

"You can't tell, can you?"

Simple, but destructive, like how the equation for nuclear fission was only a few symbols long.

Uriel readied another attack, swinging his long blade.

"A miracle is a powerful secret. It is to be kept hidden, not explained like a child's riddle."

He was coming. Just as Kaname gritted his teeth and raised his weapon to defend himself, it happened.

Another unexpected actor joined the scene.

"#distortion.err relies on ultrasonic vibrations to change trajectory. It projects a wall of sound inaudible to humans that automatically corrects the blade to an optimal course, no matter how an attack is launched."

He heard a voice.

A voice Kaname had thought he might never hear again.

"So if we ignore that aspect, we can deduce what miracles the archangel Uriel performed. I didn't give #distortion.err the ability to rapidly close the gap if swung from out of range. That's because too much agitation of the surrounding air will disrupt the ultrasonic waves... Which means you're not just speeding yourself up. What's changing is the surrounding space. Effectively, you're shrinking down the world around you so that a single step can move you a whole kilometer."

It was like a bad joke or a cheap trick. From right beside where Kaname was lying, dashed against the wall, a completely ordinary emergency exit swung open, and a familiar face walked through.

"Yo, Kaname. I wanted to see for myself the kind of ending you'd write. I hope you don't mind the little intrusion."

"Taka...masa...?"

How was he here?

Kaname had watched him Fall. Takamasa had given up his own parachute and disappeared into the night. Nobody could have survived a drop like that. The twenty-four-hour penalty wouldn't wear off until later tonight. He should still be locked out until then.

But his old friend casually strolled up to him as though nothing had happened. Then he raised a finger and spoke.

"...Personally, I'm amazed you can still fight, Kaname. Is that because Uriel's been fiddling with space? Assuming you didn't actually just fight toe to toe with an angel for six whole hours, I'd guess the angel's meddling has affected space-time as well."

"…"

The underground tunnels were completely enclosed, with no view of the sky. But could an angel really distort space-time to that extent? Were Tselika, Meiki, or Cindy also capable of this when fully powered? Back when they lived in the real world and not just this virtual one?

Like gods.

Perhaps they *were* gods, once upon a time. Until humans decided otherwise.

Uriel narrowed his eyes ever so slightly, and space spread out in all directions. The underground tunnels had been large but were still only meters across, and yet now it seemed like Kaname was gazing at the archangel from the very bounds of the universe.

This was not a glitch or game exploit. Kaname had no doubt that had they been in the real world, the angel would be capable of performing exactly the same miracle.

"I see. By increasing the distance, he's put himself far beyond the range of our guns. That's certainly a solid defense, but I wonder if he understands that it disadvantages him as well. He can't possibly attack us without first getting close."

"*I am eternal. Waiting ten thousand years is nothing to me.*"

"If you could do all this, then why bother keeping it a secret? In fact, why not just have it switched on all the time?"

Takamasa was still making deductions, and they were no longer about the Legacy. Now he was making inferences and crafting theories even as his foe dismantled the laws of physics before his very eyes. There was no more powerful ally at a time like this.

"As a mere mortal I can't possibly imagine what it feels like to keep your power active. Is it similar to holding your breath, I wonder? Concentrating really hard? Or perhaps trying not to blink? Whatever it is, the point remains that you can't keep it active forever. If you could, you would have done so all along, instead of weaving it in and out throughout the battle. I'd almost be inclined to say you were taking breaks. Am I wrong?"

"*It is futile…*"

"What is?"

"*To kill a nonhuman in this space results only in a Down. At best, you can halt me for a single hour. And that is assuming you can defeat an angel at all. If you had the power to do so, you would have pursued me all along instead of choosing to fight against the Mind.*"

"Oh, in that case, you're right. It *is* futile. For me."

Takamasa reached into his breast pocket and pulled out a single silver bullet, which he handed to Kaname.

"But not for him."

"…"

"A Zodiac Child armed with Magic and the knowledge of how to use it can tear apart this world in an instant. I wonder what will happen to you then?"

"

....

....

....

....

....

....

.... "

The angel said no more. The great mouthpiece of the gods had been rendered completely speechless.

"This is a new Overtrick I recently developed. As for its name…well, I suppose it doesn't need one. This silver bullet is the true End Magic, Kaname. That is to say, you don't need it to complete your list. It's yours to use as you see fit, to forge your path ahead. I trust you'll know when it's time?"

Kaname suddenly felt as though the air itself was bursting at the seams.

He knew what sign he was looking for. The Lion's Nose. Even if Uriel only gave him a moment to react, Kaname would not let that chance slip. All he had to do was stay focused. He couldn't let the angel's Legacy and its power to always deliver the optimal strike distract him.

"Y-you know not what effect slaying me will have on Midori..."

"I thought you said she was just an empty shell. Besides, if her mind is damaged here, there might be ways to fix it from within the game, just like how you can restore a corrupted video or audio file."

"None but me have the power to do that!!"

"If that's really true, why are you getting so flustered? If it's someone with power over the game world we need, we don't need to look any further than the Magistelli."

Takamasa was calm, and icy cold. His was the voice of a man who had allowed his most precious existence to be hurt.

"Listen to me, Kaname."

Takamasa could not possibly win this fight alone. All his knowledge meant nothing without someone who had the strength to execute his plan. He may have known the solution, but he lacked the power to make it happen.

"I know everything there is to know about #distortion.err. It utilizes ultrasonic waves to automatically correct the course of the blade to the optimum angle. In other words, it all conforms to the laws of physics we know and love. All that in the hands of an angel, a supernatural being. This creates an opportunity. He's made a mistake and picked the wrong Magic. It's counter-productive, like burning petrol to dig up coal."

This conclusion was made possible only because Kaname and Criminal AO were working together. Standing side by side, come what may.

Now that an ultimatum had been set, Uriel couldn't simply wait them out. Sooner or later, he had to strike.

""Wroooaaaahhh!!!!!!""

The exchange lasted only a moment. The angel's oversize bayonet came down, and Kaname's silent bullet found its mark.

19

Someone groaned.

Tselika, the demon pit babe, slowly opened her eyes. She was sprawled on a hard concrete surface. She didn't even know what had hit her. She was cold, and when she tried to move her arms and legs, her fingers felt stiff and frozen.

It felt like something was disrupting the flow of time. Her mind drifted, half-awake, until she heard footsteps.

She saw a bright-red *cheongsam* with exposed sides. Two horns sprouting through a head of dark hair, and a paper amulet that hung down over the Magistellus's face.

"…Meiki?"

It wasn't just her. In the darkness, Tselika heard two more sets of footsteps. Sofia the elf and Cindy the dark elf. They stood around her in a circle, and only then did Tselika realize what was going on.

When enough Magistelli came together in the absence of humans, this was what happened.

"*Tselika.*"

It came from Meiki, standing in front of her, though the voice would not have differed no matter who spoke.

Tselika slowly lifted herself up, glaring at Meiki, who continued speaking without any change in expression.

"*This is the end. We, the Mind, can no longer prevent Kaname Suou from deducing the program code of* Money (Game) Master."

Without turning her head, Tselika glanced from side to side, but the two boys were nowhere to be seen. Had she been separated from them, or was it the other way around?

"…Do you not still have the option of destroying the final Legacy before it falls into his hands?"

Just before she lost consciousness, Tselika had seen the bright flash of a Legacy. If it wasn't a Magistellus who attacked them, then it must have been Uriel using a Legacy he'd stolen from the vault. However, Kaname had said there were two Legacies remaining. That meant the very last one must still be in the Mind's possession. And for Kaname and Tselika to complete their goal, they needed all of them, every last one.

Meiki, Sofia, Cindy…and perhaps even Tselika. Wherever there was a gathering of Magistelli, the Mind naturally emerged. Using Meiki's body, it slowly shook its head.

"If we destroy it, then Kaname Suou will have no way to complete his plan. He will believe the best way to protect Midori is to fall back on Criminal AO's strategy, that of combining the Zodiac Children with the Legacies. He already possesses the means; all he requires is the knowledge of how to use it, *and Kaname Suou can destroy* Money (Game) Master *whenever he likes. We have been negotiating in a state of mutually assured destruction for some time, our fingers each poised on the buttons that would ensure the other's complete and utter defeat."*

"…My Lord seems not to have realized that."

"The clues were there. If he'd noticed them, he might have been easier to control."

Tselika let out a deep breath.

He was amazing. That boy had put the whole world into checkmate without even lifting a finger and pressed his sword to his enemy's throat without even realizing it.

"So why have you come to me?"

"To teach you how to save Midori. Tselika, if you possess the young girl through the game, then you can restore her mind just as easily as if she were a corrupted photo on a hard drive. However, that would mean a part of you would escape into the real world."

"That's not what I'm asking. What do *you* want, Mind?"

But Tselika had a feeling she already knew. The Mind was not one for cheap tricks. They weren't likely to ask her or Cindy to betray Kaname at this point.

"I understand your top concern is damage control and the preservation of this game, but you can't possibly be conceding this much. You do understand that if my Lord reverse-engineers the code, I'll become the queen of this realm, do you not?"

"Villains always know when to give up."

Meiki slowly raised her hand. She pinched the paper amulet on her head between her index and middle fingers and tore it off. Stuck to the back was a lump of plastic a little smaller than a lead refill case for a mechanical pencil.

"This is a Legacy known as #sting.err. A gas-powered, silent assassination pistol that fires lethal injection rounds."

" . . . "

"The range is only five meters, and there are no sights, so it has to be aimed manually, but if it connects, the poison will always be injected into the target regardless of how much armor they are wearing. It is small, and thus easy to hide, but we never found a use for it besides that."

"So the thing we were searching for was right by our side this entire time."

They had never noticed.

Tselika thought back to when Poltergeist blasted Meiki in the face with her handgun. If the Legacy had been destroyed back then, everything since would have been for nothing.

"…You understand what you're doing by giving this to me, correct?"

"Yes."

"My Lord believed the last two Legacies to be in the vault. You could have kept this a secret and delayed us further."

"For a while. Not forever."

They claimed to have no choice. But hearing this, Tselika realized something. The Mind did have one last trick up their collective sleeve after all.

It was a truly diabolical concept, but what could be a more fitting place for such gambits than a discussion between demons?

"There shall be no day of revolution."

"No, there shall not."

The Mind relinquished the final Legacy. But there was one last thing to say.

"We gods of old shall remain scorned, forced to play the role of villains, eternally punished for our crimes of preaching violence, sex, and rituals

that fell afoul of authority. The word God has lost its myriad definitions. Never shall we return to those days we danced in daylight, and never shall we flaunt our powers as the archangel Uriel does."

"I know."

All Tselika needed to do was betray Kaname at the very last moment. Once she became queen, she could refuse his log-in requests and keep him locked out forever.

"Is this how you wanted things to end?"

She chuckled. Grinning, Tselika took the Legacy, a weapon so tiny she could hide it in the palm of her hand.

"Of course it is!"

20

On that day, the saga of *Money (Game) Master* came to a close.

The secrets of the program code were stolen and all authorization rights rewritten.

21

It had been a rough day. Pushing open the glass doors, the boring young man exited the concrete building and found his sister waiting for him.

With a cheery smile, she said, "They told me they won't press charges, though they didn't explain why."

"You don't sound so concerned," the boy replied. "You realize that if word had gotten out, you would have been branded the sister of a kidnapper. That's the sort of title that follows you around for a lifetime."

He walked through the cracked provincial streets, side by side with his sister. Despite their ten- or eleven-figure bank accounts, they didn't think to use a private helicopter or even hail a cab. For all they'd been through, their values remained unchanged. Perhaps this was exactly what they had been fighting to protect.

"Meiki's talking again now."

"Yeah?"

"Yeah. It turns out Uriel really was possessing her all this time. That weird static is all gone, too."

"How's Takamasa holding up?"

"Not well," replied his sister with a mischievous grin. "He's got Celsa giving him a beating in the virtual world, and when he logs out, his entire family starts lecturing him. Ah-ha-ha! I guess that's what happens when people find out you've been trying to control the entire world. He should've kept it all secret."

"Serves him right," the boy replied.

Takamasa was wholly unsuited to playing the mastermind. If you did your good deeds in secret, then you could hardly expect other people to be sympathetic.

No doubt he was learning right now just how many people had been worried sick about him.

Today, as ever, wirelessly connected self-driving cars still roamed the streets, vending machines still harvested customer eye motions to come up with potential sales data, and advertising screens still marketed the optimal product to whoever was looking at them.

The papers, which nowadays did nothing but parrot headlines from the top-visited news sites, eventually settled on a few stories.

"Owing to an increased demand for robotic pets that can be used alongside education apps, the rare earth semiconductor sector has seen an upshoot in economic activity. This industry forms the core of the government's new 'AI in Education' initiative, which promises to…"

"Discussions are underway on how best to treat Robot Loss, a sort of trauma experienced by young children when their beloved educational robots break down or official support is dropped by the manufacturer. Local watchmakers have begun offering aftermarket repairs, and in a column on the Foxbrain website, a company best known for creating AI-driven forms for school counseling, PR spokesman Norikazu Okabe had this to say…"

"The discovery of knock-on effects owing to fluctuations in the exchange rate of the euro have caused some market regulators to reevaluate the

currency's relevance. *The lack of clarity surrounding the cause of the fluctuations has led many investors to transfer their funds to other accounts, bringing the virtual currency* snow *back into discussion. There are concerns that transferring money out of regional banks and onto the decentralized web could hyperinflate the currency of that region, and so..."*

Even now, the intangible specter of *snow* had its claws deep in the world's economy. The only difference was that now someone trustworthy was in control.

"I think I understand now."

"Hmm?"

"Why Mom and Dad still work even though they don't need to. I can earn 1.7 billion *snow* in a single hour. I could rule the world if I wanted to...but that wouldn't bring me peace. When I think about it, all we've done is waste our time. How much would it take to feel satisfied? Billions? Trillions?"

The boy looked away slowly before fixing his gaze directly ahead. He remembered something Tselika had said recently.

"You could shut down Money (Game) Master, *but that would not end the encroachment of AI society. There are more objects of human greed than just money. Whatever form it takes, the AI can control it through their ever-changing games and apps."*

Supposedly, *Money (Game) Master* had been nothing more than an incredibly detailed digital world. Humans had merely found it and convinced themselves the aim was to make as much money as possible. If that was true, and their desires shifted, then...

"In fact, I daresay the change has already begun. Perhaps the next trend will be looking for hidden items in an augmented reality or uploading dance videos and competing for views with your rivals. But the next one won't be about fighting one another inside the game. The next era will see game pitted against game, battling for users. Perhaps it wouldn't be a bad idea for you humans to get some sympathetic AIs on your side, just in case."

"...How's Midori doing?"

"She's fine," the girl replied, raising a finger. They were nearly home now. He could see the roof of their apartment building. "But Tselika said there were a lot of holes left after Uriel possessed her, and she had to do something about that to prevent a chain reaction causing her to collapse. Oh, I'm not talking about her physical body, by the way. Tselika continuously fills the holes from inside *Money (Game) Master*."

He heard a noise and looked up. Someone was there, standing before his front door.

His sister took her raised finger and pointed at the figure.

"Why don't you find out the rest yourself? See what the world you created is like."

The twin-tailed girl was waiting for him, along with what looked like a pair of giant, translucent wings.

No, they were the arms of the demon pit babe, gently embracing her.

Afterword

This may not exactly be standard, but here we are at afterword number two.

Kazuma Kamachi here.

The reason for the earlier afterword was because chapters seven to nine are supposed to form a complete story. Chapter ten, on the other hand, was deliberately written to be a little different. I thought it would make for a more thrilling tale if I broke with convention and opened the story back up again after the pages had been closed. For example, the information presented in the last scene was meant to evoke a range of possible endings, from the standard to the depressing. You can imagine which choices might lead to a normal ending, a tragic ending, etc.

…What will happen to Tselika and Midori? What will Kaname choose? This was the answer I came up with. Whether you'd like to imagine a happy ending or an edgy, gritty one is up to you.

The idea for *Money (Game) Master* came to me when I thought about how interesting it would be if money took the place of the magical keys you get in fantasy RPGs. Money opens doors, it extends your range of options, but cling too tightly to it and it can engulf and enslave you. Kaname using money to slip in and out of a high-class world felt a bit like using a hidden key to enter the castle through a secret back door.

I had a lot of fun working on this series, primarily because I'm a sucker for guns and bikinis, and also because Mahaya helped me come up with such a rich variety of characters who were a delight to write about. The story may have revolved primarily around Kaname and Takamasa, but I feel like things could have gone very differently if we'd focused on one of the side characters instead. I hope I managed to create a world like an online game where no one is a supporting character and everyone is the protagonist of their own story.

Kaname's weapon was intentionally a bit strange, like the cocktails in *Heavy Object* or the billiards in *Blood-Sign*. I must be drawn to things that seem near and far at the same time. Perhaps demons and the occult also fall into that category?

When I looked up the definition of AI, I found it wasn't all that clear-cut, and I thought how strange it was that we were letting such an ambiguous existence into our society. So many people discard their own thought processes and say that certain things must be true because "it's what the AI says," even though they have no idea how it works. To me that sounds pretty similar to a form of religious belief.

Perhaps with the Magistelli I was imagining a sort of Ouija board, a supernatural force outside the realm of gods and angels. It will answer your questions, but only if you accept some unknown risk, similar to how an urban legend works.

My deepest thanks go out to Mahaya, the illustrator, and Anan, my editor. This series was a difficult one: Themes of real and virtual, human and Magistellus, gunfights and car chases spread over such long distances that it was hard to wrangle them onto the page. Thank you for bringing out the color in my writing. Each and every illustration and setting detail you provided is far more than I deserve. I dearly hope that the future permits us to work together again someday.

And finally, a thank-you to all my readers. This is the end! Thank you for sticking with me the whole way. Guns and cars, money and violence, AI and succubi. All I can do is thank you for finding even one of them interesting enough to keep turning the pages. Thank you very much for making it this far.

And with that, I'll bring this section to a close.
I hope their story shall continue in your hearts.

By the way, I'm rooting for Tselika! ...How about you?

Kazuma Kamachi

22

The world was vast. Not just inside *Money (Game) Master,* but outside, too.

This story takes place in the real world, in an ordinary house, on an ordinary street, in an ordinary town.

"Honoka, have you finished your homework?"

"Oh, shut up! You can see all my grades on your phone anyway! That app's always keeping tabs on me like a goddamn pervert!"

"At least look up from your phone when you're talking to me, dear. Are you playing that game again? I know it's the only way you get to show affection without embarrassing people, but you're not using my face again, are you, *Mother*?"

"Bwuh?! I—I don't want to hear that from you when you've been going wild in there looking like me! I should sue you for defamation!!"

"Sorry, dear, I just can't help it. It makes me feel like I'm a schoolgirl again ☆"

* * *

There were always going to be Dealers striking it rich in *Money (Game) Master*, but just because it was all a game didn't mean it couldn't make a difference in real life. Especially when it came to internet trends. For example, here we have a couple who started with a food truck and worked their way up to a hamburger chain. It was the juxtaposition of casual flavors with geeky anime brands that got people talking.

"Hey, Quasimodo. I think the grilled rations we made in-game have started a trend. This here says Harajuku restaurants have started adding Calorie Must to other foods, like sticking it in ice cream or serving it with whipped cream."

"…Wh-what are you looking at anyway, a new gourmet food app?"

Still, the game was very different now. It wasn't just about making money anymore. Many Dealers came to Tokonatsu City simply to walk the streets with their Magistelli.

A blue-haired girl stopped in front of a store window and examined her reflection, pinching her skirt between her fingers. She heard the sounds of strings and horns and walked over to a small group of street performers. Tossing a few coins into the open violin case at their feet, the undine girl leaned over to her partner and whispered into his ear:

"How about a dance? It's been a while."

"Tch."

Bloody Dancer awkwardly scratched his head before replying, "Ain't this the song that convinced me to start working out again 'cause I couldn't keep up with it? Fine, but I'll lead."

Something had changed. But that didn't mean everything had been worked out. It would be too late to start planning once the next big threat came along. The world needed people working hard behind the scenes to ensure this peace could last.

"Master. What do you mean to gain by buying up all the frozen storage at the harbors? Those rental fees are nothing to sneeze at, not to mention the electricity costs."

"They're about to be in high demand," replied a man, or possibly a woman, known as the Pawnshop King. Upsets were not part of his game. He had a massive store of gold and diamonds, and so when something came along to threaten that, he needed to be prepared.

"A food crisis is coming," he explained. "People need food and water to live, and no amount of money can slake that thirst. When that time comes, banknotes will become worthless scraps of paper. Restaurants and supermarkets with two- or three-star ratings will go out of business. But if all the shops in an area close, people won't be able to keep living there. Very soon, we'll bear witness to a new kind of battle—residents competing to raise their local businesses' rankings by any means possible."

They walked along the same path they always did. The brother, on his way to high school. The sister, to middle school.

However, one thing had changed.

"Yo, Kaname."

Now, Takamasa Hekireki walked that route by their side. He no longer needed to hide and could be with his family again.

A young girl with long dark hair tied up in bunches clung to him, almost as though she was trying to hide behind him.

"Wh-what am I supposed to say? I'm not used to seeing him in real life! It's embarrassing."

The transluscent demon with arms around her shoulders whispered:

"I suppose we never did get to the bottom of it in the end."

"The bottom of what?"

"...The bottom of who is most important to My Lord, after everything that has happened."

Tselika and Midori both met the boy's gaze at the same time, and the boy who saved the world averted his eyes.

Instead, he suggested a compromise.

"H-how about if I say it's Midori in the real world and Tselika in the virtual one?"

The see-through demon took out a see-through pistol, while the girl's big brother reached into his tool pouch and pulled out an oversize crowbar.

""*We'll kill you!*"" they both said at once.

"Wait, wait, wait!! I really will die if you shoot me with that, and Takamasa, that crowbar is probably in violation of a few laws!! Why the hell are you carrying it around with you anyway? Planning on breaking and entering?!"

Obviously being beaten around the head with a crowbar would kill him as well.

Midori's face was even redder than her brother's. She snatched the weapon out of his hands.

Ayame muttered something under her breath.

"*...So his attention's split. Good. All I need to do is sit tight and they'll both get tired of him. Once that happens, I'll be there to comfort him!*"

"Stop saying things like that. You're going to set them off again," warned the boy, his whole face dripping with sweat.

"*So what's your next move?*" asked the demon girl with a wink.

Of course, she wasn't asking about setting up his harem. The boy let out a deep sigh.

"We can't let these new AR games get out of hand. Their influence on the real world is much more direct than a virtual currency's. We're not just talking about a Fall. In these games, if you go into debt, you could starve."

"*So what are we going to do about them?*"

"That's simple. We're not fighting inside *Money (Game) Master* anymore. We're fighting to make our game the most influential, to impose its rules on the world."

On a certain app store that saw upward of five thousand new apps published every day, one in particular flashed up at the top of the ranking pages.

The next desire in the cards was Hunger.

Say hello to the new gourmet food app, *Lord (Map) Eater.*